THE
ENGLISH
BOYS

A MYSTERY

JULIA THOMAS

MIDNIGHT INK
WOODBURY, MINNESOTA

FIRST EDITION
First Printing, 2016

Book format by Bob Gaul
Cover design by Kevin R. Brown
Cover image by Shutterstock.com/34230646/©Beata Becla

Midnight Ink, an imprint of Llewellyn Worldwide Ltd.

Library of Congress Cataloging-in-Publication Data
Names: Thomas, Julia, 1959.
Title: The English boys: a mystery/Julia Thomas.
Description: First edition. | Woodbury, Minnesota : Midnight Ink, 2016. |
 Description based on print version record and CIP data provided by
 publisher; resource not viewed.
Identifiers: LCCN 2016007206 (print) | LCCN 2016018176 (ebook) | ISBN
 9780738749020 | ISBN 9780738750514 ()
Subjects: LCSH: Actors—Fiction. | Best friends—Fiction. | Secrets—Fiction.
 | Murder—Investigation—Fiction. | GSAFD: Mystery fiction | Love stories
Classification: LCC PS3620.H6286 E54 2016 (print) | LCC PS3620.H6286 (ebook)
 | DDC 813/.6—dc23
LC record available at https://lccn.loc.gov/2016007206

Midnight Ink
Llewellyn Worldwide Ltd.
2143 Wooddale Drive
Woodbury, MN 55125-2989
www.midnightinkbooks.com

Printed in the United States of America

To Will, with love

ONE

The Book of Common Prayer, as any good member of the Church of England knows, is rife with dark and fearsome parts. Daniel Richardson had inherited a copy from which he liked to quote obscure passages, often the odd phrase from *For Those at Sea*. Bellowing "Safely from the boisterous main, Bring us back to port again," never failed to amuse his friends when they were drunk. Some parts, however, were frightening, particularly one line in *The Solemnization of Marriage*, which called forth the "dreadful day of judgment when the secrets of all hearts shall be disclosed." Just what secrets there were to be discovered, he wasn't certain, but it was terrifying nonetheless. He thought of it now as he stood leaning against the stone wall outside Westminster Abbey where his two closest friends were about to be married. They were still in their twenties, and as far as he was concerned, much too young to wed. In fact, to Daniel, the thought of marriage itself was as inexplicable as the Bermuda Triangle: people disappeared there every day, but still, there was no preventing others from boarding ships and setting out for the exact same waters.

Restless, he plucked at his collar. It had rained the night before and puddles formed along the walkways, but the sky had cleared and only a wisp of gray cloud remained. He thrust his hands into his pockets, listening to the bells chime half past five. Looking about, he took a cigarette from his pocket and lit it, trying to ignore Tamsyn's voice in his head demanding that he put it out. She lectured him about the risk of cancer whenever he smoked, almost always going into the danger to the ozone layer while she was at it. It delighted him when she made passionate little speeches. She had opinions about everything, unlike most of the women he knew who were content to let someone else think of social issues. Tamsyn argued the dangers of overfishing the North Sea and voting the Labour Party back into power and the plight of the homeless, despite the fact that when he'd met her less than a year ago, she hadn't had a pound in her pocket. She was, without a doubt, the best thing in his life and, unfortunately, moments away from marrying his best friend. No matter what anyone said, marriage changed things. The bond they shared was unbreakable, and yet he knew nothing would ever be the same again.

Daniel dropped the cigarette on the pavement and squashed it with the toe of his freshly polished shoe, relieved he hadn't caught the notice of the photographers clustered in front of the building. It was a nice afternoon, and he wanted to chuck his coat, walk over to Bridge Street, and look out over the Thames. The London Eye was just across the river, and though some felt it spoiled a perfectly good view, he thought it interesting in its own monstrous sort of way. It would have been a good day for a sail on the river, or perhaps riding in Hyde Park. Whenever he stayed with Hugh's parents in the country, they always went riding, and though he hadn't been on the back of a horse until a few years ago, it had become one of his favorite pastimes. The desire to escape was strong, but Tamsyn and Hugh were counting on him. He straightened his tie and walked back into the church. As best man, he had last minute duties to perform, but Hugh was nowhere to be found. He was probably talking with the bishop. On impulse, Daniel decided to find the bride instead.

He wandered the halls until he heard a rustle of satin, following the sound to a slightly opened door. Tamsyn stood there alone in a dressing room, looking into a long mirror, her auburn hair pulled back from her face with a few strands falling about her cheeks. Her lips were full and broad, with just a hint of lipstick. He couldn't help but smile at the dress, which was more conservative than he had expected from her usual Bohemian appearance, a confection of a gown that was every young girl's dream. Although he thought the Abbey a wretched place to pledge one's troth, she and Hugh were proud to have a formal wedding here, with every one of the two hundred and twelve seats spoken for and a bishop of the church reading the text. She looked up in surprise when she caught him staring.

"What are you doing here?" she asked, smiling. She wasn't conventionally beautiful, but her smile, which seemed to him in turns both cunning and artless, arrested him each time he saw it. "Spying on the bride, are you? Come on. Give us a kiss."

He hesitated for a moment before walking over to stand in front of her. "Shouldn't I wait until you're a married woman before I kiss you?"

"It's never stopped you before."

"That was before you decided to marry my best friend." In spite of the rebuke, he leaned over and kissed her on the cheek. "Mmm. Lavender. I'm thinking fields in Provence."

"You're thinking you'll shag a bridesmaid."

"Such talk. And on your wedding day, no less." He glanced up at the window, noting that the first of the guests had begun to arrive. He couldn't help but think of last autumn when the three of them had been shooting the final scenes of a Thomas Hardy film in Dorset, talking for hours every day and spending inordinate amounts of time in the local pubs. It had been wonderful; the best time of his life, in fact. He realized she was staring at him, so he cleared his throat and tried to look serious.

"Tam, are you sure you're ready for this?"

"Of course I'm ready. Why wouldn't I be?"

"You know what I mean. Marriage to Hugh isn't just a two-person affair. You'll be marrying his family, too. I swear I saw you curtsy the last time you spoke to his mother."

"You're just jealous," she answered, reaching for a pair of gloves. "Obviously, I've broken your heart."

"And many others, I'm sure."

His mobile vibrated against his thigh and he retrieved it from the pocket of his trousers, frowning. It was another text from Sarah, whom he'd been dodging for the last week. He hadn't gotten seriously involved with anyone since he'd met Tamsyn Burke and then lost her to his best friend, and he certainly didn't consider one ill-advised night with Sarah Williams any sort of relationship. It was another of Tamsyn's idiosyncrasies, introducing people and herding them in groups to organized events: the theatre, parties, even an absurd afternoon boating on the Serpentine. Sarah had accompanied them on two or three occasions. She was pretty enough, but he'd known it was a mistake even before it happened, and now he wouldn't be able to avoid her. Sighing, he looked at his mobile.

Are you here yet? I need to talk to you.

It was simple, straightforward, and it scared the hell out of him. He wanted to reply, *You too—I can't wait to introduce you to my fiancée,* or something equally harsh, just to make her stop.

"Who is it?" Tamsyn asked.

"No one," he answered. He deleted the message without replying.

"It was Sarah Williams, wasn't it?"

"You did have to invite her today, didn't you?"

"How involved are you getting with her?" she asked, with a look that jabbed him in the heart.

"I'm not involved with her," he argued. "You know she's not my type."

"I didn't know you had a type." She arched a brow and turned back to the mirror to adjust a strand of hair.

"I still can't imagine why anyone would want to get married in Westminster Abbey," he said, changing the subject. They had argued about it a dozen times in the last few weeks, and somehow it felt comforting to resort to their usual sparring at a time like this. "The place reeks of history and gloom and death."

"The Tower was booked," she replied.

God, he thought. She was perfect. He wanted to whisk her away like they did in films, consequences be damned; but of course, real life wasn't like that. He was about to reply when he noticed her younger sister standing in the doorway.

"Hello, Carey," he said, nodding.

He had met her on a couple of occasions when Tamsyn could coax her out for a drink. At twenty-three, Carey was younger than her sister, but in every way more serious and responsible. For the last two years, she had been a medical student at King's College studying something so terminally boring he could never remember what it was. He looked at the two of them now and the contrast was as stark as ever. Tamsyn was wild and unpredictable, while Carey was sensible and disciplined. It was hard to believe they were sisters.

"I couldn't find hairpins," Carey said, still looking at Daniel. "But Mum should be here any minute, and she has some with her."

"Do you mind waiting for her?" Tamsyn asked. "I don't want my hair coming loose halfway down the aisle."

Carey nodded. "Of course. I'll be back in a few minutes."

"I could get the pins, you know," Daniel said, watching her leave. Knowing Tamsyn, she had probably sent Carey on a dozen errands already.

"She doesn't mind," she answered. "Well? What do you think of the dress?"

She swayed the voluminous skirt left and right, like a ten-year-old seeking her brother's approval. Daniel shrugged. In no way did he see himself as her brother.

"I expected something a bit saucier, if you must know," he said. "A corset and fishnet stockings, perhaps. This is positively bridal."

"Can't you be serious? I'm trying to get married today."

"Marriage is serious, all right. A year from now and you'll be talking nappies and breastfeeding." He gave a mock shudder. "And you'll probably want Uncle Daniel to babysit, which I must tell you now will never happen."

She cocked her head and smiled. "Go find Hugh. I'm sure he needs you more than I do."

"All right, then, I'm leaving. Break a leg."

"This isn't a play, you know."

"No, I suppose it isn't," he said. "Still … "

He flashed a grin before closing the door. As he glanced at his watch, a fresh wave of regret overtook him. It was going to be difficult to witness this wedding, not to mention spend another two or three more hours in this blasted tuxedo, making mindless conversation with people he'd normally try to avoid. Pull yourself together,

Richardson, he told himself. No matter how he felt about it, he didn't want to ruin their day. Preoccupied, he collided with Hugh's father in the corridor, grazing him with his shoulder.

"Excuse me, sir," he said, bringing up an arm to steady them both.

Noel Ashley-Hunt nodded, mumbling something indecipherable. In spite of the fact that he'd known the man for years and had spent holidays at his country house, they were hardly close. Hugh's father's celebrity and natural reserve kept everyone at a distance.

"Have you seen my son?" Ashley-Hunt asked, toying with his cufflink, his face etched into a frown. The Ashley-Hunts were not thrilled at the idea of this wedding either, Daniel knew, from the few remarks Hugh had made on the subject.

"I'm looking for him myself."

"Damn this old pile. Too many places a person can get lost. If you see him, advise him that his father is waiting."

"Of course," Daniel replied, watching Ashley-Hunt march down the hall glaring into open doorways.

A minute later, he found Hugh sitting at the back of the chapel in a pew behind a column, bent forward as if in prayer. It was an unnatural pose for someone so self-assured. Daniel sighed. It was ridiculous the way everyone was behaving out of character today, Tam playing the blushing bride and Hugh the serious bridegroom contemplating their future. The whole thing was more than he could bear.

"Having second thoughts there, old chap?" He said it in jest, but he almost wondered.

"Ah, the best man!" Hugh said, ignoring the question as if he hadn't heard it. "I was wondering where you went."

"I couldn't find you, so I went to make myself a nuisance to the bride."

"How is she?"

"Radiant. Persephone, come to life."

"Ready to become the fawning wife, I suppose?"

"Tamsyn wouldn't fawn over anyone."

"No, she wouldn't, would she?" He turned and looked at Daniel with interest. "Father told me you landed a role in the new Trollope film."

"As luck would have it. I found out yesterday. Are you still taking off a few months?"

"That's the plan, not that he's too keen on it. It seems like a good idea to settle into marriage first, before I'm tied up with another project. How was the script, by the way?"

"Fine. True to the book." Daniel smiled. "Perhaps a little less dull."

Hugh stood and began to fumble with his tie. "How's this? Do I look the part?"

"Here," Daniel said, reaching out and taking hold of it. "You never could tie a decent knot. Speaking of your father, he's looking for you."

"Then I'd better not disappoint him any more than I already have. I'm sure Mother's probably worked herself into a state by now. Are your parents here yet?"

"I haven't looked. Slipped my mind completely." He clapped his friend on the shoulder. "It'll be great, you know."

"I'm sure it will," Hugh said, heading for the door. "See you at the altar in ten."

"Just think," Daniel called after him. "By this time tomorrow, you'll be getting drunk on a beach in Fiji."

"Your lips to God's ear," Hugh called back.

Daniel could almost feel the words echo in the empty, vaulted room.

TWO

CAREY BURKE FOUND HER mother, borrowed the necessary hair-pins, and turned back in the direction of the room where her older sister was getting ready. She and Tamsyn hadn't been as close as she would have liked in the past few years, but she wanted her to be happy and to settle down to an ordinary life. Nothing, however, about this wedding was ordinary. The groom was a well-known and respected actor, and his father even more so. Half the guest list had appeared in *Hello!* magazine, dined with royals, or snagged top film awards. In fact, she wondered how many of them Tamsyn had even met. She and Hugh had only been engaged for a few months.

Their parents had driven over from Wales, and though she had hoped her best friend, Nick Oliver, would come with them, he had declined the opportunity. She didn't blame him; an occasion of this magnitude was completely out of their sphere. In fact, she hadn't even wanted to be in the wedding, but because Tamsyn never asked anything of her, it was the least she could do.

Hugh Ashley-Hunt was, if not a shocking choice for her sister, at least a complete surprise. None of them had expected her to settle down so quickly. Of course, Carey could understand the attraction. Hugh was handsome: tall, with cropped blond hair and startling blue eyes. Though he had a formal manner, he also had a way of putting people at ease. He'd charmed their parents, and their father in particular wasn't easily charmed.

His friend, Daniel Richardson, was no less attractive. He was tall, though not as tall as Hugh, with dark, wavy hair and a bemused smile. However, Carey was not as easily impressed as her parents. She had no time for film stars. She barely had time to attend her sister's wedding. As far as she was concerned, it would take a long time, years perhaps, to develop relationships with her new brother-in-law and his friends. She didn't let people into her life easily, or without a great deal of thought.

She didn't approve of the Abbey for the wedding either, though clearly the Ashley-Hunts had insisted on it. Carey believed a wedding should be small and personal, including only the people one loved most, in a place that had a special meaning to the bride and groom. Nevertheless, she made her way through the halls and found Tamsyn to deliver the hairpins.

"Thank you," Tamsyn said, taking two of the pins from her and securing a lock of hair into place. She turned and looked at Carey with a smile. "How do I look?"

"Perfect," Carey answered, and it was true. No one would have eyes for anyone but the bride today, which was just as it should be.

Tamsyn reached out and squeezed Carey's hand. "I just need a moment to myself, and I'll be ready."

"Of course." Carey nodded and slipped out the door.

She had done the right thing. Tamsyn had wanted her to be in the wedding, and she was fulfilling her promise. That's what a sister was for.

———

Daniel stood at a window in the corridor, watching cars arrive. A couple got out of a vehicle, the woman in a frothy, feathered hat that obscured her face and the man in a formal suit and top hat. He recognized them at once: Hugh's longtime friend Marc Hayley and the American actress Anna Parrish. Their arrival in England had caught the notice of the press the day before. In fact, the guest list had excited a great deal of attention. He thought about going down to greet people as they arrived, many of whom he knew, but changed his mind. He had no desire to shake any more hands than necessary.

"It's going to be a long evening," a voice said behind him.

He turned to find Carey at his elbow, her arms crossed. She was an unexpected ally in the war against weddings, and as far as he could remember, she had never initiated a conversation with him before.

"I'm not sure why Tamsyn and Hugh insisted we get here so early," he said.

"They probably wanted to make sure everything goes well."

"We've got a bride, a groom, and a church. What more could they want?"

"A guarantee would be nice."

He stopped and gave her a second look. There was something about her eyes that held his for a moment. They were intelligent eyes, clinical in their intensity. This was a girl who was precise about everything. Her face was rounder than Tamsyn's with a hint of a dimple in her right cheek, and he wondered if she ever smiled to show it.

"What do you mean, exactly?" he asked.

"Nothing," she answered, and he realized that she did not want to confide in him. He suddenly wanted to keep her talking.

"Weddings are a miserable business, aren't they?" he asked.

"I don't know. I don't often go to weddings."

"I've been to too many. I don't see the attraction, myself."

"Neither do I," she replied. "I can't imagine sacrificing education and career to tie oneself to a kitchen and a man who leaves socks lying about."

Daniel laughed. "What are you studying, again? I'm sorry. I keep forgetting."

"Neuromuscular diseases."

"Good lord. Why on earth would anyone want to study neuro-muscular diseases?"

Carey shrugged. "Someone has to."

He nodded, eyeing the dress she had no doubt agreed to wear only for her sister's sake. The traditional white silk dress, chosen so that the bride is not singled out by evil wishers who might curse her for her happiness, had cap sleeves and a bodice that hugged her thin frame. The skirt ballooned over a slip of petticoats, falling just below her knees. It was a considerable change from her normal uniform of jeans and woolly cardigans. Her pale hair fell to her shoulders, not quite blonde, and not quite brown. On the few times he had seen her before, she had always seemed as if she wanted to blend in with the crowd, which was the opposite of Tamsyn, who did everything to stand out.

"You're in love with her, aren't you?" she asked suddenly.

"Tamsyn?" he sputtered. "No, of course not. We're friends, you know that. Just friends."

He examined the tips of his shoes to keep from looking at her. How had she known? He'd never said anything to anyone, and yet she stood there, probing him with those piercing eyes as though she could see into his soul. He was trying to think of a way to change the subject when he saw Sarah Williams approaching them. Fuck, he thought. Could this day get any worse?

"So, you won't take my calls," Sarah said, brushing Carey aside. She was attractive enough in her blue satin gown until one looked her in the eye and saw the Valkyrie within.

"Sarah," he began, trying to think of a way to prevent an argument right there in front of everyone.

"Excuse me," Carey said. She turned with surprising dignity and walked away.

Daniel took a deep breath, watching her retreat before he looked back at the girl before him. "Look, I'm sorry if I have offended you."

"Offended?" Sarah said. "Really? You've slept with me and that's all you can say?"

Heads turned at the end of the hall.

"Keep your voice down, please."

"I'll do whatever I like," she answered. "I'll scream to the whole bloody world that Daniel Richardson doesn't give a damn about anyone."

"I think most people who know me already realize that."

"You're a bastard, you know that?"

"I don't think we should get into this here. Why don't we meet somewhere later and talk?"

"No. You'll stand me up, that's what you'll do. It's all you're good for. Running out on people."

She made a fist and punched his shoulder, and the jab, while it did not hurt, knocked him against the wall.

He held up his hands as if in surrender. "You're right. We need to talk. Tell me where and I'll meet you, I promise."

"Why should I trust you?" she asked.

Daniel looked down the corridor and noticed several people whispering and nodding in their direction.

"I wanted you to take my calls," she continued. "I didn't sleep with you to be another of your conquests."

"One night does not constitute a relationship," he snapped, regretting it the moment the words tumbled out of his mouth.

"How dare you?" she replied. For a wretched moment, he thought she might cry.

"Sarah, I—" he began, but she turned her back and marched away.

Daniel tapped the pocket that held his cigarettes, wishing he could have a smoke. He couldn't go back toward the crowd gathering in the direction Carey had gone. There was nothing for it but to meet Hugh at the altar. He wouldn't make eye contact with Sarah during the ceremony but would stand, circumspect, thinking of his evening, when he would finally be at home. Nothing sounded better than sitting alone in his quiet flat, although he knew that when he got there he would be plagued with thoughts of Tamsyn and Hugh on their wedding night. He comforted himself with the thought that he would see Tamsyn often. It would be enough, hearing her voice and watching her laugh, drinking in the essence of her. One could befriend a married woman, and he would be good at it. He was an actor, for God's sake. It would be painful, but he could bear it just to be near her.

Suddenly, a scream pierced the stillness of the Abbey, echoing through the empty halls. Daniel turned and ran in the direction from which it had come. A crowd had materialized outside the nave and he skirted it, running instinctively to the room where Tamsyn had been. He found a knot of people already crowding outside the door.

"Ring the police!" someone shouted.

Out of the corner of his eye, he saw his parents come up beside him, but he ignored them and pushed his way inside. Tamsyn was lying face down on the cold marble floor, surrounded by members of the wedding party. He pushed forward, brushing everyone back. Hugh knelt beside her. Daniel took her shoulder to roll her gently over, gasping when he saw the blood soaking the front of her gown and slicking onto the floor. Her eyes were half-open and lifeless.

"What happened?" Hugh cried. "Did anyone see what happened?"

No one answered. Tamsyn's mother fell to her knees and took hold of her daughter's wrist, searching for a pulse. The crowd was silent, afraid to move. Eyes darted from person to person as every mind formed the same unspoken question: who had killed a bride on her wedding day? Daniel couldn't tear his eyes from the sight of Tamsyn's body, which moments ago had been so full of life. Beside him, Hugh began to groan, a low, animal-like sound that was answered with a chorus of moans and cries from the huddled groups behind them.

"Get back, everyone," someone shouted. Daniel looked up to see his father taking command in the panicked room. "Give them some room!"

Daniel's hands were shaking. He wondered how he had known to run to her. Had it been a premonition, or had he wanted to protect the one he loved? He leaned back to give Hugh and Tamsyn's parents more room, but he was damned if he was going to leave her side, no matter what anyone said.

Tamsyn was gone. The person he loved most was lying dead in front of him. And just like that, without a single warning, his entire world came crashing down.

THREE

THE CROWD BEGAN TO react. Some of the women were crying; others had to sit to prevent themselves from fainting. Someone was sick in the corner of the room. Daniel felt ill himself. Hugh still crouched on the floor, clutching Tamsyn's limp hand, leaning forward to prevent anyone else from coming near. Blood seemed to be everywhere: on their clothes, the floor, and the wall. Daniel stood, heart pounding in his chest, unable to accept what had happened. She couldn't be dead. It wasn't possible.

By the time the police arrived, someone had taken him by the shoulders and sat him down in a chair. People were speaking to him and around him, but the words didn't make any sense.

Everyone who had not been seated in the church was then led down the East Cloister into a room that looked as though its chief function was for storage. Unlike in the formal rooms of the Abbey, there were no Waterford crystal chandeliers, no votive candle stands depicting the Christ or the Blessed Virgin Mary. There were no stained glass windows; in fact, there were no windows at all in the dimly lit room, where folding chairs that had been propped against the wall long ago were now being dusted off to seat the crowd.

Suddenly, Daniel was angry. The police were wasting valuable time. Family and friends were being rounded up like suspects while whoever killed Tamsyn had slipped right past them and was probably miles away by now. He glanced at his watch. Barely half an hour had passed since the police had been summoned. Beside him, Hugh stared at the blank wall, unseeing, his crisp white shirt stained red with blood. Carey's face was wooden, unlike the painful displays of emotion around her. She stood with one arm around her mother, who had begun to weep. Daniel brought them both chairs. Mrs. Burke allowed herself to be helped into one, her husband taking the one beside her.

"Thank you," Carey murmured.

He nodded, looking at his own parents and brother, Alex, who sat at the back of the room, talking in hushed tones. Cliques formed among the anxious crowd, people already growing suspicious of one another. The Ashley-Hunts sat nearest the door, as if desperate to escape, and assorted cousins and friends stood in groups of three or four talking amongst themselves. Before long, a detective entered and stood in the center of the room.

"Have a seat, everyone," he said, gesturing to the chairs. He was a short but elegant man, a far cry from the bleary-eyed, coffee-stained sort of policeman they might have expected. He looked to be around fifty, and his calm demeanor might have soothed everyone had the crime been less shocking. "I'm Detective Chief Inspector Murray, and we're going to take statements. I have three constables here who will speak to you, one or two at a time. This can be a fairly quick process if everyone cooperates. Find a chair and cease talking for a few minutes as we prepare to begin."

"What are you doing?" Mr. Burke called out. He struggled to his feet. "Why aren't you trying to find out who's done this?"

"There may be witnesses in this room, sir," Inspector Murray replied. "We have to find out what was seen and heard in the minutes prior to Miss Burke's death. It is important that we speak to everyone present."

Owen Burke looked at his wife and sat down, allowing the inspector to continue.

"Each of you has your own story to tell," the inspector stated, "but if you talk to others, you're going to change their stories, and they yours. So I want you to think about everything you can remember and keep it to yourself until it's your turn."

There was a murmur of assent. Daniel looked at Hugh, trying to keep his eyes off his friend's bloodstained jacket and hands. He loosened his tie, unbuttoned the top button of his shirt, and sat down next to his brother. The two of them hadn't gotten along in years. In fact, he wished his mother hadn't insisted Alex accompany them to the wedding. She had probably told him he'd never have another chance to see a wedding in Westminster Abbey, or some other rot like that.

"Christ, can you believe it?" Alex said, ignoring the inspector's request. "I mean, a murder in a fuckin' church."

Daniel held his tongue out of respect for his mother, who frowned at Alex.

"Watch your language," she whispered. "We're in a place of worship."

"More like a war zone, init?" He looked at Daniel, daring him to say something about his deliberate use of lower class speech, flexing his wiry shoulders under his jacket to antagonize him.

"Exactly like a war zone," Daniel replied. Had they been at home, he'd have gotten him in a head lock. "Full of bloody criminals." He glanced at Alex's coat, wondering if there was a bag of cocaine tucked inside.

"Boys," Sheila Richardson hissed. She looked at her husband with irritation. "Gerry. Say something."

"Why bother?" he grumbled, stuffing his hands into his pockets. "No one's listened to me in years."

Before Daniel could reply, another police officer stepped into the room. He murmured something to Murray and then left.

Carey rose from her chair. "Inspector, surely my parents don't need to be present for this."

"Miss Burke—"

"I'm sorry, but you'll appreciate how unbearable this is for our family. Could you let them go first, please?"

Inspector Murray cleared his throat. "Certainly. Will you need someone to drive you home afterward?"

"No, sir," Owen Burke answered. "I have my car."

"Dad, are you sure you can drive?" Carey asked.

"I can drive," he declared. "Anything to get out of here."

"Are you going to fingerprint everyone?" Alex interrupted, shifting in his chair.

Murray shook his head. "Not at present, no. Just be prepared to answer a few questions, and then you'll be free to go."

Noel Ashley-Hunt finally broke his silence. "Our son has also been through a devastating shock. We'd like to take him home. And my mother-in-law—for God's sake, she's in her seventies. She's certainly not a suspect."

Ashley-Hunt's temper, though Daniel had never seen it, was legendary. Even Hugh clashed with his father on occasion. The man was used to getting his own way.

Murray looked at one of the officers. "Take the Burkes into the next room and get a statement from each of them so they may leave. Then talk to the Ashley-Hunts."

A quarter hour later, another officer was assigned to interview the Richardsons. Alex leapt out of his chair, eager to state his non-involvement. Sheila Richardson tried to repair her face with a tissue while her husband held her handbag. Daniel was rising to follow his brother and parents into the next room when Inspector Murray put a hand on his shoulder.

"Not you," he said, shaking his head.

"What?" Sheila asked, tissue poised in mid-air. "Why not him?"

Daniel looked at his mother and shrugged, conscious that everyone in the room had looked up. "It's all right, Mum. You go ahead."

"But we're a family. We should go together."

"I'll be fine. I'll ring you tonight."

Under Murray's scrutiny, she nodded and followed her husband out. The room bristled with an uneasy silence as minutes ticked by on the clock. The bridesmaids sat together, eyeing everyone else in the small room. Nearby, Sarah Williams looked lost in thought. Daniel distanced himself from her as much as possible, relieved they had been told not to speak. An interminable twenty minutes later, a constable came into the room, clipboard in hand.

"Miss Williams." He looked up from his notes as Sarah straightened her skirt and stood. She gave Daniel a self-satisfied smile and followed the officer out of the room.

The two other young women still sat huddled together, texting furiously as they were forced to wait. He wasn't the only man in the room who noticed them. A striking, muscular man in a leather suit jacket was propped against the wall, brooding. He narrowed his eyes, frowning in Daniel's direction. Daniel recognized two people in the corner as old friends of Tamsyn's from her days in the theater. She had mentioned Dylan Cole and Lucy Potter to him on more than one occasion. They were an odd pair from what he could see, unconnected to the rest of the party. He knew that in earlier days, they and Tamsyn had made a hard-partying lot, with her the center of attention. In recent months, they were more a fringe group hanging on as Tamsyn made her way up the hierarchy of the British acting community. They might be scorned by the respectable members of the party, but, in turn, they seemed to disdain everyone present even more.

The film producer Sir John Hodges and his wife, Antonia, with whom Daniel had become familiar, regarded the proceedings with something bordering on outrage. The Hodges had produced the Hardy film in which he, Hugh, and Tamsyn had starred, and they were now in post-production, making arrangements to promote the picture. A great deal had been expected of it. On the other side of them, Marc Hayley sat next to his date, Anna Parrish, who was talking in a low voice on her mobile.

One by one, they were called in to speak to the police, until eventually Daniel was the only person left in the room. In spite of himself, his heart beat faster as he wondered if the police could possibly think he would kill someone he cared for as much as Tamsyn.

He waited to be assigned to a police officer, practicing his statements in his head in spite of himself: *I have no idea what happened. She was perfectly fine when I saw her; eager to get married. We talked, like any normal day.* While thoughts swirled in his tired brain, Inspector Murray himself walked over, and rather than taking Daniel into a separate room like everyone else, he pulled up a chair and sat next to him. The poor lighting threw shadows in the tracery of lines on the older man's face.

"You're Daniel Richardson," he stated.

"Yes, sir," Daniel replied, waiting for him to take out a pen and pad of paper, but the Inspector merely crossed his arms.

"How long have you known Miss Burke?"

"Almost a year," he answered.

"I understand you were close."

"Yes," he managed. "I introduced her to Hugh, in fact."

"And you've been friends with Hugh for a number of years."

"Yes, since we were young."

Murray's eyes narrowed. "How did you feel about them becoming a couple?"

Privately, Daniel had thought them mismatched, but he wouldn't say that to the inspector. Instead, he answered, "They were happy. They were my friends. I was happy for them."

"Can you tell me what happened this morning?"

"I have no idea. I went to talk to her, to wish her luck. I don't think I was in there more than five minutes, if that."

"What did you talk about?"

"How beautiful she looked, mainly. She seemed anxious about the dress." He neglected to repeat Tamsyn's assertion that he was jealous of Hugh. It would only implicate him unfairly.

"Did you see anyone else in the corridor before or after you left?"

"I don't think so." Daniel leaned forward, his shoulder muscles tense. "No, wait. I did see Noel Ashley-Hunt. He was looking for Hugh. In fact, we both were."

"And then?"

"He asked me to look for his son. I found Hugh a few minutes later in the chapel."

"How long did you and Hugh talk?"

"Not long. A few minutes at most. It was almost time for the ceremony."

"Did you notice anything out of the ordinary? Anyone running or rushing away from that room?"

"I've wracked my brain, but I can't think of anything. I was a bit distracted."

"Ah, yes," Murray said. "You were having a rather public quarrel with Sarah Williams."

Daniel looked at the inspector. "We went out last week, but I realized right away it was a mistake and I don't want to see her again. Unfortunately, she took it personally."

"She's definitely a very angry woman. Quite a number of people interviewed mentioned that she struck you in the hall. You're fortunate that it establishes your whereabouts near the time of the murder." Murray touched his lip in thought. He reached into his coat pocket and extracted a business card. "If you think of anything else, I want you to give me a ring."

"That's it? I can go?"

Murray nodded. "You may go, but I'll be in touch."

———

It was late by the time the cab pulled up in front of his building, and he was exhausted.

Daniel turned up his collar as he got out of the taxi. The mild weather had been interrupted by a burst of cold wind and the threat of rain. He walked up the steps to the entrance, relieved to be home, and took the lift up to his flat.

It was his first flat, this cavernous set of rooms in the white stone building off Kensington High Street, just around the corner from his favorite pub. It was sparsely furnished, which suited him, a contrast to Hugh's more formal house in Holland Park, which resembled a nineteenth-century gentleman's club full of jardinières and walking sticks and good leather chairs. Daniel had often wondered how

Tamsyn fit in there. She cluttered up the place with pink and purple knitted scarves and boots littering the floors and gaudy bangles lying atop Hugh's first-edition copy of *Daniel Deronda*. What did they see in each other, really? he wondered as he unlocked the door and stepped inside. He turned and bolted it behind him, as if to lock out everything that had happened that day. He went straight to his bar and looked at the dismal contents before shrugging off his jacket and collapsing on the sofa, his fists tucked into his eye sockets.

After a few minutes, he rubbed his face and opened his eyes. He had no idea what he was going to do. A world without Tamsyn Burke was unimaginable. She had been the only one who could make him laugh at any time or any place, particularly the wrong place, simply with one of her devilish looks.

"You're going to go mad if you sit here and think about it all night," he said aloud to himself. However, he didn't stir. Instead, he stared at the large empty wall across from the sofa, on which Tam had once threatened to paint zinnias. He ought to have let her. He suddenly wanted something of hers, like one of her endless scarves, something he could hold in his hands. He would ask Carey about it at the funeral. God, he thought, groaning. She'd have him in church twice in one week. It was one more bit of proof of her hold over him.

There was a knock at the door. For a moment, he didn't move, imagining Tamsyn on the other side in one of her mad miniskirts and Aran Isle cardigans. Knowing it wasn't, he was tempted to leave it. It was probably his mother, with his father and brother in tow, worried that he wouldn't eat.

"Richardson," came a call from the other side of the door.

Daniel recognized Marc Hayley's voice and raised a brow. Hayley was Hugh's friend, and for a moment he wondered how he had gotten his address. Then he remembered: Tamsyn had thrown a party at his flat a few months before. She'd strung lanterns from the ceiling and thrown open windows, despite the fact that it had been the middle of winter. She'd pranced about the room pouring vodka and speaking in a Russian accent all evening, acting like a prostitute trying to get someone to take her home for the night. She'd been ridiculously wonderful and his chest grew tight thinking about it.

"Richardson, are you in there?" Hayley called again.

"Hold on," he answered. He forced himself to get up from the sofa and go over to unlock the door.

Hayley stood there with his dark, curly hair flopped down in front of his face like one of the characters he played in films. All that was missing were the breeches and boots. "What a day," he said, heaving large breaths from running up the stairs. "What a fucking bad day. There's only one thing for it."

"What's that?" Daniel asked.

"Getting pissed."

He stared at Hayley for a long moment, realizing he was right. Anything would be better than sitting here choking on every small memory, even having a drink on an empty stomach with a prat like Marc Hayley.

"All right," he said. "I'll get my coat."

They tumbled back out into the street, where it was now dark. Shopfronts were lit, enticing buyers inside to buy their wares. It had begun to rain, and couples ambled about under umbrellas, looking in windows and talking in low voices. In fact, the whole world seemed to be going about business as usual. It was infuriating. Everything was different now. From this day on, Daniel would divide his life into two parts: Before Tamsyn, and After. And After was a place he really didn't care to be.

FOUR

THE DUKE OF MARLBOROUGH public house was just a few streets from his flat, and though Daniel hated bringing Marc Hayley there on the principle that one doesn't shit where one eats, he was too tired to think of another decent pub. Rain soaked the collar of his coat, but he ignored the insistent drizzle and walked alongside his companion, looking at familiar sights along the way for comfort on this dreary night. They passed St. Mary Abbots Church, and though he had never attended services, nor was he religious, there was something he liked about the ancient building with its tall archway and heavy wooden door. It gave him comfort when he needed peace. He sometimes walked inside the gate and sat on a bench, buffered from the bustle of the High Street. He had occasionally met Tamsyn there, bringing large cups of coffee on chilly days, and though they were hardly removed from the street, it felt as though they were in another world. A flower shop had taken up residence against one wall, with buckets of roses stowed behind the stone walkway. It was a quiet place to sit, unmolested by hordes of shoppers or the occasional rabid fan. Then there was the highly entertaining game of Fashion Disaster, when he would listen to Tamsyn rate the attire of various passersby, even while she herself wore great woolly boots with tassels and amorphous gypsy frocks. It always made him laugh, because she did it with a straight face. He once told her she frightened mere mortals.

Daniel pushed his fists harder into his pockets. Nearing the pub, he realized his mobile had been silent all day. Most of his calls lately had been from Tamsyn or Hugh. Tamsyn, in particular, had spent the last month bothering him relentlessly with wedding details. Her mother was in Wales and Carey was occupied with her studies, but Daniel knew that even if her sister could have spared the time, she wasn't the sort to worry about particulars like cake and beaded slippers and what size font was appropriate for the invitations. Hugh, meanwhile, was openly disinterested and frequently told Tamsyn "whatever you want," a phrase Daniel had thought would serve him well once the two were married. Tamsyn didn't seem to mind her bridegroom's reticence.

"Men hate planning weddings," she'd said once.

Daniel had laughed at the irony. "Precisely."

Even though he hated it as much as the next man, now he was glad he had been there for her when she'd needed him most. At least he could say that.

"This is it," he said, nodding toward the large green door in front of them. There wasn't anything special about this pub, but he liked it all the same, from the plain bar towels down to the pictures on the wall: bland images of Surrey, with sheep dotting the hillside and clouds hanging low over a green valley. The frames were nondescript and ordinary. In fact, everything about the place was ordinary, as if one were walking into one's mother's kitchen, where every glass and plate and even the cracked ceiling overhead were familiar and comforting.

Daniel glanced over at the man behind the counter who ran the place. He poured pints without ever changing his facial expression, whether it was for some of their actor friends or a group of beautiful girls. When he wasn't wiping glasses or pulling pints, he leaned against the bar, talking on his mobile to his wife. Daniel placed their order and went to sit at one of the sturdy wooden tables, studying Hayley as he did so. They didn't know each other well, though they had been thrown together now and again. At the Ashley-Hunts' house, there were a few framed photos of Marc and Hugh together when they were much younger. Occasionally, Daniel wondered if he had usurped Hayley's position in Hugh's life.

Hayley sat down beside him without removing his dripping coat, his leonine curls shaking much as they did on the big screen. He was a tall man but moved with fluidity and grace, and his Roman nose and square jaw never failed to attract attention. There was something hard about his hazel eyes. He had been successful in his acting career, but more often than not had been cast as the villain in American films. He had the perfect looks for it: good-looking enough to engender sympathy, but also cruel-looking enough to be the picture of evil when his character's true motives were revealed. One couldn't trust a man like that, Daniel thought: too self-assured, too forceful.

He waited for Hayley to begin, rather than encourage him with pointless questions.

"What a fucking awful day," Hayley repeated, taking a draw of his bitter and sucking in the foam.

Daniel nodded, wondering why he had bothered to come. If the flat hadn't seemed so damned empty, he wouldn't have consented to be the sounding board for Marc Hayley's morbid curiosity. He realized that he didn't want to be alone, either.

Hayley looked at him from the corner of his eye. "Blasted luck for Hugh. It'll scar him for life. I keep seeing the blood on his wedding kit. He'll never get over it."

"He's gone home with his parents," Daniel said, not certain what else to say. "They'll look after him."

"Yes, they'll take care of everything. But the long term. It's a nightmare. Will he even want to act again?"

Daniel put down his glass, surprised. "Why wouldn't he?"

Marc snorted. "He's just lost the woman he was going to marry. I imagine that will change everything."

"Perhaps it will."

"You knew the girl well, didn't you?"

"Yes," Daniel said, wondering what he was implying.

"I only met her once. What was she like?"

"She was unique, to say the least. I've never met anyone else like her."

"Yeah. They broke that mold, didn't they? I don't mean to malign the girl's character, but she was a bit of a one-off, if you know what I mean. I couldn't believe it when Hugh told me he was marrying her."

"When was the last time you spoke to Hugh?" Daniel asked, trying to change the subject.

"He called me a few days before the wedding. He seemed fine."

They sat in silence for a minute, pulling on their pints. Outside, the rain began to slam against the window and a bolt of lightning reflected on the bottles behind the bar. Daniel might have thought it an omen if the worst hadn't already happened.

"Before that," he pursued, feeling rattled. "When had you last spoken to him?"

"I was here in February, although we email occasionally. I've been in LA doing a vampire film. They're fucking obsessed with vampires there. You can hardly get away from it. Anyway, I asked him if he wanted to try his luck there."

"Is your film going to be released this year?"

"In a few months, if all goes well."

Daniel understood what he meant. He'd already been involved with a few producers who were struggling to make ends meet and having difficulty getting the product into the public domain. It was a tricky business. He'd been lucky, considering the relatively short time he'd been acting, but there were plenty of others he'd known who couldn't get anything going at all. Even Tamsyn had been given her breakout role due to Hugh's clout and power of persuasion.

"And when did you meet Tamsyn?" he asked, though he had an idea.

"At one of your parties, I should think." Hayley smirked. "I remember thinking, *Who the hell is that, hanging all over Richardson?* She hadn't targeted Hugh yet."

"By then, they were already together. We were just friends."

"I don't think the poor bastard knew what hit him. I mean, could she possibly have been less suitable for a man of his class? Now, you or I, that might have been understandable. But Hugh? He doesn't usually mix with the less desirable elements of society."

Daniel ignored the multiple insults and concentrated on finishing his pint. He wanted to sit there and drink until the back of his neck went numb, then lay his head upon a table and sleep for hours. If only he could wake up the next day to find it Saturday morning all over again. Had Tamsyn truly been killed by one of the twenty-seven people the police had interviewed that day? Someone who had been brazen enough to risk being caught in front of family and friends? Did Marc Hayley have some obscure motive of his own? Had he been jealous of Hugh?

"I keep thinking we were probably in the same room as the murderer this evening," Hayley said suddenly.

"It hardly seems possible," Daniel replied. "It must have been someone who escaped out a window or something."

"No. She was stabbed in the chest. That's face to face, a crime of passion. Imagine being killed by someone you invited to your wedding."

Hayley got up and ordered another round, bringing the drinks and setting them on the table with a slosh. He was already a little drunk. "Who was the last person to see her alive? I heard someone say it was you."

Daniel put down his pint. "That statement precludes the existence of someone else as the murderer, does it not?"

"I'm not suggesting—"

"I don't know what the hell you're suggesting, but I didn't have anything to do with it."

"We're a bit testy, aren't we?"

Daniel tried to calm down. It was pointless getting into it with the likes of Marc Hayley. "What do you expect, after what we've been through?"

"Fair enough," Hayley answered. "I just meant, did you see anything unusual? Did you see someone else go into that room?"

"That's what the police wanted to know."

"What did you tell them?"

"I don't think I'm supposed to discuss it. Isn't that what they told us when we were being questioned?"

"What does it matter, if you had nothing to do with it?"

"I didn't. Just leave it at that."

"I thought we could figure it out together."

"You've jumped to a lot of conclusions: Hugh didn't love her, she wasn't good enough for him, maybe I had something to do with it.

You don't know what you're talking about, Hayley. I think this conversation is over." Daniel started to rise from his chair.

"Wait," Hayley said, waving him back into his seat. "Look, I'm sorry. Really, I am. I didn't mean to imply you killed the girl."

"Stop calling her 'the girl,' for God's sake."

"All right. I didn't mean to imply you killed Tamsyn Burke."

"Then what the hell is this all about?"

"We've been through something hideous today. I want to get my mind around what happened. I suppose I just wanted someone to commiserate with."

"Someone besides Anna Parrish?"

Hayley leaned back in his chair. "Believe me, mate. Anyone besides Anna Parrish."

Daniel looked at him, raising an eyebrow. "The papers have the two of you as quite the item."

"Yeah, well, don't believe everything you read."

"But you brought her all the way from LA to attend the wedding."

"She bloody begged me to come. Said she needed to talk to Tamsyn. Why, I have no idea." He stretched his legs under the table. "We've had a bit of a thing, Anna and me. It's about run its course. When I made arrangements to fly to London, she insisted on coming with me. I thought she might make a pleasant diversion, but after what happened today, she's locked herself in her hotel room and hasn't stopped making calls."

"What sort of calls?"

"I have no idea."

"That's a bit odd."

"Everything about this day is odd, Richardson, in case you haven't noticed."

Daniel's mobile rang. He pulled it from his pocket and saw Hugh's name flash across the screen.

"Excuse me," he said, rising. He walked out of the pub and huddled against the doorway of the building to answer the call. "Hugh … Are you all right?"

"I need to talk to you," Hugh said in a low voice. "Where are you right now?"

"Standing out in the rain, actually."

"Listen, the police have just left and they're headed straight for your flat. How fast can you get over here?"

"Depends on whether or not I can find a cab at this hour." Daniel asked. "What's going on?"

"I'll explain everything when you get here. Come round the back and I'll meet you at the door."

There was a click on the line and Daniel's mobile went dead. For two seconds, he debated going back into the pub and telling Hayley he had to leave, but instead he turned up his collar against the wind and whistled at a passing cab. Nothing was more important than the fact that Hugh needed him.

FIVE

OF THE MANY TIMES Daniel had visited the Ashley-Hunts' Mayfair home, none of them had involved stealing in through the back door under cover of darkness, the threat of arrest hanging over his head. The house was Regency, with a white-painted stucco façade and an impressive black entryway framed by two tall columns. He had never stepped over the threshold without imagining carriages pulling up to the door and nineteenth-century women lifting their crinolines to avoid puddles. The wrought-iron balconies provided a fine view of Berkeley Square, though he doubted they had ever been used by the present owners. The bow windows had heavy velvet curtains that enclosed the inhabitants in a cocoon of comfort and privacy. It was the sort of place where men were offered port and cigars in the library and discussed politics and world affairs. In fact, he himself had been present on at least three such occasions, although as the junior members of the set, he and Hugh had contented themselves with sitting in the corner and listening to their elders speak. The foyer boasted the requisite vertical-striped wallpaper, as well as more furniture than he had in his entire flat and Caroline Ashley-Hunt's prized collection of Sevres, which rivaled that of the British Museum. To Daniel, the house lacked the warmth of their Gloucestershire home, which, despite an enviable array of Louis XIV chairs and four-poster beds, smelt of wet dogs and horses. He himself had never had any aspirations to such grandeur; more likely he'd be terrified every moment that it was about to be burgled.

When he arrived, the electrified gate was ajar, and even though he moved through it without a sound, sure that no one had seen him, it closed behind him. Hugh must be watching from the security room, he realized, with its half-dozen cameras trained on every side of the house, vigilant against intruders. The rain had stopped, but the wind whipped around his legs and stung his eyes, and he put his head down as he walked around the house. A few dim lights illuminated the exterior, but the ground floor rooms were dark. When he turned the corner, the light was on and Hugh was waiting for him on the step.

"Come in," his friend murmured, ushering him into the house.

"What's going on?" Daniel asked.

"Let's go in the kitchen. I imagine you could use a cup of tea."

Daniel shrugged off his jacket and ran a hand through his hair.

"Hang your coat there," Hugh said, indicating the hook on the wall. "It's dripping."

"Marthe will mop in the morning. She's relentless."

Daniel hung his coat on the hook and followed his friend into the kitchen, where Hugh filled a kettle and leaned against the counter. He looked exhausted, no doubt having spent hours analyzing the situation from every angle. It was the way Hugh coped with things, not that it would work this time. If he expected a rational explanation for what had happened, he was certain to be disappointed. As far as Daniel knew, Tamsyn didn't have enemies, and even if she had, they were certainly not numbered among family and friends at the wedding. There was no sense to be made of it. Her murder defied logic.

"I've gone over and over it," Hugh said. "I didn't see anyone in the corridor. No one at all. Of course, they could have gone out the other side, but it would have been difficult to avoid the family."

"I don't know how you can think anymore. It's all going hazy for me."

"Probably because it's eleven o'clock at night and you've been drinking. Have you eaten anything?"

"No. Have you?"

"I may never eat again."

"How long were the police here?"

"A couple of hours. It was ghastly trying to hash back through it all. I've made a list, you see," Hugh said, producing a crumpled paper from his pocket. "Everyone who was in that part of the Abbey is there. The police are adamant that it was someone on this list."

"Have they any particular suspect?"

Hugh put the paper on the table. "They find it somehow significant that you were the last person known to have seen her."

"Thank you for adding the word 'known.'"

"Of course you didn't do it. I'd stake my life on it. In fact, you were half in love with her yourself. I said as much to the police."

"They didn't believe you, I suppose?"

"They're looking at motives."

"What possible motive could anyone have?"

"The seven deadly sins: greed, envy, lust; but I don't see how any of them apply here."

"There were people present that I certainly don't like, but I still wouldn't accuse them of murder," Daniel replied.

"One of the bridesmaids, for example."

"Exactly. Or that odd couple, Dylan Cole and Lucy Potter."

"They're peculiar, certainly, but insane enough to do something like this?" Hugh tapped the paper with a finger.

Daniel frowned. "May I have a look?"

Hugh slid it over to him. "No one on this list would have hurt her. No one."

"It's all family and friends." Daniel sighed. "Do you mind if I hold on to this for a while?" He wanted to look at it later when he hadn't been drinking, but more importantly, he didn't want Hugh obsessing over it when there was nothing he could do.

"All right."

Daniel refolded the paper and put it in his pocket.

"I'm cursed," Hugh said, standing. "Literally, I think. I've got the Montgomery curse, passed down on my mother's side. You know—my grandfather was shot by my uncle while they were hunting, and his father was ruined in business. There are stories up the line as far back as you want to go."

"You're thinking of Lizzie Marsden."

"God help me. I'd actually thought I'd got over my run of bad luck with that one."

Six years earlier, they had been friends with a peer's daughter named Elizabeth Marsden. Lizzie was a young hedonist who had pursued them both at Oxford: Diana the Huntress come to life, with bleached blonde locks and a perfect china-doll face. She was an exquisite clothes horse, flashing about in the newest and most risqué designs. She could have had any man she wanted, and often did. During the month or so when Hugh and Daniel had escorted her about London, they were the focus of everyone's attention. Daniel was less than enthralled; she was too perfect, in his eyes, a little calculating and cold. Hugh hadn't minded her frosty demeanor, possibly because he himself was somewhat aloof. The two of them would have made an attractive pair, both tall and blonde and striking, though Lizzie preferred to go about with one of them on each arm. During that time, both Hugh and Daniel were on the stage, Hugh in *Twelfth Night* and Daniel in a contemporary play. It was their first brush with fame and they were enjoying it. They frequented clubs, where they were recognized for the first time, and it didn't hurt to have the most beautiful girl in London at their side.

"Hey, Flirty," she'd always called Daniel, and though he certainly flirted with beautiful girls from time to time, he had never flirted with her. One didn't need to. In his opinion, she was dangerous. Unfortunately, he didn't follow his instincts and have done with her. The inevitable incident took place at a party in London. There was a raucous crowd, with most of the cast of his play present and some of the other men eyeing him with envy. He'd been talking to a girl who painted sets, and Lizzie had gotten jealous.

"Look what I've got," she announced, interrupting their conversation. She'd started to pull something out of her handbag, and when Daniel realized what it was, he'd taken her hand and pushed it back in. She had laughed. "Of course. You're right. Let's go somewhere more private."

"I'm sorry," he murmured to the girl. He hadn't even gotten to ask her name.

Lizzie had taken him by the hand and dragged him into a bedroom. She took the bag out of her purse and put it on a table, kicking off her shoes before forming snaky little powder lines on the dresser.

"Have some?" she asked.

He shrugged it off. He hated the jitteriness and then the stupor that came over him when he did drugs. He'd worked too hard for what he had to piss it away now on something pointless like cocaine.

Lizzie pulled her blouse over her head and turned toward him. Before he could say a word, she had pushed him down on the bed. Her perfect breasts were visible beneath the sheer bra and he found his hands on her waist, settling her on top of him. It was the only time he slept with her, and he regretted it afterward.

"How long have you known Hugh?" she'd asked while they were still naked.

"Since we were boys," he said.

"Dirty little boys, I'm sure," she'd answered, running her finger in light circles over his chest. "I'll bet you were quite the naughty thing."

Instead of answering, he'd sat up, or tried to, moving her off his chest and onto the bed with a heave.

"I've struck a nerve," she said, laughing. "What sort of mischief did you get up to? Tell Lizzie all about it."

"I need a drink," he'd replied, ignoring her. He'd pulled on his clothes and darted back out to rejoin the party.

A few weeks later, Lizzie had shown up at Hugh's house, drunk again, and tried to cause trouble. Daniel couldn't get out of there fast enough. Hugh had called a cab for her shortly before Daniel left. The next morning, her body was found floating in the Thames. Both men were questioned by the police, but from the amount of drugs in Lizzie's system, it appeared she had committed suicide. She was the tarnish in their crowns, a tale dredged up now and then in *The Sun* or in a *Tattler* column. Hugh rarely spoke of her, even after all this time, but for Daniel, it was a scar no different than the one he had on his arm from an automobile accident years before. The pain might go away, but the reminder was always there.

Neither of them had been intimate with anyone for a long time afterwards, taking particular care not to get involved with anyone who used them for their looks or fame as they rose through the ranks, being chosen for plum roles over other actors. They were closer than brothers, looking out for each other more than ever. In fact, Daniel had often thought it a shame that Alex had never been half the brother to him that Hugh was. After her death, no one like Lizzie Marsden figured in their lives again. There had been various girls throughout the years, but none who had really mattered until Tamsyn Burke. She had captivated them both, in a way that the likes of Lizzie Marsden could never do. But now she, too, was dead.

Daniel began rooting about in the pantry, emerging with two potatoes. "I think if we're going to deal with this, we oughtn't do it on an empty stomach. Crack a couple of eggs there and I'll make the chips."

They chopped and fried in Marthe's spotless kitchen. Hugh stirred the eggs, and Daniel reached over to hand him the salt, bumping him in the arm, an unspoken way of relating his sorrow. In spite of his own grief, he was devastated for Hugh. To be moments away from marrying the girl you loved, only to lose her forever, was an unimaginable tragedy.

After eating a few bites, he pushed his plate away. It was nearing midnight, and for whatever reason, the police apparently wanted to see him. "Speaking of cursed … "

"Ah," Hugh murmured. "The police."

"I suppose I should go round and have a word."

"It's the middle of the night. Go in the morning." Hugh raised a brow. "Besides, there's something I haven't told you."

"What is it?" Daniel asked. He suddenly had a sick feeling in the pit of his stomach.

Instead of answering, Hugh took out his mobile and began jabbing at icons with his finger. After a few seconds, he handed it to Daniel.

"What is it?"

"A death threat, sent to me by anonymous email."

Daniel stared at him for a moment before taking the phone and looking at the screen: *You don't deserve to live. I'm coming after you.*

"When did you get this?" he asked.

"About ten days ago. I didn't think much of it at the time. I wasn't even sure it was meant for me."

"Did you tell the police?"

"Yes, I told them tonight. I had all but forgotten it until … " He looked down, unable to say the words.

"What did they say?"

"They consider it a credible threat under the circumstances."

"What are you going to do?"

"Father's stepped up on that one. He's hiring bodyguards even as we speak. The police are looking into it in the meantime."

"Is it connected to Tamsyn?"

"What other answer could there be?"

Daniel shook his head, trying to take it all in. "What can I do?" he asked.

"Just being here is everything."

Daniel stood and slipped on his coat, which was still damp. Hugh held out his hand and Daniel took it, looking at the grim expression on his best friend's face. He would do everything in his power to help him. He didn't know how, but he did know one thing: there was nothing he would rather do than find out who had killed Tamsyn Burke.

And then he'd do everything he could to make that person pay.

SIX

An hour later, Daniel came out of the police station knowing little more than he had before he arrived, although he did learn that Inspector Murray had not been among the policemen who had been at the Ashley-Hunts' that evening. According to the desk sergeant, Murray had taken statements at the Abbey, then worked at his desk for a couple of hours and left at nine o'clock.

"So who went to my flat?" Daniel asked, confused.

"No one from this borough," the sergeant said. "I'm sure you'll be contacted if any further statement is required."

Without any way of discovering which investigators had been looking for him, the only thing to do was to go home and try to sleep. That hour of the night, it was an effort to find a cab. Daniel walked for a couple of blocks, wishing he had driven his own car. The city showed scant signs of life at a quarter past two in the morning. When he hailed a taxi, he found that obtaining transportation did not improve his spirits. It felt as though they were flying at warp speed, taking half-mile leaps as he stared blindly through the windows. The food at

Hugh's house had sobered him, although not as much as the conversation. He had focused so much on his own feelings of loss that he hadn't appreciated how Hugh felt until then. Perhaps Marc Hayley was right—Tamsyn's death could damage his career. Not that it mattered from a financial perspective. Hugh hadn't chosen acting for the money, and Daniel had sometimes wondered if he loved acting for its own sake or if he was competing with his father's stellar career. Most actors he knew were compelled to do it, though of course some fell into it by chance. Daniel considered himself one of the latter. He was good at a few things, like literature and grammar, and his mother had hoped for quite a long time that he would teach, but he had never seriously considered it. He enjoyed acting because he liked being immersed in a world apart from his own, a false world in which he looked better and sounded wiser, and where everything came out right in the end. Hugh didn't seem to feel the same about it, but Daniel had never been certain.

Finally deposited in front of his building, he paid the driver and hesitated on the step before going in. He lit a cigarette, wondering how life could change so drastically in twenty-four hours. After a few minutes, he went inside, taking the lift up to his flat. He locked the door behind him and went into the bedroom, where he fell upon the bed. He tossed and turned for nearly an hour until weariness overtook him.

The following morning, Daniel woke late. His head pounded as though he hadn't slept at all. It's the first day without her, he thought, staring at the window across from his bed; the first day when the sun will rise and set without Tamsyn alive to see it. As he poured his first cup of coffee, his mobile buzzed, and he peered at it before answering. It would be his mother, of course, wondering how he was doing. Instead, Tamsyn's face stared at him from the screen.

"Tam?" he said, his heart hammering once again. Had it all been a nightmare after all?

"No," said a matter-of-fact voice. "It's Carey."

It took a moment for Daniel to calm down and realize it was Tamsyn's sister. "Good God, you called from her phone!"

"I didn't have your number."

"I'm sorry. It startled me." He tried to recover himself. "How are you?"

"Holding on. Just."

"And your parents?"

"I haven't seen them this morning, but they're devastated. They don't understand how this could have happened."

"I'm sorry," he repeated, not knowing what else to say.

"I can't think of a motive, Daniel. There's no reason why someone would want her dead."

"Nor can I."

"Can you meet me?" she asked. "We need to talk."

He hesitated, hating himself as he did so. Did Carey blame him somehow for her sister's death? "When?" he asked. "Today?"

"This morning."

"Yes, of course. Shall I come round to your flat?"

"No," she answered. "My parents are coming over. They'll be making arrangements."

"I can meet you anywhere. Just name the place."

"There's a café in Arundel Street, Angelo's."

"Near the university. I know it." He'd dropped Tamsyn there once when she'd met Carey for lunch. "I'll be there in half an hour."

Daniel hung up, wondering if he should ring Hugh. Instead, he locked the door and made his way to the Underground. It was cold outside, hardly the spring day the previous one had been, and beneath the streets it was colder still. He exited near King's College, hurrying down the Embankment. He found the café and went inside to wait. She arrived two minutes after him and spied him the moment she walked through the door.

Daniel stood as she approached the table. For some reason, he found it unbearable waiting to hear her speak. As different as Carey was from Tamsyn, he knew that her speech patterns and expressions would conjure her sister's face. She wore a brown hooded cardigan and jeans, looking more like a teenager than a medical student. The impression wasn't improved when a lock of hair fell over her face and she brushed it back.

"Have a seat," he said, pulling out a chair. "I've ordered coffees."

"Thank you," she answered, sitting down. "Let's get straight to the point. I think we should reconstruct the scene to try to figure out exactly what happened. We need to make a list of everyone who was in that part of the Abbey yesterday."

"I already have one," he said, tapping his pocket, where he had tucked the list from Hugh.

"May I see it?"

He paused for a moment and then handed it over, watching as she read it through twice.

"Are you certain this is everyone who was in that room? I didn't think to look."

"Oh, I looked, all right. I was the last one questioned, so I had plenty of time to watch people being called in. This is absolutely correct."

"It's hard to imagine someone she knew this well ... "

"I know," he said, cutting her off. He wasn't certain he could stand this, and he had no idea how she could, either. "Perhaps you shouldn't try to get involved with things. I'm sure it must be painful."

"Don't tell me what to do."

"I only meant—"

"Oh, I know what you meant," Carey snapped. "You meant, 'Leave it to the police.' Well, I can't. Tamsyn was the only sister I had. I can't do nothing. And I should think you, as her friend, would be glad to help."

"Of course," he stammered.

"Good. I'm sure we can figure things out."

"We can't interfere in the police investigation, you know," he said. "They take that sort of thing quite seriously."

"If we leave it to the police, it will take forever, if it gets solved at all," Carey said. "I'm not going to have my parents sit through a protracted investigation while the whole thing is rehashed in the papers every day. Someone out there killed my sister, and I intend to find out why."

"That's admirable. I'm just not certain how effective it will be."

"Either you help me or you don't."

Daniel could see it was no use. She would not be dissuaded. Then again, in her position, he probably wouldn't be either.

"All right," he said. "But there's something you need to know. Hugh received a death threat about a fortnight ago. The police are looking into it."

"Oh, god. What about Tamsyn?"

"This threat came to him, not the two of them. He didn't even know if it was a serious threat."

"Even more reason for us to get started," Carey said. "Let's divide up this list: family, friends, acquaintances. Hold on, I have some paper."

He watched as she fumbled in her bag and took out a pen. The coffees arrived and he took a gulp of the scalding liquid to fortify himself.

"Family," he repeated, trying to expedite matters. "That would mean you and your parents. None of whom, of course, are suspect. I say we go straight to some of the others, like Cole and Potter."

"You mustn't jump to conclusions. Inevitably, they're wrong. I could have hated her for all you know."

"But you didn't."

"You can't know that for certain. You don't know me very well."

"That's true, I don't," Daniel agreed. "But I'm still certain you had nothing to do with it. Otherwise you'd never be here trying to find out who did. Now, back to family. That would include Hugh, wouldn't it? I mean, they were minutes away from becoming man and wife."

"Next you'll say his family counts as her family, too."

"Well, say what you want about the Ashley-Hunts, but they're no murderers. I've known them for years."

Carey set her pen on top of her paper. "Perhaps this was a mistake after all."

"All right," Daniel said, sighing. "It's just hard to think of anyone on this list as a cold-blooded killer."

"Then think of it as eliminating them, one by one, as possible suspects. We're exonerating those who are innocent of a crime."

Her jaw was set with such determination that he couldn't even begin to argue with her. What would Tamsyn have wanted? he asked himself. And suddenly he knew that if she could, Tamsyn Burke would come back from Purgatory or Heaven or wherever her soul now resided and insist that he help her sister in this impossible, final act of sisterly love.

It was the least he could do.

"How long have you known Hugh?" Carey asked.

Daniel put the list on the table. "We met when we were thirteen, when we were both recommended for Junior Guildhall, an acting class. I wasn't having an easy time of it. You know, the kid from Brighton without money or connections, a complete outsider in a cutthroat environment. I was on the verge of quitting just to escape the bullying when Hugh rescued me. We've been as close as brothers ever since."

"Tamsyn loved him, too."

Daniel sighed. "When's the funeral?"

"The day after tomorrow."

"So, if one of these people is a murderer, are they more likely or less likely to come?"

"More likely, I think," she said after some hesitation. "They wouldn't want to be conspicuous by their absence."

He had to admit she was right, but the thought of sitting through the funeral with a killer in their midst was more than unfathomable. It was terrifying.

———

Detective Chief Inspector Gordon Murray of Scotland Yard held the same opinion. He had rung Tamsyn Burke's parents and inked the funeral into his agenda book. In the meantime, he had men following three of the wedding guests: Marc Hayley, Alex Richardson, and Ciaran Monaghan, although if nothing unusual turned up within the next forty-eight hours, he would turn his attention elsewhere. For the moment, he was not monitoring the activities of the other Richardson brother, Daniel, who had been seen by a number of witnesses arguing with Sarah Williams shortly before the body was found. It had been a heated conversation, and from the witnesses' perspectives it was clear that Sarah Williams was angry over being jilted by Richardson. The murder inquiry was also complicated by the death threat that Hugh Ashley-Hunt had received, but of course at this early stage it was impossible to tell if it was related to his fiancée's murder. Now they had to find the source of that email and determine if there was any connection.

Tamsyn Burke had been stabbed with an ordinary knife, which had been stashed in a plastic bag and then stuffed in an urn. Unfortunately, there were no discernible prints on the weapon, which the lab had confirmed. It was damned unfortunate when there was no physical evidence left behind.

Murray looked up when he heard a knock at the door. "Come in."

It was his subordinate, Detective Sergeant Ennis, with a handful of files. "As you requested, sir," he said.

Murray looked back down at the form in front of him and signed his name at the bottom. "Did you find anything interesting, Sergeant?"

Ennis was an earnest young man of twenty-eight, eager to learn as much as he could from Murray. He'd become indispensable in the six months they had worked together. His mother, a native of Jamaica, had married an Irishman; the couple had settled in London, where an interracial marriage was more acceptable than in his father's Gaelic village. He was tall and wiry, with a wide, prominent nose and short, cropped black hair. Since working for Murray, he'd become something of a clothes horse, and it had elicited comments among his peers, none of them complimentary.

For the last few hours, Ennis had been running background checks on the twenty-seven people on the suspect list. Murray was interested to see if there had been any previous arrests or convictions among them.

"A few of them have had priors," Ennis said, handing over the files. "It goes way back. Owen Burke had four arrests for drunkenness in the '80s and '90s."

"The victim's father."

"Right. More recently, Lucy Potter was arrested for theft but not convicted. Alex Richardson has a few minor drug charges. Ciaran Monaghan and Marc Hayley have each been charged once with assault."

"How recently for Hayley?"

"Three years ago. He lost his temper and got into a fight with a reporter in a wine bar in Ealing."

"Not exactly unexpected behavior for an actor." Murray flipped through the files, and after a couple of minutes set them on the corner of his desk. Nothing appeared to point to anyone as a murderer.

"What do you think, sir?"

Murray tapped his finger on the desk, frowning. "One thing's for certain. No one could have stabbed that girl to death and been so nonchalant about it unless they'd killed before."

After Ennis left, he looked at the clock on the wall. It was already after six. He hadn't moved much in the last two or three hours and his neck was getting stiff. Leaving the files on the desk to review in the morning, he took his jacket from the coat rack behind the door and made his way through "A" Division, mulling over what he had read. Something seemingly unimportant, some minuscule fact, perhaps, would filter through the long list of suspects and motives and make its way to the top. He just had to sift through things until it happened. In the car park, he made his way through the sea of dark vehicles and unlocked his Audi. His brow furrowed in concentration as he started the car. Who stands to benefit from this murder? he wondered. As he pulled onto Broadway, he saw that the traffic was bad again. It was always bad these days. When he went out on a case, he usually had Ennis drive him. As it was, he was thinking of giving up the car and relying on the Tube.

Murray headed north on Grosvenor Place toward Belgravia, to the tall white row house he called home. It had belonged to his Uncle Roger, who had left it to him twenty years earlier. As a young constable, he could never have afforded such a home without the bequest, but it suited him perfectly now. Inside, it was as neat and orderly as it had been when his wife was alive, and he had changed nothing about it from the furniture placement to the dishes in the cupboards.

When he discovered it had been left to him, it had been quite a shock. He and his wife had been living in a second-floor flat in Islington, surrounded by noisy neighbors with too many children, and had never expected to inherit anything, much less a house. Ingrid, a tall Swedish blonde he had met at university, was the sort of woman he'd never even looked at during his bachelor days. She was too beautiful, too perfect, for an ordinary man like him. Yet somehow, she had loved him. They had been married five years when they'd moved into this house, and though she'd kept all of his uncle's furniture, she had swept away the stuffiness of the house and filled it with a lightness he had never imagined.

They had spent years trying to get pregnant, and it was his greatest regret that he had not been able to have children with her. Then, four years ago, she had found a lump in her right breast, and six months later he was a widower.

When he arrived at the house, he parked the car in the street and went inside, observing his rituals: hanging his coat on a hook, sifting through the mail on the hall table, touching the surface of the buffet in the sitting room where the drinks tray was laid. Ingrid had painted that piece, as she had a few of the others, a Carl Larsson blue. It made him think of their last trip to Sweden and her parents' home in Katrineholm, where they'd gone shortly after her diagnosis. It had been summer, and they had eaten gravlax and dumplings and walked among the shops, sitting outside on the long summer nights as he listened to her talking about his life without her. He had found it unbearable to speak of such a thing, but living without her had been immeasurably worse.

Sighing, he picked up the telephone and ordered his usual Monday takeaway to be delivered, and then poured a glass of wine, a Bordeaux that was Ingrid's favorite, and waited in the sitting room. When the food arrived a half hour later, he took out a pen and paper and began to make notes while picking at his lamb tikka and bombay aloo. *Who killed Tamsyn Burke?* he wrote at the top of the page. Then he scribbled a name on the paper and circled it. It was process of elimination now, and one might as well start at the top.

SEVEN

TAMSYN BURKE HAD COME into Daniel's life unexpectedly, and all because of an opportunity for him to work with Hugh in a film. Despite their close friendship, Daniel and Hugh had never been cast in any production together since their days at the Royal Academy of Dramatic Art. Their interests, like their personalities, ran along dissimilar veins: Hugh preferred to act in historical pictures when the opportunity arose, while Daniel opted for contemporary films. From time to time, Hugh had mentioned the possibility of working together, but Daniel had privately thought himself far too competitive to star in any film opposite his best friend. He was surprised that Hugh would welcome it either.

As they were establishing themselves in the public eye, they were known to be friends, but until Sir John Hodges contacted them, no one else had approached them for the same project. Daniel supposed this was inevitable. Although there existed an incredible wealth of acting talent on their small island, theirs was a field where nepotism mattered almost as much as ability.

"Come down for the weekend, Daniel, so we can at least discuss the possibility," Sir John had insisted when he rang. "Ashley-Hunt seems quite eager."

Daniel had decided that a break from London after the long, wet month of June was in order, as long as Hugh was so keen to go. They'd taken an early train to Paris, where they rented a car and drove to the Hodges' home a few kilometers south of Lille. Daniel had been to France a number of times, most notably a couple of years earlier when he'd been involved with an attractive French chef from Perpignan. For one brief weekend he had considered settling down in the Pyrenees, where they would open a restaurant and raise enormous dogs. The relationship, while more serious than any previous one, eventually ran its course, and he smiled to himself when he remembered how he'd avoided the continent for a while after that. Regardless, it was good to be back. The landscape of northern France had awoken from the dormancy of winter and everything was in full bloom. Thick, verdant beech trees lined the road and wildflowers were scattered across the fields.

They arrived mid-afternoon, pulling up to a late-nineteenth-century house. It was pink stucco adorned with weather-beaten green shutters and ivy, a crumbling, timeworn French maison. Sir John and his wife were perfect hosts. The food was excellent, their rooms comfortable, and there was no talk about films. As a matter of fact, a very satisfactory day passed without any mention of it at all, and when at last the subject did arise, it was more tempting than Daniel had expected.

"I want to do *Under the Greenwood Tree*," Sir John told them over a good Pinot Noir in his library.

"Hardy," Hugh said. "A vicar and a farmer vying for the same girl. Is that right?"

"Yes, that's the one."

"Who'll play the girl?"

"I haven't cast the girl yet, but we're looking at a number of suitable actresses. It would have to be someone well known, to balance things out with the two of you."

"I don't believe we've accepted just yet," Daniel said, swirling the wine in his glass.

"Oh, but you will. Think of it. It will make the film. Everyone will want to see you together."

"I presume you'll film in Dorset?" Hugh asked.

"Yes. I've already found a location. We stayed there a few weeks ago and discovered a rather unspoiled village that would be perfect. I have people there now making arrangements."

"I'm still not convinced it would be the best idea for us to be in the same film," Daniel said.

"Why not?" Hugh asked. "We've talked about it before."

"True, but I didn't really take it seriously. It would be rather like doing a movie with someone you're married to."

"We could handle it. Besides, we'd each bring different strengths to the film."

"You must do it," Hodge's wife, Antonia, said as she entered the room. She was a tall, perfectly coiffed dyed blonde of a certain age who wore what Daniel considered dangerously high heels. She went over to the cabinet and poured herself a small sherry. "You're bookends, you see. Light and dark. Good and evil. I, for one, would kill to see you both in it. Do consider it."

"I believe that makes you the evil one," Hugh said to Daniel, laughing.

"It's a nice afternoon for a swim," Sir John interrupted. "Why talk business when there's fun to be had?"

"Excellent," Hugh said, rising from his chair. "Just the thing for a pleasant afternoon."

The subject didn't come up again until they were about to leave the following day. Sir John followed them to the car and shook their hands.

"I'll have scripts sent round," he said, as if they had come to an agreement.

Daniel was ready to protest when Hugh intervened. "That would be wonderful. Thank you for considering us."

"Yes," Daniel echoed as he opened the car door. "And thank you for the weekend, as well."

Three hours later, they had deposited the car at the rental agency and were on the ferry to England, and Daniel, after some persuasion, had agreed to make the film. The mast flag flapped in the breeze, which, while not quite a gale, was nevertheless strong enough to encourage most people to go inside. Daniel stood alone at the rail, staring at the retreating coast of France and not really thinking of the Hodges or the film they were producing or of Hugh's enthusiasm for the project, but of the satisfaction of days like this. He liked the disconnected feeling he had just now, as if he were cut off from everything in the world. Even his mobile couldn't get reception in the middle of the Channel. No one, neither agent nor family nor friends, could bother him in any way. It felt majestic having the deck to himself, and he was very glad he hadn't let Hugh talk him into taking the Eurostar back to London.

"You're missing one of the best experiences a person can have," he'd chided when his friend announced his intention to get a drink and brace himself from the elements, such as they were on a sunny day in July.

"God, no," Hugh had replied. "I still say we should have taken the train. Give me champagne and hake with gruyere in first class any day over a stiff wind and a plastic molded seat."

"You don't sit on a ferry, gobhead. You beat your chest and feel the wind in your face and, for this one hour, you own the Channel and everything you see."

"You're a romantic of the worst kind. Never deny yourself the odd bit of luxury. Life can be so cruel."

Daniel laughed. "Yes, I imagine it's been very hard for you. Best go find sustenance in the form of alcohol."

"Thanks, I believe I shall."

From the deck, Daniel took a last look at the pier and lighthouse growing smaller in the afternoon sun and then turned to face north. With only a thin band of clouds hovering high in the sky, the white cliffs of Dover were visible, even at this distance. Studying them, he felt an unexpected rush of pleasure. He didn't think of himself as a nationalist, but certain images, these cliffs among them, gave him a strong sense of pride. The day was beautiful, and he was fortunate after a weekend's freeloading to be here experiencing it instead of trapped in some office or even on location for a film. It would be an agreeable hour contemplating the gulls and watching the water ripple where the cod and plaice nipped up to the surface, the sort of thing that he would think about on rainy autumn days to take his mind off the bone-numbing chill.

He didn't notice the girl at first. She sat on a bench several feet away from him, a small thing wearing a sundress and sandals with an enormously wide-brimmed hat on her head. She hardly moved. In fact, it was almost as if she were asleep behind the dark sunglasses she wore. Yet, even though she sat so still, something about her arrested his attention. When she suddenly moved to look at him, he realized he'd been staring.

"Why aren't you inside, like everyone else?" she asked.

Daniel made an expansive gesture and smiled. "I'm taking this all in, of course. It's far too nice a day to spend it indoors."

"That's what I think, too." She removed her sunglasses and placed them on her lap. "What were you doing in France?"

He was surprised at her directness, almost as much as he was by the enormity of her deep brown eyes. "Business," he said, shrugging. He didn't get personal with people he didn't know.

"I was day-tripping. That's a fun word, day-tripping, isn't it? I went shopping and treated myself to lunch."

"Alone?" he couldn't help but ask.

"Yes," she admitted as she stood and walked over to stand by him at the rail. "I had a look around Calais. It was my first trip to France."

She could do a good job better than Calais, he thought, although his answer was more civil. "There are a lot of nice things to see in France."

"Oh, I'm sure there are. Maybe one day you'll show me."

In spite of himself, Daniel smiled. "We're to become great friends, are we?"

"Of course. And it's not because you're a film star that I'm adding you to my list."

"Your list?" he asked, uncomfortable now that she had recognized him.

"Yes, my list. I'm putting you on because you have a nice face."

"As do you," he replied, wondering if he could make a graceful escape. He didn't chat up strangers. One never knew what they might want. Suddenly a Pimms with Hugh and a molded plastic seat sounded almost appealing.

"I'm Tamsyn," she said, adjusting her hat. "Tamsyn Burke."

"That's a good name," he said. "Not the sort someone could forget."

Her face, with its large eyes and Cupid's bow lips, was not forgettable either. There was something about her. Perhaps it wouldn't hurt to talk to her a little bit longer. After all, he couldn't help but feel sorry for her. Nothing was more wretched than taking a day trip to Calais on one's own.

"So, did you see the sights?" he asked. "The Hotel de Ville is very nice. A classic example of Flemish Renaissance architecture, if I'm correct."

"You're bound to be," she said. "But I'm afraid I was more interested in flower stalls and poky little junk shops. And there was a café, facing the Channel, with the wind ruffling the edges of the umbrellas and the smell of the fishing boats coming in from the sea."

"And most people just think Calais is a good place to score cheap booze. It's nice to see someone who can appreciate it for its intrinsic value."

"You're laughing at me," she said, in such a way that he wondered if she were laughing at him. "So, what shall we see in Paris when we go?"

"Oh, Paris," he mimicked, trying to imagine an adventure with this improbable girl. "That depends on your personality. You see, if you're the serious type, we'd walk through the Père Lachaise looking for Édith Piaf's grave, or spend interminable hours in the Louvre uncovering the mystery of why there are so many portraits of Josephine Bonaparte. Or perhaps we would sit at Les Deux Magots drinking bad coffee and reading Sartre or Hemingway and pretending they make sense."

"But I'm not like that, of course."

"Oh, you're not like that at all. You're a free spirit. You know: the sort to lean over the deck of a bateaux mouche to see if you can see your reflection in the Seine. Or eating melting ice cream on the Île Saint-Louis. Anything but ordinary."

"You know, I thought you'd be a pompous arse. Actors generally are."

"I beg your pardon?"

"I should know. I'm an actor, too."

He gave her a skeptical look while trying to keep a straight face.

"Oh, I'm not in the Jane Austen set like your lot," she explained unselfconsciously. "I do the odd science fiction television program. You know, dinosaurs taking over the earth and mummies coming to life in the British Museum, that sort of thing."

"Is that what you meant to do when you were at school?"

"I've changed my mind. You are a pompous arse."

"At least we have that sorted. Would you like a drink?"

Tamsyn pulled off her hat and rested it on the railing. "I'd love one."

He left her to purchase two lemonades from the mini café inside, pausing to exchange a smile with Hugh, who was observing his tête-à-tête with the girl. Hugh raised his glass in a mock toast, and Daniel shook his head. She wasn't the sort of girl one chats up and takes to bed two hours later. He knew better than that. She was the sort you leave almost immediately after meeting and then wonder why the hell you can't get her out of your mind.

EIGHT

In spite of its location off Trafalgar Square, amidst the angry snarl of Charing Cross Road and St. Martin's Lane, the National Portrait Gallery remains a haven for deep thinkers and scholars who come primarily to transport themselves to other places and times. The massive stone walls shelter their inhabitants from the strident London traffic, which shunts incalculable numbers of passengers to and from various means of employment, meals, and business dealings of every kind. The gallery provides a place to contemplate the faces contained therein, some of which were fashioned of paint, others in pen and ink, not to mention observe the stark contradiction between the grandness of bronze sculptures and the more modest plasticine medallions. All are capable of inspiring interest and giving the viewer the ability to recreate, at least in the mind's eye, the exact mental picture he or she hopes to attain.

It was shortly after agreeing to appear in Sir John's film that Daniel found himself doing precisely that as he stood in front of the portrait of Thomas Hardy, oil on panel, by William Strang. The portrait was how he'd imagined it: entrancing. Hardy's slightly balding head was captured bent in thought, eyes downcast, sad, almost, as if he were grieving or thinking of a love that he had once possessed but now lost. His full, bushy eyebrows dominated the upper half of his head, his even more voluminous mustache the lower, and the subtle play of hues behind his dark suit set the tone for an ominous mood. Certainly, if the author had been contemplating one of his characters, he was thinking not of *Under the Greenwood Tree*'s resilient Fancy Day but more likely of his heroine Tess, for the miseries with which he endowed her poor character would indeed have the power to cause him tremendous pain.

Daniel wasn't overfond of portraits, or pictures of any kind. They were antithetical to the dramatic arts. He did, however, see the activity of searching out any and all relevant information as an important exercise in the preparation for a role, not unlike memorizing lines of dialogue or watching a previous version of a film in order to determine what, if anything, might be useful to him in his art. Hardy's expressive face spoke volumes in the silent room. He had been a man who cared deeply about the people he created in his novels, and if he were able to see them now, would have opinions about every aspect of their depiction on film. At any rate, taking the odd hour in the NPG made Daniel feel he was substantiating his claim on his current undertaking.

He preferred the Victorian portraits to the other collections, for although he found photography somewhat more interesting, actors were frequently the subject of the newer collections and it was an odd sensation to see life-size photos of people one knew or with whom one worked. Hugh's likeness had recently been added to the collection; he could be seen posing with a glass of champagne on a perch at Stonehenge. That in itself was certainly worth avoiding. It was fine to celebrate the works of actors like Sir Laurence Olivier or Dame Judi Dench, who had created a body of work which could be nothing less than deeply admired and who perhaps deserved, after decades of honing their craft, to be showcased in just such a manner, but to have his contemporaries, even his own friends, portrayed thusly, the people he got drunk with and ate with and spent half his time with … well, it was unimaginable.

He sat down on a bench, having accomplished his plan for the morning. He'd done what he had come to do—taken a serious look at the face of Thomas Hardy—and now he had to decide what to do next. Daniel was rarely bored; the innumerable activities provided by a city the size of London practically forbade it; but, nonetheless, he hadn't found anyone available to join him for lunch and he didn't like to eat alone. His mother had asked him down to Brighton for the day, but he had begged off. In fact, for the last two years, he had seen his family only at Christmas and once or twice in the summer, when he would take the morning train down and the earliest return trip back to London that he could manage. He didn't mind seeing his parents, but his brother was an irritation he preferred to avoid. He had also been invited to spend the day with Hugh's family, but he had done so recently and felt he could forego that particular duty. He had looked forward to a day of complete self-indulgence, and yet, now that he had it, he had no idea what to do with it.

After sitting for a few more minutes, he resolved to get a curry on the way back to his flat and spend the afternoon watching old videos. As he stood, he heard a voice call out to him.

"Daniel Richardson!"

He turned, and though he had no idea whom to expect, it certainly wasn't the familiar face that beamed up at him, which belonged to the girl he'd recently met on the ferry. She looked even younger than she had before, wearing an absurd vintage frock that must have been quite the rage in 1962. If she had been wearing go-go boots instead of bottle-green ballet flats the color of her dress, she would have conjured images of the Beatles singing "Love Me Do."

"I see you're stalking me," Daniel said. He couldn't help smiling.

"In a city of eight million people, that seems rather impossible."

"No doubt. What are you doing here? I hadn't pegged you as the sort to spend Sunday mornings looking at portraits."

"I was supposed to meet someone for lunch. It looks like I've been stood up."

"Then why don't you have lunch with me?" he said, the words erupting from his lips before he had even considered what he was saying.

"Do you often come here to pick up girls?" she asked in mock disapproval.

"Every day." He shoved his hands into his pockets. "Come on. It'll be fun."

She smiled, her broad, full lips devoid of any lipstick. Her hair was a riot of red waves, sun-streaked and natural, reminding him of girls at school. He wondered how old she was. Surely she was nearly his age. She looked younger, but there was something knowing in her eyes.

"Where would you like to eat?" he asked when they were out in the street, standing on the pebbled mosaic outside the door.

"Let's have a picnic."

He was pleased with her suggestion. Anyone else would have named a posh restaurant where she might have been seen with him. He was used to that by now.

"Well, I haven't a blanket, for one thing," he argued, hoping she would at least choose a respectable café. "Or a hamper from Harrods full of smoked salmon and caviar."

"You're just spoiled. Anything can be a picnic if you eat it outside in the fresh air."

They settled for a lump of Stilton, a loaf of bread, and two apples purchased from a nearby shop, taking their finds to a bench overlooking the Thames. It was a bit Parisian for his taste. Meals were meant to be eaten with a knife and fork, and wine was meant to be poured into glasses rather than shared in sips from the same bottle. Yet at the same time there was something pleasant about sitting with her and staring beyond the London Eye to the violet clouds beyond. Rain threatened overhead, but for now, there was a stillness, almost an air of expectation.

"We'd better go," he said a half hour later, trying to think of a way to ask if he could see her again.

"What are you doing tomorrow night?" she asked. "Some friends are having a party."

"Sorry. I can't."

"Of course not. You're too famous to mingle with the average Briton."

"No, I mean, I'm going to Dorset tomorrow. I'm leaving early."

"Oh! Well, I'll come with you."

"Oh, you will, will you? No other plans to keep you here? What about the party?"

She wrinkled her nose. "Never mind about that. It would have been dull anyway."

"Be that as it may, I'm not going away for the day. I'll be gone weeks."

"Take me along anyway. The minute you're tired of me, put me on a train and send me right back to London."

"And what might you do in Dorset, may I ask?"

"Work, presumably. I assume you're there to do a film, and as it's Dorset, it's bound to be a period drama. I could get a part as an extra. 'Girl With Sheep' or something."

"How very Bouguereau of you. Do you have your own little crook?"

"Doesn't everyone?"

"Still..." he said, looking up again as he heard the first crack of thunder.

"I won't impose on you, really. I'll find someone to room with when I get there. I just need a change."

"I can't believe I'm even considering it."

"Of course you can. It's inevitable. We're going to be great friends. Might as well start now."

To Dorset, she came. The following morning, he picked her up in front of the flat she shared in Paddington and stowed her two battered bags in the boot of his car. She wasn't talkative, preferring to nurse a cup of coffee, though whether she was hung over or deep in thought, he wasn't sure. After they were out of London, she lowered the window to feel the breeze on her face. Twice, she asked him to stop the car so she could get out and look at the view. He was happy to comply. It was a warm day, and he took off his jacket and rolled up his sleeves. Occasionally he glanced at his wristwatch out of habit, but in actuality he was unconcerned about the time. It had been a year and a half since he had been out of London to shoot a film in the country, and he had forgotten the elation he felt to be forced out of his usual habits and routines and given the opportunity to live life at a different pace. Acting was a hurry up and wait sort of job, with a great deal of preparation and action at the beginning degenerating into a measured, thoughtful activity of getting the retakes exactly right.

The second time Daniel and Tamsyn stopped, they were deep in the countryside. They got out of the car, she walking ahead of him, entranced by the sight in front of her.

"Look!" she cried, examining the blackthorn, which grew some distance from the road. "They're beautiful. You'd never see this in London."

"You're Welsh, aren't you?" he asked.

"Yes. My family still lives there."

She was almost beautiful then. Daniel smiled, bending over the flowers for a moment as she turned and walked deeper into the meadow. The air was still and quiet, and even a few steps from the road one could forget that modern civilization was there behind them. He was used to the din of the city, the constant noise of the modern industrial society from which untold millions never had a rest and knew no other way of life. Hardy himself in *Greenwood* spoke of the blooming apple trees and fallen petals of the Dorset countryside, and though Daniel could never express with the same elegance or fineness of feeling what he saw before him, he felt it now, reaching his very bones. No sound could be heard apart from the wrens and thrushes warbling the occasional mid-flight tune. They were as alone as Adam and Eve, and as innocent as the biblical pair before Shame entered their souls and filled them with the need to cover their naked bodies.

Tamsyn ran through the grass, enveloping herself in the exquisiteness of it as though Daniel weren't even there, pausing for a moment to gaze ahead, where the European Chalk Formation gave way to the sandstones of east Dorset. The downs rose and swelled in perfect, damp greenness, a glorious postcard of beauty, making him wish he had a camera with him. Yet he knew that no man-made, artificial device could record what he saw in that moment. The clouds crouched low upon the farthest hills, as if heaven reached out to bless the earth in just that very spot, along with the frail mortals who had stumbled into Paradise.

He waited while she took her fill, and then without a word, they returned to the car and continued on their way. They arrived not long after in Colebridge, a village perched on sloping hills and dotted round with trees. There, they drove up to a row of stone houses, gray and white and tan, their colors muted and fading against the deepest cobalt sky. Daniel pulled a paper from his pocket and consulted his notes before turning at the first church he came to.

"What are you looking for?" Tamsyn asked. She hadn't spoken in some time, lost in a reverie he had been loath to interrupt.

"My friend's house. Well, not really his house. It's been rented for him during his stay. I thought I would stop in before I go to the hotel."

"Why don't you stay in a house, too?" she asked.

"Not my style." Daniel glanced at her as he pulled in front of a thatched-roof cottage and parked the car. "I like my freedom."

"Doesn't everyone?"

They stepped out of the car. Daniel pocketed his keys and knocked at the door, which swung open almost at once.

"Ah, you made it," Hugh said, stepping aside for them to enter.

The house, certainly a Grade I and possibly a Grade II, looked as though its owners had been booted out, leaving everything in a state of elegant comfort. There were deep armchairs and shelves of books and even paintings on the walls of peonies and English dales and the ubiquitous spaniels of which middle-aged persons are so fond. Someone had assembled a household of possessions selected with great care over many years, and it would be lived in for weeks or months as though it were a mere backdrop for the conversations that would be held within its walls.

"Hugh, this is my friend Tamsyn. She's hoping to get a small role in the film."

"We'll have to put in a word for you, then," Hugh answered. He held open the door. "Come in. I have lunch ready. I hope you're hungry."

"Always," Daniel said, watching Tamsyn as she walked across the stone steps and into the sitting room.

"Straight through," Hugh called to her, indicating the open door that led to the garden out back. He stopped and looked at Daniel, arching a brow. "So, who is she? I'm surprised. This is not your usual style."

"It's not what you think," Daniel argued. "It's a lark. She's fun, that's all. She dabbles in acting and asked to come along."

"She can stay here, unless you're taking her in."

"I'll get her a room at the hotel for a couple of nights."

"Nonsense. I have all this space. Why shouldn't she stay a night or two, as long as you've dragged her all this way? For that matter, why don't you stay, too? You can play nurse."

"Thanks, but I prefer to keep things simple." Daniel laughed. "If I took a house, I'd probably end up inviting some girl I hardly know to stay with me. We'll be busy, anyway."

There were a great number of things to be accomplished within the first few days: wardrobe fittings, rehearsals, finding some kind of bit part for Tamsyn. Daniel was suddenly wondering how he had been so easily talked into bringing her along. Hugh led him out onto the terrace, where a cold supper had been prepared. Daniel opened the bottle of wine.

"This looks yummy," he said, pouring it into three glasses. He handed one to Tamsyn.

She accepted the glass with a smile. He felt her eyes on him throughout the meal, during which it was decided that she would stay in one of the empty rooms upstairs.

"Will you be all right?" Daniel asked later, when he was ready to leave.

"Oh, yes," she answered. "Hugh's great, letting me stay. I'll look for a room with someone once I've settled in."

"Good," he pronounced, relieved. "I mean, it will be good for you to have someone to hang about with."

"Are you trying to get rid of me?" she asked, turning her face toward him.

"Maybe you're trying to get rid of me, moving in with someone else."

"You know you'll always be my first love," she said.

He thought, then, that he might kiss her, but at that moment, Hugh walked through the door.

NINE

THE CARTESIAN CIRCLE, LIKE Daniel Richardson's current under-
standing of things, was a mistake in reasoning. In 1641, Descartes
laid out a framework for the meaning of life based on the truth, or
assumption of truth, that a benevolent God exists. Accordingly, God
exists because he has given human beings a mind with which to
think (*Cogito ergo sum; I think, therefore I am*); if God does not control man but has given him a mind to think for himself, he is not a
deceiver; if God is not a deceiver, he is benevolent; therefore, this
benevolence proves that God exists. The philosopher wrote that he
had discarded perception and used deduction as a method of proof.
Yet who amongst us can claim methodical proof that God exists?
Does not even Scripture claim, "Faith is the substance of things
hoped for, the evidence of things not seen"?

Daniel's mistake in reasoning was that one could know the mind
of any other human being. He thought he knew Tamsyn Burke and
Hugh Ashley-Hunt. He thought he knew himself. Instead, he brought
into their lives the catalyst for future life disruption, if not destruction,

however innocent he was of that notion. His personal Cartesian Circle was based on certain assumptions: a perception of Tamsyn Burke blowing the stale sameness out of his life; a perception of Hugh being the Hugh he had always known and could rely on to be his normal, diffident self; and a perception that he himself was at a point in his life when he could arrange events to suit himself for amusement purposes only, without the entanglement of emotion being brought to bear. In each of these opinions, he was to be proven wrong, and it all began with a single statement.

"I think Tamsyn would make an incredible heroine."

Hugh was drunk when he made this declaration, but Daniel, who was not quite as drunk, took it for the omen it was.

"What do you mean?" he insisted, putting down his pint so forcefully it sloshed onto the counter of the bar.

Hugh nodded, as though he had been thinking of the idea for months instead of the brief time he had known her. "There's something about her. She has no business playing some silly bit part when she has such talent. Why, she should star in the bloody picture. I'll bet she would outshine us both. Besides, the part of Fancy still hasn't been cast."

From the beginning, Daniel had thought of Tamsyn as his friend, and the friendlier she became with Hugh, the more concerned he became. It wasn't right for Hugh to steal her right out from under his nose. Nevertheless, he had hidden his feelings from both of them while he struggled to sort them out. He was now feeling a sudden resentment toward her. Who was she, anyway, unsettling his life like this?

For once, Tamsyn wasn't with them. The three of them had so frequently been seen together by the cast and crew in the last few days that they were being referred to as the Trifecta. In the past, whenever Daniel had what might technically be referred to as a dalliance on set, he'd seen less of Hugh and they had spoken on the phone more, dissecting the object of his fancy until she was in such tatters that the relationship was soon ended. Neither of them had ever brought a girl into the other's life, not since the affair with Lizzie Marsden. Now Tamsyn had done the impossible. She had broken through both of their reserves at once.

"Are you sleeping with her?" Daniel asked. He hadn't meant to say the words aloud, but somehow hadn't been able to stop himself.

"Tamsyn Burke? Are you kidding? I've never met anyone more like a kid sister than her in my life. Besides, have you seen that girl who works for the caterer?"

"The chatty blonde?"

"That's the one. I'm thinking of looking into that."

Daniel chuckled into his beer glass, relieved. He gazed around the room. There were a few people from work there, having drinks, too. It was a congenial group of people for the most part, as was evidenced by the fact that they were allowed to enjoy a pint in peace. No one had wandered over, ostensibly to ask some irrelevant question about tomorrow's shoot or to seek an autograph for some nonexistent relative. In fact, things were how he'd hoped they would be. A few friendships had sprung up; a couple of meaningless flirtations were taking place. There was always the odd affair or two among people who have had to uproot their lives for a few weeks and were forced to take rooms in strange towns. There was a little casual sex, a few drinks, a lot of laughs; it was part of itinerate work, whether they were cameramen or wardrobe consultants or actors. The pub was part of the scene, an anonymous place in London or Dorset or wherever they happened to find themselves for the duration, sitting at tables full of half-filled glasses and listening to so much laughing and talking one couldn't take anything seriously. An idea was only half-meant if it was shared in a pub, especially in these conditions.

It was almost August, and the heat from the crowded room was beginning to get to him. Outside, the sun had set and it had begun to cool off, and Daniel found he needed a breath of fresh air. In a village this size there wasn't anywhere else to go in the evening, and he wasn't the sort to hang about his rented flat. He knew that when the cast and crew got to know each other better, they would begin to congregate in one or two people's rooms, but that was something he had always managed to avoid. He kept his distance, allowing himself an occasional, safe flirtation, and stayed in the pubs where nothing could go wrong.

He glanced at his watch. It was after ten.

"I think I'm drunk," Hugh slurred into his ear.

"Good job we're not driving," Daniel replied. "We can walk it off."

They each took a last drink for good measure and then stumbled out into the road, putting their arms around each other to prevent the other from falling. They could hear the buzz of laughing and talking in the pub growing weaker as they walked down the lane. The village was living up to the rustic vision Daniel had concocted, not merely as a perfect place for the sort of film they were shooting, but as a place where they could have the occasional binge without attracting any notice.

"Do you ever read Hardy?" he asked Hugh.

"Hardy? God, no. Not since university, and that was only when forced. Besides," he added, "why bother reading it when people like us are making perfectly good films about it?"

"Hmmm," Daniel murmured, tightening his grip on his friend. The fact that Hugh was slightly taller made it harder for Daniel to keep him upright.

It was a short walk to Hugh's rented house, and as they approached the door, Daniel asked him for the key. It was produced after a minute of searching the same pockets twice, and then duly handed over. As soon as they were inside Tamsyn appeared, clad in a terry robe emblazoned with enormous coffee cups and looking half her age.

"I think you need a hand," she said, giving them both a look.

"Thanks," Daniel answered.

They dragged Hugh into his bedroom, where Daniel helped him onto the bed and pulled off his shoes. Tamsyn took a blanket from a cupboard and settled it over him, and then the two of them left, shutting the door behind them.

"You didn't come out tonight," Daniel remarked, as if he didn't really care one way or another.

"I didn't feel like it," she said, picking up a cup. "I've made tea. Would you like some?"

"Why not?" he said, following her into the kitchen, where he leaned up against an old beam. It was a rustic room, but one fitted out for the avid cook. Copper pots hung from a rack on the ceiling and French olive jars were filled with spatulas and spoons. It was a kitchen for making shepherd's pie or bread and butter pudding. It was a shame none of them knew much about cooking.

"The water's still hot."

He watched as she poured, an odd feeling coming over him. This was the sort of thing he preferred, when it came down to it; a sense of normalcy that had long been missing from his life. Of course, that feeling wasn't attached to her in particular, he assured himself. It was just one of those sensations he had from time to time, which usually went away if he ignored it long enough.

"What do you think of the film so far?" he asked, trying to keep his mind off her figure, which was fortunately obscured by the robe.

"Amazing. The *Woman with Child* is strategically important to the village scene," she said, winding her hair with her hands and tying it up, leaving feathers of red locks loose around her face.

"A standout part, I'm sure. Never mind those forty or fifty other people milling about, trying to look busy."

She tossed a cushion in his direction. "That was your opportunity to be gallant, and you missed it."

"Sorry, I don't use a script on my off-hours. You'll have to cue me."

"You've had a lot to drink too, haven't you?"

"Thanks for noticing, Captain Obvious." He closed his eyes and watched the small dark spots that swirled in front of his eyelids make odd, Rorschach-like patterns. He wondered how psychologists analyzed the difference between psychotic and nonpsychotic thinking, and then wondered whether or not he even believed in that rot.

"By the way, I've found a place to stay," Tamsyn said. "Olivia, one of the assistants, invited me to move in with her and a couple of friends."

"You're not going to stay here?"

"No. This was only temporary, remember? I'll be happier with a bunch of other girls."

"That sounds grand." Daniel clasped his hands behind his head, stretching.

"You're not even listening," she accused him, scrutinizing his face as though she were his mother. "Do you want to sleep here tonight?"

"No, thanks. I'll make it back all right."

She handed him a hot mug and sat down in a deep chintz armchair. "It's not what I expected, exactly. The film, that is."

"Well, you've got a part, anyway."

"For a couple of weeks at least."

"I'm sure they'll find something for you to do if you want to stay a little longer."

She shrugged. "Unless something more interesting comes along."

"I'm not sure something interesting could possibly happen around here, unless you shag the producer or something."

"Not my style."

"I didn't think so." He took a drink of the tea. It was far too sweet for his taste. Smiling, he set the mug on the table. "I should go."

"Thanks for the company. It was rather quiet here tonight."

"Any time."

He made his way down the path and closed the gate behind him. He wasn't certain if it was the cool night air, but he felt better as he walked through the empty roads on the way back to his flat. He liked this girl; he really did. And soon Tamsyn would move in with girls she'd met on the set. Maybe then, without Hugh acting as some sort of 1950s chaperone, he would feel comfortable asking her out.

TEN

"I'M GOING TO LONDON for the weekend," Hugh said a few days later, setting a dish of cold prawns on the highly polished table. He was an effortless host, feeding his friends and planning various forms of entertainment on a regular basis. Daniel found it a trifle irritating at times. "Marc's come down and we're going to meet up with some people he knows. Why don't you come with us?"

Daniel leaned back in the sturdy wingback chair, which he appropriated every time he came over. It had been a long, boring day of work, and even the book he was reading between scenes hadn't begun to hold his attention. "Actually, I thought I'd stay here for the weekend."

"I know you don't particularly care for Marc, but he can be very amusing when he wants to be."

"I know," he answered, watching Hugh take a slick little prawn from the plate with his fingers and drop it into his mouth like a seal at Regent's Park Zoo. "I'm just a bit tired."

"Or you've got plans with someone," Hugh said, eyeing him with curiosity. "I noticed you speaking to Hodge's assistant, Jenny."

"I have no plans other than to find a good bookshop, if possible, and get something decent to read. The novel I'm reading at the moment is very dull."

"What about that scrummy brunette in Wardrobe … Kate, is it?"

"There's no one, really."

Hugh looked up, his eyes widening. "It's not Tamsyn, surely?"

"God, no. What made you say that?"

"I just wondered." Hugh picked up a bottle of wine and inspected it. "Well, suit yourself. Stay in boring Dorset if you like. But I'm leaving at four o'clock tomorrow, if you change your mind."

"Thanks. Maybe next time."

They both looked up as they heard the sound of a key in the door. Tamsyn walked in and heaved her backpack onto the floor. Apart from the odd bit of messiness, she had been an admirable boarder, according to Hugh. Still, Daniel was relieved that she was finally moving out.

"Have a prawn?" Hugh asked as he took another from the tray.

"I think I will. Thanks," she answered.

"Daniel?"

"Not on your life." He hated the slimy things. No matter how attractively they were presented on a tray or how much wine he'd had to drink, he couldn't stomach them.

Tamsyn laughed. She was dressed in a long, airy skirt that had likely been purchased at a jumble sale and a plain blue T-shirt. Daniel wondered how long it would be until she earned a proper paycheck, and if she would buy decent clothes when she did. He wasn't altogether certain she would.

"How about a nice glass of champers after a dreadful day?" Hugh asked.

"A small one, I suppose," she answered, sitting next to him on the sofa. "Although I really must go and pack."

"You're moving into Olivia's?" Daniel asked.

"That's right. It's going to be a few of us in a house in the middle of town. We'll be cottagers."

"I'll help if you need me to," he said.

"I didn't bring that much with me, you know."

"Still, easier to get around in a car, isn't it?"

"Yes. That would be nice. Thank you." Tamsyn took one of the prawns between her fingers and sucked it down, chasing it with the champagne Hugh offered. She gave him a wry look. "I may miss being spoiled, though."

Hugh gave a mock bow. "You're welcome any time."

"How generous of you," Daniel said. "You sound like Parson Maybold. I think the film's rubbing off on you."

"All the more reason to get out of town for the weekend." Hugh turned to Tamsyn. "Don't let that rush you, though."

"It won't."

"Now that that's all settled, let's think about dinner," Hugh said to them both. He stood, as though he were a force that would move them from their comfortable chairs. "Sir John told me about a good restaurant nearby. What do you say? Shall we give it a try?"

"Why not?" Tamsyn said.

Daniel nodded. Although he wasn't really in the mood to do anything, he couldn't very well refuse since he had chosen not to go to London for the weekend. He drove them to the restaurant at the Dove Cote Inn, where they ate a respectable meal of roast lamb and herbed potatoes. Daniel drank stout while Hugh and Tamsyn consumed cheap wine, the only options available at the establishment. He listened as they talked, mostly about films and plays in which Hugh had starred, and wondered if she fancied him. Then she turned her attention to Daniel, though he steered the conversation away from his career. He found the topic far less interesting than finding out more about her. At last they put down their glasses and Hugh took out his wallet and paid the bill.

"Enjoy yourself this weekend," Daniel told Hugh when he dropped them off.

"I will, thanks."

"And Tam, I'll see you tomorrow."

"Tomorrow, then."

He went back to his hotel room and flipped on the television. He sat in bed, changing channels, though nothing captured his attention. He turned it off, opened his book, and then closed it again.

"What's wrong with me?" he muttered, though he knew the answer. Tossing the book on a chair, he leaned back and stared at the ceiling until his eyes grew heavy and he finally fell asleep.

The following morning, Daniel knocked at Hugh's door just after nine o'clock. It had rained in the night, and the roads and hedges were damp and glistening. Wet white stones surrounded the beds of hybrid tea roses in various shades of tired pink, their petals frayed by the rain. For a moment, he thought of gathering a few for Tamsyn, but of course, if he did, she would get entirely the wrong idea.

Just then, she opened the door. A blue scarf was tied around her head, and the ends fell in silky waves to her shoulders around her curling hair. "Look at you," she said, her full lips curling into a smile. "Always there when I need you."

"What shall I carry?" he asked.

"Everything's here," she said, indicating her few belongings, which were heaped by the door. "Too bad we're not off to Paris today."

"You know, I was thinking of going to Brighton, just for the night."

"That sounds like fun."

"You could come along, unless, of course, you have other plans."

She hesitated for a moment. "I could ring Olivia and tell her I'll move in tomorrow."

Daniel was pleased. "Perfect."

He loaded her belongings into the boot. As he started the car, he handed her a map, smiling as it became a tangle when she tried to open it. It took a few minutes for her to refold it again and find Dorset, with a few panels opened to the east in order to track their progress.

"Look for Southampton," he instructed, pulling onto the motorway in the midst of the Saturday morning traffic. With beautiful weather like this, people were bound to want to get away for the weekend. "Then we'll go through Portsmouth and Chichester. Do you see it there?"

"Oh, yes. Sorry. I rarely travel by car."

"It's nice to stop whenever you like."

"Why didn't you tell Hugh?"

"I didn't decide until just now."

"Well, I'm glad you did."

Daniel studied the countryside as he drove over the cobbly hills. The fen to the south seemed to stretch on for miles, its peaty tufts nearly obscuring the toadflax and goat willow that grew there. The moor, even viewed through plate glass, had a calming effect on him. His mind felt free and clear for the first time in months. He almost forgot Tamsyn. She, too, was deep in thought, scribbling in a cheap French notebook with a bright orange cover, the sort pupils used.

"What are you writing so furtively there?" he asked, breaking the silence.

"None of your business. Keep your eyes on the road."

He didn't pursue the subject. She was a curiosity, and he preferred it that way. While he had known Hugh to recommend someone for a role before, he had never known anyone as unconcerned about it as she seemed to be. In fact, for someone who had unexpectedly landed the lead, she was as nonchalant as if she had done it dozens of times before. He wondered if she would take it seriously enough.

"Why Brighton?" she asked.

"My parents are there. We can stay with them and look at the sights, such as they may be."

"That will be fun."

"I forgot. You're little Mary Sunshine who appreciates the true beauty of something in spite of its wretchedness to the objective observer."

"Do you think it wretched?"

"Well," Daniel said, winking, "it's a carnival sort of town, but if you're in the right mood, it can be fun."

"You're in that mood."

He smiled. "How can you tell?"

In answer to his own question, he hit the accelerator, speeding along the motorway with the windows down. Tamsyn removed her scarf and then laughed as the gust of wind blew her hair about her face.

They arrived in Brighton before noon. Instead of taking her to his parents' house, Daniel drove about showing her the sights: the West Pier; the Grand Hotel, where he had lost his virginity to a chambermaid, though this fact of his personal history he would reveal to no one, especially not Tamsyn Burke; and the insane or possibly romantic Royal Pavilion—he had never decided which. The weather was fine apart from the wind, which whipped her skirts about and repeatedly lashed the ends of her scarf into her eyes. The beach was crowded and he didn't want to swim. It was a day for walking and talking and following whims, a true mini break from their work, such as it was.

She toyed with the ends of the blue scarf and looked at him. "This reminds me of home."

"Where's home?"

"Llandudno, by the sea. My family is there; everyone but my sister, Carey."

"Why aren't you there as well?"

"I'm making it big in acting, remember?"

"Yes. We mustn't forget that. Listen, I'm starving. Do we want to find a café or have a bratwurst right here?"

"Do you even have to ask?"

"A girl after my own heart," he said, walking up to a stand. It was hot in the sun and he shielded his eyes, wishing he had his sunglasses with him. He would have to buy a pair in one of the shops.

They ate, perched on a large rock, listening to the sound of the wind whipping the towels of the swimmers farther down on the beach. Tamsyn kicked off her sandals, and when he took the trash to a bin and came back for her, she still hadn't put them on, hooking them instead over a finger and slinging them over her back like a pack.

"There's a French film at the cinema," he said, toying with the keys in his pocket. "I noticed it when we drove past."

"Which one? I might have heard of it."

"Does it matter? They're either wildly sad or wildly funny."

"Then, let's."

They sat, at Tamsyn's insistence, near the front of the empty theatre. The film, a drama, was one he had seen before. He preferred foreign films, usually French or Scandinavian; the Danes particularly could emote well on screen; anything as long as it wasn't American, which he often found insipid, or Spanish, which was even worse. There was a peculiar anonymity in going to foreign films as well. He was never approached there, as though people who prefer them desired an intellectual high that could not be achieved if one broke the reverent silence and introspection required after its viewing. Tamsyn, however, was not content with merely watching the film. She whispered some of the lines after they were spoken, as though she were practicing schoolgirl French. He couldn't decide if he found it amusing or annoying, but in any case did not interrupt her, forgetting after a while to read the subtitles and watch the tragedy unfold before him but listening instead to her concentrated repetition: *Tu sais que je t'aime; Je n'oublie pas; Tu es le mien toujours.*

Then, after, they walked through the streets to his parents' house, where they were welcomed despite the late hour with cocoa and biscuits as though they were teens who had been out on a first date. Tamsyn ate and drank politely and then went to bed in his old bedroom, no doubt surveying his books and cricket bats and old jackets while he took two spare pillows and a blanket and went to the sofa. There, in the darkness, he thought of the last girl with whom he had slept, a bank employee by the name of Sybil. He'd slept with her in spite of the mild revulsion he'd felt toward someone who would try so desperately to go to bed with a film star, and he showered as soon afterward as possible. He hated being fawned over and decided, then and there, on his mother's sofa, not to go to bed with any more ridiculous girls. He would save himself for someone fresh and original and real, like the girl lying in his childhood bed now. He imagined himself beside her, stroking the tattoo on her ankle and staring out the window at the yellow crescent moon. It was the first time he fell asleep feeling relaxed in a very long time.

ELEVEN

THE FOLLOWING MONDAY MORNING, Daniel awoke with a feeling of satisfaction. In spite of a good weekend spent with Tamsyn, nothing had really changed. There was still work to be done and a professional image to foster, although, as he reminded himself occasionally, he didn't have to work in the film industry. He had squirreled money away for some indeterminate day when he might need it, which allowed him the random fantasy of pouring cappuccinos to earn his keep and living an anonymous life that would make fewer demands on him in general. In fact, he needed very little: a roof over his head, food to eat, and a relationship with Tamsyn Burke. All he had to do was tell her.

The weekend had been a success. He had managed to forget his nearly unlikable character, Dick Dewy, not to mention Thomas Hardy and work in general. His parents had been glad to see him; surprised, perhaps, that he had arrived with a girl in tow, but prepared to accept her, as he had known they would. His mother once gave him an inquiring glance, which he rebuffed with a shake of the head and a frown, indicating Tamsyn was merely a friend, though she didn't look altogether convinced. He left Tamsyn at Olivia's cottage late Sunday night, wondering what they might do together next weekend. Llandudno came to mind. He'd never been to the Welsh coast, and he wanted to see where she had grown up now that he had shown her Brighton.

It was a boring day on the set. Retakes were necessary for every scene. Everyone had taken it in stride for the first hour, but a ripple of irritation began to build on each subsequent occurrence. Unable to concentrate on a book, Daniel drank too many espressos, feeling the blood pump harder and harder through his veins until he thought they might burst. To counteract it, he drank two bottles of water over the next hour. Hugh was lucky enough to be relieved of the tedium by noon.

"Come by later," he said, pulling on his jacket. "If they ever let you go."

By six o'clock, Daniel had begun to wonder. Tamsyn had gone by two thirty, saying nothing but pulling pins out of her hair from thick, gelatinous layers of hair spray as she walked out of the building. The temper of the cast and crew deteriorated over the course of the afternoon. An argument broke out between the writer and director over the use of a line that was not taken directly from the book. One of the wardrobe girls complained when she had to re-hem a trouser cuff that had torn when Daniel became entangled in a knot of cords while trying to reach for a cup of tea. In the late afternoon, they filmed the bloody choral scene, and the shriek of the pipes was almost enough to drive him mad.

All day he had expected his agent to ring about another film he was eager to do, yet his mobile never vibrated in his pocket. He chafed at the general lack of action while trying not to betray his emotions to the crew. He was no dilettante. Normally, he kept a book in his pocket and his mouth shut. Things happened, often when one least wanted them to. The best and worst parts of his job were one and the same: no matter how much one loved or hated a particular job, it would end within a few weeks. Nothing lasts forever.

It was approaching seven thirty before he was finally able to leave, by which time he despised the entire project. He needed a drink. He would go to see Hugh, and talk, or rather, let Hugh talk while the alcohol numbed his mind just enough to forget the horrible day, and then after a pleasant hour had elapsed, or possibly two, he would excuse himself and ring Tamsyn. He had watched her more than usual all day. Her hair had been piled into a knot, insouciant curls escaping from every angle. She had worn a high-collared frock that was tight at the bodice and hips, and her belt had a small mother-of-pearl clasp. Brown boots were barely visible beneath her full skirt. Her ears were like two Imperial Venus shells plucked from a Jamaican beach: perfect twin bivalves, from which dangled pearl-drop earrings, obviously genuine antiques, screwed as tightly as possible onto her lobes. He couldn't decide if she looked Victorian or not. Probably not, he decided, in the end. She was far too saucy to play such a pure, if self-centered, character like Fancy, and it was shocking that Sir John hadn't realized it. Although, on reflection, perhaps he had, and merely hired her to capitulate to Hugh's whim. He wouldn't have been the first.

The evening was fine. A warm summer breeze blew around him, making him long for the beach. Tamsyn had enjoyed Brighton, as he had hoped. But now he wanted to take her to Spain or Morocco, somewhere along the Mediterranean, to stay in an enormous white hotel flanked by banana trees and desert palms stretching out toward the clouds. They would visit markets and buy fruit from wobbly stands and lie under umbrellas in the hot sand, staring for hours at the sea. Holidays in the past had been dominated by family or friends, and for once he wanted to have a companion like Tam, who could truly understand how to enjoy life. They'd drink cerveza through the night, looking at the stars overhead as though they were a newly discovered phenomenon, and dance in the moonlight to the sound of a Spanish guitar. Then, and not before, they would kiss. It would be a long-awaited moment, as their friendship, so bright and unexpected, evolved into something more. He wouldn't rush it, of course; these things had to develop naturally; but he knew from the effortlessness of their relationship and the fact that she was in no way impressed by his money or position that she was someone he could truly love. She cared for him as well. He knew it.

Daniel got into his car and sighed. Starting the engine, he looked back at the manor behind him where they had been filming all day: an enormous pile of limestone and bricks that had been built more than a century ago. One wing had sustained some damage, which was evident by a low pile of rubble left on the west side of the house, a macabre reminder they had survived the war. The house was still owned by descendants of the original owners, although it wasn't lived in; it was hired for weddings and corporate events, and the kitchen had seen an inordinate number of catering firms in the last thirty years. Several of the larger rooms had been set up for filming and, despite its grandness, he sometimes felt he was the only one immune to its attraction. It was just a house, albeit a large one; one he would be leaving in a few weeks, never to think of again. The drive was a long, graveled crescent and the tires of his car crunched as he eased down the path. Hugh's house was on the other end of the village, past the shops and greens and a minor bustle of activity on a rugby pitch. It was warm, hot even, and he put down the windows of his car to feel the breeze on his face, leaving them down as he pulled up to Hugh's house.

He got out of the car and knocked at the door. No sound could be heard from inside, but that wasn't unusual. Hugh, who rarely did anything as prosaic as reading, could often be found with headphones listening to Strauss or Grieg, as if music were a commodity that could not possibly be shared. In all of the years they had been friends, Hugh had never played music aloud. Daniel waited, and then after a while, opened the door.

The house was empty. He wondered if Hugh had asked him to meet him at the pub and then rejected the idea. He'd have a quick look round and then ring Tamsyn. The kitchen was empty, too, but to his surprise, her handbag was on the floor.

"Hugh?" he called out, without receiving a reply. He was about to open the back door when something, instinct perhaps, brought his eyes up to look through the small window, where he saw them together outside.

They were reclining in a lounge chair. Hugh lay back on thick cushions, and Tamsyn sat astride his long body, her dress clinging to her frame. It had come loose at the neck and had fallen aside to reveal a cool white shoulder dotted with freckles, and below, it was pulled up to her thighs; and though it was impossible to see what was happening, there was no mistaking the throes of passion, the pitch and thrust of their bodies together.

Daniel had never been the jealous sort who suspected every woman he dated of infidelity. He had never really cared for anyone enough to experience jealousy. He had conducted himself, if not entirely wisely, then at least discreetly in his affairs, and attachments had never been made, at least not on his side. Sex, too, held no mystery; he had either seen or done or discussed nearly everything there was to know. He had never committed himself seriously, even for a moment. Until now.

A wave of anger crashed over him. It was a blow to realize that Hugh's having sex with this mad, improper girl could make him feel as though bricks had been dropped on his head. He stood for a moment, head tipped back against the wall with his eyes tightly closed. He was breathing harder than normal, his fists clenched as though ready for battle. But instead he composed himself, and then called Hugh's name, waiting a few seconds to give them time to spring apart with their knowing smiles, to cover themselves, and to prepare to welcome him into their little tête-à-tête as though nothing had happened at all. No one knew or even suspected the shattering of his heart.

TWELVE

AUTOPSIES WERE A FACT of life for any police detective, as commonplace as the ubiquitous bad coffee and bureaucratic jumbles of paperwork that plagued all investigations. Inspector Gordon Murray had seen dozens of corpses posed in the standard anatomical position awaiting the first cut of the Y incision to determine the precise cause of their deaths. Still, one never really got used it. Dr. Charles Hanson, one of the best coroners in London, had taken the Burke case, and Murray knew from experience he would be thorough. Though he didn't always personally inspect the body, something about this case troubled him more than usual. He left his office and knocked on the open door shortly after Hanson had finished.

"Photos and stats over there," Hanson said, tipping his head toward the desk before continuing to scribble his notes. Most people used computers these days, but Hanson was of an age that would not give in to the inconvenience of learning modern customs, no matter how commonplace they had become.

Murray walked over and gave the file a cursory look. *Well-developed Caucasian female. Weight, 8.02 stone; Height, 63 inches; Body Marks: one tattoo above left ankle, one 3 cm birthmark on right buttock. Fixed Rigor Mortis.*

He put down the file and turned back to the body. It was his second look at Tamsyn Burke, and what a difference twenty-four hours made. A day ago, there had still been some color in her face, and she could have passed for being unconscious. Now, however, she was as gray as if she had been dead for years. He looked at her auburn hair, which had been pulled back. It must have been quite striking with her pale complexion when she was alive. Murray walked up to the table and took a closer look. Occasionally, victims looked younger in death than they even had alive, and this one most certainly did. She had been petite, and no match for her killer. Her hands had been quite beautiful, with long pianists' fingers, small knuckles, and well-maintained nails. She had probably held them up in the days and weeks preceding the marriage and imagined her wedding band sparkling like the Hope Diamond, and looked forward to showing it off to her friends. He sighed, thinking of her parents' grief. As long as he lived, he would never understand what possessed someone to take another human life, particularly the life of an innocent like her. No matter who she was or what she may have done, she was still but a girl who needed love and protection. The sight of her decaying corpse angered him to the core.

"Only one stab wound, I see," he said, looking at the point of entry.

"That's right," the coroner answered, putting down his clipboard. "He got her in one thrust."

"At precisely the right angle to end her life."

"That's correct. The weapon went through the skin and the subcutaneous tissue, and between the left fifth and sixth rib straight into the left ventricle. The cause of death was hemorrhage from the stab wound."

"Damn the luck. A little left or right and she might have lived."

"Damn the luck is right. She also had a few contusions on her hands, defense wounds. She had mere seconds to react. Not long enough to stop the thrust of the knife. It's a simple wound, really. The perpetrator knew precisely where he could cause the most damage."

"So you believe the killer is a man?"

"Not necessarily. I use the word 'he' in a theoretical sense. Due to the close proximity of the killer, anyone could have done it had they known what they wanted to do. Surprise, not force, was the main element in this murder."

"Reinforcing the concept that she knew the murderer."

"It had to be someone she trusted."

"Presumably," Murray said, more to himself than to Hanson, "every one of the twenty-seven people in that wing was someone she trusted. Only the immediate circle had been admitted to that part of the Abbey."

"I don't envy you that," Hanson said, setting his pen on the counter and closing the file. "All I have to do is find the cause of death. The reason for it is a different matter altogether."

Murray thanked him and left the office, deep in thought. The key to solving this murder was to understand the victim. Who precisely was Tamsyn Burke? Did people like her or not? Did she incite feelings of jealousy or hatred in the people she knew?

Murray himself was accustomed to being hated. One couldn't be a Detective Chief Inspector without it, he supposed, considering the type of people one had to deal with. Suspects hated the police when they were guilty, and even more so when they were innocent. Half of his subordinates were envious of his position. The public viewed the police as a necessary evil, sometimes fearing them as much as the criminals they caught.

During the course of a murder inquiry, most people, even mere witnesses, were afraid to talk in case they implicated themselves. It seemed that everyone had secrets. This case would undoubtedly prove no different, particularly because several had ties to the film industry.

Back in his office, Murray turned his attention to the reputation of the famous stage and screen actor, Noel Ashley-Hunt. He had actually seen him once in *Much Ado About Nothing* in the role of Leonato at the Old Vic, but when he had met him at Westminster Abbey, he couldn't imagine anyone less suited to play a comedy. Ashley-Hunt was a professional who took his life and career seriously. According to his résumé, he had acted with the Royal Shakespeare Company and won a number of awards, including a Tony for his portrayal of Don Quixote in *Man of La Mancha* in New York, but it wasn't until a series of popular instamatic camera commercials in the '70s that his face became recognizable in every home in England. He was known for many years for his boyish good looks, and while he had aggressively gone after but not gotten the role of James Bond, he'd played similar playboy types in both American and British films. As he matured, he took on heavier roles in World War II pictures and other epic films, once playing the dual roles of George V and his look-alike cousin, Nicholas II, in a landmark mini-series, which solidified the English love affair with the handsome actor.

Through several newspaper articles, Murray discovered that Ashley-Hunt had been born in Yorkshire to a poor family. His mother, Mary Alice, had left his father when Noel was seven, taking the child with her to London where she sought a life on the stage. She had very modest success; she was employed enough to keep food on the table, yet never became a star. Instead of discouraging the young

Ashley-Hunt, this whetted his appetite for fame. He was raised behind the scenes and had been coddled by the actresses his mother knew. He was accepted by the Royal Academy of Dramatic Art at twenty and began to carefully craft a career, one of solid roles and an excellent reputation.

At thirty, he had married a cousin of the royal family, Caroline Montgomery, and from all accounts it was a serious love match. The beautiful Mrs. Ashley-Hunt, a tall, blonde society girl, was a favorite of the tabloid photographers, even more so after marrying the dashing actor. She suffered three miscarriages before giving birth to Hugh, whose birth was heralded like royalty in the London newspapers.

When his career was established, Ashley-Hunt became a philanthropist, giving generously to various charities as well as to the British Museum. There was talk that he was soon to be awarded an Order of the British Empire, thus giving him a title as well as his wife. On paper, he was formidable; in person, even more so.

Murray looked at his watch. It was one thirty. He had a two o'clock appointment with Noel Ashley-Hunt to discuss Tamsyn Burke's murder. He picked up the phone and dialed Ennis's extension.

His sergeant picked up on the first ring. "Yes, boss?"

"I have an interview in half an hour."

"I'll bring the car around, sir."

"Thank you." Murray replaced the receiver on the telephone and stood, pulling on his coat. He wasn't star-struck like most people. Men like Ashley-Hunt did not intimidate him in the least. The actor might have a distinguished reputation, but in a murder investigation he was no better or worse than anyone else. Apart from the Queen, he knew of few individuals who were better than his peers. Murray often thought if he hadn't been such a monarchist and a political conservative, he would have made a fine democrat.

Outside, it was raining, and he unfolded his umbrella as he waited for Ennis to bring round the car. It was typical May weather; sunny and warm one day, cool and drizzly the next. Today, it felt more like March than May. Rivulets of rain dripped from the nylon, and he shook it vigorously when Ennis pulled up. He slid into the passenger seat.

"The Ashley-Hunts, sir?" Ennis asked before he had a chance to tell him. Sometimes he wondered if his sergeant was clairvoyant.

"That's right. We've an appointment with the father, but I plan to have a word with the son as well. I want to talk to him about the death threat he received."

"I've got IT working on the link to the source, sir. So far, all we know is that the email account was established two months ago on one of those free webmail sites. It'll take some tracking to see if we can find who opened the account."

Ennis went silent, focusing on the traffic while Murray considered the case. Twenty-seven people were on the suspect list; all family, friends, or acquaintances. No one else had been seen apart from in the public areas, where guards protected the artifacts. Even though none of the twenty-seven suspects had serious criminal records or a history that pointed to murder, the killer was certainly among their number. Someone had gotten close enough to stab Tamsyn Burke without alerting her to danger.

Motive, method, and opportunity, he thought; the three factors one had to identify in every case. The method, of course, was obvious: stabbing with an ordinary knife, the likes of which was sold at Marks and Spencer and virtually dozens of other shops that traded in kitchen wares. The opportunity had presented itself in the minutes preceding the ceremony that had been about to take place. That left the infinitely more difficult part of the equation: motive. Some clue would make itself known if he looked hard enough. He pointed as Ennis pulled into Edgemore Street.

"Just there."

Ennis pulled the car up to the curb and they opened their umbrellas against the rain. The sun was obscured by dark, charcoal clouds, and a ripple of thunder could be heard in the distance. Two men stood discreetly on either side of the door, as innocuous as the gendarmes outside the Palace Elysée in Paris. The first time he had seen them, Murray hadn't even realized he was passing the residence of the President of France until the cab driver mentioned it. At the moment, he was pleased to see that Ashley-Hunt had taken the threat seriously and provided a security detail for his son's benefit.

The door of the house opened as he and Ennis approached, and they were ushered inside by a housekeeper. They sheathed their umbrellas in a stand and were shown into the study where Noel Ashley-Hunt was waiting.

"Inspector Murray, won't you come in?" Ashley-Hunt said, looking up from his desk.

"Thank you for seeing us today," Murray answered. "Will your wife be joining us?"

The man gave an apologetic smile. "Unfortunately, Caroline is organizing flowers for the funeral."

Murray knew that powerful men like Ashley-Hunt began difficult interviews with a false cordiality; in fact, the more cordial the greeting, the nastier the conclusion was likely to be. Ashley-Hunt stood and went over to the fireplace. Murray noted it had just been lit. The logs showed little sign of ash, and the room was still cool. Ashley-Hunt had set the stage in order to control the situation.

He waved them to a pair of club chairs and went to perch on the edge of his mahogany desk, crossing his legs at the ankles and folding his arms.

He's impatient, Murray thought. Good. He took out a notebook, which he did not open, and a pen.

"How long have you known Tamsyn Burke?" Murray asked, studying Ashley-Hunt's face for any change in expression. There was none, of course.

"My wife and I met her for the first time at Christmas."

"Here in London?"

"At our country house in Gloucestershire."

"And when did your son meet her?"

"They met when Hugh began filming *Under the Greenwood Tree* several months ago. She was working as an extra and Hugh persuaded Sir John Hodges to consider her for the lead."

"Did your son often recommend people for parts in his films?"

"Of course not."

Murray sat back in his chair and folded his hands on top of his notebook. "Can you tell me what you thought of Miss Burke when you met for the first time?"

"Hugh occasionally brought friends to the house. It was not unusual. I didn't think much about it."

"But you must have known that she was more than a friend if he brought her at Christmas, am I right, sir? Had he ever brought home a girl for Christmas before?"

"I don't recall. I am not in the habit of cataloguing my son's friends."

"Surely a father would remember his son bringing home a serious girlfriend for the holidays."

Ashley-Hunt's brow creased into a frown. "Then, no, I don't suppose he ever had."

"Did you get the impression at the time that they were serious about their relationship?"

"They showed signs of being in a relationship, but I never expect these things to last. Certainly not at his age."

"What was her behavior toward the family?"

"She was polite enough."

"I understand she was quite different from your son, from her upbringing to her recent life."

"Yes, she was a different sort of girl."

"Not exactly the sort you'd choose for him yourself, then?"

"Where are you going with this, Inspector?" Ashley-Hunt growled. He stood up and walked around to sit in the chair behind the desk.

"I'm just trying to determine if you and your wife approved of Miss Burke."

"What difference would it make? Young people date whomever they wish these days."

"But for the record, you did not approve of her?"

"No," he admitted. "She wasn't the sort of girl we wanted him to see. Frankly, she was beneath him."

Murray looked at the French doors over Ashley-Hunt's left shoulder, remembering what he had read about the man's own humble beginnings. It was hypocritical, to say the least. The velvet curtains were opened and he watched the torrents of rain beating against the pane. "When did they become engaged?" he asked.

"In February."

"That's short notice for a wedding at Westminster Abbey," he remarked.

"My wife is a member of the royal family," Ashley-Hunt said. "But it was still difficult to secure the location. I had to call in a few favors."

"Twelve weeks," Murray counted. "So many details. The dress, the caterers. Who made most of the arrangements?"

"She did." Ashley-Hunt had not once used his wife's name, Murray noticed. "With my credit cards, of course."

"Who decided to have the wedding at the Abbey?"

"We did. They would have gotten married anywhere, Trafalgar Square, Regent's Park, a Register Office. I don't think either of them cared, and as long as they didn't, we preferred that they do it right."

"Of course." Murray opened the notebook at last and jotted a few scrawling lines across the page before closing it. Would Ashley-Hunt have gone to the trouble of securing Westminster Abbey if he had wanted to kill the girl? he wondered. "Did you see them often during the engagement?"

Ashley-Hunt shook his head. "We're both busy men. We met occasionally for dinner."

"Would you say you grew fond of Miss Burke during that time?"

The man's face turned to stone. "We really didn't know her that well. She spoke little when we did see her. I suppose she was minding her p's and q's."

"Do you have any idea who might have wanted her dead?"

"Until the day of the wedding, I had never met any of her family or friends. I have no idea who could have done such a thing."

"Did you speak to her on the day of the wedding?"

"No, I did not."

"I understand you were in the area where she was getting ready. You were seen coming down the hall approximately fifteen minutes before the body was found."

"Are you suggesting I had something to do with it?" Ashley-Hunt demanded, rising from his chair. "I'll admit I didn't particularly like the girl. I didn't see her as a suitable wife for my son, but things have a way of taking care of themselves. If she was as unsuitable as I believed her to be, the marriage would have dissolved within a few months. As a matter of fact, I'm sure it would have. She lacked the essential qualities that would have suited Hugh for a long-term relationship."

"Did you ever say as much to your son?"

Ashley-Hunt's mouth hardened to a thin line. "I've learned that one can give advice but it is rarely taken. The older you get, the more you have to regret. I did not wish to add my son's ire to that particular list."

"Did you see anyone acting suspiciously that morning?"

"Not that I recall."

Murray tucked the notebook into his coat and stood. "I understand the funeral is also to be held at Westminster Abbey. Who decided to have it there?"

"The use of it was offered in light of the circumstances."

"That was most kind, I'm sure." Murray took a card from his pocket. "If you think of anything else, you can ring me at this number."

"I'm sure I've told you everything I know. I think the police should be out looking for real leads instead of bothering the family at a time like this."

"Unfortunately, in a crime of this nature, no one is exempt from scrutiny, Mr. Ashley-Hunt." Murray paused for a moment. "I'd like to have a brief word with your son while I'm here."

"He's home, of course," Ashley-Hunt said, "but I thought it best he not join us for this meeting. I don't want to distress him further. I'm sure you understand."

"As a matter of fact, he may need to talk about it. I'm sure he is anxious to see the killer identified as quickly as possible."

"Of course he is. We all are," Ashley-Hunt snapped. "But he's distraught. Anyone can see it's a bad time."

"There's never a good time to talk to someone during a murder investigation, sir," Murray said, tapping the arm of the chair. "Like anyone who was present, he may have seen something inadvertently without realizing a connection, something that might have bearing on the case."

Ashley-Hunt didn't move for a few seconds, and then with a loud sigh left the room in search of his son.

"What do you think, sir?" Ennis asked in a low voice, his eye on the door in case Ashley-Hunt made a sudden return.

"I don't care for the man, but I don't believe he's involved in the girl's death. It obviously was premeditated murder, and you can't convince me he would have hired the greatest church in Christendom as a place to kill a future daughter-in-law. A man like that wouldn't want the publicity, would he?"

"But wouldn't publicity be good for an actor's prospects?"

"Not for a man like Ashley-Hunt. He's already established. He seems like a man who would avoid controversy rather than create it."

They heard footsteps in the hall and waited for Hugh to come into the room. Murray was curious to see him again. They certainly were intriguing, these young actors. Hugh was already successful, even at his age. He could afford to marry someone for love rather than merely to please his parents, if he so chose. Not all young men could say the same.

Hugh came into the room and walked straight to Murray, who stood and shook his hand. "You wanted to see me, sir?" he asked. His face was drawn and his complexion naturally pale. He looked tired, as if sleep had eluded him since Tamsyn's death.

"Thank you for seeing me," Murray said. He glanced at the door to be certain that the young man's father hadn't followed him into the room.

Hugh noticed and nodded. "I told him I didn't mind talking to you. Have you found out anything? Have you got any leads?"

"No," Murray answered. "But we will. By the way, do you happen to have her mobile?"

"No," Hugh said, looking surprised. "I thought you had it."

They each found a seat and Murray continued. "Tell me what you remember about that last hour."

Hugh looked at Ennis and then back at Murray before taking a deep breath. "I was in the chapel for quite a while. I was nervous, you see. We probably should have run off together, but my parents wanted a 'real' wedding, and we didn't want to disappoint them. It's fairly intimidating to stand in the middle of Westminster Abbey and realize you're about to get married in the same spot where kings tie the knot."

"Had you seen Tamsyn earlier in the day?"

"No, she stayed at a friend's the night before. I thought it was a little absurd, because we were already living together, but she wanted to do it right."

He struggled to maintain his composure. Murray gave him a moment before he asked the next question.

"Did you speak to anyone while you were in the chapel?"

"One of the assistants came in and spoke to me about the music, and then I was alone for a while until Daniel came in."

"You're good friends, if I'm not mistaken."

"He's like a brother to me. He came to make sure I was all right. He'd seen Tamsyn a few minutes before and said ... he said she looked beautiful and she was anxious for the ceremony to get started, like I was."

"And then what happened?"

"Daniel told me that my father was looking for me. He probably wanted to give me some parting word of encouragement or something, but I couldn't find him. It's hard to find your way around the place. I ran into that old friend of Tam's, Monaghan I think it is, and then I heard a scream. I really don't remember anything after that."

"Did you speak to Monaghan?"

"No. I've only been introduced to him once."

"Have you had any thoughts about who might have sent the death threat?"

Hugh shook his head. "None at all, sir. I've racked my brain since this happened. I can't think of a single person who would have threatened either one of us. If you knew Tam, you'd know what I mean. She had such a good heart."

Murray nodded. "Thank you for talking with me. I'm sorry to have troubled you. It's just important for us to know everything that happened that day so we can get to the bottom of it."

"I understand," Hugh replied.

Murray could tell that Hugh was the opposite of his father in terms of personality: he was someone who easily related to others. "If you think of anything, ring me at once," he added, standing. He shook hands with Hugh once again.

In the hall, he and Ennis were given their umbrellas and stepped outside into the rain, which had not abated during the brief conversation. They hurried out to the car.

Ennis turned up the heat, while Murray wished for a cup of tea. As the car pulled away from the curb, he looked up at the house, where his eye caught the flutter of a curtain up on the first floor. It was Noel Ashley-Hunt, frowning down at them from his study.

"I'm anxious to see who turns up for the funeral," Murray said, turning to his sergeant.

"You don't think the killer will be there, do you?" Ennis asked, surprised.

"He'll have to be," the inspector replied. "Otherwise, he's implicating himself in her murder."

THIRTEEN

It was the tics that bothered Nick Oliver the most, the rapid, involuntary muscle contractions in his right arm that beleaguered him hourly. It was ruining his life. He couldn't throw or catch a ball. He couldn't write a letter without that dreaded jerking motion wrecking the page. Not to mention that one couldn't hide a thing like that. It was evident to everyone who saw him. Most people had the presence of mind not to comment on his disability, but nevertheless, their eyes were drawn to it anyway. He could see them watching, waiting to see when it would happen next.

It had been distressing when he was at school, but now that he was a university student, he chose distance learning instead of living among his peers. He was stringing his education out slowly, taking only one or two courses per term, in no hurry to graduate. Graduation implied doing something with what he had learned. He had hoped to study horticulture or environmental studies, something approachable like agriculture, a solitary occupation, but his mother had insisted on computers and finance, which he despised. She thought, mistakenly, that he was going to get up his courage and rejoin the world, make something of himself, but he wanted to dig in the earth and grow things, not put on a suit and tie and watch people watch his ticking arm and wonder when another insensitive idiot would say something to him about it. Sometimes the tics would disappear for a few minutes and he could almost pretend that he was normal. Those blissful moments were invariably shattered by reality. His reality was that he still lived at home with his mother at twenty-three years of age, a borderline agoraphobic due to the disease that was ravaging his nervous system.

He only had one real friend, Carey Burke, who had lived next door to him his entire life until she had gone to university in London. They had shared everything: every secret, every dream. Between their houses at the back of the garden was a high shrub into which he had trimmed a passageway they called their maze, and they would slip through it to see one another even though they could have easily knocked on one another's front door. He had been distraught when Carey left, though they spoke on the phone and emailed frequently. Now, he sat on the bed, looking at the letter in his hand that had arrived in the morning post. It was her way; important things were always written by hand, her crisp, no-nonsense letters committed to paper as though they were too sacred for electronic transmission.

She had written to break it to him that Tamsyn was dead, though he already knew it from his mother. The whole country probably knew by now. For Nick, the news had evoked a variety of emotions. He was devastated for Carey, who was the best person he had ever known. There was nothing she wouldn't do for someone, even a complete stranger. In fact, if she had a flaw, it was that her compassion caused her to be too involved with people she didn't even know. Carey and her parents, who had gone to London expecting a wedding in Westminster Abbey and were instead mourning the loss of their eldest child, deserved his concern. Tamsyn, however, did not. It was hard to imagine two sisters more dissimilar. He'd once heard Carey called "the plain one," which had angered him because it couldn't be farther from the truth. Hers was an innocent beauty, as far as he was concerned. Tamsyn was brash and irreverent, but she could also be cruel. She had taunted him from the earliest age, calling him "Spaz," and he'd despised her as much as he cared for her sister.

"She doesn't mean it," Carey used to say, ever the peacemaker. She also believed that the meek would inherit the earth.

"Of course she does," he'd argued. "Why else would she say it?"

He had never been able to convince her that Tamsyn wasn't the same sort of person she was. Carey loved unconditionally, refusing to believe anything but the best in people, and although Nick had even benefited from it himself, he did not think it should apply to someone who had the capacity to laugh at the misfortunes of others. Agitated, he looked at the letter in his hands, which was crumpling at the edges.

I can barely breathe, Nicky. I can't believe she's gone. I know she wasn't always as good to you as she should have been, but she was my sister, and I loved her. Who could have done such a vicious thing?

It was eerie, of course; someone he'd known well dying at so young an age. Even though he hadn't liked her, Nick had to admit it was terrible luck to be killed on one's wedding day. No one deserved that. He moved over to turn on his computer and sat down in the chair in front of it, tapping his foot as it displayed the logo and took the usual two and a half minutes before he could log on to the Internet. When at last he was connected, he looked up the Westminster Abbey website, picturing, with something between fascination and repugnance, Tamsyn's bloody body in a wedding gown. What a vile way to die. He wondered who killed her. Was it another poor soul who had been tormented by her as he had? Someone who was jealous of the sudden happy turn of events in her life? He had followed, with some perplexity, her minor television career, and he thought it staggering that she had been offered a major role in a film. Carey had never expressed any surprise whatsoever.

I always wanted to please her, to make her laugh. Her laughter was the most magical sound on earth. When she was happy, she lit up the whole room.

And when she wasn't, Nick thought ungraciously, she could be a real bitch. Even so, he had to admit that men everywhere were attracted to her. Who wouldn't be, when she went out of her way to be noticed by everyone in her trajectory?

Nick slid the letter back into the envelope and put it on the corner of his desk. Tomorrow he would take the train to London for the funeral. His mother wanted to go but she couldn't get leave from work. It would be difficult, making such a long trip on his own. He hadn't done it in years, and then, Carey and his mother had been with him. At least Carey would come home for a while in June, after her term, to be with her parents. That was something to look forward to.

It was a beautiful afternoon. Nick went downstairs and through the back door. He needed to weed while the sun was out. He had always been one to plant things, but over the last five or six years, he had taken over the garden entirely. His mother had never cared for it much anyway, and it was cathartic to create something beautiful on his own. In the shed, he took down the hoe and went out into the yard. Weeds sprouted around the brick paving stones that surrounded the roses and dianthus. He stepped on the hoe's blade with the toe of his Wellington boot, pushing it into the wet ground.

Their house had been built in 1953, and as with most homes of that era, its period details were both charming and annoying, for everything, sooner or later, broke and then broke again. It seemed they were always fixing things: roof tiles and exasperating leaks with no certain origin and cracks in the plaster. His parents had bought the house the year he was born. The Burkes had moved in the year before, when Tamsyn was a toddler, and Carey was born seven months after Nick. He'd been an only child. Neither of his parents had ever told him the reason why, but he'd speculated for years that they didn't want another handicapped child. Many neuromuscular diseases were genetic, he'd learned as he had gotten older. He had always tried to be a good son to make up for his affliction, and he'd been particularly close to his father, who had died four years prior from a heart attack.

His parents had lived a quiet life. His mother was a teacher in a local primary school; she often brought home drawings from her pupils and put them on the bulletin board over her computer, in the office where she had been struggling to write poetry in her free time since he was very young. She'd had no success, but wrote on without complaint, amassing stacks of unpublished poems in neat folders on her desk alongside stacks of rejection slips. She was perhaps too well-adjusted for the melancholia he suspected was required to write great poetry, though poetry was, in his opinion, a lost art. There were no more Plaths or Audens or Keats on the literary horizon, no budding Yeats who could shake one to their very core. Modern poets whined of dull suburban life, of various and sundry complaints like dealing with children who grew up with handicaps, of the temptation to drink or fight or break out of the boring nothingness of life and feel something for a change. He found it exhausting and was happy his mother rarely complained. She was a stoic sort, quiet and self-contained, and they kept out of each other's way. She prepared the evening meal, where they had their one brief if pleasant interaction of the day, and spent much of her free time at the computer. The keys were not often heard clacking, for she stared out of the window a great deal, possibly wondering where her life had gone.

Nick worked for over an hour on the flower beds. There was a light wind, and the sky, which had begun to darken overhead, occasionally blew a few drops of rain onto the brim of his hat. *It can't make up its mind,* his mother sometimes said. *Just like me.* He never asked what she couldn't make up her mind about. It wasn't done.

He raked some of the leaves, kicking them into a pile. This time tomorrow, he would be in London with Carey. He wished to God that she hadn't gone into medicine. It took forever to graduate and then to qualify, and who knew what hospital she would work at when the time came. It wasn't likely to be in Wales. In the meantime, however, he would get his degree to satisfy his mother and then move wherever Carey was to look for a job in a garden center. He was relieved to have a plan.

———

The following morning, he bought a ticket to London and boarded the train a little after nine. It wasn't crowded, for which he was thankful, and he made himself as comfortable as he could in his seat, clutching her letter in his hand and a knapsack full of magazines and snacks that his mother had insisted he bring. He wasn't sentimental about most things, but this journey had a sense of importance about it. Carey was meeting him at Euston Station, giving him the opportunity to support her during the worst crisis of her life. He put aside any feelings he had regarding

Tamsyn. Carey had mentioned in previous emails that she wanted to take him to Covent Garden and Leicester Square, and he knew she was fond of the British Museum. She wrote about it often enough. For him, however, she was the only thing worth seeing.

The trip was long and hot, the train car jarring and uncomfortable. He hadn't been able to concentrate on reading, worrying instead about how things would go when he arrived.

"You're here," Carey said, approaching him as he got off the train.

She kissed him on the cheek. He knew she appreciated how much effort it had taken for him to make such a trip. As they walked out of the station into the harsh afternoon sun, she tucked her hand inside the crook of his arm. The tremor stilled the moment she touched him. Without a word, she led him through the crowds rife with noise and confusion, people coming, people going, things for sale, things to eat, all of it contained in one huge, stifling place. He hated it at once.

"I don't want to go home yet," she said. Carey was always quiet, but there was something else evident in her demeanor, a deep sadness he had not expected, though she had written about it. She looked up at him, concerned. "That is, if you don't mind. If you're tired, we can go back to my place."

"I'm fine," he lied. Shifting his pack on his shoulder, he wanted to get away from the noise and traffic and find a quiet place for a meal. In spite of himself, he couldn't help resenting that she normally would have remembered his likes and dislikes, crowds being something he loathed. Of course, she had suffered a recent shock. She wasn't herself. He would have to understand.

"Are you hungry?" he asked.

Carey shrugged. "I haven't been able to eat much."

"You have to eat."

"I could drink some tea, I suppose."

"Do you know a place we could go?" he asked, glancing around.

Carey rubbed his arm. "Of course. We'll take the tube to Russell Square. I know where we can get you a good cottage pie."

Twenty minutes later, they were seated in the corner of the Sheffield Bistro and a strong pot of tea had been placed on the table. Nick watched Carey arrange the cups and saucers and begin to pour. He pushed his pack under the chair and sat back, pleased when he saw she remembered the sugar.

"This is nice," he said, accepting the cup she offered. "Being here with you."

She tried to smile. "I'm glad you're here. It's been ghastly."

"I can hardly believe it's real."

"It doesn't feel real, and I was there." Her voice broke for a second.

"What do the police say?"

"The only people in the vicinity besides the bishop were family and friends. They talked to everyone at the scene, but they haven't discovered who did it."

The food arrived and Nick watched as Carey picked at her meal, jabbing her fork into a stringy piece of lamb.

"You have to eat something," Nick said.

"I can't. Really."

"Trust me," he said. "You need to keep up your strength. Who knows what's ahead?"

She reached across the table and touched his hand. "I'm glad you're here."

She smiled at him, and he was suddenly very glad he had made the trip to be here for the person he loved best. Things were meant to happen, sometimes.

"I'd do anything for you," he answered. Even as he said it, he wondered if she knew how true it was.

FOURTEEN

TAMSYN BURKE'S FUNERAL TOOK place in the very spot where her wedding was to have been, a *mea culpa*, it seemed, from the Dean and Chapter of Westminster Abbey for having lost her so tragically on her most important of days. The service drew a large crowd. Apart from the family and friends who had been present on the day of her murder, there were other relatives and business associates who had never even met her. Inspector Murray and Ennis were in attendance, scanning the room for suspects. Outside the church, onlookers gathered on the pavement with mobile phones held over their heads, snapping photos when Hugh stepped out of his car and walked head down into the building. The Hardy film was weeks away from release and Tamsyn had not been well known enough to have real fans, but such circumstances bring out the morbid. The Burkes followed Hugh inside and sat across the aisle from the Ashley-Hunts, nodding stiffly as they took their seats.

Carey sat with her mother on one side and Nick on the other. She was glad he was there. It was an ordeal only to be managed on the arm of a good friend. She avoided looking at the casket in the front of the room. The first notes from the organ jangled her nerves, echoing in the hollow recesses of the room. Even the murmur of people greeting one another or trying to take a seat was distressing. The majesty of their surroundings did nothing to help, and even before the service began, Carey knew she would never darken the door of the Abbey again. She glanced at Hugh, who sat red-faced and silent between his parents, and at Daniel beside him, who was as stony-faced as anyone in the room. Her own parents sat numbly, having done their weeping at home.

Throughout the difficult parts of the sermon, Carey placed her hand on Nick's arm for support, where the irregular vibrations of his tics passed through his arm and into her fingers like a stream flowing into the mouth of a river, gently but steadily, pulsating and alive, comforting in its constancy. As the service began, she couldn't listen for fear of crying. Instead she shut it out, mentally quizzing herself on the parts of the Central Nervous System: brain, brain stem, mesencephalon, tectum, cerebrum peduncle, pretectum, mesencephalic duct. She imagined the soft pink and white tissue inside Nick's brain and the damaged part that caused the tics, what it would look like to the naked eye, if it could be surgically repaired. Anything was better than listening to the funeral of her only sibling. Occasionally, the sound of sniffling broke her concentration. She was a reserved person by nature, prone to analytical thought and ruled by common sense, but suddenly she felt herself sliding into the Slough of Despond; not just a place of despair, but despair tinged with guilt. She could have been a better sister. She hadn't judged Tamsyn, but she had often feared for her, and now, the worst had come true.

She longed, suddenly, to believe in prayer, to be washed in something pure and true that would cleanse her from the filth of this wretched mess. She believed in God; as a member of the scientific community she believed that adaptation was measurable and therefore indisputable, and that evolution did not occur universally but in fits and spurts; but the thought that an ultimate Creator had time for one among billions of human beings seemed improbable, to say the least. Too many millions suffered every day for him to hear and to acknowledge the cries of one, though believing in God allowed her the hope of heaven, where Tamsyn surely deserved to be.

The service droned on. Carey became sore from sitting motionless for such a long period of time. She massaged her neck during the final prayer and then took her mother's cold, unresponsive hand.

"Are you ready?" she asked.

She looked at her mother. Miranda Burke was young, not yet fifty, with only the slightest hint of gray beginning to show in her hair. Her face, when the girls were growing up, had been creased with laugh lines, though Carey knew the last ten years had taken a toll on her. When Tamsyn had turned fifteen, she had rebelled against authority, and her mother had been left to deal with the consequences. Carey had the sudden wish to see her smile again, but now that wouldn't be possible until she was back in Llandudno, sometime in the distant future when the painful memory of their beloved Tamsyn on the floor in a bloody dress had begun to fade, if that was even possible.

Her mother roused herself from her thoughts. "I suppose so."

She was wearing a black suit quite proper for someone of middle age, though Carey had refused the custom and donned a green jacket she would have worn to class on any ordinary day. She could imagine Tamsyn would have wanted them to wear something as colorful and irreverent as her own personality, and though Carey had none of her sister's verve, she had made an attempt. Black seemed so final; green, on the other hand, reminded her of leaves and trees and fields, of heaven itself, which lay just beyond their reach.

"Do you want to go to the pub, Mum?"

Miranda shook her head. "Not especially. But we should go anyway, for Tamsyn."

Carey was disappointed, but there was nothing to do but go with them. She squeezed her mother's arm. Of course, even if she didn't feel like making small talk, she could spend the time observing the attendees. Was it possible that the murderer would come and sit among them and lift a glass in Tamsyn's honor? The thought revolted her, and yet, anything was possible if someone was hardened enough to stab the sharp end of a knife into a beautiful living being.

Most of the people walked from Westminster Abbey to the Regency Arms several blocks away, but the Burkes and Nick Oliver squeezed into a cab and jostled through traffic to arrive at the pub a few minutes early.

"I suppose I'll have to talk to people," Carey remarked to Nick as they walked through the door.

"I suppose," he agreed.

She looked at him for a moment. "I'm sorry. This is awful, I know. Especially this, crammed in a small room with lots of people we don't know."

"Or want to," Nick added.

She watched her parents and Nick find a table and sit down. She didn't care for alcohol but ordered a half pint to be socially correct, wondering how long they would have to stay. She never went to pubs. For one thing, there was never time. She was either in class or studying; even her mobile phone was always set to vibrate so that it wouldn't interrupt whatever sentence she happened to be writing and make her lose her train of thought. For another, she rarely socialized beyond the study group she had joined. They were an interesting lot who had come together during their first term at university: Jared Chin, a Chinese student from Guiyang whose father, a worker in a small umbrella factory, wanted him to become a doctor; Roddy MacInnis, who was studying medicine to best his brother, a barrister; Gillian Stewart, who was a few years older and had returned to university after losing her parents in an accident; and Fiona Dickson, who had inherited a fortune from her great-uncle and decided to pursue the career she had dreamed of since childhood. All of them were serious, apart from Roddy's occasional and generally unwelcome attempt at humor. From time to time they would get into arguments over a method of diagnosis or treatment, but mostly they were a congenial group in which there were no weak links. Carey had originally suspected that she might have to carry the load when someone faltered, but they had proved sound and reliable, all of them getting excellent marks.

She saw that her friends had come to the Regency Arms to support her on this dreary afternoon. They huddled around a table in the corner and nodded at her in sympathy, as unused to taking time off or having a drink as she was. Carey went to greet them, though she didn't feel like engaging in conversation with anyone. It was too much effort.

As she lifted her glass to her lips, her mobile began to vibrate in her coat pocket, startling her and causing her to slosh ale on her sleeve. She reached for a napkin and dabbed at it, her back to the crowd. Irritated, she took the phone from her pocket and saw there was a message from Daniel Richardson.

Don't talk to me here.

Although she hadn't seen him arrive, she could suddenly feel his presence somewhere behind her. She fought the impulse to turn around and scan the crowd. Instead, she fumbled with the keypad to send a reply.

How did you get my number?

I have my ways. Does anyone look suspicious?

Right now, everyone does.

He didn't reply. Carey longed to abandon her glass, but it served as a means of avoiding conversation. It was odd, seeing Daniel's name on her mobile. She knew that half the girls in London would have taken her place in a heartbeat just to have the chance to talk to him, but she was different. Anything relating to sex or the male species was nothing more than a distraction when one was studying medicine. Waiting for his response, she felt a hand on her shoulder.

"Miss Burke. I'm sorry for your loss."

She knew the deep, elegant voice before she turned around. It belonged to Dr. Henry Landrake, one of her biology professors. He was unusually attractive for a university professor, so unlike the balding academes she vastly preferred. His forceful personality and reputation among the students caused her to avoid as much contact with him as possible.

"Thank you," she managed, just.

"She was a lovely girl."

Carey had forgotten that Tamsyn once met her after Landrake's class. He had demanded an introduction, which she had reluctantly given. Landrake was like that, prying into her personal life. She'd had the sickening feeling all term that he was trying to sleep with her.

Carey gave a tight smile and lifted her glass, only to freeze when he put his warm, smooth fingers around her wrist.

"Don't forget, I'm always here for you should you ever need anything."

"School's going well," she said, avoiding his meaning.

"I meant in a personal capacity as well."

"Thank you," she said again, hardly daring to breathe until he removed his hand from her arm. Over the glass, she caught Fiona's raised eyebrow. She hoped Fiona didn't think something was going on between them. Surely the sheer number of hours they spent working together contradicted that possibility. As if sensing her discomfort, her friend moved toward her, and Landrake left to get a drink.

"I was up half the night," Fiona said. "Even though we're between sessions, I'm desperate to work ahead for next year."

Carey was relieved that she hadn't offered condolences or made some sort of vague, prying remark. It was tiresome, trying to respond to them. "I'm anxious to get started, too."

"That's understandable. Maybe we can get together next week. I wouldn't mind staying ahead of the boys."

Jared and Roddy were engaged in a spirited discussion behind them, possibly about boating. Roddy had been trying to get their whole group organized for a picnic and outing in the country, which everyone else in the group had resisted.

"We need the occasional change of scene," he'd said.

"No, we don't," Gillian had replied.

"Of course you don't. Who would want to waste time relaxing?"

Gillian had nodded. "We don't need to develop lazy habits."

He'd been disappointed, but reliably good-natured the next time they'd seen him. Carey caught his eye now and smiled. He was the odd man out sometimes, but well-meaning.

She was lucky to have friends who would drop everything just to be there for her when the bottom dropped out.

Her mobile began to vibrate again. She slid it out of her pocket and looked at the screen.

There's someone you need to talk to. Meet me on
the Blue Bridge, St. James's Park, 20 minutes.

Carey glanced across the room at Nick. He was a good friend, talking to her parents and her aunt and uncle. She made her way through the crowd until she reached their table.

"I'm feeling a bit tired. I'd like to go now."

Nick stood. "I'll come with you."

"No," she said. "I just need some air. Can you please see Mum and Dad back to the hotel?"

"Of course," he answered.

"I'll ring you later, then."

Carey kissed her mother's cheek and touched her father's arm before turning to leave.

She didn't even have to look in his direction to know that Daniel Richardson was watching her every move.

FIFTEEN

AT ST. JAMES'S PARK, Carey walked out onto the bridge, which spanned the length of the lake. Daniel Richardson was nowhere in sight. A band of tourists took photographs of Westminster Palace at the other end, their cameras glinting in the glare of the sun, which had suddenly appeared between the clouds. She closed her eyes and lifted her face to the sky, listening to the flap of wings overhead and the water slapping against the bank below. She took a deep breath and realized she was hungry. Usually when she imbibed the rare pint, it dulled her interest in food, but now she thought of rich pasta, pesto, and garlic, things she rarely craved. She studied the water, trying to put the thought out of her mind. Nearby, a flock of pelicans flapped their feathers in the sunshine as if to assert their dominion over the lake, St. James's Park, perhaps even London. For one futile moment Carey wished it were just a normal day, not the day her sister was being buried. She felt guilty being alive.

She turned, looking for Daniel, wondering if she had imagined the whole exchange.

She was scrolling through her texts when he appeared at her shoulder.

"You startled me," she said. She took a step back and stuffed her mobile into her pocket.

"Sorry. I couldn't walk out with you," he said. "I didn't want anyone to notice."

She didn't answer. An elderly couple walked past, smiling and relaxed. It was easy to forget that normal life was still taking place all around them. She thought back to a week earlier, when she'd ended the term with good marks on her exams and was looking forward to buying new textbooks for the autumn term. She had been happy, as happy as she'd ever been. Life had a rhythm and routine that was comforting, but all of that was gone now.

Daniel took her arm and began to steer her along the bridge, northwards through the traffic of the Mall. Crossing to Marlborough Street, he hailed a cab. Carey waited for him to give the driver directions.

"The Dorchester, please," he said, settling back into his seat.

"We're going to a hotel?" she asked. She had no idea what she had expected, but it certainly wasn't that.

"I've figured out how to start. There's someone you need to talk to."

"Who?"

"Anna Parrish."

"Anna Parrish? The actress?" Carey asked, surprised. "Why do you want me to talk to her? Aren't you the one who knows her?"

"I've never met her, but Marc Hayley says she insisted on coming to the wedding with him, that she wanted to talk to Tamsyn. We need to find out why she was so keen to come. I think because you're a woman, you might have more luck with her."

"How would I go about it?"

"Go into the hotel and ask to speak with her alone." He looked over the lake. "Look, I know it's awkward, but she could turn around and get on a plane to go back to the States tomorrow and we'd have missed our chance."

"Then what?"

"If she doesn't shed any light on the situation, we'll decide what to do next."

Carey looked at her watch. "It's after five."

"Perfect time to catch her. It's too early for supper."

The traffic was dense. Carey rarely rode in cabs, which felt stuffy and close compared to the Tube. It was an unnecessary expense as well, and she could hardly stop herself from watching the meter ticking away pound after pound. Daniel seemed unconcerned.

"What do you know about her?" she asked, turning to study him.

"Well, she's American, obviously. Not exactly top tier in the acting game, though she's very well known. That's probably due more to her, shall we say, lifestyle than to talent."

"And they came all the way to London just for the wedding?"

"Yes. I mean, it doesn't surprise me that Hayley flew back for it. He's an old friend of Hugh's. But Anna's different. I made a couple of calls and found out she even asked for a few days off from the show she's working on in Toronto."

"Oh," Carey said. "What does that mean?"

"Trust me, it's difficult to stop production and take off a few days. Who knows what she had to do to get it."

The cab eased to a stop in front of the hotel and Carey got out.

"Aren't you coming?" she asked.

"I'll wait for you at the pub on the corner."

She leaned back into the cab. "I don't know what to say."

"Look, this woman might have had something to do with your sister's murder, or know someone who did. Anything you can find out will be helpful."

Carey drew her jacket around her and stepped back from the cab. She turned to face the hotel, nodding at the doorman as she entered. The lobby was crowded with patrons, some of whom had enjoyed afternoon tea in the Promenade and were leaving the building. She wracked her brain for a mental image of Anna Parrish, whom she had glimpsed at the Abbey: average height, with a preference for high heels and a round, curvaceous body, not one of those waifs one saw on the television who existed on yogurt and tofu. She had dressed to attract attention at the wedding, in an expensive red silk dress. A woman like that would be easy to pick out of a crowd, but she was nowhere to be seen. Carey would have to inquire at the desk. Then something caught her eye: a shiny black crocodile Hermes handbag.

She looked up at the owner of such an extravagant item and saw that it was indeed Anna Parrish. She was sitting in a gold brocade chair, sending a text.

Carey took a deep breath and forced herself to walk toward the actress. The woman had shoulder-length dark hair that fell around her shoulders and green, cat-shaped eyes. She wore a black blouse over a pair of jeans with tall, black pumps.

"Miss Parrish?" Carey asked.

Her voice sounded more confident than she felt. Perhaps it was wrong for her and Daniel to investigate, independent of the police inquiry, though it had been three days and the official investigation had turned up nothing so far. If she couldn't even approach someone in a public place without feeling every nerve in her body revolt, she wouldn't be able to pursue it at all.

"Yes?" Anna Parrish gave her a cursory look and then a second glance, her demeanor changing when she recognized Carey. "Oh, I'm sorry, Miss … Burke?"

"Yes, I'm Carey Burke." She dug her fingers into the strap of her bag. "Look, I apologize for being blunt, but did you know my sister?"

Anna Parrish studied her for a moment before speaking. She glanced about the lobby at the dozen or so people talking and reading magazines. "Perhaps it would be best if we had some privacy."

Carey nodded, following her to the lounge, which was almost completely deserted this time of day. A couple of men sat in a corner conducting a business meeting. Anna walked over to a pair of club chairs tucked out of the way and looked at Carey.

"Is this all right?"

"Of course."

She watched as the actress sat down in the chair and kicked off her four-inch heels. She set the shoes next to her handbag on the table between them and sighed.

"I hope you don't mind. These shoes are killing me. I couldn't get a cab and had to walk several blocks in them."

"Not at all."

"Well?" Anna asked. "Do you want a drink or something?"

"Not really, thanks. I wanted to ask you a few questions, if you don't mind."

"Why? I mean, aren't the police working on the case?"

"Yes. Of course. It's just that I want to understand a few things for myself."

Anna sighed. "It must have been awful. I don't know how you're coping so well."

"I'm not sure I am."

Anna looked around at the nearly empty room. "Do you think I could smoke here?"

"There aren't any ashtrays."

"Then I probably can't. The world is becoming a totalitarian state when you can't have a simple cigarette. What is it you wanted to ask me, anyway?"

"Did you know my sister?"

"I hate to go all Bill Clinton on you, but define 'know.'"

"Had you ever met her?"

"No, I hadn't. This is my first trip to England."

"You came as a guest of Marc Hayley, didn't you?"

"Yes," she answered, tucking a few falling strands of hair behind her ear. "Marc and I have a sort of casual relationship. We've known each other for a couple of years."

"And he invited you to the wedding?"

"Well, not exactly." She shrugged her shoulders.

"What do you mean?" Carey leaned back in her chair and crossed her arms.

"I mean, I asked him if I could come with him. I knew he was close to Hugh. Pardon me for saying so, but it's a big deal to bag a social event as big as this one."

"I heard you asked Marc Hayley to come because of Tamsyn, not because of Hugh. Is that true?"

"Marc must have said something to you."

"No. Actually, I've never met him."

"Then how ... ?"

"Does it matter?"

Anna shrugged. "I suppose it doesn't. It's not that important, really. I had a letter from your sister, oh, about a year ago. It intrigued me, and when I found out she was marrying Hugh Ashley-Hunt, I wanted to come and meet them."

"You had a letter from Tamsyn?" Carey asked, incredulous. "A year ago, before she was even involved with Hugh? What sort of letter?"

"It was odd. She wanted to know if I had any background information about Marc."

"I'm sorry, I don't understand."

"Well, neither do I, really. That's one thing I was going to do: ask her what kind of information she wanted."

"Did you reply to the letter?"

"Yes. I told her I had only known Marc for a couple of years and hadn't ever met his family. I didn't even know he was friends with Hugh until after I got the letter. I have no idea what she was getting at."

"Do you still have it?"

"At home, back in LA. But I haven't been there in over a month. I've been shooting a sitcom in Toronto."

Carey frowned, taken aback. What information could Tamsyn have wanted from a complete stranger about someone she had never met before?

"Is it possible that I could have it after you get back?"

Anna shrugged her shoulders. "Sure. Why not?"

Carey reached into her handbag, a canvas catch-all that was meant for carrying as many university textbooks as she could lift, and drew an envelope from its recesses. She extracted the letter inside it before writing her address on the back of the envelope. She held it out to Anna.

"I don't know exactly what my sister was trying to do, but it may be important." She stood. "Thank you for your time, and for being kind enough to answer my questions."

"I'm really sorry about everything." Anna reached out a sympathetic hand.

Carey shook it briefly. "Thank you."

She turned to leave, slinging her bag over her shoulder and stuffing her hands into her pockets, puzzled. What an odd thing it had been for Tamsyn to do, contacting Anna Parrish about Marc, especially before ever meeting Hugh. Maybe the letter would shed some light on it, but somehow she doubted it. She stepped out of the hotel and headed in the direction of the pub down the street, where Daniel would be waiting. Perhaps he could make some sense of it all.

SIXTEEN

LE PETIT CAFÉ WAS nearly a mile's walk from Scotland Yard, but when it wasn't raining and he wanted to stretch his legs, Gordon Murray often headed for its familiar green awning to buy lunch. It was nearly one o'clock and he had ordered a meal for Ennis, too, who'd spent the morning punching at the keys of his computer. When he returned, he placed one of the bags on the sergeant's desk and headed for his office.

"Thank you, sir!" Ennis called behind him, suspending whatever he had been typing to inspect the bag's contents.

Murray closed the door behind him, leaving the lights off. There was just enough light coming through the blinds. Fluorescents gave him headaches and inhibited inspired thinking. In less than an hour, Sir John and Antonia Hodges would be coming to his office to discuss the murder of Tamsyn Burke. He'd prepared his questions and put them in the drawer. For now, he spread a small cloth across his desk and arranged the food items upon it: a thick ham sandwich, a cup of mushroom risotto, and a fat, crusty baguette. He looked up when he heard a knock at the door.

"Yes?"

"Tea," Ennis replied, placing a hot mug on his desk.

They were so simpatico that Murray hoped they would work together until he retired, even if it meant Ennis wouldn't be promoted. He thanked him for the tea and tasted it. Just the right amount of sugar, he thought. Ennis had closed the door behind him by the time he turned his head. With skills like that, it was inevitable that the sergeant would eventually be kicked upstairs.

Murray's father had been a Detective Chief Inspector, too, of whom he was enormously proud. In his desk at home, he kept clippings of his father's greatest cases, his favorite of which occurred in 1956 when he had located and arrested a Nazi who had been hunted since the end of the war for his crimes at Auschwitz and Birkenau. From the moment Murray learned of it, from a retired colleague of his father's rather than from his father's own lips, he knew he wanted to join the Metropolitan Police. The case had taken six years from the first tip to the actual arrest, a notion that comforted him now when cases weren't quickly solved. It was the persistence, the resolve that one must finish no matter how long it took, that Murray admired most. Of course, everyone preferred the tidy cases: murder weapon recovered, incriminating evidence at the scene, swift retribution to the guilty party; but he also loved the puzzles. The Burke murder case was certainly that: twenty-seven suspects, none of whom were obviously the murderer. In this case, the motive ran deep.

There was another knock at the door.

"I've dug up something for you," Ennis said, poking his head into Murray's office.

"I've been making calls about the Hodges, and thought you might like to see this."

Murray took the proffered sheet of paper and read it. "Do you have any confirmation?"

"Not from a bank, *per se*. My source was a director who'd quit this last film before it started. He was eager to talk, I can tell you."

"Thank you, Sergeant. That is most helpful."

After Ennis left, he ate and read through the note again before putting it in his desk with his list of questions for the Hodges. He wouldn't have to look them over again; once he had written things down, he would remember.

The Hodges were a glamorous pair, like many of the suspects in this case. Sir John was sixty-four, an outspoken man known for his lavish excesses. His wife, Antonia, was a decade younger than he. She was his third wife, and the only one with whom he had no children. In all, he had fathered seven offspring: three by his first wife, and four by his second. He was known for his charming hospitality and was a favorite among those who had worked for him, for if one were in his good graces, he could be quite accommodating. Hodges was obviously a man who enjoyed the company of the much younger stars in his orbit. It was a noisy, social world he inhabited, very different from the solitary life that Murray knew so well.

The Hodges arrived on time, at two o'clock. Lunch had been eaten and cleared away, and the offending fluorescent light switched on. Murray opened the door and waved them inside.

"Come in and have a seat," he said. "Thank you for coming."

"Anything we can do to assist in this nasty business," Sir John replied.

Murray waited a moment while the Hodges settled themselves in the chairs opposite his desk. He had considered taking them into one of the boardrooms, but he preferred the intimacy of his office, with its maps of London on the wall and the window overlooking Dacre Street. He sat down behind his desk and took out his pad of paper.

"So. We're here to talk about Tamsyn Burke, as you know. Could you tell me how you met her?"

Sir John was a huge man both in personality and size, a man who could intimidate if he so chose. His wife, on the other hand, while polite, was cool. She balanced a large handbag on her lap and looked at him with apprehension.

"We were casting a part in *Under the Greenwood Tree* a few months ago," Hodges answered, clasping his hands around his ample stomach. "I had picked out a girl I thought could do the part, but I wasn't in love with her, if you know what I mean. Then Ashley-Hunt asked me to take a look at one of the girls we'd hired for some of the village scenes. Actually, I'd deferred that hiring job, so I hadn't seen her before. She was quite lively, and I decided to give her a try at the part if it meant that much to Hugh. After I saw her on the rushes, I was glad I'd listened to him. She made the camera fall in love with her."

"Did you get to know her personally?"

There was an awkward pause, and Murray looked up from his notes. Hodges was a heavy man with a flushed complexion, but it wasn't his imagination that the man looked even more uncomfortable than usual. He wondered if he had stumbled onto something significant. Perhaps Hodges was the kind of man who seduced his leading ladies, young women who were trying to make a name for themselves and advance their career.

Hodges cleared his throat. "I didn't know her terribly well, no. There were a few parties, but I didn't spend much time with her. Did you, Toni?" He turned to his wife, whose arched brow said more than enough. They were hiding something, whether it had to do with Tamsyn Burke or not.

"No, I didn't. She only had eyes for Hugh. They had gotten serious about that time."

"How well do you know Ashley-Hunt? Are you friends with his father?" Murray asked.

"Well, I've run across Noel at events, of course, but I've never worked with him or had a meaningful conversation with him," Hodges said, glad to be on more comfortable ground. "I didn't know Hugh before I began working with him on this film, either. I happened to see him in something Antonia made me watch—"

"*A Midsummer Night's Dream*," she interrupted.

"Yes, well, that then. I saw him and liked his looks immensely. He's quite tall and has that long, hangdog look about him that is so appealing to women. A few weeks later, I saw a photo of him and Richardson in some rag—"

"*Hello* magazine," Antonia supplied.

"Whatever," Sir John said, waving his hand. "The important thing is that when I saw that picture of the two of them at an equestrian event, looking ever so dashing, I knew right then their friendship needed to be transposed to the big screen. They have a chemistry that most producers would die for."

"It's Richardson," Antonia said. "He positively smolders."

"Let's get back on track, shall we?" Murray asked. "Now, you met them how long before you began working together?"

"Was it July?" Hodges asked, turning to his wife. "I called and invited Hugh and Daniel to the house in France. They were quite good company, I can tell you. The house simply sings when it's full of young people, doesn't it, dear?"

She nodded.

"Is the film finished?" Murray asked.

"Everything but post-production."

"When did the filming end?"

"Well, we began in late summer, and it went on for eight weeks."

"To your knowledge, did anyone show any sign of disliking Miss Burke throughout the production of the film?"

"Little tiffs flare up in almost every production," Hodges answered. "Remember last year, Toni, when Finn Brody got drunk and took a swipe at Dominic Cooper? That turned into a major fracas."

"Were there any during this production, particularly involving Richardson, Ashley-Hunt, or Tamsyn Burke?" Murray asked.

"None that I'm aware of. They were friendly with the crew, and it seemed a pretty amiable lot this time."

"Did you ever notice anything unusual about Miss Burke?"

Hodges threw his head back and chortled. "She was an odd one, no mistake. Strange fashion sense. I wondered if she was color blind. But she kept the hours, didn't complain a single time, and didn't cost a bomb. I consider that a roaring success."

"Cost a bomb?" Murray repeated. "Unlike Richardson and Ashley-Hunt, I assume?"

The conversation ceased and the Hodges exchanged a look.

"Of course, if you get actors of the caliber of Richardson and Ashley-Hunt," Hodges said, "it will definitely cost you. But the film wouldn't be as big without them, especially with an unknown heroine. That's always a gamble. Sometimes it pays off. We needed them both."

Murray drummed his fingers on the table. "But you've had difficulty financing this film."

"Where did you hear something like that?"

"Please answer the question."

"What has that to do with anything?"

"That entirely depends. This film of yours could be a success. You've cast two well-known actors in the lead roles. It could be an even greater success after the murder of Miss Burke."

Hodges's round face began to turn red. If anything, his wife went paler. "That's preposterous," he protested. "You aren't suggesting I killed this girl for the publicity?"

"I have twenty-seven people present at the time of the murder," Murray replied. "One of them had a motive strong enough to stab her in the heart. People have killed for far less than earning millions from the morbid curiosity of the film-going public."

"You're wrong," Antonia Hodges snapped. "Oh, not that there weren't financing problems, but that we could have had anything to do with her murder."

Murray frowned, remembering the girl's body crumpled in a grotesque heap of wedding dress stained in blood. "Through which entrance to the Abbey did you arrive?"

"The north door," Sir John replied. "Just like everyone else."

"Were the two of you alone when you entered the building?"

"No," Antonia said. "There was a young woman in the doorway, and some of Tamsyn's family arrived at the same time."

"Were you acquainted with any of the other guests at the wedding?"

"No," Sir John answered firmly. "None apart from Richardson and Ashley-Hunt."

Murray tapped a pen on his desk. "What was the relationship between Tamsyn Burke and Daniel Richardson?"

"They were thick as thieves, all three of them. It was hard to tell who was dating whom. They'd probably known each other all their lives."

"Not quite," Murray said, studying them both. "In fact, Ashley-Hunt and Richardson met Tamsyn Burke after they met you."

"Really?" Hodges asked, looking surprised. "I had no idea."

Murray stood and walked over to look out of the window. "When did you arrive at the Abbey?"

"Almost a half hour early. Toni wanted to get a good seat. As you can see, a man of my size needs considerable room."

"So, you were there before most of the other guests?"

"Yes. We spent the time looking at some of the tombs while we waited."

"Which was your favorite?" Murray asked, raising an eyebrow.

Hodges paused. "I don't suppose I have one. Let's say John Milton, for argument's sake."

Murray let it pass. "Did you see anything unusual at all while you were there? Anyone acting out of character?"

"No, but we were occupied. A friend of Hugh's, Marc Hayley, introduced himself and a terrible American girl who kept pushing us to put her in a film. She assumed because we gave Tamsyn a part we must be giving roles away."

"And of course, that's not the case."

"I resent your tone." Sir John heaved himself out of the chair. "We've cooperated, sir. I can't think of anything more to say at this time."

Murray stood and the two men glared at one another for a moment. "Make certain the sergeant outside the door has the information about where you are staying," Murray said.

Sir John gave a curt nod and then squeezed his wife on the shoulder. They walked out, leaving the door open behind them.

Murray followed them to the door, watching them leave. Money was a powerful motive, but whoever had stabbed that poor girl in the heart had been driven by something far more compelling. He was certain of it. His job was to find what that could possibly be.

137

SEVENTEEN

CAREY JUMPED WHEN HER mobile rang in her jeans pocket. She was sitting on the lumpy mattress in her flat, jotting notes on a piece of paper she had torn from a notebook. Across from her, Nick looked up from her laptop, where he had been typing.

"Who is it?" he asked.

"Daniel Richardson," she answered. She put the mobile up to her ear. "Yes?"

"I'm three streets away from your flat," Daniel said. "May I come up?"

"Hold on." She put it up against her chest and looked at Nick, who was engrossed in what he was writing. "He wants to come up. Do you mind?"

"No," Nick answered, although the look on his face told her he did. She ignored it.

"All right," she said to Daniel. "It's in St. Matthew Street."

"I know where it is."

"I'm on the first floor." She ended the call and put the mobile back in her pocket.

Nick had stopped typing on the computer. "He's that actor, isn't he? What does he want?"

"I didn't tell you before, because I thought you might not approve," she said. "I asked for his help."

"Doing what?"

"We're looking at the suspects in the case."

"Don't be stupid, Carey!" he protested. "That's a job for the police."

"Well, they haven't come up with anything, have they?"

"How do you know? They're not going to tell you. And this sort of thing takes time and resources."

"I can't sit around waiting for something to happen."

"What can an actor do anyway?" Nick asked. "He's not an investigator. Oh, wait. I suppose he played one in a film."

She ignored the remark. "We're just talking to people, that's all. Sometimes you can get a feeling about someone."

"That's what I'm afraid of."

Carey looked about the small, two-room flat. The kitchen had a small refrigerator, a stove, and barely enough cupboard space for a few pots and pans and tins of soup. In the main room, her bed was shoved against one wall, next to a small table and a sofa that had seen better days, if not decades. It wasn't a place to entertain friends. It was one thing having Nick there, who had practically grown up in her house, but Daniel Richardson was another matter. She didn't even study there with her friends. They usually met at the library or a café, and on the rare occasion at Gillian's posh Chelsea digs, where no one dared sit back on the furniture.

Within minutes, Daniel knocked at the door. Carey got up to answer it, ignoring the withering look Nick gave her.

"Come in," she said, stepping back so he could enter. "Daniel, this is Nick Oliver. He's a friend. He lives next door to my parents."

Nick nodded. Carey knew he was hoping he wouldn't have to shake hands and betray his tic to a complete stranger, a famous one at that.

"I assume you're here to talk about what to do next." She saw Daniel raise a brow at Nick and she tried to smile. "Don't worry. He's reliable."

"There's someone I'm concerned about," Daniel said, still eyeing Nick.

"Who?"

"That tough-looking bloke who was at the wedding. You remember. Spiked hair and a leather jacket, sitting by himself. Is he a friend of the family?"

"Ciaran Monaghan," Carey answered. "We knew him in school. He went out with Tamsyn when they were young."

"What do you know about him?" Daniel asked, picking up a book that was lying in a stack on the floor and examining the cover: *Immunological and Autoimmune Disorders in Developing Nations.* He put it back quickly.

"He works in London now, somewhere not far from here, I think. I run into him sometimes."

"Can we get his address?" Daniel asked.

"I can probably get it," Nick replied, shrugging. "My mother teaches with his aunt. Not that I think we should get involved."

"I'm surprised Tamsyn didn't tell me he was coming to the wedding," Carey said. "And I do think you should find it, Nick, if you don't mind."

"I have to talk to my mum anyway, I suppose," he replied. He stood and went into the corridor to make the call.

"What ended the relationship between Tamsyn and Monaghan?" Daniel asked when Nick was gone.

"I don't know. She never told me."

"And who is that, anyway?" Daniel asked, cocking his head in Nick's direction.

"A family friend from Wales. I told you."

"He wasn't at the wedding."

Carey hesitated. She didn't want to tell him about Nick's problems. It was too complicated to explain with Nick standing ten feet away. "He couldn't come, that's all."

"Was he close to Tamsyn?"

"They didn't like each other," Carey admitted. "They never have."

"How do you know he wasn't already in London?" Daniel persisted. "He could have slipped into the Abbey without anyone noticing and killed her."

"I doubt that, because I picked him up at Paddington Station on Monday."

"He's got a guilty look about him."

"You're acting like he's a suspect."

"Right now, everyone's a suspect."

A minute later, Nick came back and sat down on the sofa. "My mum will try to get the address and email it to me. If she can figure out how to do that."

"Tell me about Monaghan," Daniel said, leaning against the wall near the window.

"He's a wanker," Nick answered.

Daniel folded his arms. "Would Tamsyn have asked him to the wedding, or do you suppose he crashed?"

"I don't know," Carey said. "I never saw the invitation list. But why would he do that? Do you think he was still in love with her?"

"Maybe he was blackmailing her, to get to Hugh's money," Daniel said. "Or he could have decided to talk her out of it. His last chance, as it were."

"I can't imagine that Tamsyn invited him," Carey said after a moment. "She wasn't the sort to look back."

"I wish we could look through her emails," Daniel said.

Carey froze. "Nick, you're computer savvy. You could probably hack into anything."

"No, I can't," he said. "You're overstating my abilities. I've taken a couple of courses. I know about as much about it as you do."

"If someone was threatening her, there could well be some kind of electronic trail," Carey continued. "There might even have been threats made against her. Why didn't we think of this before?"

She pulled her laptop off a shelf and turned it on, then glanced up at Nick. "Would you mind making tea? I have the feeling we'll need it."

"You don't happen to know her password, do you?" Daniel asked, sitting down beside her.

"I might, actually," Carey said. "She mentioned once that I would know it from a clue."

"What was the clue?"

"She said it had to do with her favorite book as a teenager."

"What was that?"

"*The Scarlet Letter.* I assumed she meant the author's name was her password."

"Who wrote it? Melville? I'm afraid I'm not up to date on nineteenth century American authors."

"No, Melville wrote *Moby Dick.* Hawthorne wrote *The Scarlet Letter.*"

She went to the web mail site and typed Tamsyn's email address in the appropriate box. Then she tried a password.

Hawthorne **Invalid ID or Password. Try again.**
Nathaniel **Invalid ID or Password. Try again.**
scarletletter **Invalid ID or Password. Try again.**

thescarletletter **Invalid ID or Password. Try again.**

"This is impossible," she said.
Nick grunted from the kitchen. "There are endless variables."
"Keep trying," Daniel answered.

nathanielhawthorne **Invalid ID or Password. Try again.**

"What were the names of the main characters?" Carey asked.
"No idea, but you could look it up online."
"Of course." She opened a new screen and typed *The Scarlet Letter* in the search box. Within three seconds, there were thousands of websites offering information. She clicked on a book site and scanned the page. "Here we are."

hesterprynne **Invalid ID or Password. Try again.**
dimmesdale **Invalid ID or Password. Try again.**

"I think that's too complicated," she concluded. "Let me try something else."

ScarletA **Welcome to your inbox. You have four new messages.**

"Perhaps I should look at these alone," Carey murmured, glancing at them.
"I cared about her too," Daniel argued. "I want to know what happened."
She paused for a moment and then nodded. Of the four new messages, two were from the bridal shop where Tamsyn had purchased her dress, one was from their mother, and one from Ciaran Monaghan.
"I can't believe it," she said. "I thought he was completely off the radar."

Ignoring the others, she clicked on Monaghan's email.

April 1
From: Ciaran Monaghan
To: Tamsyn Burke
Re: Wedding

Yes, I can be there. But I'm not sure I understand. Want to enlighten me?

"What does it mean?" she asked.

"Look in her Sent Messages box," Daniel suggested.

Carey pressed a few keys and found the original email from Tamsyn. It did nothing to elucidate matters.

April 1
From: Tamsyn Burke
To: Ciaran Monaghan
Subject: Wedding

Thanks for talking to me this afternoon. Have you made a decision yet?

"She must have answered his last email in person. Are there any other messages between them?" Daniel asked.

Carey scrolled back through the email listings. "Nothing to or from Monaghan. Absolutely nothing."

"What about that email Tamsyn got from your mother?"

"Would you mind if I read that one alone?"

"Of course," he answered. He stood and went to the window, giving her space.

Carey turned away, taking her laptop to the opposite corner of the sofa for complete privacy. After a few minutes, she began tapping away.

"What are you doing?" Daniel asked.

"I'm deleting some of the messages."

"What for?"

"Because now you know the password, and there are some things in here that are strictly private."

"Were there messages from anyone else on our list?"

"Yes, and I'll show those to you. There are two from Lucy Potter, and one each from the bridesmaids we know from Wales. I'm afraid they don't explain much."

April 3
From: Lucy Potter
To: Tamsyn Burke
Re: News

I can't believe you asked. The answer, of course, is yes. And I would like to bring Dylan, if you don't mind.

April 1
From: Lucy Potter
To: Tamsyn Burke
Re: News

So surprised to hear from you. I didn't know they had computers where you come from. Oh, is that bitter? Didn't mean to be. It's just been a long time, hasn't it? I've seen you in the magazines, of course. Who would have thought one of us would have made it to the top? So, what's the question you wanted to ask me?

From: Natalie Swindon
To: Tamsyn Burke
Re: A surprise

*Tamsyn! How are you? I couldn't believe it when I saw your
email! We've been absolutely thrilled for you, all the news we've
heard in the past year or two. Things are busy here. The shop's
doing great. Did you know Marianne works here at the shop
with us? We're having a grand time. Oh, I saw Jasper Cornwall
a couple of months ago. You remember him, I'm sure … best
looking boy in school. Married now, though, drat the luck, to
some English girl. They were in town to see his parents, with
their two-year-old son in tow. I have to admit, I was glad it
wasn't me that was tied down with a kid already, no matter
how attractive Jasper is. I miss you! I miss you! I miss you!
Next time you're here, we'll go out for drinks and have a
splendid time. I can't wait to see you. Love, Natalie*

"Jasper Cornwall," scoffed Nick. "What a tosser."
Carey ignored him and kept on reading.

April 17
From: Marianne Gaines
To: Tamsyn Burke
Re: Bridesmaid

*I'm sorry it took a while to answer your email. It was such a
surprise to hear from you. I think it's very nice of you to ask
Natalie and me to be in your wedding, if you're sure you
haven't got smarter friends in London who would want to*

do it. I've never been to London, but Natalie says it will be
fun. Of course, Natalie makes everything fun, doesn't she?
Thanks again for thinking of your old friends.—Marianne

"Nothing else?" Daniel asked.

"Nothing."

"What about her mobile?" Daniel asked.

Carey looked at him. "I have it. I can check the history."

"It's worth a look, but don't get your hopes up. We know she most likely spoke to everyone on our list. You should check it for messages, though."

Carey closed the computer and glanced at Nick, who was staring at her. The kettle suddenly shrieked at its boiling point just as he got a text.

"I have it," Nick said, looking at his mobile. "Monaghan's address."

"What do we do?" Carey asked.

"We go there," Daniel said. "Then we'll see."

"I'm coming with you," Nick said, pocketing his phone.

Carey pulled on a jacket and glanced at Daniel, trying to gauge what he was thinking, but she couldn't.

"All right then," she said. "Let's go."

Outside, Daniel insisted they take a cab though it was only a ten minute walk. They stood under the eave of the shop across the road from Monaghan's flat, Daniel smoking while Nick sulked. Carey wondered if the door of Monaghan's building would ever open.

"Why don't we just ring him?" she asked.

"It would be better to run into him," Daniel answered, tossing his cigarette on the ground.

"You shouldn't smoke."

"You sound like—"

"Like what?" she asked. "A doctor?"

"Never mind."

Nick touched her sleeve. "Look, there he is."

Daniel stood with his back to Monaghan, looking at Carey. "Is he coming this way?"

"No," she replied. "He's going the other way."

Daniel turned and began walking after him, with Carey and Nick a short distance behind. They followed Monaghan three blocks, but when he turned a corner, they lost him.

"We need to split up," Daniel said, pointing to the right. "You try that direction. Ring if you see him. Don't talk to him without me."

Daniel watched as Nick followed Carey into a lane crowded with restaurants, and then he turned and went in the other direction. The shops and cafés were bustling with midday activity. Restaurants were serving meals out of doors, and patrons clustered in noisy groups around small tables. He scoured the crowds, wondering which way Monaghan had gone. He noticed a movement in the doorway of a small shop and plunged in, working his way through tables of merchandise to reach the door to a back room. A couple of employees were working at a large desk, and they sat up in alarm when he burst in.

"Oi!" one of the girls shouted.

He paid no attention, striding through to the back door and letting it slam behind him. In the alleyway, he moved faster, breaking into a sprint. He skirted the bins and boxes littering the pavement until he came to the end of the alley, where he found a slightly open door. It was a tall, dark building, and he pushed the door fully open without stepping inside. As his eyes adjusted to the darkness, he entered the room and looked around. It was some kind of warehouse. There were boxes everywhere, alongside abandoned chairs and tables. Then suddenly, he saw a figure coming out of the shadows.

Before he could react, Monaghan punched him in the stomach, a hard blow that left him gasping for breath. Daniel hadn't fought since primary school, but he threw a fist at Monaghan's jaw, which made contact. It felt like iron, but he saw that it drew blood. Monaghan jabbed back, catching him in the shoulder, and then reached a hand up to wipe the blood trickling from his lip.

"What the fuck are you following me for?" Monaghan asked, leaning in close. His hair was short and spiked, and he had a stud earring in one ear. He was tall and muscled, the sort who would be a problem if the fight escalated any further.

"I need to talk to you."

"Get out. I've got nothing to say to you."

"It's about Tamsyn."

Monaghan spit some of the blood onto the floor. "What makes you think I know anything about Tamsyn?"

"You were at the wedding."

"Guess they just let anyone in."

Daniel ignored the sarcasm. "Carey and I are talking to some of her friends about the last time they spoke to her."

"Carey has no business looking into this mess, and if you're encouraging it, you're putting her in danger."

"Are you threatening me?"

"Hell yes, I'm threatening you. Stay out of it. You're not the fucking police."

"When was the last time you saw her? Just tell me that."

"Are you accusing me of something?" Monaghan asked, narrowing his eyes and taking another step closer. "Do you think I hurt her?"

"Did you?" Daniel asked, staring into his black eyes.

"Fuck you."

Daniel didn't see the last blow coming. This time, it completely winded him. He sank down on one knee to catch his breath. After a couple of seconds, he stood, but Monaghan was already gone. He took his mobile out of his pocket and dialed Carey's number.

"Found him," he said, holding an aching rib.

"Is he with you?"

"He's gone. Where are you?"

"We're in front of Archer's. Do you know it?"

"Yeah," he muttered. "I'll be there in a minute."

He found the café nearby. The building was an anonymous gray brick, espaliered with thick ivy that made him think of the country-side instead of a restaurant in the middle of busy London. Inside, it was almost empty. A middle-aged American couple sat at a table having an argument, and in the corner, an older woman sat alone, taking the occasional drink of tea and knitting to pass the time. A couple of young girls stood in the corner, texting instead of talking. They chose a table and ordered coffees.

"He won't cooperate," Daniel said, trying not to look at Nick.

"What happened?" Carey asked, looking at him closely.

"Nothing," he answered. "He refused to talk."

"He's always been a bastard," Nick said.

"But still, he went to her wedding," Carey said, shaking her head. "Maybe he was jealous of her relationship with Hugh."

"You're wasting your time," Nick said. "Like I told you, let the police handle this. That's what they're paid for."

Daniel caught Carey's eye. They were thinking the same thing, he knew. They had to keep on, but first, they had to get rid of Nick Oliver before he got any more involved.

EIGHTEEN

ON A SEPTEMBER DAY not long before the shoot was finished, Daniel changed out of the over-starched nineteenth-century get-up and into his blue button-down and jeans. It always felt good to get back into his own clothes. Shed of character and dialogue, he felt more like himself, able to focus on his own problems. Most of the crew had dispersed for the lunch hour, although a couple of cameramen were setting up equipment for the early afternoon takes while the light was still good. Tamsyn had the day off, but Hugh was sitting in a chair in a dusty corner, eyes closed, listening to music. He hadn't seemed to notice everyone trickling off the set. Daniel walked up to him and waited until his friend's eyes opened.

"What are you listening to?" he asked.

Hugh pulled off one of the earbuds, looking up at him. "Nina Simone."

"Which song?"

"*Just in Time.*"

"That's one of Tamsyn's favorites."

Ordinarily, Daniel found Tamsyn's music preferences too eclectic—he hesitated to say juvenile—for his taste, but now and then, she played something decent. Hugh was looking at him cautiously, and music was the right way to open a conversation with him. Lately, Daniel had kept to safe topics. Everyone knew that Hugh and Tamsyn were seeing each other now, but neither of them had said anything about it to him, and he wasn't going to be the one to bring it up.

"Are you hungry?" Hugh asked, turning off the song.

"Pretty much always," Daniel answered. "You know me."

"I don't really feel like going out. What's left on the cart over there?"

They wandered over to see if anything had been left from the bounty that had been placed there hours ago. There were stale bagels and squelchy fruit, but actors learned to subsist on whatever was put out before them. They picked around at the edges, putting a few things on their plates before going back to sit down. Daniel pierced a large strawberry with his fork and ate it in a single bite.

"Are you as sick of Hardy as I am?" Hugh asked.

"Maybe more," Daniel admitted. "But I think the film was a good idea, all told. I'm glad we did it."

"Ah. I believe the phrase is, 'I told you so.'"

Daniel smiled. "Rub it in."

"What do you think you'll do next?"

"I'm looking at a couple of offers, but I haven't decided which, if either, to take. What about you?"

"You know what I'd really love? A break from everything. I'd like to spend some time sitting on a beach, figuring out how to get the milk out of a coconut."

"Have you ever thought of writing a screenplay?" Daniel asked. "You could take whatever you're interested in and create a whole script around it. I've been reading about the life of Robert Louis Stevenson.

He spent a few years in Hawaii and befriended King Kalakaua and his niece. I think that would make a great story. Just think of it: romance, sweltering Hawaiian nights, and tropical paradise. It's tempting."

"You write it, and then cast me, and my dream of coconuts on the beach will be complete."

"Maybe I will. We could use a little sand and sun after this."

Hugh's mobile rang, and he pulled it from his pocket to peer at the screen. "It's Tamsyn. Do you mind if I take it?"

"Go ahead," Daniel answered.

He stood to give Hugh some privacy and went back over to the food cart, stabbing a piece of melon with a little too much force. He could hear Hugh's low, rumbling voice murmuring behind him.

It had gotten away from him, the relationship with Tamsyn. He analyzed it sometimes, wondering precisely how she had become more interested in Hugh when it was obvious there was chemistry between them. He had envisioned a different type of woman for Hugh: industrious, elegant, and capable, the sort that wore a chignon and a Chanel suit with Jimmy Choos. Not Tamsyn, who looked as though she would be more at home on a low-rent production of *Sweeney Todd* with buckets of blood than doing a respectable Hardy film with a well-known producer. The thing that troubled him the most was the weekend they'd spent in Brighton. They'd fit together in a way he never had with anyone before. He was certain Tamsyn had felt the same way. He'd never misjudged any relationship with a girl before. About one thing he was certain: she would never be dishonest. She wouldn't lead him on only to go with a bigger prize.

He went back over to sit down next to Hugh, hoping he wouldn't have to listen to Hugh fawning over her.

Fortunately, Hugh was ringing off. "Until then," he said.

Daniel didn't hear Tamsyn's response, but Hugh laughed. "No doubt," he replied. "See you in a couple of hours."

Daniel busied himself with spreading the cream cheese on a hardened bagel as if it were the most interesting thing he could possibly do.

"Sorry about that," Hugh said.

"It's fine," Daniel answered. "It was a good time to get a call, anyway."

"No, I mean, I'm sorry if it bothers you about Tamsyn."

"What do you mean?"

"I mean, obviously you two are friends, and now I'm seeing her. Is that a problem for you?"

"No," Daniel said, a little too quickly. "Of course not."

"I feel a bit guilty about it," Hugh said.

"You shouldn't. People get attractions for all sorts of reasons, and if I like someone you're dating, so much the better. It would be worse if I hated her."

"You could never hate Tamsyn. I've never seen you so taken with anyone before, ever."

There was no good answer to that, so Daniel decided to drop the matter. He wouldn't bring up the Stevenson script idea again either. There was no reason to let Hugh have everything. "What are you doing tonight?" he asked, to change the subject.

"She wants to go to the pub. Of course, you'll have to join us. She isn't happy if you aren't there. Sometimes I wonder if she thinks we're a package deal."

"Don't even go there."

"Ouch. You're right. But you know what I mean."

"What are you going to do when we shut down here?"

"You mean, what am I going to do about Tamsyn?"

The question hung in the air between them. It had been a matter of some concern to Daniel. In the past, Hugh had dated girls for a while and then had conciliatory breakups, lavishing the girl with a nice leaving present like a monstrously expensive handbag. Then he went back to his bachelor ways without a backward glance. Daniel had hoped this would be the case with Tamsyn as well. He had no idea what the two of them saw in each other, but he had little doubt it would run its course like every relationship either of them had ever had. In fact, he'd speculated to himself that after the inevitable end, he would wait a respectable amount of time and then resume his attentions toward her, if she was still interested.

"Well," Hugh said at last. "I thought I would ask her to move in."

Daniel was shocked. Hugh had never lived with anyone before. Not that there weren't plenty of nights of sleeping here or there, but in general, he guarded his privacy and had never allowed a girl to breach the gap.

"How does she feel about it?" Daniel asked, when he could finally speak.

"I haven't asked her yet."

Hugh sounded unconcerned, and Daniel stole an appraising look at his best friend. Perhaps even more astonishing than Tamsyn's involvement with Hugh was Hugh's interest in Tamsyn. It was an utter mystery. Hugh was fastidious and particular. It was more than Daniel could imagine, having this gypsy-like creature move into Hugh's elegant house. She lived out of a knapsack, for God's sake. She begged rides from total strangers, like Daniel, to go to Dorset without any idea of what she would find when she got there. Her clothes were eccentric, her background was sketchy, and she had betrayed no interest whatever in being the girlfriend of a major English star. That is, until she'd started dating one. Daniel shook his head at the whole idea.

"You're serious?"

Hugh looked at him. "I've never been more serious about anything."

Daniel put his fork on his plate and set it on a pile of scripts on the floor. He couldn't eat another bite. He wished there were a way he could excuse himself and end the conversation. He wished his mobile would ring. He wished the door would open and everyone would flood back in, ready for the next round of torture.

"If it makes you happy," he finally said. "That's what's important."

"Which pub do you want to go to tonight?" Hugh asked.

"Either one is fine," he said, relieved at the change of topic. There was another pub in the village they hadn't gone to as often, but their usual place was noisy enough to keep him from thinking too much. Both spots had plenty of drinks to drown his troubles.

"She likes the Crowned Goose better, so I suppose it will be that. But I think it gets awfully hot in there."

Daniel couldn't have cared less. He was ready for a drink. He was ready to feel the buzz and the blur of alcohol, and then he would watch Tamsyn entertain them and everyone else with her terrible impersonations and silly jokes. He was ready to sit back and drink her in and fall in love with her all over again.

That evening, it was raining, a fine mist that did not require an umbrella. If it hadn't been for Tamsyn, it would have a mild deterrent to going out. Daniel paced around his room, wishing for once that he had been smart enough to take a house and have actual space to live in. He didn't especially care to waste money, and posh digs in a remote Dorset village where he would spend little time qualified in his mind as a waste indeed, but now he felt like a caged bear at the zoo. He wondered if he should stay away, but trying to come up with alternatives to the pub was an unfruitful exercise.

He ran through a mental list of some of the people he liked among the crew to invite out, but it was so near the end of filming that he didn't want to disrupt plans. Two newly formed couples were already fighting or in tears about going back to their London lives and respective significant others, and most others were merely irritable at having been away from home so long and weren't especially good company. In fact, the only person that Daniel really wanted to see was Tamsyn. He wondered if he would feel like that forever.

If only he hadn't been so reluctant to let her know how he felt about her. He had been too cautious, though in retrospect he couldn't imagine handling it any other way. Eventually, he decided to join them. If he didn't, he would be thinking about them anyway.

Tamsyn, however, was not in the mood to amuse anyone that night. She was quieter than normal, though neither of them said anything to her about it. Hugh ate a plate of scallops and played darts with a couple of local men, and Daniel, who wasn't hungry, nursed a pint and was occupied answering questions from a curious barmaid. Tamsyn caught his eye once or twice, and he longed to pull away and talk to her, but just as the woman tired of asking him about London and acting and life in general, Hugh returned and coerced him into a game.

Tamsyn pushed her dinner around on her plate and then put down the fork. Before Daniel could think of a way to extricate himself, she tossed her napkin onto the table and walked over to them.

"I'm going back to Olivia's," she said, stretching up to peck Hugh on the cheek. "Stay and enjoy yourselves."

"I'll come with you," Hugh offered.

"No, that's all right. I'll have a hot bath and forget about the long, ghastly day."

"If you're sure."

She looked up at Daniel, who was suddenly struck mute. He couldn't very well offer to go with her with Hugh standing right there. She smiled, as if enjoying his obvious discomfort.

"See you tomorrow," she said.

He watched her turn and retrieve her handbag from the chair where she'd left it, and then walk out of the pub. When he realized he'd been staring, he turned back toward the dart board, throwing one for all he was worth. Hugh whistled as the dart clipped one of his own, very near the bull's eye. He raised a brow and caught Daniel's eye.

"Some friend you are," he said. "You're trying to steal the game right out from under me."

That's the least of it, Daniel thought to himself. If he had his way, he would steal a great deal more than just the game.

NINETEEN

GORDON MURRAY WAS METICULOUS about shelving books in his study at home, always collecting those he had pulled for reference during the week, jotting pertinent notes, and then putting them back where they belonged. He didn't think of himself as compulsive; naturally tidy people, he believed, observed systems of behavior that led to productive thought and actions. He wanted his books where he could find them at all times, and on Saturdays, each was returned to its proper place. The maid, Josefine, had carte blanche to clean every room in the house apart from this one. He even dusted it himself. The shelves, which ran from floor to ceiling along two walls, held books he had accumulated since childhood: dog-eared copies of Stevenson and Kipling; novels he had loved during his years at university, the Iris Murdochs and Evelyn Waughs and Virginia Woolfs; the sonnets and poetry he had chosen when he was first working in London and spent rainy afternoons in musty shops purchasing volumes to round out his literary education. The library his uncle had left to him was substantial, though culled for the best and most interesting books, like those on fly fishing on the River Test; it was something he had never done, but he kept the book in case the opportunity ever arose. The other, less interesting ones were given to charity to make room for his growing collection. All of Ingrid's books were kept on two shelves. She hadn't had many, being a woman who preferred magazines, and he always wished there had been more.

The desk in his study had belonged to his Uncle Roger: an impressive William V mahogany writing table that he considered the best piece of furniture in the house. His uncle had rarely used it, and the chair he had left behind was an ordinary sort, which Ingrid had replaced early on with a tufted green leather chair with a high back and wide arms. Murray had been distressed at the expense, not unwilling to use the rickety chair of his uncle's, but over time, that chair at that desk had become his favorite spot in the world. A few months after buying it for him, Ingrid had purchased a small chintz armchair and tucked it in a corner with a lamp so they could read together. There were always piles of magazines that she had strewn on the floor beside it, which would probably be there still if the housekeeper hadn't removed them while she was in hospital at the end. That incident had caused a row, and the woman was fired in a rare moment of anger on his part, Josefine replacing her a few weeks later. He remained ashamed of the episode. It was unlike him to become so irate, but losing Ingrid had caused reactions within him that he had never expected.

On the desk was a blotter; one of Roger's inkwells, made of etched glass and sitting on a silver tray tarnished from no longer being polished; a datebook nearly devoid of dates; and a Dundee marmalade jar he had confiscated from the pantry years before to use as a pen cup. As usual, there were files on the desk, this time of suspects from the Burke case. He planned to look them over after dinner.

His mobile rang, and he plucked it from his pocket to answer it.

"Inspector Murray? This is Peter Flanagan. I'm a Fingerprint Lab tech from Forensics."

Murray hadn't worked with Flanagan much, but knew his reputation. He was one of the younger, highly talented men that the Metropolitan Police were currently recruiting.

"I hope you have something for me."

"I've been on the team doing DNA analysis for the Burke case. We've found a problem and hopefully corrected it, sir. A sample taken at the scene wasn't properly stored with the rest of the evidence in the case."

"What sort of sample?"

"There were two hairs taken from the wedding gown that did not belong to Miss Burke. Both were long, almost white female hair."

Murray did a mental calculation of the women he had interviewed. There was Carey Burke, the bride's sister, and three young female guests: Natalie Swindon, Marianne Gaines, and Sarah Williams, the woman who had argued with Richardson before the ceremony.

"Can you give me a description, please?"

"Color: dyed blonde, peroxide, approximately fourteen inches long."

Natalie Swindon was the only match among that group.

"Can you give me anything more specific?"

"Whenever hair has been chemically treated—dyed—with peroxide, it makes it almost impossible to get a positive DNA match. Peroxide degrades the DNA in hair, especially after washing or exposure to water. A good shampoo and all DNA is stripped from the hair fibers."

"So you can't make any positive identification."

"I'm afraid not. Also we have to take into account the way it was collected and stored, along with the age of the sample. Hair DNA is highly vulnerable to external forces like high temperatures such as a hair dryer, or any cleaning agents or corrosive substances. Given all this, all we can go by is the physical appearance at this point."

"Thank you, Flanagan. That's still useful information. I appreciate the call."

Murray walked over to his desk and sat down in his green chair, digging through the files to look through them again. None of the young women present seemed as though they would have been friends with Tamsyn Burke. Natalie Swindon and Marianne Gaines were from Llandudno and had known Tamsyn in school. She had met Sarah Williamson in London a few months before her death. He browsed through the records and notations he had received from Rachel Quinn, one of the clerks on his floor.

For a moment, he allowed himself to think of Miss Quinn, who had worked in his department for at least fifteen years and was someone he relied on for informational support in addition to Ennis. Although there were a number of capable people working with him, he had a tendency to depend on as few of them as possible. Miss Quinn was discreet, efficient, and self-effacing, all qualities he admired. She was around forty, a slender woman with a penchant for thin cardigans and whose dark hair was always pulled back. Lately, he had noticed her cardigans, due entirely, he was certain, to their understated but attractive jewel tones. She wore a dark pair of glasses when typing or peering through the files, but removed them whenever she spoke so that she could look one in the eye. Her shoes were always attractive but of a medium-height heel, sensible enough to stand in all day but high enough to be flirtatious, if she was so inclined. To his satisfaction, she was not. She wore no rings and only occasionally a pendant around her neck. She was more elegant than many of the women who worked there, but so unobtrusive a human being that unless one worked beside her, one wouldn't even know she was there. She was steady and reliable, and he wondered if she were lonely too. He tried to put it out of his mind. This was not the time to think of himself, when there was a case demanding his attention.

Taking his reading glasses from his pocket, he looked at the name on the first file: Marianne Gaines. Marianne came from an ordinary working-class family. Her father drove a lorry; her mother was a hairdresser at a shop called *Colour Me Red*. Richard and Elise Gaines had four children, of whom Marianne was the eldest. She had worked at various jobs as soon as she was old enough to earn a living, until she had been convinced by Natalie Swindon to come and work with her.

Natalie, whose parents owned Swindon's Flowers and Ephemera, was an only child who worked in her family's business. Marianne had joined the company four years ago. According to both of their statements, the two were inseparable. They worked together, spent Friday nights with a series of harmless young men, and went to mass on Sundays. They each told the police that they had not spoken to Tamsyn since she'd left Wales until two months ago, when Tamsyn had contacted them out of the blue and asked them to be bridesmaids. Why had she asked them? And even more troubling, why had they accepted? To get a free trip to London? To go to the biggest society wedding of the year? Or was there something more calculated behind their attendance? In all likelihood, they were jealous of Tamsyn Burke. She had come from the same middle-class childhood as Swindon and Gaines, gone to the same schools, and only had a minor acting career until she was discovered by Hugh Ashley-Hunt and Sir John Hodges. She had gotten a decent salary for her role in *Under the Greenwood Tree*, not to mention the fame of appearing on the big screen with two of the hottest young stars in the British film industry. And not least, she was marrying one of the most eligible bachelors in England, a man with looks, wealth, and power. Jealousy was a common motive for murder. Women were just as devious as men, Murray knew; perhaps more so. These girls, in spite of how bland and innocent they seemed, would have to be interrogated further.

Sarah Williams, who was neither bland nor innocent, was not to be discounted either. According to her file, she had left her home in Bristol at the earliest opportunity, living in a decrepit flat in Hackney for several years until she was able to afford to share a nicer one with two friends. Her work history was sketchy. There was some modeling, a little secretarial work, and periods of living off the gifts of generous older men. A complaint had once been lodged against her for trashing a man's house after being spurned. He had dropped the charges in order to hide his indiscretion from his wife, but Murray knew the girl was capable of retaliation when provoked. Her life appeared to consist of sitting in bars most evenings, allowing men to buy her drinks and who knew what else. In this manner, Sarah Williams had met Tamsyn Burke and become a peripheral element in her world.

Murray was still not certain how the girl had become close enough to Tamsyn to be invited to her wedding. Likewise, it seemed as if the two bridesmaids had been plucked out of thin air. With the exception of the Hodges, Daniel Richardson, and Hugh and his family, there was no record of the victim seeing or speaking to any of the guests or the bridesmaids at her wedding for months or even years.

Murray put down the pencil and stared out of the window. Would the girl have simply invited everyone she knew to fill the pews at Westminster Abbey, regardless of how she felt about them or how little she knew them? If so, why? Was she trying to impress the Ashley-Hunts, who would have no trouble filling seats on the groom's side with well-known and important guests? He believed in Occam's Razor: the simplest explanation was most likely true. Still, questions troubled him. If she'd reached back to the people from her past whom she thought she could trust, it had been a deadly mistake. Whoever killed Tamsyn Burke had killed her deliberately at that place and at that time, not the day before or the day after. The person chose to kill this girl minutes before she was to walk down the aisle on her father's arm.

To what possible end? he wondered. To prevent her from marrying Hugh Ashley-Hunt? Or perhaps because she had thwarted someone else's romance or plans for marriage? Had the killer chosen that day and that hour because he or she wanted to kill Tamsyn Burke at the most hurtful moment possible? Or was she killed then because the murderer wanted it merely to appear to be a vengeful killing?

He stood, closing the file on his desk. He needed fresh air. Shutting the door behind him, he went downstairs, through the kitchen, and out onto the terrace. He looked over the garden, where he would have been planting a new rosebush if time had permitted.

Overhead, the sky was dark, but it had not yet begun to rain. The breeze had picked up, but the clouds hung above them, as stationary as if they had been pasted onto the sky.

Lonely. The word hung over him like a fog. On impulse, he took his mobile from his pocket and dialed Ennis's number. It was Saturday afternoon, and he made it a habit not to bother his sergeant on the weekend unless there was a break in whatever case they were working on at the time. However, his junior officer didn't appear in the least surprised when he answered the call.

"I'm sorry to disturb you, but I wanted to know if you remember which of the young women at the wedding were found leaning over Tamsyn Burke's body."

"Her sister, Carey Burke, and Marianne Gaines both leaned over the body after the attack. Of course, her parents were there, as well as Hugh Ashley-Hunt and Daniel Richardson."

"Not Natalie Swindon?"

"Not according to her statement, or anyone else's taken at the scene."

Which meant, Murray thought, Swindon had spoken with Tamsyn earlier. He would have to find out precisely when.

"First thing Monday, I'd like to have you meet with Miss Swindon. I'll prepare some questions for you. Oh, and Ennis, I wonder if you would mind doing me a favor."

"Of course, sir."

"Well, it's rather of a personal nature."

There was no hesitation on the line. "What can I do, sir?"

"I want a dog, Ennis."

"A dog? What sort of dog?"

"I don't know. Something not too large or messy."

There was a pause. He could almost hear the sergeant's mind cogs turning. "I may know of something, boss, but I'll have to make a call first."

"Of course, this is your weekend. You mustn't trouble yourself right away."

"It's no problem. My girlfriend's sister's dog had a litter a couple of months ago. I'll see what I can find out and ring you soon."

"Thank you."

It was only afterward that Murray realized he hadn't asked any pertinent questions, such as what sort of pups they were. Instantly he regretted his request. He would wait until Ennis called later and tell him he'd changed his mind.

For now, he went inside and poured a drink to go with the meat pie and chips he had purchased the night before at a takeaway. He unwrapped the brown paper packet and set the pie on a dish. He suddenly remembered the holiday he was scheduled to take the following week, a guided tour of the Lake District. He wasn't fond of tours, with the shabby coaches, the mechanical-sounding guides, and the thought of sitting in cramped quarters for days at a time with perfect strangers, but he had faithfully taken a holiday each year, a deathbed promise to Ingrid. Of course, he had seen through her thinly veiled attempt at putting him in the way of other women, but even Ingrid would have laughed at the thought of him wooing one of these serious-minded pensioners with their PVC totes emblazoned with photos of Blenheim or Woburn Abbey and their arms full of brochures. He was not looking for a wife, but he was able, for small periods of time, to enjoy the beauty of a Cornish port or a visit to a cheese factory in Somerset or a tour of the Horse Center in Norfolk. On Monday, he would cancel the trip, but he would also check his calendar for the best time to reschedule. She had been right. It was good for him.

Ennis didn't ring him. Relieved, Murray put aside all thoughts of the case and settled in for an evening of serious reading. He was delving into Uncle Roger's collection on the Boer War and studying the depiction of the concentration camps when there was a knock at the door. When he opened it, Ennis was standing there with a wriggling blanket in his arms. Before he could protest, the sergeant had moved past him and deposited it on a chair. Curious, Murray went over to see it for himself. He would say something nice and then politely refuse. But when the blanket was pulled back, he couldn't help smiling at the long, sad face on a pup so young.

"What is it?" he asked.

"A Springer spaniel. There were six in the litter, and this was the runt. They couldn't sell him. Were they ever relieved you could give him a good home."

Murray looked at the lopsided ears and the liver-colored spots on the thin puppy fur. In spite of himself, he began to rub one of the ears. The small creature turned and sniffed his hand and then licked it.

"There you are, sir," Ennis said, smiling. "Looks like it 'took.' I'll get his things out of the boot. They've sent along everything you need for the first few days."

Murray watched him go out to his car and then turned to the dog.

"What was I thinking?" he muttered. "I hope Josefine will know what to do with you."

The dog wagged his pencil-thin tail and cocked his head as if he understood.

TWENTY

THE THEORY OF CHAOS VS. Determinism had long been a bone of contention between Carey and Tamsyn, with Carey unexpectedly taking the side of determinism. Despite her scientific background, and the incontrovertible evidence of cacti whose leaves have become spines or fossils found in sedimentary rock at different stratigraphic levels, or even the homologous similarities in higher organisms that strongly suggest a common ancestry, she did not subscribe to the theory of evolution. It was as impossible for her to believe in the Big Bang Theory as it was the notion of time travel. Nothing in her experience proved that any living cell or sentient being had ever been created through chaos. She had combed *On the Origin of Species* for clues, affirming her notion of adaptation but remaining unconvinced of the idea of evolution. Darwin himself had expressed doubts in his writing, and if he did not believe that the organism of an eye could be reproduced rapidly enough to evidence evolution—an eye, which is the one sense that leads one to truth quicker than any other—then how could she believe?

Tamsyn rather emphatically took a romantic view, preferring chaos in its infinite simplicity. Life was huge, random, uncontrollable, meaningless, unpredictable; and as long as it could be defined as such, so could she. Carey was methodical, predictable, perhaps even a bit boring; the sun rose and set, the chicken laid an egg; there exists in all known things a beginning and an end. Therefore, by process of elimination through the examination of facts as she saw them, Carey accepted the existence of God, for without a sense of meaning, she did not want to live. However, for her, God, who knew all and would come again to judge the world for its sins, was as remote and unreachable as the dimmest star. Without it, the night sky might be only a little darker, but there existed the hope that billions of light years away it burned brighter than the sun, illuminating everything in its path. She might not pray, but she wished to sometimes.

She rubbed her tongue against her upper left cusped and stole a glance at Nick, who was typing on her computer.

"What are you doing?" she asked, setting down her mug of cold coffee, wondering how long she'd been lost in thought.

"Ah, you're back," he said, not answering her question. His hair was getting a bit long, and he pushed it out of his eyes, frowning.

"You know what I think?" he said at last.

"No," Carey answered, dreading his response. She could tell by the look on his face that she wouldn't like what he was about to say.

"It's stupid, that's what this is. Really bloody stupid." He closed the top of the laptop and looked at her, frowning again. "You'll get yourself killed."

Carey was taken aback by his tone as much as by his words. "We're asking questions, that's all."

"And if you ask them of the wrong person, you've stepped on a land mine. No one can save you."

"Daniel says—"

"That's another thing. Who the hell does Richardson think he is, anyway? He's got no more idea what he's about than you."

Carey's shoulders slumped and she sat down.

"I'm sorry. I didn't mean it, Carey. It's just that I'm worried for you. If you keep on with this, you'll get hurt."

Nick's mobile, which was sitting next to him on the bed, began to ring. He looked at the screen and then declined the call.

"Who was it?" Carey asked.

"My mother," he said, shrugging.

"You should have answered it."

"She probably just wonders when I'm coming home."

"Do you know what you're going to do?" Carey tried to keep her voice even and unconcerned, though she was finding Nick's visit far more tiresome than she could have imagined. His checkered history with Tamsyn made him a difficult person to confide in at a time like this.

"That's the thing," he said. "We should both go home. Your parents could use you right now, I'd say."

Carey turned away and tried to get her emotions in check. He didn't understand how she felt about this, the most horrific thing that had ever happened to her, and he certainly wasn't going to help unravel the mystery surrounding her sister's death. She suspected he was trying to get her to leave London altogether. It was no secret that he wanted things to go back to the way they'd been when they were young. For the first time, she was truly concerned about Nick. If he didn't figure out his future soon, he would become a complete agoraphobic.

"I don't—" she began, when his mobile began to ring.

"It's Mum again," he said. "I'd better take it."

She stood to give him privacy and took her mug to the kitchen to rinse it in the sink. The stream of tepid water from the tap drowned out his conversation, and she tried to think of a way to get out of going home. It wasn't easy for her to say no to anyone, but with Nick, it was especially difficult. She wondered, perhaps, if it was only now, when he was trying to stop her from something she wanted to do, or if it had always been that way.

Even if she and Daniel had done all that they could do, she resented Nick saying it. She couldn't get on that train, not now, even though they had no idea how to proceed. She realized that at this moment she preferred the company of someone who had truly loved her sister to the one person who had resented Tamsyn all of his life. She dried the mug with a cloth and set it carefully on the shelf.

Nick ended his call and cleared his throat. "Well, that's that. We have to go. Mum's gotten herself hurt and needs me."

"What happened?" Carey asked, coming back in to sit down across from him.

"She fell and broke her arm. Of course, it's her right arm. She won't be able to do anything for weeks. I'll check the train times."

"I'm sorry you have to leave," Carey said.

He'd been opening the laptop and paused with the top half-open. "You need to come too."

"I will," she said, "but there's something I have to do first."

"What?" he asked, eyes narrowing.

"Something at university," she lied. "I was in the process of filing papers, and I have to get it done before I can go."

"How long will that take?"

"Two or three days, I think."

"I can't wait that long."

"No," she said, taking control of the situation. "You have to go without me. I'll follow as soon as I can."

Reluctantly, he agreed, and after ordering a ticket, called his mother to let her know.

Carey tried not to show her relief as she helped Nick get his things together.

"Do you want a cup of tea first? Or a sandwich?" she asked.

"No, thanks," he answered, clearly peeved. "If I want something, I'll get it at the station."

Any other time, she would have tried to reason with him, but now she couldn't wait to see him out the door. She put on her jacket and walked him to the Tube, growing more anxious by the minute in case he changed his mind.

They said an awkward goodbye at Charing Cross Station. He hadn't been in the building thirty seconds before she found herself dialing Daniel Richardson's phone number. She didn't even stop to wonder why.

———

An hour later, Carey watched Daniel swirl the stout in his glass, erasing the foam that clung to its sides while she looked around the room. She'd never been in this pub before. It was all chrome and glass and wine spritzers, the sort of place she hated. She wondered if it was Daniel's sort of place, or if it had merely been a convenient spot to meet. Even now, this late in the day, she wondered why she had asked him to help her. She'd never seen any of his films and had no great appreciation for actors. He wasn't formidable or amazingly brilliant. Perhaps it was merely the comfort she felt in the solidarity of their union against the wrong that had been done them. Daniel felt it as keenly as she did, she was sure.

"I should go," she said. "It's getting late."

"Stay," he answered, putting his glass on the bar and signaling for another drink. "We'll come up with something."

"You don't want to be alone," she said, glancing up at him.

"Neither do you."

He'd called her bluff, leaving her to wonder if she was that easy to read. Still, the fact could not be escaped that the moment Nick was gone, she had called him.

"Damn," she said, pushing away the glass. She rarely drank, and it was beginning to affect her already. She picked up her mobile and punched in a number on speed dial.

"What's wrong?"

"Nick was angry when he left. He won't answer my calls." She tried to imagine him making his way through the crowded station, fuming all the way back home.

"You can't beat yourself up about it. We've got a lot on our minds right now. It's not exactly easy to take care of old friends when we're trying to get somewhere with this bloody case."

"You shouldn't·say that. He came all this way, and it was difficult for him."

"Why?" Daniel asked.

She stared at him, wondering if he was truly so obtuse. Surely he had noticed the tic in Nick's arm, as much as Nick always tried to hide it. He had developed defense mechanisms for obscuring it from view: holding his hand in his pocket; putting his arm on the back of Carey's chair, fingers grasping the wood tightly; throwing his jacket over his shoulder in a way that concealed his arm. As long as she'd known him, she had never been able to forget it or his awkwardness in dealing with it. But she found she couldn't explain to Daniel that Nick was the most self-conscious person she knew, or that he hated people and crowds, or that he was in serious danger of becoming a recluse.

"It just was. Let's leave it at that," she said.

They sat for a minute without speaking. The music playing in the background was beginning to give her a pain between the eyes. It had been wrong to ring him up, and she had no idea why she'd bothered. There was nothing he could do about Nick or Tamsyn or anything. For that matter, there was nothing she could do either. She stood, a little wobbly, and tugged on her jacket.

"Let me help with that," he offered.

"No, thanks," she answered, moving away from him. If she'd gone just a touch farther, she might have toppled over. "I'm leaving."

"I can see that."

Daniel stood, threw a few coins on the table, and put on his own coat, following her out of the pub. They walked for a block until she reached the Tube station, stepping up to the machine to purchase a ticket. He reached in his pocket for change as well.

"What do you think you're doing?" she asked.

"Getting a ticket. That's what one usually does at a ticket machine."

"No, I mean, why? You can go back home. We haven't accomplished anything today."

"Do you think I'm letting you go by yourself? You're drunk."

"I am not," Carey protested. "I'm just tired."

"Let's get a cab."

"No thank you."

Below, the station was nearly empty, but the sound was deafening when the train roared up to the platform and the doors slid open. She clambered up the steps and sat on the edge of her seat, holding on to the metal bar and doing her best to appear sober. He slid into the seat behind her, bracing his feet on the floor before the train slid forward once again. When it came to a stop at Charing Cross, they got off and found their way out onto the pavement.

"You're stalking me," Carey pronounced, crossing Villiers Street and heading toward her building.

"You could say that, I suppose. I prefer to think of it as personal protection."

She said nothing more, letting him walk her to her building and then up the stairs to her flat, where she took out her key and after a moment's fumbling, opened the door.

"I need an aspirin," she said, kicking off her shoes and hanging her jacket on an ancient coat rack by the door. "What about you?"

"No thank you," he answered. "Another drink would be nice, though."

"I don't usually keep anything around," she said coolly. "I don't drink much."

"I can see that."

A rickety chessboard sat on the edge of a dresser and Daniel picked up the white queen, tapping it against his palm. He couldn't even imagine what sort of girl played chess, or for that matter studied medicine, or appeared to be a terminal virgin at the ripe age of twenty-three. Carey Burke was an anomaly, and while some men might find it an irresistible challenge to their masculinity, he did not. Instead, he felt protective of her; more so with each passing day.

"Do you play?" she asked, before tipping back her head to swallow the pill.

"Not well, and not for years. Hugh went through a phase where he made me play endlessly at school. He finally tired of it, thank God."

"Let's see how bad you are."

"No, really, I can't. I'm drunk, and you're a brain, two reasons you'll enjoy an unfair advantage."

She, like Hugh, refused to be dissuaded, setting the board on a table and placing the pieces on the squares before holding out her hand. Reluctantly, he relinquished control of the errant queen.

"That's the last control I'll have in this game."

To Carey's surprise, it was not. She followed a plan when playing chess: second left pawn, forward one space; bishop to the pawn's spot, blocking the rook; mirroring the moves on the right; waiting for the overeager player opposite to make a bolder move and jeopardize his queen. Daniel was far too haphazard a player for that and held his own, strategizing at her level if not beyond. He appeared to play by instinct rather than reason, but he was good at it. It was impossible to predict what he would do, because even he didn't know what his next move would be.

While he contemplated moving a knight that could, if he saw it, put her king in check, she watched him. He was self-deprecating and often prevented people from seeing his intelligence, perhaps in order for them to feel better about themselves. She could see why he had been so close to Tamsyn. She herself wasn't interested in a relationship while she was in medical school. For one thing, men were rarely intelligent enough for her, and when they were, their personalities were infused with the quirks and eccentricities of men like Jared and Roddy, whose sense of humor was submerged so deep as to be nearly nonexistent. In fact, she hadn't thought that a sense of humor was something she would relish in a partner or friend, but spending time with Daniel over the last few days had made her realize its power. He was kind, and he had cared about Tamsyn, loved her, perhaps, and he was trying to help Carey believe that this heinous crime would not go unpunished. She reached over and tipped her king onto his side.

"You lied," she said, yawning. "You're good, and I can't keep up with you tonight."

He leaned back, his eyes betraying the fact that he was tired too. She got up and pulled a quilt from the wardrobe and handed it to him. "It's late. You can stay on the sofa, if you like."

"You don't mind?"

"Of course not. It's not much, but … "

"It's great. Thanks."

She went into the toilet and came back, toothbrush and toothpaste in hand. "I don't have an extra toothbrush. Sorry."

"That's all right." He held out his index finger and she squirted some of the paste on it, but instead of following her into the loo, he went into the kitchen and bent over the sink.

She changed into black shorts and an old sweatshirt, and he untied his shoes and set them neatly on the floor by the sofa. Then she brought him a pillow and crawled into the small bed on the opposite wall, pulling the quilt up to her chin. Afterward, she turned off the lamp, and neither of them uttered a word, each falling asleep within minutes, the weight of their struggles with their personal demons lifting in the comforting black of night.

———

When Daniel woke the next morning, he felt somehow different, knowing he would see Carey as soon as he opened his eyes. The feeling shocked him. He heard the shower being turned on and could smell the coffee she had made and put on the table beside him. She must have come close to him, and he wondered if she'd put it down quickly or lingered over him. He tried to get hold of himself. He had an unnaturally strong feeling for her because of what they were going through. The two of them were on a lifeboat in the middle of the sea; they would either both drown or both be saved, but it was something they would experience together. No one else could help them through the storm they were facing now.

"Shall I make breakfast?" she asked when she came out of the shower, tucking a strand of hair behind her ear. She pulled the tie of her robe tighter, smiling.

"No, thanks," he said, collecting himself. He took a quick gulp of coffee and stood, folding the quilt and placing it on the sofa. "I have things to do this morning."

In fact, he didn't, but it was time to leave and think about what the hell they were playing at. The morning intimacy with Tamsyn's younger sister was somehow more than he could stand.

TWENTY-ONE

IT WAS TWO DAYS before Christmas when it all fell apart. Daniel was standing by the fireplace at the Ashley-Hunts' house in Gloucestershire, a drink in hand, listening to a toast being made by one of Hugh's cousins at the annual Christmas party. It was the one time of year when sloppy sentimentalism was tolerated by Hugh's father, and a round of toasts and long litanies of family history were recited by half of those present as they drank copious amounts of wine. Tamsyn sat in a chair on the other side of the room, listening, as he was, with half an ear. She wore a form-fitting black sweater over an ankle-length skirt of red and green, a sort of patchwork contraption where the fraying seams were on the outside of the garment rather than the inside. He smiled. She was a rebel to the core.

He yearned to check his watch for the time, but caught Hugh's mother's eye and didn't dare. Tomorrow, he would drive down to Brighton. He could hardly think of anything he less wanted to do. Not because his parents were there, of course, but leaving Tamsyn here, in the warm little circle of Ashley-Hunts, to enjoy Christmas Eve and Christmas Day as a family was a difficult cross to bear.

When the three of them were in London, things were different. He often met Tamsyn on her own for lunch and they took long walks in their favorite places. She was fond of Kensington Gardens, which happened to be near his flat. One of the pools, although manicured within an inch of its life, had a natural effect that both of them enjoyed. There was also, within a long expanse of the wall, a small door, barely four feet tall, with a square window set on the diagonal and boarded up. He argued the door was an entrance to the lawn equipment, but she disagreed with him. The Duchess of Cambridge, she was certain, was just on the other side, probably feeling cooped up and restless in spite of the massive renovations that had been undertaken to make it a perfect royal home. He loved that about Tamsyn. She made him look at everything differently.

The idea of leaving her in Gloucestershire was more than depressing. If they were on their own, he could have discovered what she really wanted to do for Christmas, and he didn't for a moment think she would choose a poncy Ashley-Hunt holiday. Daniel had the strong suspicion that Hugh was going to propose to her, and he was afraid that he would find out about it days later when they'd gone home and settled back into their ordinary routines.

He took a couple of steps back, and when that did not attract attention, he turned and went into the kitchen. He set his glass of wine on the counter and put his hands in his pockets, turning toward the window, feeling black and miserable. A moment later, he heard footsteps behind him.

"The toasts go on forever, don't they?" he heard Caroline Ashley-Hunt say.

He turned to face her. 'I'm sorry. I didn't mean to leave. I've had some things on my mind."

"I hope everything is all right," she said. She put her glass on the counter as well and walked over to adjust a few canapés on a tray. "Do you think we have enough shrimp?"

He glanced at the tray and nodded. "The food is amazing. You're the perfect hostess."

"May I ask you a question?"

"Of course."

He knew what was coming, and he didn't want to answer it.

"Are Hugh and Tamsyn serious?"

Daniel was terrified of saying the wrong thing. He didn't want to lie to Mrs. Ashley-Hunt, who had been generous and kind to him through the years and genuinely interested in his life as he got older. He also didn't want to reveal any of Hugh's thoughts or motivations to his mother. It was for his friend to decide what to tell his parents and when, though it seemed clear enough to him that Hugh and Tamsyn were heading for an engagement. Perhaps most importantly, he didn't like to discuss Tamsyn with anyone, no matter how well he knew them.

"I don't know," he answered.

It was true enough. With Tamsyn, one could never be certain how serious she was. She had her little secrets, he knew.

"Would you mind helping me with this tray?" she asked.

If he wasn't going to tell her anything, she wouldn't continue to press him. He gave her his most charming smile.

"I'd be happy to. You throw a wonderful party."

By the time they arrived back in the living room, the toasts were over and people were chatting and having another glass of wine. Three or four people reached out to take an hors d'oeuvre from the tray as if he were a waiter, and it was a couple of moments before he managed to set it on the large table with the others. Caroline had disappeared into the crowd, and he hoped the matter would be forgotten. He thought he would be fine, and then Tamsyn walked over to him.

"I have something for you," she said, pulling a package from behind her back.

She didn't wait for him to open it. Like a child, she pulled away the paper herself. It was a book: a pristine, shiny copy of *The Age of Innocence*. Daniel had never read it, but he had seen the film, a tragic story of unrequited love. He looked up at her. She wasn't sending him some sort of message, was she? Did he even want her to? Wouldn't it be simpler for all of them if he carried a torch for her without anyone suspecting?

"It's perfect," he said, taking it when she held it out. "You know I love to read."

Hugh came up beside them and didn't seemed to notice any particular significance to the gift.

"Where's mine?" he asked, his eyes glittering.

"Oh, you'll get yours," Tamsyn said, making them both smile.

"My gift for you is under the tree," Daniel said. "You can have it on Christmas, and not before."

"Tell me what it is."

"Doesn't that spoil the surprise?"

"That's fine with me. I hate surprises."

"It's that horrid little scarf you liked so much, that we saw last week. The one with the metallic things dangling on the ends."

"I love that scarf!" Tamsyn cried. "You went back and got it? Aren't you wonderful!"

"Well," Hugh said, reaching into his pocket. "If we're giving gifts early…"

Tamsyn took the posh little box wrapped in a black velvet bow. She slid off the ribbon and lifted the lid, revealing a diamond bracelet inside. The diamonds were round, alternating large and small stones, set in platinum. Daniel couldn't resist raising an eyebrow.

"Merry Christmas, indeed," he said, putting a hand on his friend's shoulder.

"Nothing but the best for our girl, eh?" Hugh said.

Tamsyn clapped the lid back onto the box and smiled. "It's beautiful. Thank you."

"Come on," Hugh said, taking her by the arm. "I haven't introduced you to my aunt and uncle yet."

Tamsyn was pulled away into the crowd. Someone, possibly Hugh's father, had turned on music and the golden tones of Frank Sinatra filled the room. Daniel went to the back of the house and let himself out the door. Standing on the step, he patted his pockets, located his cigarettes, and lit one. It was trying very hard to snow. There were light, tinkling bits of drizzle but he withstood it, fixing his eyes on the trees beyond. It was dark now, pitch dark, with only the muted illumination of the lights from the house splaying across the lawn. The moon was hidden behind the clouds.

He realized suddenly that he was angry. If he had been Hugh, he would have waited until a private moment to give Tamsyn something as expensive as a diamond bracelet, not whipped it out in front of someone else for effect. But perhaps, Daniel thought, it was for his benefit, not Tamsyn's; a message to stay away from what was rightfully Hugh's. Never, in all of the years he had known Hugh, had a girl ever come between them. Daniel had promised himself in Dorset that it wouldn't happen this time either, but the situation was becoming more difficult by the second.

Did Hugh really love her? Or had he seen that Daniel was falling for her and stepped in to claim the prize? Hugh was competitive, the way any healthy, successful twenty-nine-year-old was competitive, but that didn't mean he was out to deprive his best friend of the girl he wanted most.

Maybe it was best, after all, that he was headed to Brighton in the morning. He needed time to think. He certainly couldn't do that here, with diamond bracelets being unwrapped under his nose. Daniel took a last puff of the cigarette and then let himself back into the house, going up the back staircase up to his room. He lay down on the bed and stared at the ceiling, trying to think about nothing.

After a while, he heard a knock on the door and it opened slowly. Tamsyn peered around the edge with a smile.

"Want some company?" she asked.

"Of course."

He propped himself up as she sat down on the foot of his bed, pulling her legs under her and plucking at one of the frayed seams of her skirt.

"Where's Hugh?" he asked.

He had expected a long night, knowing their room was next door. He could handle their relationship as long as they were reasonably discreet, when it was something he didn't have to think about on an hourly basis, but knowing there was a single wall between them would be harder to bear.

"The men are having cigars. I'm sure they're wondering where you are."

"I'm tired," he said.

"What's the real reason?" she asked. "Too chummy in there for you?"

"I just didn't feel like it," he answered. He didn't want to get into specifics with the one person who was the reason for his mood swings.

"I loved the scarf," Tamsyn said, kicking off her shoes and tossing them onto the floor. The thick carpet muted the sound. "I opened it after you disappeared."

"It's hard to shop for the girl who has everything," he teased.

"You know what I like."

"Where's the bracelet?" he asked, even though he knew that he shouldn't. "I didn't see you put it on."

"It didn't go with this outfit, did it?" she demurred.

He was hard-pressed to think of anything she owned that it would go with at all. There was an unspoken thought hanging in the air. Why didn't Hugh understand exactly what sort of girl Tamsyn was? Or did he see something in her that Daniel just hadn't seen yet, the future lady of the manor house and film star? Somehow, Daniel couldn't imagine her any differently than she was at this moment.

"Those were some pretty boring toasts tonight," he remarked. "You put a brave face on it, though."

She laughed. "I think that's my future, right there."

"No doubt."

"Do you always come to the Ashley-Hunt holiday party?"

"Most years, yes. But I don't stay on through Christmas."

"You're leaving in the morning," she said.

"Have to put in an appearance at my parents'."

"I wish you didn't have to leave. If you stay, we could take a snowy ride tomorrow or do something adventurous, like build a bonfire."

"You'll have plenty to keep you busy here," he assured her. "Hugh will see to that."

She moved from the end of the bed to sit next to him. Without a word, she reached up and touched his chin with her hand and turned it gently toward her. She lifted her face to his and their lips met. He was powerless to stop her. He knew then that anything she wanted from him was hers. He didn't want to betray Hugh, but his friend was so far from his thoughts as to be completely inconsequential. She kissed him fully, and the spark was as sharp as an electric current. Daniel's heart began to pound. As he moved his hand to cup her precious, elfin face, she suddenly pulled back. She smoothed back his hair for a lingering moment, and then stood, retrieving her shoes from the floor. Then she slipped out of the room without a word, closing the door tightly behind her.

TWENTY-TWO

It was difficult, after so many years of being out on his own, to live in the same house with his parents, but Hugh knew it was the best thing at the moment. He felt raw and moody, and the house, if not his parents, soothed him. There was a stillness here that belied the fact they were in the middle of London. Each of the rooms had a settled, relaxed feel, and the familiarity of many long years spent in them. He knew how soft or how hard each chair was; and while he enjoyed the art his parents had collected over the years, which included a couple of Cecil Kennedy florals and a William Biscombe Gardner, he preferred the antique furnishings his mother had collected: the mahogany tables and secretaries and enormous bedsteads that reached to the ceiling. The generous size of the rooms might not have been noticeable to him had he not found so many houses wanting when he had been searching for his own. The Mayfair house served as a guide to what any good home in London should be.

He especially loved the kitchen, run by Marthe. She had been their family's cook as long as he could remember, and she was a marvel.

Trays of chocolate biscuits always lay cooling on the counter alongside bowls of berries ready to be cooked into jams. Meals were stately affairs with numerous courses, and the refrigerator was always stocked with his favorite things regardless of whether he was there or not.

Since Tamsyn's death, he had perched on a chair in this kitchen for a part of each day, watching Marthe work. It was the only place to grieve. Though the old woman said very little, she commanded the room and used it in its entirety. Every bit of silver was polished and checked; china rotated so that one didn't tire of eating off the same plate; small, modern appliances were suitably stored in the pantry along with enough food to feed an army. For Hugh, being there kept his mind on something warm and real instead of Chief Inspector Murray and the excruciatingly slow investigation. He had never had any patience, anyway, but something of this magnitude was almost too painful to bear.

His parents were little distraction, neither of them knowing what to say to a bereaved son. They had been disappointed in his marriage to Tamsyn, he knew, but now that she had been murdered, things were different. They were sympathetic, though not overly solicitous. An Ashley-Hunt was expected to grieve in peace and come to terms with things in his own way. This was something he had to deal with in private.

The police hadn't yet discovered who had sent him the death threat. Every day, Hugh checked his email to see if another one had come, relieved each time to see that none had. He wasn't aware of making enemies. In fact, he usually went out of his way to be friendly to everyone he worked with, and of all his friends, he was the most polite to people who worked in bars and shops. Their lives were miserable enough without those like him making it harder. No, the death threat was truly a mystery. His present situation made him worried and anxious, and he even resented the bodyguard posted near the front door. It was Carson today, he noted. He had come to know each one. He'd told his father not to bother, he didn't feel threatened; but of course, the old man had insisted.

The sun was shining, making puddles of sunlight on the floor where Duke, the old yellow Labrador, was lying, eyes closed, perhaps imagining his younger days when he was able to run about on a leash and ferret out rabbits and mice in the park. Hugh knelt down and rubbed the dog between the ears, which was acknowledged by a slight lifting of his eyelids and a vague wag of his tail. If Duke hadn't been flagging lately, he would have taken him for a walk, but the old fellow was now beyond such simple pleasures. He could barely drag himself outside twice a day to attend to nature. Hugh made a sudden decision, going up to his room and wheeling his old bicycle from the closet. He had to get out of the house, even for a short time. Restaurants and pubs were off-limits; it would draw negative attention to be spotted out having even a simple meal or drink so soon after the funeral. He didn't feel like talking to anyone, so his London set were crossed off the list as well. He couldn't imagine how long it would be before he could have a conversation with someone that didn't focus on the horrific situation in which he now found himself. He wasn't a filmgoer, per se, unless it was the premiere of one of his own bits of work or possibly Daniel's, so he couldn't see himself sitting in a half empty, darkened theatre in the middle of the day simply to get out of the house. Still, he couldn't be trapped inside another day.

Tucking a pair of sunglasses into the pocket of his hoodie, he maneuvered the bicycle down the stairs, remembering many previous admonishments from his mother regarding the state of the paint on the walls. Making certain no one was there to see, he parked it behind a settee and went in search of Carson, who, as he had suspected, was in the library looking at book titles and listening for sounds from the front door.

"Marthe's made something marvelous today," Hugh said, watching the man turn around. "Fresh lemon curd and hot scones. Perfect with a cup of tea."

He had noticed that Carson preferred tea to coffee, having spent a few days learning each bodyguard's personal idiosyncrasies. This one was rather old-fashioned, a solid Brit who loved golf played with woods instead of irons and probably stood in the privacy of his own home when the Queen gave her Christmas speech.

"That sounds rather good," Carson answered, putting the book back on the shelf with a smile. "What about you?"

"Thanks, I've had some. I'm going upstairs to read for a while."

"Then I may nip in and have a look."

Hugh smiled and headed for the staircase. Upon seeing the man walk toward the kitchen, he turned around and eased the bike out of the front door. No one else was in the house. His mother was having lunch with one of her endless friends and his father was on the links, where he could be found most sunny spring days when he wasn't in the middle of a project. Hugh turned toward Hyde Park, as he so often had when he was younger. His limbs were stiff, so he took it more slowly than he otherwise might have, crossing Park Lane and South Carriage Drive through thick traffic. He hadn't put on his sunglasses yet, which seemed as though it invited people to look at his face rather than grant him the anonymity he preferred. He pumped the pedals, his calf muscles tightening as he increased his speed.

Before he reached the curb, he heard the sudden squeal of brakes and the scraping sound of metal on metal behind him. Shaken, he turned to see that he had narrowly missed being hit when someone had made a right turn into oncoming traffic. Three vehicles were affected, and no one appeared to be hurt, but his heart was thumping anyway.

"Oy! Are you all right?"

Hugh looked up to see a young man near his own age yelling at him through an open car window.

"Fine," he replied, reaching for the sunglasses.

"Close shave, that."

Keeping his head down, Hugh walked his bike into the park, away from the gathering crowd. Inside the safety of the gates, he steered clear of other cyclists and pedestrians, riding down abandoned paths while searching for a bench. He couldn't find one that wasn't taken, so instead rode toward a remote bank of trees and alighted to sit in the cool shade. It was possible to think here. He removed his hoodie and rolled it up for a cushion under his head, looking up at the sunlight that filtered through the tall, leafy oaks. He was alone in the world, and he felt it. He didn't even want Daniel's company now. Perhaps especially Daniel's. He couldn't stand the look of abject grief on his friend's face. Tamsyn had changed him in those few months she'd been in their lives. The truth was, she had changed them both.

By the time Hugh had met her, any hope of dating someone anonymously was long since gone. He had kept to his personal vow of eschewing public displays of affection and had never, ever smiled for the cameras that waited around every turn. The beginning of their affair, in Dorset, was the calmest their relationship would be, with the privacy of a countryside film shoot and getting to know each other slowly over several weeks. Back in London, as far as the press had been concerned, the gloves were off. He and Tamsyn had been photographed often, and in spite of the fact that she hadn't dealt with it before, she'd had an instinct for handling the press. It took a great deal of sangfroid to pull that off, he knew, and he had a healthy respect for anyone who could do it.

Above him, birds made raucous noises. The swallows and swifts were back in force after their African and Mediterranean winters, populating trees and building nests, making general nuisances of themselves. Summer was coming, he thought, without Tamsyn there to see it. The warm sun on his face made him think of his last trip to Greece, two years ago. Daniel had planned to go with him, but a last-minute opportunity to do a film prevented him from tagging along, so he had talked Marc Hayley into accompanying him. Marc was always a stalwart companion. Hugh hadn't seen him since February, when the weather had been abysmal. The cold, from which they'd had no respite, seeped through cracks in the doorways and windows of old houses, even some of the grander ones. Hugh's home had a few, in spite of the fact that he'd had contractors seal as many as he could before the onset of winter. The bedrooms upstairs were particularly drafty and hard to heat. Drizzle had tapped at the windows, threatening snow. Marc had come with him to a party at Daniel's that night, and they'd resolved, inclement weather or no, to go out the next day for drinks and dinner.

Tamsyn was off somewhere the following evening, in spite of the weather. Hugh had no idea where, shopping perhaps, but more likely she was with Daniel. She saw a good deal more of his friend than he did, but he never worried about them being together. In fact, he encouraged it. Daniel was more trustworthy than the Pope. When he'd chosen a best friend, he had chosen well.

Marc had come to the house that evening to pick him up. "Traffic's fucking atrocious," he said as he walked through the door.

"Want to take a cab?" Hugh had asked, pulling on his coat. "It's too far to walk."

"Yeah. Then we won't have to leave the car when we've had a few too many."

They had to walk three blocks before a cab finally stopped for them, and Hugh gave the driver directions. A few minutes later, they were deposited in front of the restaurant. Watley's, which had opened within the past year, was bustling with eager patrons. A waiter took their order and the two of them settled back in their chairs.

"I'm starving," Hugh said. "It's been a while since I've had a really good meal."

"What, the new fiancée doesn't cook?" Marc asked.

Their wine arrived and Hugh poured for them both. "I'm pretty sure she hasn't even been in the kitchen yet," he said with a laugh. "I think she still feels like a guest."

"I can't believe you let someone move in with you, let alone got engaged." Marc gestured around the room. "Look, there are pretty girls everywhere. Why give it all up for just one?"

"When you find the right girl, you'll see what I mean."

"I'd rather die, thank you very much."

"What about Anna Parrish?"

"Anna?" Hayley shrugged. "We see each other when we're in the same place. When I'm on another continent, I consider myself unattached. Don't you?"

Hugh smiled. "Marriage vows are serious things. Why bother with them if you don't plan to hold up your end of the bargain?"

Marc shook his head. "Really, Hugh, I'd never have expected it from you."

"You underestimate me, Marc."

Hugh listened to a brief rundown of the past year of Marc's career, along with his friend's hopes for the next. He was suddenly tired. Spending time with Marc in the past had been great fun, but after the stimulation of his time in Dorset with Tamsyn and Daniel, keeping up with him was more of a chore than he'd expected. After they finished the meal, he raised his hand to signal for the waiter.

"Let's have a coffee."

"Forget the coffee, old man. Let's hit a bar."

Hugh paid the bill while Marc hailed a cab, already regretting his decision to go along with him. A quiet coffee would have suited him better; that and getting back to the house to see if Tamsyn had returned. He thought of texting her, but they'd made it a point not to check on each other constantly, as if there were no trust in the relationship. Instead, he got in the cab and they went to one of Marc's favorite bars nearby. They ordered drinks and sat back on the stools.

"So, how is your mother?" Hugh asked. The last he'd heard, a couple of months before, she had been undergoing radiation treatments for something rather serious. The liver, if he remembered correctly.

"She's doing better, actually," Marc answered. "The treatments were successful, at least for now."

"She must be relieved." Hugh couldn't imagine going through that. His mother wasn't particularly strong, and dealing with a life-or-death situation would take every ounce of fortitude they could muster. Yet it wasn't such a far-fetched idea. He was nearly thirty, and although she didn't look it, his mother was almost sixty. He couldn't expect her to be in perfect health forever.

A female bartender came over to wipe the counter in front of them, no doubt to get a closer look at a couple of film stars who had wandered in off the street on a cold, wet night. Hugh was tired of the conversation before it even began.

"What can I get for you boys?" she asked, looking up at them from under dark fake lashes. It was one of the bad things about being an actor; he could always spot artifice in women.

"I'm fine," he murmured.

Marc smiled and set down his glass. "Well, I'll have to think about that."

As Marc began a flirtatious banter with the girl, Hugh gazed up at the fireplace along the back wall, lost in thought. He was engaged to be married, and one didn't do unseemly things when one was engaged. At least, he didn't. It occurred to Hugh suddenly that neither he nor Marc had sisters. He was an only child, of course, and Marc had three brothers, two younger and one older. Neither of them had the deference toward the fair sex that they might have had if a sister had been raised in their midst. As it were, women were objectified. Not because they wanted them to be, but Hugh suspected that growing up with a complete lack of experience, along with the combined cultural norms of the day, had left them without the empathetic feelings they might have had toward the opposite sex.

"If only I could say what I really want," Marc teased the girl, interrupting Hugh's thoughts.

"It's getting late," Hugh said, tired of being in the line of fire.

"Just one more," Marc said, turning back to his friend. "By the way, did I tell you I'm shooting in Amsterdam next summer? A mystery. I'm playing the priest who isn't so innocent after all."

"No surprise there," Hugh remarked. He turned his attention to the girl, who was still waiting. "Looks like we'll have another."

"Haven't been to Amsterdam in a while, have you?" Marc asked as the girl turned to leave.

"It's been four or five years, I think."

"I hear there's a lot to do, and I intend to try it all."

Hugh set down his glass as the girl brought another and placed it in front of him. The whiskey looked like a beautiful amber pool, and he swirled it in the glass before lifting it to his lips and knocking back a swallow.

"That's it for me," he said.

Marc followed his example and then turned toward him, looking serious. "Can I tell you something, mate?"

"Of course."

"I admire you. I really do. It takes courage in this day and age to make a go of something, and if this girl gives you what you want, then I couldn't be happier for you."

"Thank you," Hugh said, surprised.

"I'm almost jealous," Marc said, stealing a glance at the barmaid once again. "Almost. But not quite."

He remembered those words now, lying in Hyde Park, wondering what he was supposed to do now. He needed a break from his career, the speculation in the press over Tamsyn's murder, and, not least, from his parents. Tired of thinking, he listened to the sounds around him. He could hear the muted noise of people talking in the distance, all words thankfully obscured by the breeze. Honks and screeches of traffic wafted around him, easy enough to block out when one had grown up in the middle of London. In fact, it was odd that he often slept better in the city than in the country, but then a great many things about life were odd, and when it came down to it, there was nothing he could do about any of them.

His mobile vibrated against his hip and he took it out to see that Daniel had texted him.

Carey and I are looking into things together.
    How are you holding up?

Hugh squinted at the small screen and frowned. There was no good answer for that question, as far as he was concerned. No good answer at all.

TWENTY-THREE

"MAY I HELP YOU?" a cheerful server asked, startling Daniel from his coma-like reverie in front of the array of choices before him at Patisserie Valerie. How long he'd been standing there, he wasn't quite certain. He had ventured out of his flat, desperate to get away from the silence as well as the thoughts that beleaguered him, and since his cupboard was bare, he found himself inside the café. Outside, it drizzled, and rain dripped off his leather coat onto the polished floor.

"That one, I suppose," he said, pointing.

"The almond croissant, or the brioche and butter?"

"The croissant." He hesitated, watching as she opened the case to remove the pastry from the shelf. "No, sorry. The brioche, I think."

She eyed him, the pleasant look draining from her face. Evidently she wasn't prepared to deal with dithering customers. "The organic porridge is also popular, if you're so inclined."

"I'm sure it's quite good, thank you, but I'll take the brioche."

"For takeaway?"

"Yes, with a coffee, please."

She withstood the additional information without any further complaint, tucking the pastry into a bag and shouting out an order for the coffee. He turned toward the window, wishing it were a clear day, though he knew if it were he would find himself in the garden of St. Mary Abbots again thinking of Tamsyn. He wondered if he would have to move to a different part of the city to get through a single day without a backlash of grief and despair.

"Sir?" the girl asked, getting his attention again.

He looked up to see her holding the bag and cup out to him, clearly ready to move on to the next customer, who might not vacillate in front of the pastry counter like a fool. He reached for them and then found a table anyway. It was still raining far too steadily to venture outside. His table faced a window, and he pulled the chair close enough to touch the moisture on the inside of the glass. Rain puddled in the gutters outside and tires splashed pedestrians, who scurried to their various destinations. He watched as a couple pushing a pram with a freakish plastic cover went by; he tried to imagine zipping a child into what seemed an airless prison, cut off from all humanity by a torrent of rain. What errand was crucial enough to take a child out in such weather?

Removing the lid from the coffee, he took a swallow and then reached into his pocket for his list of suspects. He had made notations on every inch of the paper, none of which made much sense or had come to fruition, pathetic attempts to learn more about the anomalous friends and associates Tamsyn and Hugh had invited to the wedding. He scanned the list until he came to the couple whom Tamsyn had met when she was first dabbling in acting: Dylan Cole and Lucy Potter. They were a curious duo. Though he had only seen them once, they had made an impression on him. Cole was darkly clad and rail thin, with dyed black hair and eyeliner. He was effeminate and refined, his hair gelled to points, with painted nails on small, bony fingers. The

Potter girl was as odd in her own way. The dress she had worn to the wedding was a vintage shop find, with matching shoes and handbag from the 1940s, and between gloved hands, she'd clutched a large handkerchief embroidered with orange geraniums. Tamsyn had mentioned them on one or two occasions, but he really hadn't paid attention. Now he wished he had.

Taking his mobile from his pocket, Daniel got on the Internet and Googled them. There were only brief mentions in the occasional improv show or low-rent theatre production, mostly avant-garde plays with an occasional Chekhov to pay the bills. Carey said she'd never met them, and the only thing more ridiculous than trying to talk to them himself would be to have her do it. He pulled the brioche from the bag and took a bite, brooding. Even with all his connections in theatre, he might not find someone who had worked with them. Daniel ran through a mental list of actors, script writers, set designers, anyone he could think of. As he took another swallow of his coffee, a name sprang to mind: Siobhan Brady.

She was one of few people he knew who worked both high-end and low-end productions. She was a costumer, coordinating vintage and specially made clothing, shoes, and scarves. She arranged alterations and scheduled fittings and repairs. She haunted vintage shops to find props and pieces to lend authenticity to whatever project she happened to be working on. Siobhan took a personal interest in each production. In fact, he had once heard it said that when stocking a bookshelf during stage productions, she only chose books that she had personally read. No one had her eye for detail.

It took three calls to get her number, and he was relieved when at last he heard her voice.

"Siobhan, this is Daniel Richardson. We worked together on *The Importance of Being Earnest* two years ago."

"Daniel! What a surprise," she said. "What have you been up to? Or should I say 'whom'?"

There was a hint of mischief in her tone. She knew his habit, even from their relatively brief association, of dating girls from the set. Although she was at least fifteen years his elder, she was an attractive woman, with chestnut-brown hair and dark glasses usually found pushed halfway down her nose. She had a bookish quality that he found appealing. If she had been a little younger, he might have dated her too.

"Nothing but trouble," he said. "Listen, I wonder if you know a couple of people. I'm trying to reach Dylan Cole and Lucy Potter. Have you heard of them?"

There was a pause on the other end of the line. "Not quite your style, I must say."

"It's personal, not professional. They're friends of a friend."

"They're working in a small company called The Players Club. Last I heard, they were doing a wretched hash of *Swan Lake*, without the ballet."

Daniel tried without success to imagine it. "Any idea which theatre?"

"The Byzantine, I think. They move around from place to place."

"So you've worked with them before?"

"A couple of times. They were all right. I never had any problems with them."

He took a deep breath. "Did you know Tamsyn Burke?"

"Not personally," she answered, "though I've seen her before."

"Did she have any connection to The Players Club?"

"Not that I know of. She visited Dylan and Lucy a few times when we last worked together, but that's all I know."

"Well, thanks for the information. How are you? What are you working on now?"

He listened as she told him about her current project, a play written by one of the hottest new writers in London.

"Impressive," he said when she was finished.

He ended the call with the promise to take her out for a drink sometime, which they both knew would never happen. Outside, the rain had stopped as abruptly as it had begun. He threw his cup in the bin and stepped out of the café, raising his hand for a cab. He was lucky, for perhaps the first time in this entire business. The nearest cab spotted him and pulled up to the curb.

"Hammersmith," he said to the driver. "The Byzantine Theatre."

As the vehicle lurched into the morning traffic, he pulled out his mobile and looked up the theatre, then leaned back in his seat and sighed. It was odd, the startling differences between the friends of Hugh and Tamsyn. They barely even came from the same world. Was it true that opposites attracted—the dominant and the submissive, the weak and the strong? In general, he doubted it. He liked to be around people more like himself, who shared his basic values and beliefs, and though Tamsyn had been different, something about her had been familiar, as if they had been friends for years.

The taxi pulled up in front of the theatre. Handing the cabman a note, he went inside, where he found it as dreary on the inside as it was from the street. It had a musty, humid smell. A hundred years old or more, it was everything he hated about old theatres: flat, faded velvet chairs, torn curtains, creaky furnishings that hadn't seen the light of day in decades, seats too small for luxury-seeking twenty-first-century human beings. It was poorly lit, with fading wallpaper peeling back at the corners of the wall. Everything about the place was depressing, but in an effort to be fair, he tried to see it through fresh eyes. It certainly had the space for them to vent their creativity upon the—albeit minor—masses. The stage was large and made of good solid oak, and though it could use a good polishing, it provided ample room for set design and staging. He wandered down an aisle in the empty chamber and opened a door leading into the back rooms. There, each space was small and cluttered in comparison. A few people were working on various projects: a seamstress stitching a threadbare gown; a girl, dressed in tight jeans and a hoodie, emptying bins while listening to her iPod; a young couple in the corner talking in low tones, obviously having a personal discussion rather than a professional one. He opted to speak to the woman who was sewing and walked up to her.

"Is Dylan Cole here?" he asked.

Her eyes widened in recognition. "He's through there," she said, nodding in the direction of a closed door to the right. "Is there anything else I can do for you?"

"No thank you," he said, avoiding her eyes and wondering what she might have meant. He knocked on the door and stepped inside.

"Good god! If it isn't Daniel Richardson!" Cole said, putting down a pen. He appeared to be writing some kind of letter, which he covered with a script. "What are you doing here?"

"I'm not sure I know," Daniel admitted. He was rather relieved to find him alone.

Cole hesitated, but then lifted a stack of manuscripts from a battered old stage chair.

"Sit down. Do you have any news about what happened yet?"

"Unfortunately, no. It's maddening. Listen, I know it's rude, but may I ask you a couple of questions?"

"What, you're an amateur detective now?"

Daniel shrugged. "I've been making inquiries, trying to establish some sort of context. Were you in regular contact with Tamsyn before the wedding?"

"Define 'regular,'" Cole said bitterly. "We were inseparable before she met Ashley-Hunt, but she didn't entirely break contact with us afterward. She and Lucy were close. They emailed a lot when she was making the film. And she called to let us know about the wedding."

"How did you feel about it?"

"How did anyone feel about it? They were a mismatched pair if I ever saw one. I only hoped the blighter loved her and wouldn't break her heart."

Daniel felt a tightening in his chest. If he was honest, he had to admit he had felt exactly the same way. "How is Lucy holding up?"

"She's miserable. Luce isn't usually a crier, but this has really torn her up. She told me she feels that if she'd talked Tamsyn out of it, she'd be alive today. How is Ashley-Hunt?"

"Same as any man who lost his bride right before the wedding. Shattered, of course. Where did you usually meet Tamsyn?"

"She came here, sometimes. Once in a while, she'd turn up at the flat."

"Did she talk about anything in particular, that you recall?"

Cole frowned. "It wasn't what she said, exactly. It was what she didn't say."

"What do you mean?"

"Well, she never talked about her life, if you know what I mean. She didn't wax on about Ashley-Hunt, or talk about the film she had made, or mention any of her new friends. When she was around, it was all old times, as if the present didn't even exist."

"For example … ?"

"You know, she and Luce talked about vintage clothes, jumble sales, ordinary stuff. It's not like we didn't know she had money now, but she didn't mention it. She preferred her old life, I'm sure of it. Otherwise she wouldn't be so keen to write off the new one. I've seen plenty of people who've made it, and they can't wait to tell you all about it. Not Tamsyn, though. I don't think she was happy with her new life."

Just then, the iPod girl stuck her head in the doorway. "Dylan, Roger needs to talk to you. Something about the set."

"I'll be there in a minute."

"I think he broke something."

He hesitated for a minute, frowning. "I'll be right back." He stood and pulled the letter he'd been writing from under the script, folded it, and put it in his pocket.

The moment he was out of the door, Daniel walked over to the desk. He pulled out the drawer and ran his hands over the contents. Bills, mostly, and notices of other plays, both past and present. He opened one of the lower drawers of the desk and then froze when he saw the photo on top. His heart gave a lurch. Tamsyn's smiling face stared up at him from the top of a stack of papers. He lifted the photo to get a closer look. She was younger, by at least four or five years. It was a publicity portrait, probably taken for some play. She looked uncomplicated and happy, just as she had been until some bastard had taken her life.

He set the photo on the desk and looked with surprise at the clippings beneath it, which had been cut from various newspapers. Most of them he had never seen before, apart from the more recent ones. One, whose headline read *Actress to Star in Hodges's Film*, jumped out at him. By the look of the stack in front of him, Cole had followed every mention of Tamsyn Burke since Daniel had known her. What was he doing with these clippings? Was he obsessed with Tamsyn? Angry that she had dropped the two of them when she'd made it into a feature film? He could only imagine the jealousy that they must have felt to see her get everything she wanted without any trouble at all.

He heard footsteps in the hall and stuffed everything back into the drawer just before Cole walked in. The clippings were odd, but without anything else to go on, they didn't explicitly implicate Cole in her murder.

"Thanks for talking to me," Daniel said.

"If you find out something, I would appreciate it if you let me and Lucy know. It's killing her."

"I will. Thanks."

Cole stood and opened the door to his office, then walked Daniel through the theater, no doubt to make sure everyone saw them together. At the front entrance, Daniel shook his hand. He hurried outside and dialed Carey's number.

"Meet me at the corner of Broadway and Dacre Street in fifteen minutes. There's something we need to do."

Daniel took a cab to Broadway and waited another ten minutes until Carey came into view. It had only been a few hours since he'd seen her, and he watched her approach, a bewildered look crossing her face when she realized where they were.

"What are we doing here?" Carey asked. "This is Scotland Yard."

"We have to talk to Murray. I went to have a chat with Dylan Cole, and we're getting nowhere. I'm starting to think we've done everything we can for now, and I'm hoping we can get some information from him."

Carey turned toward him, an angry look on her face. "You're giving up. And I don't think he'll tell us anything."

"It's worth a try."

He led the way into the building, where they were stopped by security before being allowed to proceed further. Cleared for entry, Daniel headed for the desk.

"We'd like to see Detective Chief Inspector Murray," he announced.

"Do you have an appointment, sir?" the sergeant behind the counter asked.

"I'm afraid we don't."

"Your names, please?"

"Daniel Richardson and Carey Burke."

"Reason for your visit?"

Carey spoke this time. "We're here about the murder inquiry into the death of Tamsyn Burke. She was my sister."

The sergeant jotted something on the paper and jerked his head to the side. "Have a seat. Could be a long wait."

They found two chairs apart from the crowd. Daniel spied a coffee machine and stood. "Want something to drink?"

Carey rubbed her temples. "Will it really be a long wait?"

"Probably. Might as well relieve the boredom with a cup of industrial police coffee."

He took his time getting the cups, then poured the scalding brew and went back to where Carey was sitting. He handed her one of the cups.

"Maybe he's too busy to see us," she said.

"Maybe he's not."

"Why haven't they done something? Every day that goes by means a smaller chance of catching whoever did this."

"I'm starting to think we should trust them. Murray looked like the kind of man who didn't let things go."

"I wish I could believe that."

"We have to. There's no other way."

Daniel leaned forward in his chair and laced his fingers. He was losing hope that they would ever find out who killed Tamsyn, though it would be the greatest waste in the world to have lost her and spend the rest of his life having no idea why.

"Excuse me," the sergeant said, having come around from his desk to stand in front of them. "Chief Inspector Murray will see you now."

They followed the directions and soon stood in front of Murray's door. Carey gave Daniel a look, and he reached over and squeezed her hand before taking a deep breath and knocking on the door.

"Come in."

He turned the knob and gestured for Carey to enter, closing the door behind them.

"Won't you have a seat?" the inspector said, rising from his chair.

"Thank you," Carey answered.

The room was plainer than Daniel had expected: a few books on the shelves and files on the desk. Nothing flashy like some of the police offices he had seen on the telly or on a film set.

"Inspector, with all due respect, we don't understand why so many days have passed without the police making an arrest in the case," he began. "There must be some lead that you're not telling us about."

"The police do not report to family and friends while things are in the investigative stage," Murray answered. "I'm sure you understand that this case is being taken quite seriously. You're not attempting to involve yourself in some way, are you?"

"No," Daniel answered. "But it's torture to wait endlessly and read the speculation in the newspapers. Who killed Tamsyn, Inspector? Was it really one of the people there at the wedding? Couldn't someone have been waiting inside the church who left the scene before she was found?"

Murray sat back in his worn leather chair and tapped a pencil on the desk. "There is, of course, that possibility, I'll admit. But I think it very unlikely."

"Why?" Carey asked, clutching her bag.

"There were people outside. If someone had left suddenly, through a window or door, it would have attracted attention. And, in fact, the

Ashley-Hunts had a small security detail outside to make certain that only invited guests were allowed inside, not to mention the press."

"Surely there were fingerprints in the room. Or some madman let out of the bin the day before, something like that."

"I wish it were that simple, Mr. Richardson. Unfortunately, it's not. For one thing, there is a complete lack of DNA evidence in the case. Of the dozen or so fingerprints found in the room, the only ones we've identified so far belong to the two of you and Hugh Ashley-Hunt, and I hardly think you'd be persevering toward the end of finding a murderer if it were in fact one of you. Another difficulty is the murder weapon. It's a common knife sold by thousands all across the country. There's no way to track down where it was purchased or by whom. I will say that I have my eye on one or two suspicious persons. At this point, I'm still sifting through information and watching everyone very closely. One must be patient in these matters."

"Who are the suspects?" Carey asked, leaning forward.

"I'm afraid I'm not at liberty to say," Murray replied. "I could, of course, be wrong about my assumptions, and there's not enough evidence yet to make an arrest. Only time will tell."

"I don't understand," Daniel said, standing. "Friends and family were in that church, not people who hated her."

"On the contrary, that's precisely who killed her," Murray said. He turned to Carey before continuing. "You see, Miss Burke, this wasn't a random act at all. Whoever killed your sister was someone who had a deeply personal reason for wanting her dead."

TWENTY-FOUR

THE TEA HAD GROWN cold, but Carey took a swallow of it anyway. The pot had been weak and tasted only of the sugar, which she had added too liberally. The saucer had a chip along the edge, and she walked back into the kitchen to toss it in the bin. She had hardly slept in the two days since she and Daniel had spoken with Inspector Murray, and she had heard nothing from either of them. It was over. There was nothing more to do. Whoever had killed Tamsyn had destroyed their lives and walked away. In spite of herself, she imagined it sometimes: the killer pulling out a knife and stabbing Tamsyn, face to face. Then he would have stashed it in the plastic bag before joining them all in the room of family and friends when the police arrived. She tried to remember if anyone had been breathing hard or seemed agitated, but nothing stood out in her memory, nothing at all.

Sighing, she picked up her mobile and looked at the blank screen. Nick still wasn't answering her texts. She thought about sending him an email, but decided against it. She would speak to him the next time she went home. He was sensitive and easily hurt, but as much as she wanted to rectify the situation, she couldn't do it long distance. She didn't have the strength.

There was no one to talk to about Tamsyn now that Daniel had given up. Carey threw herself onto the bed and lay down on her side, pulling the duvet over her shoulder. She longed, suddenly, to be home, in her old room at her parents' house. They had kept it intact, down to the last peeling Coldplay poster, for weekends and holidays when she came to stay. In fact, if she could have studied medicine in Llandudno, she would be there still, filling her sister's shoes as best she could. On her rare visits home, Tamsyn had refused to stay over, opting instead to stay with friends. Her parents had long since given up that battle.

Taking a deep breath, she closed her eyes. She thought of her room in Llandudno, with the quilt made by her grandmother and the small desk tucked in a corner, littered with favorite objects from trips with friends. She enumerated them now, like counting sheep: the mug from Cardiff Castle, full of colored pencils; a stack of drawing pads, half full of dreamy sketches of flowers and birds from walks taken with Nick; a recorder from a local festival; pennants from school; a trinket jar with a ring inside, a pretty, if modest, band with a pair of intertwined diamond chips from her first boyfriend, Evan Davies, who'd refused to take it back when she broke up with him; and various scarves and hats she sometimes still wore. It was a room resplendent with the hopes and dreams of a young girl, the girl that in some ways she still was. She pictured the ring, imagining where Evan Davies was now, and wondered if he remembered the summer they went out together.

She thought of him fondly, but without regret. Sometimes she pondered the future and had difficulty imagining herself with anyone at all. Medicine was a difficult life and there would be loans to repay and conferences to attend and articles to write, if one were to be truly successful. Even thinking about it required more energy than she could summon.

She fell asleep, waking several hours later. It had grown dark, and she lingered a few moments before sitting up and looking for her alarm clock, which had fallen off the bedside table. *Eleven o'clock*, she thought, frowning. She would never get back to sleep now. She threw back the comforter and put a kettle on the stove. The silence of her flat, which had never bothered her before, seemed almost suffocating. It was time to go home. She would pack a bag and take the train tomorrow.

While she waited for the water to boil, she snatched her phone from the seat of a nearby chair. She would text Daniel and let him know. After all, it would be unfair if he tried to contact her and discovered she'd left London without a word.

I'm going to my parents' for a while. Text if you hear anything.

Carey waited a few minutes for a reply, which didn't come. For some reason, she felt hurt. It's his fault, she thought. He'd agreed to get involved and then dropped it the second it got complicated. Then she shook herself. She was oversensitive after all she had gone through. She had relied on him, and that had to stop. He wasn't family. He wasn't even a friend, really. She set about making tea and then crawled back into bed, perching her laptop on her knees. She would order a ticket online and save herself the bother in the morning. The earliest train left Euston Station at 8:10 a.m., and she'd have to take the Tube from Charing Cross even earlier. The trip took three and a half hours, but she never minded that. It gave her time to think. After she bought her ticket, her mobile buzzed. She picked it up and saw that Daniel had texted.

When?

"Seriously?" she murmured aloud. She texted him back.

In the morning.

That's it? she thought. He isn't even going to call? Perhaps they had said everything that needed to be said. Inspector Murray had been vague, and everything looked hopeless. She tried to calm her temper. It wasn't Daniel's fault that they couldn't make heads or tails of the case, any more than it was hers. They didn't know how to start a proper investigation. Evidently, Scotland Yard didn't either. Sighing, she threw a few things into a bag, wishing she could leave tonight. She didn't relish a long night of tossing and turning.

Daniel didn't text again, and she shrugged it off. What did it matter when there were people at home who needed her? Her responsibilities would shift now, though just how, she wasn't certain. It might be necessary for her to go home more often, or look for a program in neuromuscular diseases closer to Llandudno, if such a thing existed.

She went to bed but couldn't sleep. Pulling back the curtain, she lay on her pillow, staring out at the night sky. Of course, she could see little of it from here; the buildings all around obscured most of the view, but when she was out of doors in a park or on a large green, she always looked at the constellations. As a teen, she'd been given a book on them, and she and Nick had spent long evenings searching the twilight with cheap telescopes and binoculars almost as worthless as the cardboard tubes they'd devised as children. She hated how hard it was to focus through any sort of device; her peripheral vision always drew her eye away and prevented her from concentrating. It was much easier to see what could be observed with the naked eye, and in any case, the wider view of stars and Saturn and meteoroids was much more dramatic. They had always hoped to see a comet one day. Nick had said if they only spent long enough searching, they would discover one, like Halley, and they would call it Carey's Comet. Sometimes he mentioned it even now, in his emails. *I was watching for Carey's Comet tonight*, he had written only a few weeks before, and she'd thought it touching that he remembered the silly, obscure thoughts they'd shared when they were young. It made her feel connected to him, and glad to know someone cared about her no matter what. She hadn't meant to neglect him after Tamsyn's funeral, but she wasn't herself just now. He had to understand that, surely.

———

Early the next morning, Carey was at Euston Station. The crowds were overwhelming, people pushing and shoving their way through to their various destinations. She bought a newspaper out of boredom and wished for a cup of coffee as she stood, waiting. A family with children was standing next to her, the young boys bumping into her with their toys and knapsacks. It would be hard to travel with small children during peak hours, she knew, trying not to be annoyed by them. The youngest was two or three, with a heavy tin truck he rolled back and forth on the ground, twice running over her feet and once banging her in the ankle so hard she cried out. His parents didn't even look at her. She rubbed her ankle and tried to move away from them, but the crowd behind her had grown too large for her to get far. She was about to step into the aisle when she felt a strong hand grasp her arm just above the elbow. She turned in surprise to find Daniel standing behind her. He shrugged his shoulders at her inquiring look.

"What are you doing here?"

"I'm coming with you. I want to see where you and Tamsyn grew up. Maybe there's some sort of clue there."

"Oh, no," she declared. A knot of anxiety worked its way from her stomach to her throat. "There isn't, really. Tamsyn rarely went home. And honestly, there's nothing there for you to do. I'm just going to spend time with my family. They're taking it hard."

"I want to go," he said, refusing to budge. "I need to."

"There's not enough room for you," she lied. No matter what, she couldn't let Daniel Richardson board that train. "Why didn't you ring me first?"

"I knew you'd say no."

"Well, you're right. You've gotten up early for nothing."

Daniel shrugged again. He might have been used to getting what he wanted, but she wasn't her sister. She didn't have to bring him along. In fact, she couldn't.

"I'm coming with you," he repeated in her ear.

They were deadlocked. What would her parents say? They had always gone to such lengths to keep their lives private. Nick wouldn't be happy to see him either. Carey turned away and watched as the throng of people began to move toward the train.

"I'm sorry, but there are a few things I need to take care of," she said, glancing up at him. "I'll ring you if anything happens."

"The last I heard, all citizens are free to travel," he said, moving forward along with the crowd.

She tightened her grip on her bag and followed him helplessly. He made his way through the cluster of people, his bag slung over his shoulder, and boarded the train without once looking to see if she was still behind him.

Arrogant prat, she thought. Sighing, she followed him into the car. Without a word, he took her bag and stowed it in the luggage compartment.

She looked on her ticket for the seat number, watching as Daniel moved down the aisle to find his own. She found her place and sat down with the newspaper clutched in her hands, staring out the window. How was she going to explain this to her family? She would have to ring before they arrived, because she knew Daniel wouldn't stop until he'd come to the house. Stealing a glimpse, she saw he was listening to music on his iPod, his eyes closed as if he had forgotten her existence. Carey turned, fuming, as an older man in a crisp blue-striped suit came and stood over her, holding up his ticket.

"Are you the window seat?" she asked, picking up her handbag to dig through it to find hers. She hadn't looked at it that carefully.

"It doesn't matter," he said. "I can take this one."

She gave a wan smile and then turned back toward the window. The train jerked to a start and began to move down the tracks. She focused her gaze as far in the distance as she could, knowing that if she looked at the ground rushing by below, it would make her feel ill. After they had rolled out of London, she took stock of the situation. The businessman was engrossed in a book, Daniel looked as though he'd fallen asleep, and the forward rush of the train calmed her nerves. She took out her mobile and dialed her parents' house. Her mother answered after just one ring.

"Mum, it's me," Carey murmured. "I need to tell you something."

"What is it?" Miranda Burke asked. Her voice wavered, as it had since the day Tamsyn died. They would be fragile for a long time.

"I'm coming home. I'm on the train now, but there's a problem."

"What sort of problem?" her mother asked. Carey could hear the concern in her voice.

"Daniel Richardson is coming with me."

There was a long moment of silence on the other end of the phone. "I don't suppose you invited him."

"Of course not, but I can't very well stop him either."

"I'll take care of it, then," Miranda said after a moment. "I'll talk to Karen. She'll be happy to lend a hand."

"Good," Carey said, relieved. "And I'm sorry."

"I'm glad you're coming home. It will do us a world of good to see you."

"Be there soon," she said in a low voice.

"Be safe."

The words echoed in her ears long after she ended the call. All a mother ever wants is for her children to be safe. Tamsyn's death had ruined everything. Her mother would worry every time Carey was out of her sight from now on, and she couldn't blame her. At least for now, she was relieved that the immediate concern was taken care of. She could take Daniel Richardson to her parents' home, let him have a cup of tea and a meal, and convince him there was nothing more that he could do there. Why would he want to waste his time like this anyway? The killer was in London, not in a remote corner of Wales. She closed her eyes, trying to take her mind off everything; a task that seemed, at this moment, simply too difficult to manage.

———

Sometime later, she jerked up in her seat, jostled from sleep. The newspaper had fallen to the floor, and she couldn't tell from the landscape where they were. She fumbled in her pocket for her phone to check the time and found it was nearly half past eleven. They were due to arrive any minute. A glance at Daniel confirmed he was indeed still there, engrossed in his book. She squinted in order to read the title from three rows away, but couldn't manage to do it. Instead, she accidentally caught his eye, and he smiled at her as if they were on a jolly holiday with a busload of friends and had been inadvertently separated. She tried to smile and turned back around, drumming her fingers on the armrest, wishing she had never texted him about coming home at all.

When the train stopped, Daniel stamped his foot, which had gone numb. He was grateful to get up and move around, following Carey to the luggage rack to retrieve their bags. Carey's had fallen behind some of the others and was wedged in, taking an extra effort to pull it out. They made their way through the station and found Owen Burke waiting for them near the entrance. Daniel followed Carey over to her father and watched as she hugged him hard. He set down his bag to shake the older man's hand.

"It's nice to see you again, sir," he said.

"You too, and you're very welcome," Carey's father replied. "We'd better get back."

Daniel picked up his bag and they walked to the car. The wind whipped in from the Irish Sea, making him glad he'd worn a jacket. A storm was in the offing. Carey got in the front seat next to her father, and he folded his tall frame into the back. It was such a tight fit he thought of getting out and taking a taxi to the house, but instead, he adjusted his knees as well as he could and leaned sideways into his bag, which he'd placed next to him on the seat.

Burke took a sharp right and then a left into Somerset Street, going north. They drove for a while until they came to Llewelyn Avenue. There was a church at the corner and rows of comfortable houses in every direction. Most were whitewashed, as he had expected so close to the sea, but a few had brick fronts. Cars were parked in tidy rows up and down the road. Chimneys bristled from every rooftop and it was easy to imagine them covered in snow. Even the lines on the roads seemed to have been freshly painted. Before Daniel even set foot in the house, he knew Tamsyn and Carey had had a good childhood, full of hot soups and wet, furry dogs and parties at Christmas. It made it easier to understand Carey, the dutiful daughter, but harder to understand Tamsyn.

Carey hurried ahead of them and opened the large green front door. The garden in the front of the house was small, and he could see that the next street beyond cut the size of the back gardens considerably, particularly the Burkes', which was on the corner. There were small trees and clumps of tulips in front of the house, along with a short iron fence designed, no doubt, to keep out neighboring dogs.

"We're home," he heard Carey call out as she headed toward the kitchen. Owen Burke led him into the house, and he went through the door and shut it behind him.

"They're back there," Burke said, pointing ahead of him.

Miranda Burke came into the hall, an apron tied around her waist. "Daniel, it's nice to see you. I have lunch ready if you're hungry."

"That's very kind of you, Mrs. Burke. May I wash my hands, please?"

"Of course. Through that door and to your left." She came forward, took his bag, and set it on the floor by the entry table, an indication, he knew, that he wouldn't be asked to stay.

Of course, it was presumptuous coming with Carey, but after talking to Inspector Murray, there was nothing he could do in London. He didn't know why, but he couldn't stay there while Carey went to Wales, though he already doubted there were any answers for him here. Tamsyn didn't seem to fit into this house and her family any more than she did anywhere else. What was it about people who never seemed to belong anywhere?

More than ever, he wished she were alive again, to help him unlock the mysteries of her enigmatic life. Without that as an option, he had no idea how to discover even the smallest thing about her.

He washed his hands, peering out the door to make sure no one was about. Then he stepped into the next closest room, a smaller sitting room than the one at the front of the house. He glanced around, noting nothing out of the ordinary. A pair of armchairs sat in front of the window across from a sofa, which looked fairly worn. This was where they spent most of their time, he decided, in front of the telly. A knitting basket had been tucked under a table next to one of the chairs, and an open book was balanced on the footrest. Shelves ran along the back wall, holding a few small framed photos and books and a collection of teapots.

He went over to look at the photos. There was one of Tamsyn at six or seven with a missing front tooth, standing in the back garden holding a pup. He was surprised to see that her hair had been blonde then. In fact, she looked more like Carey than he'd realized. Another frame held a photo of Carey as a teenager, her head tucked down shyly, her hands crossed on her lap. Another of Carey with Nick Oliver, who, he recalled, lived next door. He noticed that one of the silver frames, no larger than the palm of his hand and in need of polish, had had the photograph removed.

This house, while worn in spots and comfortably lived in, was not neglected. The empty photo frame felt out of place. He put it down and left the room. Carey was walking toward him, clearly coming to get him.

"Hungry?" she asked.

"Yes, quite."

She led him into the dining room, where the table had already been laid. A large tureen sat in the center with smaller ones about, a real luncheon of roast and potatoes. There were cloth napkins and a vase with three roses, which had obviously been sitting there for a couple of days already, the buds open, just before the bloom goes.

He got the feeling they ate like this every day. Miranda Burke ran her household in a proper, traditional manner, every meal an observance of the life they lived together. With some anticipation, he took his seat next to Carey, across from her father, and watched Mrs. Burke lift the lid of the tureen, steam rising above the roast. He could have asked for nothing more.

"This is very kind, Mrs. Burke. I don't often have a home-cooked meal."

"Miranda, please," she said, smiling.

"Mum loves to cook," Carey said, taking the lid from a bowl of roasted potatoes. "She could have done it professionally."

"Don't be silly," Miranda replied as she handed Daniel a bowl of Brussels sprouts dripping in butter. "How was the trip?"

"Fine," they both replied at the same time.

"Did you sleep on the train?" her mother asked. Without waiting for a reply, she said to Daniel, "She always does. She has ever since she was a girl."

"What were you reading?" Carey asked Daniel. He couldn't tell whether she was interested or just making conversation.

"A Graham Greene. It has that snappy 1940s dialogue."

"I wonder why you're not a writer, then. You're snappy yourself."

He looked up over the roast beef to see if she was teasing, but she was concentrating on moving her vegetables around the plate with her fork. Taking advantage of the momentary lull, he looked up at the wall behind her, where Miranda had hung a number of frames on the wall. Some were photographs of the family and others were prints of ivy and blackberry leaves and roses, probably cut from the pages of an old book of nineteenth-century English naturalists. He studied them surreptitiously between bites, knowing he would never be in this house again. With Carey beside him, he realized that he was sitting in

Tamsyn's chair, and she must have looked at those same photos and prints hundreds of times. The conversation picked up around him, a general discussion of who had done what in the village and people Carey knew who'd asked after her, when suddenly Daniel realized that something was wrong.

He couldn't quite put his finger on it. The Burkes were polite, but of course their manner was somewhat forced. That in itself was not unusual, so soon after losing their oldest daughter and having to entertain unexpected company. The photos behind Carey were ordinary, just as the ones in the sitting room had been, a tableau of the Burke family through the years: a photo of them all together in front of a church when the girls were small; one of Tamsyn with a couple of friends at the beach; another of Carey as a toddler, asleep on her mother's shoulder. The photos were interesting but normal, and his brow furrowed as he looked from photo to photo, trying to figure out what was bothering him.

"Would you like some more potatoes?" Miranda Burke asked. She caught his eye, and he knew she was trying to distract him from whatever it was she thought he was doing.

"I'm fine, thanks," he murmured. He kept his eyes on his plate for another few minutes before he looked up again. This time he knew exactly what was wrong.

Two of the prints had just been put there, as recently as that very morning, he was certain. Something else had hung in their place until the Burkes had learned of his imminent arrival. The sun had faded the wallpaper around each of the frames, and the new prints weren't quite large enough to conceal the darker section of wallpaper that had been covered with something else only hours before.

He was mystified. First, the empty photo frame in the sitting room, and now, two photos taken from the wall. What was it the Burkes didn't want him to see? What could possibly be so inflammatory that it had to be removed because he was coming? He felt Carey's eyes on him and turned toward her.

She knew exactly what he was thinking, he realized, looking into her unblinking eyes. All he had to do now was get her alone.

TWENTY-FIVE

ONCE DANIEL HAD NOTICED the two pictures on the wall, the meal seemed interminable. Every sound became annoying: the clank of cutlery scraping against plates, the glasses clinking on the mahogany table, the muffled flap of serviettes brought to lips and down to laps over and over. The food lost its taste and the conversation became something of an inquisition: "Tell us about your parents." "How long have you been in films?" "What plans do you have for summer?" as though he could think a couple of months ahead when the girl he loved was dead. How could they make pointless conversation, he wondered, just days after seeing their child put into the ground and dirt shoveled over her, wrenching her from them forever?

After the meal, Carey stood. "I'll take care of the dishes, Mum," she said.

Miranda Burke folded her napkin and set it on the table. "I could do with a lie-down," she admitted. "I've got a bit of a headache, I'm afraid."

"I've an errand to run, myself," Owen Burke said, looking at his daughter. "Will you be all right with the dishes?"

Daniel knew he wasn't talking about the dishes. "I'll give her a hand. I always help my mum in the kitchen."

To prove his point, he stood and began stacking plates. The elder Burkes left the room and Carey began clearing the table with a laser-like concentration she probably reserved for medical school. Daniel assessed the tasks, tucked a towel into the waistband of his trousers, and began to wash dishes while Carey put Brussels sprouts and potatoes into small plastic bowls. He needed time to think. He was glad he hadn't raised his suspicions in front of the Burkes. Regardless of the talk at the table, they were brittle. He had seen it at Westminster Abbey, and it lurked just beneath the surface now. But had they removed the photos to protect someone? And if so, who? Ciaran Monaghan? If he and Tamsyn had been in some of the photographs together, it might cause them some distress, particularly if they suspected him of her murder. Or was there something from the past that they wanted to hide. A twin, perhaps? As shocking as that would be, he failed to see how it would be something to hide. He shut off the tap and scrubbed a plate.

Carey brushed crumbs from the tablecloth and then ran a cloth over the Aga, something he was certain she would normally never do. She was avoiding him, three feet away, and as he began to dry the old Grindley transferware, he tried to work out how best to approach it. He took a guess at which cupboard held cups, correctly, and was arrested by the assortment of mugs with sayings like *Happy 50th* and *Princess* and the logo from one of the CSI programs. Which, if any, had been Tamsyn's?

On the top shelf, he saw what had to be Miranda's special porcelain collection: stiff royal portraits painted on ceramics of QEII, Prince William and Kate Middleton's engagement photo, and even one of Diana and Charles. He'd once asked Tamsyn her opinion of the royals, not because he cared but because he found her opinions so amusing.

Tamsyn had shrugged. "Dunno, especially," she'd said, "but Princess Di was an angel." His mum, though not particularly religious, had set up a photo of the late princess, ringed round with small candles for vigils of her own unmitigated grief. It hadn't moved since 1997. He found it rather absurd.

"She was a man-stalking, colon-cleansing addict with a fetish for designer clothes and shoes," he had answered.

"You're a man. You couldn't possibly understand."

"How old were you when she died?"

"Too young to remember her properly, but everyone knew she was heartbroken in spite of the riches."

He hadn't argued, for that, of course, was indisputable.

"And what do you think of the Prime Minister?"

"What's his name again?"

He hadn't met a woman yet who could remember the name of anyone who'd held the office since Tony Blair. He supposed it was because they kept making movies about Blair standing up to the queen and trying to handle the looming threat of weapons of mass destruction or utter lack thereof. He'd been considered to play a young Tony Blair himself.

"Don't trouble that pretty head of yours," he'd said. "The kingdom will survive, whether or not you care about politics."

"Most of the politics I care about are a little closer to home."

"Such as?"

"Well, I protested at a rally in Wiltshire once when a field was going to be turned into a parking lot."

"And a very good cause it was, I'm sure," he'd said.

They'd bickered endlessly then, happy as otters on a sun-streaked beach. Now, he suddenly realized he was standing in front of the Burkes' cupboard, cup in hand, staring into space like a complete idiot. He turned to see Carey watching him.

"You're doing it too," she murmured.

He set the cup on the shelf and closed the door. "It's hard not to, isn't it? Everything reminds me of her."

"I know."

She turned, placing the towel on a table, and walked out of the room. He had no choice but to follow. She grabbed her jacket from the coat rack in the hall and put it on, pocketing the keys that lay upon a side table. Without a word, she opened the door and stepped outside. He threw on his own coat and followed her, peeved about being ordered about, albeit in silence. She got into her parents' Ford, which she started, and unlocked the passenger door for him to get in beside her.

"Where are we going?" he asked. He was half afraid she was going to deposit him at the train station and send him packing, his bag still parked in the Burkes' front hall.

"To see the sights," she replied.

Llandudno had not been a place with which he had been at all familiar, and yet from the moment he'd arrived, he was surprised by its beauty. The sky, thick with vapor, held a menacing gloom. Carey drove north of town and settled on Marine Drive, heading toward the north shore. They were parallel with Liverpool on the east and Dublin on the west, he figured, south of the Isle of Man. One had to have a particular reason to venture from a place like this, and he wondered how Tamsyn had ever wanted to leave it.

Carey pulled around a bend closer to the edge of the road than he would have liked, and the tall outline of a lighthouse came into view. They came to a stop by the side of the road a distance away and she got out of the car, walking toward it rapidly.

"Slow down," he called, to no avail. He wasn't certain she could hear him.

He watched as she ran ahead, her boots clicking on the stones underfoot. She stopped short of going into the building, leaning against the battlements of the stone wall. Daniel hated gothic-looking buildings, imagining torture chambers and oubliettes where prisoners were left to rot and die until all that was left of them were rat-gnawed bones. As he approached, he looked over the side of the wall. The lighthouse was perched on a cliff, and sea waves slapped against the rocks below.

"What are we doing here?" he asked. It certainly wasn't a place she would turn to for comfort.

The mist had stopped, but the stones were slick and wet, and he had the feeling that if she were to lean over the battlements, they would both be pulled over. The morning deluge had left the sand clumpy and hard around the rocks, and the promontory jutting out broke the waves as they rushed onto shore. Gulls shrieked in the distance, swooping low over the shallow beach. It was no warmer than it had been that morning, and he zipped his jacket against the wind.

Carey turned and looked at him, strands of hair blowing across her face. She brushed them back. "Daniel, how well did you really know Tamsyn?"

He was taken aback by the question. "What do you mean?"

"Did she ever talk about her past?"

"She was too young for a past," he said, thrusting his hands in his pockets. "And obviously, you came from a good home. I've been wondering why she wanted to leave a place like this at all."

"I'm not surprised she didn't talk about her life much," Carey said, turning her collar up against the wind, which was whipping her hair into her eyes. "She never did before."

"What's your point, exactly?" he asked. "Are you trying to say we weren't really friends? That she didn't really care about me if she didn't tell me every single detail of life in a sodding little village by the sea?"

She gave him a look so stinging he thought he'd go into anaphylactic shock.

"Tamsyn was raped when she was fifteen, just there." She pointed toward the lighthouse. "Two young men dragged her into their car and drove her up here one night when she was walking home from the beach. She didn't know them. She didn't do anything wrong, but she was raped, all the same."

He was stunned into silence. He could imagine the look of fear on Tamsyn's face, could almost hear her screams. The wind and the gulls, the waves of the Irish Sea beating against the rocks, would have muffled any cry. The thought of her innocence being wrenched from her made him feel as if he would be sick.

"What happened to the bastards?" he finally managed.

Carey turned away, staring out at the horizon. "I don't know."

"What do you mean, you don't know?"

"They were English boys here on holiday." She gave a sharp laugh. "This is a popular place, didn't you know? But they were never caught."

"This is gruesome. It makes me want to kill someone."

"Now you know how my parents feel."

"Does that have something to do with the reason she moved to London?"

Carey didn't answer.

He sighed. "You'd almost think it would have made her afraid to get out on her own instead of embracing it. But then, she had a way of doing the unexpected."

"She didn't leave home right away," Carey said. "She was here for a while, and then went to an aunt's in Birmingham before going on to London later."

"Did it change her, that you can recall?"

"Of course it did, but probably not in the way you think."

"What do you mean?"

"It means she got pregnant that night, Daniel. She was carrying a child from one of those boys. Can you imagine? I can't even fathom coping with the rape, for one thing, but to get pregnant … It's a living nightmare."

"A child?" Daniel asked, shocked. "What happened? Did she miscarry? Abort it?"

"Now you're being dense."

He rubbed the stubble that was forming on his chin, shaking his head. "The photos."

"That's right. Mum had photos of Emma around the house. I called her from the train and she went around taking them down."

"She's raising the child, then?"

"Tamsyn didn't want her to, but Mum wouldn't let her give the baby away. It's why she left Wales. She rarely came back for visits and had little to do with Emma."

"Does the child know Tamsyn was her mother?"

"No."

"She wasn't at the funeral," he said, after a moment.

"No. She wasn't going to be at the wedding either. After ten years, my parents were tired of trying to push that relationship onto Tamsyn. They had to accept her as she was: someone who could never bond with the child she'd conceived during a rape."

"And what of the child?"

"She believed Tamsyn was her eldest sister, the rebel who never came home. She didn't even know about the wedding. A few days ago, Mum and Dad told her that Tamsyn has died. It didn't mean very much to her, since they were never close."

"What about you?" he asked.

"I'm close to her, of course. I was twelve when she was born. The first five years of her life, she came to me as much as Mum. We both adore her."

"Was it ever reported to the police? The rape, I mean?"

"Of course. The police were called round to the house that night, and Tam was taken to the hospital. They had few details to go on: that there were two of them, both older teens, and they were English. But it was summer, you see. Half of Llandudno is tourists in the summer."

"What about the car they drove? Were there any identifying features about it?"

Carey eyed him. "She couldn't give any information about that either, apart from the fact that the vehicle was black. She was traumatized, and young. Not what you would call an expert witness."

The last, he was certain, was not a criticism of her sister, but a mere rendering of facts. It had to have crippled the entire family to go through such an ordeal. He could picture Tamsyn's slim figure, some of which he had seen up close and intimate, but he had never suspected that she'd been pregnant. Had Hugh known? he wondered. Wouldn't there have been some sign, some remnant of physical evidence that he would have noticed?

"Did she ever talk about it?"

"Never. Not once after Emma was born."

He felt in his pockets for cigarettes before remembering he'd decided to quit. "Fuck," he said, irritated.

"Well, that's one way to put it."

"You didn't hold it against her, did you? The way she rejected her own child?"

"I could always see it from her perspective, I suppose," Carey admitted. "How was a sixteen-year-old to care for an infant? How could she be emotionally involved with a child, or separate it in her mind from what had happened to her?"

"You did, though, didn't you?"

She looked back toward the sea, where the waves were lashing higher every minute. "Emma was an innocent child. She wasn't anything to do with something so horrific. It's the hardest part of living in London, being away from her."

"What about your parents?"

"They both wanted to keep her. Mum especially, I suppose, though I doubt Dad could have allowed her to give Emma away. That's what Tamsyn wanted, and that's why she left home. She couldn't be there if Emma was there to remind her day in and day out of the worst thing that had ever happened to her."

"Where is she now?"

"Emma? At the moment, she's at her friend Marina's house. Marina's mum had her when she was forty, so she was someone older who could go through this with Mum. The girls are best friends."

Daniel paused. "I wonder how hard it must have been to trade your daughter for your grandchild."

She looked up and studied the look on his face. "This is a terrible thing to admit, but I've often thought Tamsyn would have found another reason to leave, if not this."

"You're very philosophical."

"I just don't worry about things I can do nothing about. I couldn't have made Tamsyn keep Emma and stay in Llandudno. Like everyone else, I had to let her go. Fortunately, she still loved me and kept me in her life. And I have Emma in my life, too, so I had the best of both worlds."

"So your mother named her, then? Took charge from the moment they left the hospital?"

"No, actually, Tamsyn named her. She was insistent upon the name, for whatever reason. But yes, Mum took her home from the hospital."

"This is a lot to take in," he said, shoving his hands back into his pockets. He stared out onto the sea, anything but look at the lighthouse where Tamsyn had gone through so much. "Want to go for a coffee or something?"

"I have a better idea," Carey said, looking up at him. He noticed for the first time the elfin shape of her ears poking through her blonde hair. "I think you should meet Emma for yourself."

TWENTY-SIX

"I don't think this is a good idea," Daniel said, drawing the seat belt across his chest.

Carey didn't answer. As she extracted her mobile from her pocket and began punching numbers, he looked back at the lighthouse. Now that he knew the truth about Tamsyn, he was impatient to leave. There was nothing to be gained by prolonging this excursion into her tragic past. He wasn't even sure what he'd hoped to discover. Not this, certainly, but even finding out about Tamsyn's child, as shocking as it was, wouldn't lead them to the murderer. They were amateurs playing at a dangerous game. Chief Inspector Murray didn't appear to have made any inroads into the case, but it was his crime to solve, not theirs. As far as Daniel was concerned, the police didn't need any more interference from him.

As much as he hated to admit it, Daniel knew he had idealized his relationship with Tamsyn. He had wanted her but never possessed her. It was difficult to imagine her pregnant. Of course, she would have been a mere teen, no doubt as reed thin as usual, her protruding, pregnant belly unavoidably obvious no matter how she'd tried to hide it. And he was certain she had tried, at least for a while. He recalled an article he'd read that claimed nearly all crime was perpetrated by young, rogue males looking for a good time or to satisfy an immediate need. Knowing Tamsyn had been victimized by two of them made him furious.

He suddenly realized that Carey was speaking in a low voice to her mother. Without wanting to, he listened to snippets of her one-sided conversation.

"It's all right, Mum. I told him … No, there's no reason to think that … " Her voice drifted away as he stared at the road. How stupid he had been to take Tamsyn to Brighton. No doubt it had reminded her of the worst time of her life.

Carey ended the call and looked at him.

"Is this necessary?" he asked. "I don't want to cause any problem for her. She's just a child."

"You're my friend. That's all she needs to know."

"I shouldn't have come. I can be so bloody stubborn sometimes."

"You wanted to know the truth. Now you do."

He opened the window for air. "I didn't expect anything like this."

"You couldn't have known. But now you see why it's all so complicated."

They drove back into the town, retracing their earlier route. Carey parked the car in front of a stone house with mullioned windows a few streets away from the Burkes'. A curtain fluttered in the window and a moment later, a woman opened the door. She was short and had an apron tied about her none-too-slim waist.

She ran a hand through her short brown hair and smiled at them. "Carey! How are you?"

Carey reached out and grasped the older woman's hands between her own. "I'm fine, thank you, Karen," she said.

She wasn't fine, Daniel knew. She was trying not to shatter into pieces.

"This is my friend, Daniel. We wanted to see Emma for a minute."

"Of course. She and Marina are out back. They found a turtle and were setting it free again." Karen stepped inside and beckoned for them to follow. "Go on through. You know where it is. I have a cake in the oven."

Daniel followed Carey through the house, ready to bolt. They went out the back door and saw the two girls sitting in the grass. Emma was older than he'd imagined, even at ten; somehow the image of a six- or seven-year-old child had rooted itself in his subconscious. A ten-year-old was another matter. She was more youth than child, with a face that looked wise beyond her years. Surely that had to do with being raised by parents of a mature age rather than knowing the circumstances of her conception and birth.

Emma stood when she saw Carey and started toward them. As she approached, he took in every detail, scrutinizing Emma for similarities to her mother. Unfortunately, there were few. She was taller than he had expected. She had beautiful dark hair and flecks of gold in her hazel eyes. Daniel almost felt that he had seen those eyes before, but he couldn't remember where. Her mother's eyes had been as brown as a loch in autumn. He noticed her pink patterned cardigan and the heart on the end of a thin silver chain around her neck. Her hands were her mother's, in miniature, and she wore plastic rings on her fingers. When she reached them, she threw her arms around her aunt.

"I didn't know you were coming," she said, never taking her eyes off Daniel.

He tried to smile. "Hello there."

"I know who you are," Emma said. "My friend Laura's big sister has your picture on her wall."

He flushed at the comment, once again regretting his choice of career and the ridiculous manifestations of it that sprang up at the most uncomfortable of moments. Architects or butchers didn't have their faces splashed across the pages in *Hello!* magazine.

"This is Daniel," Carey said, taking things in hand. "He's my friend. Say hello properly."

"Hello, Daniel."

"It's nice to meet you, Emma. I'm sorry we've interrupted your ... " He paused, not having any idea of how to talk to a ten-year-old.

"That's all right," she answered. She looked up at Carey, her affection obvious. "Are we going home early?"

"If you like. I decided to come home for the weekend. You can stay with Marina, if you'd rather, and come to the house later."

"Will you be doing lots of grown-up things?"

Daniel tried to imagine what she was talking about. Pubs, perhaps, or shopping? Or maybe she meant spending time with him instead of with her niece, as though he were a proper guest who needed to be entertained.

"Probably."

The girl shrugged. "I'll come with you."

"That sounds good, darling." Carey planted a kiss on the top of her head.

They watched her turn and go back to her friend. A few minutes later, the three of them got into the car and headed back to the Burkes'.

"Did your mother keep Tamsyn's room after she moved out, or has she turned it into Emma's?" Daniel asked after they pulled up in front of the house and Emma ran inside.

"She kept it, actually."

"Really? I'd like to see it, if that's all right."

"You might as well," she answered. "We have no secrets now."

They went upstairs to the first floor, and then up another narrow staircase to the top of the house. Daniel hadn't expected to find that Tamsyn's childhood room still existed, and he steeled himself as Carey reached for the knob on the old door, its blue paint peeling in places. This was it, the last of her, he thought. This was all that was left of Tamsyn Burke. The skirts and jeans she'd left behind at Hugh's weren't a permanent part of her, but this room, where she'd gazed out to make wishes on stars when she was a child, held, he was certain, the magic that made her who she was. And then something darker occurred to him; it was also the place where she'd faced her crucible after the rape, the place where she was when everything in her life changed forever. He knew the second the door opened that Miranda Burke had kept Emma because of her undying love for her eldest child, even though it would in the end make them strangers.

He followed Carey into the room, the floorboards groaning under his feet. She turned on a lamp, and he could see that the room seemed older than the rest of the house, perhaps because it had been suspended in time. There were cobwebs in the corner and a thin film of dust on the furniture. It had been cleaned, but not for a few months. The posters on the wall bore fading images of Green Day and The Killers and a hard-looking Victoria Beckham who stared into the room with piercing eyes.

"Are you all right?" Carey asked. She was holding a doll, smoothing the ruffles of the dress thoughtfully.

"Are you?" he countered. He looked around for a few minutes, reluctant to touch anything in this unfamiliar, girlish environment.

"What's this?" he asked, picking up a thick book with a cover of green Chinese silk and a bookmark that appeared to have been made from a dandelion stem.

"Her diary," Carey answered.

238

Daniel paused, the book held aloft. He was unaccustomed to things like diaries. Neither he nor his brother had been interested in recording the minutiae of their ordinary existence, but girls, he knew, were different. They seized upon nuances and ideals and trains of thought, desperate to chronicle it to make sense of their daily lives. He turned it over, examining the front and back. There was a water mark in one corner, and bent pages.

The dandelion stem had left a pale green stain dried upon the paper. Had she meant it to be a fanciful hex against the interference of fairies and elves? He didn't dare read it, not with Carey observing his every move. After a few moments, he held it out to her, wondering if Tamsyn had written about the rape or the pregnancy, or about her decision to leave her child in the care of her parents and start over in London.

Carey hesitated and then took it from him, holding it between her palms. He turned and went over to the window. The street below was silent; everyone was settled in their homes, thinking about that night's lamb or takeaway curry, reading the newspaper, watching the telly. He wished he were in one of those houses, safely tucked away, reading a book or going into the kitchen to stir a pot next to a pregnant wife, tasting the stew and teasing her by adding pepper. Anything but standing here, thinking about this, aching from the reality of it all.

"This one was the last—" Carey started.

She left the statement unfinished. Then he realized what she said.

"*This* one," he said.

"Yes."

"So, there are others."

"Yes," she said again.

"Good God!" he cried. "Have you read them?"

"Of course not. They're private!"

"Nothing's private after a murder! What about your mother? Has she?"

"I don't think so. She rarely comes up here. It makes her unhappy."

"Where are the others?"

"In the desk drawer, on the left."

Daniel walked over and pulled the drawer open, revealing four other similar Chinese silk–bound notebooks in various stages of disrepair. He thumbed open one of the covers and saw that it was marked "#3." A short glance at them all showed they were numbered in order, all written in a girlish scrawl he recognized as hers.

He put them back where he'd found them, unopened, and turned to Carey. "Aren't you the least bit curious?"

Her eyes narrowed. "Do you think it will tell us anything that would have to do with her death? I mean, that would be pretty unlikely, don't you think?"

"Yeah, I suppose it would."

"But I wonder…"

"What?"

"Well, some of the people at the wedding knew her when she was writing these. Certainly Nick and Ciaran Monaghan and some of the bridesmaids. Do you think anyone might have harbored some sort of grudge for so many years?"

"I suppose it's possible."

Carey sat down on the edge of the bed and he sat next to her. Without a word, she handed him the last journal. "Go ahead and look through it. But I don't want to right now unless there's something you think I need to know."

She stood and went over to the wardrobe and began looking through a trinket box, examining the small collection of rings and bracelets and lonely charms. "Emma might like some of this," she said, pouring it out onto the desk for a better look. "She's not allowed in here."

Daniel held the book unopened. "Are you sure it's all right?" he asked.

Carey sighed. "No, I'm not sure. That's why I don't want to do it myself. It's too much like a post-mortem."

Something in her tone made him think of the quote on Shakespeare's grave: *Blest be the man that spares these stones / And curst be he that moves my bones.* A shudder went down his spine. Sighing, he turned the fat little book over in his hands and then opened the cover. "#5" was written inside. No other name or marking was made there. No "This is the property of Tamsyn Burke," or "Keep Out," or "For My Eyes Only." No, she had made no safeguard against prying eyes. Somewhat relieved, he turned to the first page.

TWENTY-SEVEN

No doubt Tamsyn's handwriting had spurred many a teacher to lecture her on its illegibility. If it hadn't been so familiar, Daniel would have given up. He thumbed through the diary and saw that she had written on both sides of each page and had filled them as full as possible. He went back to the beginning and began to read.

March 12

I told Ciaran he couldn't come round tomorrow, but he will anyway. He always does. I think I like it, even though I don't want him to know it. He usually just wants to talk. He asks so many questions. Serious stuff. About life and if I believe in heaven and things like that. I'm not sure what to say sometimes, so I just don't say anything. He doesn't seem to mind. I like that about him.

March 15

Tomorrow is my birthday. Mum is making sponge cake, which in no bleeding way is a proper birthday cake, and Aunt Lynne and Uncle Brian are coming over with the monsters. I wish I could skip it and go to London for the day. Cara B. says they have the best shops in the world. Not that I would want her sort of clothes, but I bet I could find some really fab things. Too bad Mum would never let me…

March 18

Boring birthday as usual. Carey fell and almost broke her arm, which ruined everything. And Nick followed us everywhere we went. Boring, boring, boring!

April 3

Too busy to write lately. Besides, who wants to write when you could spend the time kissing Damian Jones.

April 8

Forget Damian Jones. Wanker.

April 9

I think I spoke too soon.

April 9

No, I didn't.

April 11

Mrs. Cadogan said she liked my poetry today. Always liked Mrs. Cadogan.

April 12

I took a walk this afternoon and found a good tree to sit under to write poems. Good, interesting stuff, like Emily Dickinson, who we are discussing at school. Too bad mine all turned out complete crap. Mrs. Cadogan must be wrong. They sounded fake and silly. Maybe I'm trying too hard. Or maybe I'm just no fucking good.

April 13

Now I know I'm no good, because Ciaran liked my poems. I told him to read Emily Dickinson and he would see what I mean. He said he would never read Emily Wanking Dickinson. We laughed until he snorted Orangina out his nose. He looked like a human juice squeezer. I'll never drink Orangina again.

<u>*April 21*</u>

It's Thursday and I want fish and chips. Greasy, gooey ones with vinegar.

<u>*April 24*</u>

I like how Emily Dickinson's poems are so pretty. I just don't understand why some of them don't rhyme. Roof and laugh aren't even close. But I do so like to think of rain dropping on things, and how there must be plenty of apples for everyone and the air is cool and fall has arrived. Her poems make me feel things.

<u>*April 26*</u>

Hannah had a new jacket today and I want one just like it. It was black leather, but not fat and ugly. It was thin and short and she wore it over a green tartan skirt with boots and it didn't even look stupid. Christ, how I want to go to London.

<u>*April 26*</u>

Maybe I should ask Dad to buy me one. He might even say yes.

April 27

Nick's family came over for dinner. I asked Mum if I could go to Diana's to get out of it, but she said no. We were forced to listen to Mr. Oliver's snorty laugh and Mrs. Oliver sat there like a stone. Why don't we know any cool people? Are there any cool people in Wales?

April 28

The Killers are playing at Glastonbury next month. I wish I could go! Brandon Flowers is BEAUTIFUL.

April 29

Ciaran says we should just hop a train and sneak over there. I would DIE if I could go to that concert!

April 30

I am SO ready for the holidays. I hate school, especially History. I can't believe I've lived through nearly an entire year of dreary Mr. Percy droning on and on about "Britain Through the Ages." Dull, dull. Mrs. Cadogan did pull me aside though and recommended that I read some T.S. Eliot when I have a chance. Or is it Elliott? I can never remember. She loaned me a book and told me to bring it back next fall. He was weird, though. An American who liked to think he was British, or something like that.

In Virginia Woolf's chummy little club. Maybe I should look that up.

<u>May 1</u>

It's Saturday. What wonderful things does this day hold?

<u>May 1</u>

Well, evidently nothing. I had to help Mum with the shopping. Her back was out again. Why isn't Carey big enough to help with anything? They treat her like a baby.

<u>May 3</u>

I bicycled down to the pier by myself this morning. It was cold and no one else was there. I like to walk down to the end and stand where I can't see anything of the promenade or the town, just the sea. It stretches out forever. I'll cross it one day and go somewhere special, like New York. LIFE is on the other side of that sea. And even though it's cold as hell, I like it best when I have the entire place to myself. It makes me feel lucky. Anyone could enjoy it, but no one else does. Just me.

<u>May 4</u>

I took a look at the Eliot book that Mrs. Cadogan gave me. It's WEIRD. Weird, weird, weird. I don't understand the title, "The Love Song of J. Alfred Prufrock."

Where did the name Prufrock come from? And drugged patients on the table? The words he uses are so creepy, like muttering and licked and insidious (I looked it up). It gives me tingles. I don't know if I like it or not.

247

I've been too busy to write. For ONCE, we actually did something great. We went to Cardiff for the weekend, and I got to pick out some new clothes! I got the greatest pair of boots! Tall ones with a buckle around the ankle. SO cute! I love them. A few ordinary things Mum made me get, but I also got a leather jacket that is even better than Hannah's. It's so sophisticated and grown-up, like a picture in Vogue magazine. I LOVE shopping!

May 10

Ciaran met me at the graveyard at St. Hilary's and we read some of Eliot's poems. Well, I did. Ciaran mostly sat back against the headstones and listened and smoked cigarettes. But he couldn't really talk about them. I don't think he likes Eliot. I'm not sure I do, either. I think I want to find another poet I like as much as Emily Dickinson.

May 16

Carey lost my favorite pen, stupid cow. Little sisters are the pits.

May 17

Mum and Dad had a row today. It wasn't loud or anything, but they were cross with each other all day, not speaking. Old people are stupid. I'll never pout about anything when I grow up.

Hannah and I went to see the new Harry Potter at the movies today. I hate Hermione's hair, but it was a good, scary, fun movie and Hannah screamed a lot. She's a baby. I didn't scream at all.

May 21

I want a boyfriend. So, here's my perfect man: Tall, handsome, smart, reads Emily Dickinson, sexy (of course), and hair like Rufus Sewell. In fact, I'll take Rufus Sewell. Too bad there's no one like that in real life.

June 1

Life is over. Shit. SHIT.

June 10

Two will suffer. One will die.

Daniel started, nearly dropping the book. Was she implying that she knew who had raped her, upon whom she would exact a deadly revenge?

He went to the window and pulled back the curtains. Small white pom-poms had been sewn along the edge of the gingham by a childish hand, probably Tamsyn's. He looked down onto the yard, where he saw Carey sitting with Emma. Carey was listening to the girl, who was animatedly telling a story. She wasn't to know that her unexpected visit to Marina's had been due to his arrival; or, in fact, his insistence at coming along to find out more about Tamsyn. Well, he had achieved that, he thought, and in the process created more pain for Carey and her family.

Looking back down at the page, he saw a final entry a few pages later, without a date:

I'll find those bastards, and I'll take care of both of them.
That's the way it's going to be.

Disconcerted, he closed the diary and put it in the drawer with the others. The world, as he knew it, had changed, even though the appearance of things remained the same. He knew things about Tamsyn now, things even Hugh didn't know. Should he tell him? Certainly not when his friend was grieving, but later, when the shock had passed?

Daniel glanced around the room one last time, to memorize it, perhaps, wishing he had never come. Victoria Beckham's sly smile caught his eye once again and he walked over to the poster. The edges were curling from the decade or more that it had been taped to the door, and he ran a finger along the edge of the poster where it puckered. It looked as if something had been tucked behind it.

"What are you hiding, Victoria?" he murmured to himself.

Peeling back the tape, he reached in and pulled out three pages that had been torn from magazines and tucked behind the poster. He unfolded them, blinking at them for a moment before the shock hit. Then his heart began beating wildly, as if he'd been given a straight shot of adrenaline. Pocketing the papers, he closed the door behind him and took the stairs two at a time. He raced out the back door to find Carey. To his dismay, Emma was sitting there alone.

"Where's Carey?" he asked, still uncomfortable speaking to the girl.

"Over here." She stood, beckoning him with her hand. He shook his head, not moving, watching as she walked toward a tall hedge behind her.

"Come on," she insisted, her voice barely a whisper.

The sound of her voice spurred him to action, and he followed, curious, every nerve pulsing. As he approached, he watched her slip through a narrow, mazelike opening in the hedge that he hadn't seen from the house. He pushed his way through, coming to a halt when he saw Carey standing on the far side of the garden with Nick Oliver.

She couldn't see him from his hidden vantage point, but she looked up at Emma and gave her a forced smile. "Run in and ask Mum to make coffee, will you, Emma?"

The girl nodded, slithering back through the passageway and into the house, and Daniel went back into the Burkes' garden. He had no desire to talk to Nick Oliver. He paced around for a few minutes before walking over to sit on a low stone wall. Extracting the papers from his pocket, he looked at them again. The first was a photo of Noel Ashley-Hunt at his home in Gloucestershire. Noel stood outside, against a fence, wearing riding clothes. In another photo, obviously from the same article, he was dressed for a party and standing between his wife and the Duchess of Kent. But it was the last clipping that stunned Daniel the most: a photo more than a decade old of Noel with his teenage son, Hugh.

They stood together, laughing, guns in hand, ready to hunt quail. Hugh was already taller than his father, and a handsome young man. His head had been ringed round with black ink.

Had Tamsyn been in love with Hugh since seeing this picture so many years before? He supposed girls did that sort of thing at the usual age. It would explain her attraction to a man even Daniel himself found an unlikely match for such an unconventional girl.

Then another, more jarring thought occurred to him: *Two English boys on holiday.* Could one of those boys have been Hugh? He taxed his brain trying to recall if his old friend had ever mentioned being in Wales. It would explain why she had circled him in the clipping. And if so, it wasn't a crush at all. But who would the other lad have been? Marc Hayley sprang to mind, the only friend Hugh had known longer than Daniel.

"Idiot," he muttered to himself. He felt a traitor for even having such thoughts. Hugh was the best person he knew, closer to him than his own brother. Hugh was incapable of committing a crime like that. One couldn't spend years in constant company with a psychopath without having suspicions about him. There was certainly another explanation, and he would find it.

A moment later, Carey slipped through the hedge and came over to sit next to him. "I saw Nick," she said, tucking her hands in her pockets.

"How is he?" Daniel asked. His voice sounded strange, even to him, but she didn't seem to notice.

"He's still upset. He thinks we should stop looking into Tamsyn's murder and that I should come home for the rest of the summer."

"Do you know where your parents keep her birth certificate?" Daniel interrupted. He wasn't quite able to say Tamsyn's child's name.

"Emma's birth certificate?" Carey asked, looking up. "I'm sure it's with their important papers, but I can't ask them to dig it up right now, under the circumstances. Besides, you won't find anything of use there."

"You've seen it?"

"Yes, once. No one is listed as the father. It only lists their names: Tamsyn Alison Burke and her infant daughter, Emma Ashley."

For a second, Daniel couldn't breathe. Surely the name was a coincidence. There was no other way to explain it. At least, none that he could handle at that moment.

TWENTY-EIGHT

MURRAY CHECKED HIS WATCH as Ennis eased the car into a narrow lane. Traffic in this street wasn't particularly busy at any time of the day. The main roads were bustling, the Strand and Fetter Lane to the south, but just a few streets north the noise and activity of London trickled down to the residents and businesses going about their daily grind. Straight down the road was the garage where Ciaran Monaghan worked as an auto mechanic; he'd been employed for two years and had maintained a clean record.

"Do you want me to go inside and get him?" Ennis asked.

"Yes," Murray answered. "We don't want to disrupt the entire place."

He watched his sergeant go into the building and walked to the other side of the road. Monaghan had a long and interesting history with Tamsyn Burke, and though the two had lost touch in recent years, Monaghan had somehow found his way back into her life not long before she was murdered. That warranted a few questions, at the least.

"You want to talk to me?" Monaghan said a couple of minutes later, approaching alongside Ennis.

Murray nodded. "Let's step around the corner."

They walked to the end of the street and down a small alleyway that led to a road with a bookshop on one end and a Starbucks on the other. Murray stopped in the empty road and watched as Monaghan leaned up against a wall, taking a packet of cigarettes from his pocket. He tapped it against his free hand, shaking a cigarette loose and holding it out to Ennis.

"No, thanks," Ennis answered.

Monaghan extracted a lighter from his pocket. Murray couldn't help but compare the two men, who were close in age. Ennis was the straight-as-an-arrow young man who had gotten high marks in school and made his parents proud. The Oxbridge education he'd clearly had and the School of Life that Monaghan had likely suffered were worlds apart.

Monaghan put the cigarette between his lips. "Is this a professional inquiry?"

Ennis laughed. "You'd be sitting on a hard chair at Scotland Yard if it were. We just want to ask you a few questions. Better yet, maybe you should tell us what you know about Tamsyn Burke. I take it you were friends?"

"What makes you say that?" Monaghan asked.

"For one thing, you were invited to her wedding."

"Well, you're right, actually. I've known Tamsyn since we were tots at school."

"Were you ever ... closer than friends?"

"Not really. We were just friends. Good friends, though."

"Good enough that if she thought someone was trying to kill her, she would come to you with the information?"

"Yeah, I think she would."

Murray eyed the man carefully. "And?"

"And what?"

"Did she ever come to you saying something like that?"

"No. I don't think she ever thought she was in any danger."

"That's a bit of a cryptic remark."

"I just mean she didn't say anything to me that showed she thought something terrible was going to happen."

"You've known each other since you were tots, eh?" Ennis asked.

"We met at school. We were a couple of troublemakers, you might say." Monaghan took a drag of his cigarette and then shook his head. "Later, when she came to London, I followed her."

"What do you mean, 'followed'?"

"I wanted to get out of Wales, and she seemed to have a good set-up here, so I asked if she could help me find a flat. She'd worked a few jobs and found her way into the theatre set, made some friends through that. I got a job at a garage and we met up from time to time."

"Was she seeing anyone?"

"She didn't seem to have a boyfriend most of the time, but that didn't really surprise me."

A line of wrinkles creased Ennis's forehead. "What do you mean?"

"You know. She wasn't after what ordinary girls want. She didn't give a fuck about dating. She didn't want a wedding dress and a manor house and a bunch of bleedin' brats. She wanted to be free and easy, with no ties to anybody or any place."

"Then why on earth would she marry Ashley-Hunt?" Ennis asked. "That's nothing if not tying her down. The huge wedding, the enormous expense. It doesn't make sense."

"Tell me about it," Monaghan said. He dropped the cigarette on the ground and stepped on it, looking annoyed.

"Why do you suppose she got engaged to Ashley-Hunt?" Murray asked.

"I think she had it in her head that she had to marry him," he said, propping his boot against the wall behind him. "It was like a mission to her, all or nothing. She'd decided on it, and she was going to do it. She picked out the bridesmaids, the clothes and everything, but the odd thing about it was that I thought, when all was said and done, her heart wasn't in it."

"Her heart wasn't in the wedding, or the marriage itself?" Ennis had turned ever so slightly toward him, as if his interviewee were a rabbit that might jump away at the merest sound.

"I don't know," Monaghan answered. "But I will tell you one thing. The bridesmaids were a joke. We sat down in a café and made a list together. She said, 'Who did I hate the most over the last ten years?' That's how she picked the girls. She hadn't been in touch with either of them in years."

"Did she say why?"

"No. I thought she got a kick out of doing something that would irritate the high and mighty in-laws she was about to be stuck with."

Murray tightened his jaw. "Was she in love with Ashley-Hunt?"

"I have no idea. She didn't talk about things like that with me. She didn't moon over him or anything, but when she told me she was marrying him, I wasn't surprised."

"People marry for a lot of reasons," Ennis said slowly. "Sometimes it's love. Sometimes it's security or money. Ashley-Hunt was in a position to offer her both."

Monaghan shook his head. "That doesn't sound like her. They weren't together long, but if she was after his money, I'd have known it. I mean, she was still carrying the same old tatty knapsack. She wore the same clothes. Do you know what I mean?"

"I suppose it's a little unusual that she didn't let him buy her a lot of things or that she hadn't tried to redecorate his house. Most girls would welcome the opportunity." Ennis cocked his head to the side. "Did it seem as though anything in particular was troubling her? What was her mood leading up to the wedding? And how often did you see her?"

"We met a couple of times a week. Her mood was good. She laughed, talked, hung about like usual. She always wanted to know about me and my life. It was a good friendship that way. Best I ever had with a girl, you know, that wasn't a girlfriend. It wasn't always just about her."

"Did anyone strike you as suspicious the day of the crime?"

"I thought the lot a bunch of fucking imbeciles. The groom and his family were pompous arses, the bridesmaids a joke. I almost thought she would..."

"She would what?" Murray prompted.

"I almost thought she would laugh in their faces and leave him at the altar. I wouldn't have put it past her. I can't explain it. She didn't say anything like that, but it had the feel of a set-up to me."

"Did you ask her about it?"

"No. I thought if she wanted to tell me, she would. Now I wish I had."

"What will you do when the investigation is over?" Ennis asked. "Stay in London?"

"Does that mean I'm not a suspect?"

"Everyone who was in that wing of the Abbey is a suspect," Murray replied.

"My cousin has a garage in Ireland. I was thinking of going there. London's getting a bit tiresome."

Murray extracted a card from his pocket and handed it over. "If you remember anything else, give me a ring. In the meantime, don't leave London just yet."

Monaghan took the card and tucked it into his wallet before turning on his heel and walking away.

"What do you think?" Murray asked Ennis, watching Monaghan leave.

"It's curious that he implied the wedding was some kind of set-up. And obviously he didn't like anyone at the wedding. They're a little out of his league, I suppose."

"Let's get back to the office, then," Murray said as they walked back to the car. "A set-up is an intriguing idea. But the question is, for whom?"

TWENTY-NINE

THE NEXT DAY, CAREY and Daniel boarded the train to London at Llandudno Station. They found their seats without a word. Telling Daniel about Tamsyn's past had hurt him, and reliving it had unleashed a wave of pain within Carey herself, the likes of which she hadn't experienced in years. She remembered, even now, the sleepless nights after the rape, the feeling that they were no longer safe in their own beds. Her mother hadn't let her out of her sight for years. Their family, which had once been so average, had been torn apart trying to decide what to do about the baby. As much as Carey hated to admit it, it had been a relief for all of them when Tamsyn had left Emma with their parents and gone to London. Yet life was never truly normal again, and the guilt, at times, was unbearable.

She wanted to touch Daniel's arm, but held back. Since Tamsyn died, he had been the only one who had given her any comfort. She wondered if he felt the same. Sighing, she glanced around at the people chatting. A couple nearing sixty caught her eye. They sat next to one another with a newspaper spread out between them, pointing to something and enjoying a vigorous conversation. It made her realize how much she craved the ordinariness of life. She wanted to sit on Sunday afternoons with someone she loved in a café, having a cappuccino and reading to each other from *The Hound of the Baskervilles* and *Possession*, arguing the merits of Conan Doyle and A.S. Byatt; with someone who would spend the afternoon lazily in bed, dreaming of a life together while wide awake in the fugue of lovemaking and shared whispers. She had rarely thought beyond her immediate existence: the classes she took, the next lab or study session, trips home to Llandudno to see Emma and her parents. She didn't ordinarily wish for love and normalcy, perhaps even thought it beyond her. Instead, she had focused all of her time and energy on the goals before her. It had helped her achieve everything she'd set out to do with a high rate of success, but it hadn't brought happiness.

Happiness, which had always seemed rather fleeting, now had been crushed in every sense of the word. It had been denied her sister for whatever reason: fate, sin, the fragility of human nature, her sister's lack of ability to find contentment. It didn't matter which, but if happiness had been out of reach for Tamsyn, who had tried so hard to find it, then surely it was out of reach for someone like her, who hadn't thought about it much until now.

"I shouldn't have come home," she murmured to Daniel. "Mum and Dad are trying to keep things normal for Emma. I didn't need to make them dredge up everything while they're dealing with Tamsyn's death."

"It's my fault," Daniel replied, staring out of the window. "Sticking my bloody nose in where it didn't belong."

"It's not your fault." Carey tensed as the train pulled out of the station and the ground began to rush beneath their feet. "They've lost Tamsyn twice, you know. Once when she had the baby and now for good. They'd always held out hope that they could reconcile with her, and now that's gone. And they'll never know if they did the right thing by keeping Emma. It only drove Tamsyn farther away."

"Will they ever tell her the truth?" he asked.

"I don't know. How do you tell someone they were a product of rape and that her real mother couldn't even bear the sight of her? Mum thinks she'll never forgive them if she finds out."

"The older she gets, the harder it will be."

Carey looked at him, remembering the stunned expression on his face when she'd told him. It was clear how much he had cared for her sister, leaving her once again to wonder why Tamsyn had decided to marry the aloof Hugh when Daniel had feelings for her. There were so many questions that would never be answered. Some people led messy little lives, and others, like Carey, with their rigid, sanitized sensibilities, tried to make up for those who would or could never be conventional. She realized for perhaps the first time that the structure and sense with which she ran her life was a direct reaction to the disaster Tamsyn had made of hers.

"I blame her, sometimes," she admitted. "I actually blame her. She never did anything the way I would have. She gave up her baby and abandoned her parents. What the hell was wrong with her, anyway?"

"She was too young to be a parent."

"I don't care," Carey said. All of the forgiveness and affection she had given her sister over the past ten years dried up like a well in a drought.

"Of course you care. You're exhausted," Daniel said.

Suddenly, all of the anger she'd held onto for so many years rose to the surface. Carey hated her sister for the first time in her life. She hated the murder and dealing with the police and trying to figure out who might have done it. She hated the secret her parents kept and the knowledge that it could destroy them all sometime in the future when they least expected it. She hated the way Nick had tried to bully her into staying, afraid she had encouraged his dependence on her. She hated sitting next to Daniel and knowing that when they disembarked from the train, the one person whom she'd been able to talk with to help her make sense of things would walk straight out of her life. He would go back to his empty flat and she to hers.

"There's something I want to talk to you about," he said, interrupting her thoughts. "I've just been trying to decide if I've gone mad. I took something from Tamsyn's room."

"What do you mean?" Carey asked. Had he taken something to remember Tamsyn by? She was surprised, but she didn't blame him. She had a few mementoes of her own for private remembrances.

"There was something stuffed behind one of her old posters, and I pulled it out to see what it was."

Daniel reached into his pocket and retrieved the folded newspaper cuttings, opening them to show her. They were yellowed and wrinkled, but she could see they were articles with photos of Hugh and his father. She looked at him, shaking her head.

"I don't understand."

"I'm not sure I do either."

She picked up the clipping of Noel Ashley-Hunt and checked the date, which was more than ten years old. "Why would these have been hidden in her room?"

"I was wondering that myself," he answered. "The clippings themselves are old, not photocopies of articles from old newspapers. And I gather she hadn't gone back to Llandudno after she began to see him."

"Is it possible that Hugh was one of the two English boys…?" Carey couldn't finish the sentence.

"No," Daniel said. "Hugh could never have done something like that."

"What about the other boy? Who else was he close to ten or eleven years ago?"

"His only other longtime close friend is Marc Hayley."

"Marc Hayley!" she repeated. "He was at the Abbey! But if it's true, would Tamsyn have remembered them? And what was she doing?"

"Is it possible she saw these photos and just thought Hugh good-looking? He's the son of a famous actor. Their faces must have been in all the magazines and newspapers. Girls do that, don't they?" Daniel asked. "Fixate on rich people and stars?"

Carey gave him a solemn look. "It's a little far-fetched that she would have had a crush on someone she would later marry, you know."

"There's something else I didn't tell you."

Carey felt a moment of alarm. "Oh, god," she said. "The diary."

"It doesn't name names," he said, "but there were a couple of entries after the incident at the lighthouse. She didn't describe the attack. She just wrote that her life was over. And she mentioned the two boys, that she wanted to find them and seek some sort of revenge. Of course, she was too young to do anything about it."

Carey suddenly felt ill. "How did she meet Hugh? On the set of the film?"

He shifted in his seat. "Hugh and I were in France at the Hodges's estate last summer. On a whim, I talked him into taking the ferry back instead of the train. When I went out to the deck, Tamsyn was sitting there and approached me."

"Tamsyn? In France?"

"She said she had gone to Calais for the day to go shopping."

"And you introduced her to Hugh?"

"Not that day, actually. She talked me into bringing her with me when I reported for filming a couple of weeks later. I'm the one who got her a bit part, but Hugh met her and before long recommended her for the lead."

"But why would she do that?" Carey asked, looking around at the other travelers, who seemed oblivious to any conversation but their own. "Was she following Hugh? If it's true, he would have recognized her."

"I don't know."

"Or perhaps he didn't," Carey said. "Her hair was blonde then. There's a world of difference between a fifteen-year-old girl and a grown woman. She wasn't the same person anymore. Do you think she reinvented herself in order to go after him?"

Daniel sat back in his chair. "I'm not sure what to think. There must be some other explanation."

The train jostled them back and forth around curves and hills. Daniel stared at the seat in front of him. Carey closed her eyes and tried to block out the world. As much as she hated to admit it, she could imagine Tamsyn hell-bent on revenge. But surely, she thought, it can't be true. To seek revenge was madness.

Daniel put on his earphones, though whether he was listening to music or just blocking out the world, she didn't know. Eventually, they reached Euston Station. When they collected their bags and made it to the street, Daniel hired a cab and gave the driver Carey's address.

That's it, then, she thought, too knackered to care anymore. She wanted to go home, pull back the covers, and flop into bed and never get out again. When they arrived at her flat, however, Daniel turned to look at her for what felt like the first time in hours.

"Shall I take your bag?"

"No thanks, it's not heavy. You don't have to walk me to the door."

"Yes, I do."

They went upstairs and Carey unlocked the door, dropping her things on the floor.

"Do you want a coffee?" she asked.

"No," he answered. He was facing her, close enough to touch her, but his hands stayed at his side.

"Wine? I think there's a bottle from last week."

Shaking his head, Daniel pulled off his jacket, and suddenly he was kissing her. It was a long, urgent kiss that sucked something out of her. Before they knew it, they were on the bed, kicking off shoes, tugging off clothes. His mouth found hers, and it was breathless, sweet. His hands roamed her body as if they were old lovers coming together after a long, excruciating absence. Carey was unaccustomed to intimacy, but everything about it felt right. For a while, time was suspended. She wasn't Carey Burke, Virgin Sister of Murdered Girl, and he wasn't Daniel Richardson, Famous Playboy Actor. He was her only confidant, the person she had trusted with her life, the one she had somehow fallen in love with.

Afterward, they lay on the narrow bed, his feet sticking out one side. She brought her body up against him, breathing in the smell of his skin. It was a long time before either of them spoke.

"I have another thought," he said, "if you'd like to hear it."

She buried her face in his shoulder. "I'm not sure I can stand it."

"Remember Tamsyn's diaries?"

"You didn't take one?" she asked, propping herself up on an elbow to look at him.

"No. But I was thinking, on the train, that if she kept diaries for such a long time when she was a girl, perhaps she did the same as she got older."

Carey frowned. "I don't know if she did or not. I don't remember seeing anything like that in her old flat. But of course I wasn't looking for one."

"Wait," he said, snapping his fingers. "The day we went to Brighton, she was scribbling in some kind of notebook."

"She gave up her flat, remember? Her things are at Hugh's."

"We'll have to go over there and see if we can find anything."

"What about Hugh?" Carey said, sitting up, pulling the sheet around her. "Is he back there now?"

"He was still with his parents a couple of days ago."

"Do you have a key?"

"Not exactly," Daniel said, stroking her arm.

"What do you mean, 'not exactly'?"

"I mean, I've had one before, when Hugh needed me to take care of something once or twice, but afterward I returned it."

"Tamsyn would have had one, but her keys weren't in her bag."

"Where could they be?"

"I don't know. Lost, maybe."

"Well, I'm sure we can get in somehow," he said.

"You mean, break in?"

"If it's the only way. It won't take long to search the place, and then we'd know for sure."

"If the gods aren't against us," Carey said. She could feel her muscles tensing up and down her naked spine.

Daniel gave her a cheerless smile. "Well, as Kipling said, 'England is a bad country for Gods.'"

THIRTY

"Do you still want the car?" Ennis asked, as he retrieved a stack of discarded files from Murray's desk.

It had been pouring all morning, a hard, driving rain that flooded gutters and streamed down windows, reducing the visibility to naught. Murray had spent two hours sifting through records, trying to come up with something new as he waited for the weather to abate. It would be a shame to ruin a new pair of leather brogues without a very good reason. His mackintosh hung in a small closet behind his desk and a hat lay on the shelf above it. His good umbrella stood in the stand next to the door, a Classics City umbrella from James Smith and Sons in New Oxford Street. It was the finest money could buy and one couldn't ask for anything sturdier in a downpour, but he hated using it in the worst sort of weather.

"I think not," he said. It was a disappointment to plan a day in the field only to have to delay it.

When Ennis walked out, Murray stood behind his desk. He stretched, aware he had been sitting too long. Glancing at the notes he had written during the last hour and a half, he decided to pursue the possibility of a connection between Daniel Richardson and a deceased socialite named Lizzie Marsden. He opened the door to speak to Ennis, but found the sergeant, efficient to a fault, had already left to return the files. Murray walked out into the outer office and went to stand by his sergeant's desk. A hum of noise hung in the air as work went on all around him. Secretaries were making copies in the copy room; clerks filed and typed forms; DI Patel and Sergeant Morrissey were laughing over something in a magazine and drinking the tepid coffee that kept the office smelling rancid. No matter how many notices were put up, people continued to pour the last cup of coffee and put the glass pot back on the burner, where the remains burned until the stench clung to the very walls. Even if he had not preferred tea, Murray wouldn't have dared touch the coffee in this office.

Sighing, he went down the corridor and looked into the small library where Rachel Quinn could usually be found. His favorite clerk stood in a corner, her reading glasses pushed halfway down her nose, pulling a copy of *Blackstone's Civil Law* from an upper shelf.

"Is there anything I can get for you, Inspector Murray?" she asked. Her voice was unusually pleasant. It held just the right timbre of lightness and professionalism he admired in well-spoken women.

"Have you seen Detective Sergeant Ennis?" he asked.

"No, I'm afraid I've been searching for a few things the Superintendent needs this morning. Is there anything I can do for you?"

"No, no, it's quite all right. He'll turn up again in a few minutes."

Murray didn't want to admit that he had come to the library with the express purpose of finding her, although now that he had, he wasn't quite certain what to say. *How about a drink after work?* sounded nothing less than crass. He had enjoyed the luxury of being pursued by Ingrid when he was younger, which had taken the pressure off him so that he could enjoy the budding relationship. Even though women occasionally tried to get his attention, he found it so off-putting that he was not even tempted to take advantage of the opportunity. They weren't Ingrid, that was for certain.

He went back down the hall and into his office, pulling a file from his desk. Then he turned to his computer, where he typed in an image search for Lizzie Marsden. Dozens of pictures of a beautiful girl stepping in and out of nightclubs and limousines leapt onto the screen. She was exactly the sort of girl *Hello!* magazine kept popular with a constant stream of full-page photographs. Every few years, it propelled a face into the public arena until someone more outrageous came along. Elizabeth Marsden fit the criteria perfectly: a socialite who was known for nothing more than looks and style and the impressive list of famous men she'd dated. That she had died under mysterious circumstances six years earlier made her story all the more thrilling, he was sure. Flipping through the file, he saw with some surprise that both Daniel Richardson and Hugh Ashley-Hunt had been questioned by the police the day after her body was found, having been the last two people known to have seen her alive.

Newspaper reports suggested suicide. The *Sun*'s headline, "*Heiress Had Nothing to Live For*," and the *Daily Mail*'s, "*Lizzie Marsden Suicide Heartbreak*," surely convinced the public that this privileged young woman with her questionable moral compass had tired of her life of parties, drugs, and men. Somehow, it didn't quite ring true. As much as the public would like to believe it, a life of parties and spoiling oneself did not inevitably lead to regret, and if it did, a week spent helping orphans in tent cities in the Philippines with cameramen in tow soon put things to rights. Murray stared at the enigmatic face on the screen, searching her features for clues.

Turning to the file, he read Richardson's report first. It appeared straightforward enough. During the investigation, both men had offered their full and complete cooperation. Marsden had shown up uninvited at Ashley-Hunt's house the night of her death and tried to get them to go with her to a party in Mayfair, which they had both refused. Ashley-Hunt called for a taxi for Marsden, while Richardson, as witnessed by several local residents, left on foot to go home. Although the toxicology report showed both illegal and prescription drugs in Marsden's system, neither of the men had been doing drugs and none were found in their possession. A quick check of the records showed that Ashley-Hunt had made two calls to a cab company in West London that night, although the driver did not remember the girl later. Ashley-Hunt, according to his file, gave the same information as Richardson, and also stated that his second call to the cab company was to hire a ride to a restaurant a few miles away for a late meal. There were no holes in the story, no reason to question its veracity.

However, looking again at the high cheekbones of the well-born Marsden, who had, like Ashley-Hunt, enjoyed a childhood of wealth and ease, Murray could ill imagine a life of self-loathing. No, indeed, he thought, narrowing his eyes. She had the look of a narcissist, one who loved the attention she received. If that were true, she was not a candidate for suicide at all, which left only two options: either her death was a tragic accident or a staged murder.

Her body had been found in the Thames, two miles or more from Ashley-Hunt's house. Of course it was possible, in fact probable, that the effects of the drugs found in her system had impaired her judgment and actions. It did not escape his notice that Richardson and Ashley-Hunt, being actors, might be able to lie in a somewhat more convincing manner than someone without their training. If that was true, then discovering a motive would be the next step.

He worked at his desk for the rest of the day, thinking over the details of Marsden's death and staring from time to time at the rain. It was one of those days for thinking rather than for concentrating on paperwork. He knew it, yet he still made an effort to make sense of the notes before him.

Shortly after six o'clock, he let himself into his house with a feeling of relief. Brooks, the Springer, leapt toward his trouser leg as he came through the door. He reached down and scratched the pup between the ears, murmuring in an attempt to calm him down. He had to admit that sitting in a chair after dinner with a book in hand and Brooks lying at his feet brought him a sense of satisfaction that few things had in recent years. There had been a few problems, mostly with chewing, particularly an incident with a book he had left on a low stool where the dog had been able to get it, as well as the antique barley-leg table in the front room. He noticed it every time he went in there and promised himself he would fix it, but hadn't gotten around to it yet.

Murray walked into the kitchen and was pleased to find that Josefine had made a shepherd's pie. He helped himself to a slice, eating at the same table where she had peeled the potatoes a couple of hours before, and then cut another slice. Afterwards, he wrapped cling film around the pan and put it in the refrigerator so he could reheat it the following day. Filling the kettle, he picked up his book, *The Master of Ballantrae*, and waited for the tea to boil. He filled the brown betty he'd had for decades with the tea and water hot from the Aga and then took the book and tea and went to sit down, Brooks at his heels.

The Master of Ballantrae was an old favorite, and though he did not admit it to himself, it was often pulled from the shelves when he needed the familiarity of a favorite book to read during troublesome cases. He tried, unsuccessfully, to concentrate on the page where the Master had returned to Durrisdeer under the alias "Mr. Bally," and then closed the book and set it upon the table. It was a rare evening when he couldn't take his mind off the events of his day or the case on which he was working. He reached down and pulled Brooks onto his lap for a moment, and the puppy lavished kisses upon his face for the attention.

"All right, all right," he said, stroking the silky hair about the pup's snout. He got up, carried the dog into the kitchen, and put a little of the shepherd's pie in a saucer, watching as Brooks lapped it up. Then, rinsing the teapot and the dish, he righted the kitchen, turning out the light behind him as he left. Upstairs, he changed into walking shoes and telephoned for a cab.

It took fourteen minutes for the taxi to arrive. He had been surprised. He rarely went out in the evenings, and if he did, he took his car. London was quiet; the glow from the windows all around him in the darkness indicating that most people had settled in for the night.

Fourteen minutes, he thought, his brow furrowing as he bent his head to get into the cab. What might have happened in the time it took for the taxi that Ashley-Hunt had summoned to arrive at his house? Richardson, he was certain, was not involved. There were witnesses who had seen him, good, solid witnesses that included the barrister next door and his wife, who had arrived home as Richardson was leaving. That left Hugh Ashley-Hunt. The girl had had drugs in her system, likely before she'd even arrived at his house.

"Where to?" the driver asked, and Murray gave him Ashley-Hunt's address in Holland Park. He wasn't certain if the posh address was a result of the young man's success in his chosen career or if it had been provided by his wealthy parents. Either way, Ashley-Hunt was living a very privileged life.

Murray sat back in the seat, looking for signs of activity. The main thoroughfares were still busy, though the shops were for the most part closed. Restaurants seemed to be doing brisk business, and he was certain that the theatre district was easily filling seats on such a pleasant evening. In Holland Park, he instructed the driver to stop the car some distance away, paid him, and got out of the vehicle.

The moon was high and the stars burned red and gold against the cloudless sky. He walked past Ashley-Hunt's home, to the end of the road, and back again. He was surprised that it appeared empty. Perhaps Hugh's parents had insisted that he stay longer in Mayfair, in light of the circumstances. Taking a left into Earl's Court Road, Murray followed it until it turned into Redcliffe Gardens, and then into Edith Grove. From the house to the Thames was nearly a mile's walk, and Lizzie Marsden's body had been found over half a mile farther down, on the Chelsea Embankment.

Of course, it was possible a cab had been rung for but paid off when it arrived. But why, he wondered, would Ashley-Hunt do something like that? Richardson had already seen Marsden at the house. Murray didn't like it. The young woman couldn't possibly have staggered that far on foot while under the influence of drugs. If she hadn't gotten into the cab, someone else had to have driven her closer to the river. Years had passed since then, though; too many for it to be realistic for Ashley-Hunt to still be driving the same car. Otherwise, he might have asked for a warrant to search it.

THIRTY-ONE

EVERY CASE GORDON MURRAY had ever successfully completed had been solved by the process of elimination. Prove someone couldn't do it, and the number of suspects who could became that much smaller. In spite of all the large and even famous personalities involved in the Tamsyn Burke murder, the cold, hard facts remained the same. Men were more likely than women to stab, and although women used knives in rare cases of self-defense, men were more prone to use them. Also, relatives and friends who had traveled a long distance to be at the wedding were less likely suspects than someone who had been close to the victim recently, and the likelihood of Tamsyn knowing the person who killed her approached nearly one hundred percent.

Therefore, the killer was a man who was close to her, someone whom she knew well. Though there had been other men present that morning, men who could excite some interest in a police inquiry for their past histories, their unlikable natures, or their reticence to cooperate with the police, it had come down, in Murray's mind, to two main suspects: Daniel Richardson and Hugh Ashley-Hunt.

Murray tapped his pencil on the desk, thinking. Of the two, Daniel Richardson seemed less likely. He had been something of a lapdog of Tamsyn's, though lapdogs had sometimes been known to bite. Murray had the strong suspicion that Richardson was in love with her and would have done anything for her. In his conversations with him, he had got the feeling Daniel had been pained to watch the budding relationship between Tamsyn and his best friend. On the other hand, Murray had heard no account of a true, deep love between Ashley-Hunt and the murder victim, and his demeanor on the occasion of their meeting indicated a man with no emotional attachment. Ashley-Hunt was a calculating sort of man, and the last person it seemed he would ever entertain the notion of marrying was precisely the girl he intended to marry. Therefore, there was the possibility that these two young people had not been marrying for passion, but for other motives. Perhaps they had brokered one of those private deals one hears about in Hollywood: a marriage of convenience for limited duration with a cash settlement afterward. If so, something had scotched the plan.

Blackmail crossed Murray's mind. If Tamsyn Burke had known something about Ashley-Hunt, something about Lizzie Marsden, perhaps, she could have negotiated for money. An actual marriage between them was more difficult to understand. Blackmailers generally wanted huge sums of cash, which would have been easy enough to obtain from someone as wealthy as Ashley-Hunt, but the status she might have gotten through marrying him didn't seem at all the sort of thing she would go after. Choosing marriage over money was a far more dangerous game, one that kept her in the constant company of a man who probably had murdered at least once before.

Then again, Tamsyn might not have known about Elizabeth Marsden, in which case there had to have been another reason to get involved with Hugh. She may have seen a marriage to him as a way to reach her ambition to act on a national or even international level more quickly. However, from his research, it seemed clear that she had happened into the opportunity for the Hodges' film by chance.

Ennis had uncovered only one unusual fact about Tamsyn Burke: that she had been raped ten years earlier by two English boys in Wales. No identification of the boys had ever been made. The initial police report said that the victim could provide little or no help in finding her assailants, merely that there were two, and they had driven a black car. She had been young and traumatized; an innocent casualty of a violent crime, who had become pregnant and had given birth to the child instead of having an abortion. It had changed her life in more ways than one.

What did Hugh know about Tamsyn's past? Murray doubted the girl would have been forthcoming after an incident like that. And perhaps her parents, who were raising the child, didn't want anyone to know it wasn't their own.

Ever since seeing Tamsyn's corpse on the slab in the morgue, he had itched to bring the killer to justice. He couldn't bring the girl back, but he would see that justice was done. Another interview with Hugh Ashley-Hunt was now a certainty.

After that, Murray resolved, he would get about the business of putting his personal life in order. At home on his desk were two tickets to the Royal Ballet for the following week. All he had to do was pluck up the courage to ask Rachel Quinn to go with him. Though there was some work to be done on his part, to woo and win her, there was hope, after all, that he wasn't to be a single man forever.

His phone rang as he mulled the situation. "DCI Murray."

"Sir, this is Constable Jay Langley. I've been assigned to surveillance on the Ashley-Hunt home, and for the last two nights, Hugh Ashley-Hunt has left by the back door and gone for a short walk in the park nearby. I thought you'd like to know."

"Yes, certainly," Murray said, his attention piqued. He had never met Langley but had heard of him after he'd been wounded during a robbery a couple of months earlier. It had been in all the papers and was the talk of Scotland Yard. "You were right to call. Did he leave at the same time both nights?"

"Eleven o'clock sharp, sir, both nights."

"Who's watching the house tonight?"

"I'll be there with Constable Grisham at the usual time, ten o'clock."

"Thank you for letting me know."

What reason could Ashley-Hunt have for leaving the safety of his parents' house, which was nothing less than a fortress with its gates and armed bodyguards? Was he feeling so confined that he would risk being seen by the press or even harmed by a misguided fan?

Whatever the reason, Murray would be there to follow him that night. If nothing else, it would provide material for his interview. He worked at his desk until six o'clock, and then took his coat from the hook and locked his office door.

Traffic was average for this time of day, and Murray threaded through it, considering his next move. As far as he was concerned, Hugh's behavior was a red flag. How the young man had evaded the press, he had no idea, but he would find out.

When he reached his house, he went inside to find out what Josefine had made for supper. There were lamb chops in the oven. He wasn't fond of lamb chops, but Brooks was certain to appreciate the scraps. He unwrapped the meal and took it to the table. The dog followed, lying patiently at his feet. He knew that if he waited long enough, he wouldn't be forgotten. Murray likened the quality to being a good detective. Watch and wait, and sooner or later, the reward would come. After the meal, he cut the trimmings off the meat and put it on a saucer for the dog. Then he took him outside one last time. It was a good night for reconnaissance. The sky was clear, the ground dry, and there was no wind to interfere with proper detection. He brought the dog back into the house and locked the door behind him. Then he went upstairs to change.

It was always difficult getting information from a suspect, but he had a particularly bad feeling about Ashley-Hunt. If he was correct, the man had murdered that girl in cold blood, a crime that had been premeditated and planned to the last detail. Ashley-Hunt had wanted to see the look on Tamsyn Burke's face, to see whether she showed surprise or shock or fear. Later, after the funeral, he had stood with her parents as her body was buried deep in the plowed earth, his arm around her mother. It was a contemptible move, no mistake.

The street was empty, the sky dark. Murray got into his car and started the engine, but before he could put the car into gear, a rope was snaked around his neck, pinning him to the headrest. Looking up at the rearview mirror, he could see Ashley-Hunt behind him.

The rope was so tight about his throat he couldn't speak. He grasped it with his hands, desperate for air, but Ashley-Hunt had wrapped each end around his fists securely.

"Inspector Murray," he said in his ear. "I decided to pay you a visit. Or perhaps I should say that 'Constable Jay Langley' did."

Constable Langley. Ashley-Hunt must have read his name in the paper and impersonated him on the phone. It was clever, Murray had to admit. The man loosened the rope just enough for Murray to cough and try to speak.

"Tamsyn Burke," he rasped. He tried to wedge his fingers between the rope and his throat, but there was no room.

There was a moment's hesitation. There was no sound but the distant rumble of cars in the next street, which felt worlds away.

"Tamsyn Burke," Ashley-Hunt repeated after a moment. "God, I'm bloody sick to death of hearing about Tamsyn Burke."

"Did you kill her?"

"Who wouldn't want to kill her? She was the world's most infuriating human being."

"Blackmail?" Murray asked, keeping his eye on him. If Ashley-Hunt started talking, he might be able to pull away quickly enough to reach his gun, though he felt his fingers going numb.

"No," Ashley-Hunt said, shaking his head. "She was going to kill me."

"Kill you? Why?" he asked. "Had she figured out about Lizzie Marsden?"

"Lizzie Marsden?" Hugh asked with an incredulous laugh. "Actually, I was surprised you made the connection."

"A better question is, how did you know I was on to you?"

"I had someone watching my house. You were followed all the way to the Thames. There was only one thing you could be thinking to do something like that."

"What did Tamsyn want from you?"

"Well, for one thing, she was still pissed about what happened when we were young."

The light began to dawn. "The rape?" Murray asked, hoarsely. "Were you one of the boys who raped Tamsyn in Wales?"

Ashley-Hunt's eyes narrowed before he spoke. "Well, you can't really prove rape, can you? A couple of underage kids having a lark; that's not a crime."

"Why did she go after you?" Murray asked.

"The virgin's wrath, I suppose. She was probably saving herself for some disreputable little bugger at school."

Murray was stunned. Tamsyn Burke had been no ordinary victim. She had gotten close to a man who'd raped her to exact some sort of revenge of her own.

What had really happened between them, after all?

Ashley-Hunt laughed in his ear. "She fooled you, didn't she, Inspector? Did you really take the side of the poor little dead girl?"

For a moment, Murray thought of Ingrid. She had been supportive of his career, but nonetheless had feared for him in certain circumstances. Although he was careful not to take too many calculated risks, occasionally they were unavoidable. This situation had to be taken in hand. He hadn't expected to face a sociopath in his own vehicle. He should never have believed a call from someone he hadn't even seen before.

The rope was tight and he was running out of time. Murray pulled forward with all his might and reached for his gun, but Ashley-Hunt jerked the rope tighter, pinning him to the seat and cutting off his windpipe. He'd heard dozens of stories from policemen recounting tales of being shot, but he had never considered that he might be strangled. After a couple of moments, black spots began to appear before his eyes, and the man leaned closer, watching him.

Murray tried to move, but he was losing consciousness. He took one last look at Ashley-Hunt in the mirror, with the same wonder that Tamsyn Burke must have felt. Everything felt disconnected; his arms and legs were suddenly too heavy to move. He thought again of Rachel Quinn; of the tickets and the ballet and the lost opportunity. He had wasted so much time. Pain shot through his body, a pain unlike anything he had ever felt before. For a moment, he thought he heard Ingrid's voice calling him, and he strained to hear it. He closed his eyes, listening for the voice that had been so dear. She was waiting, he knew. Well, he thought. Perhaps there would be ballet after all.

THIRTY-TWO

DANIEL FOLLOWED CAREY INTO the back of the cab, gave the driver Hugh's Holland Park address, and then pulled out his mobile to look at the last few photos he'd taken of the happy couple at a restaurant a few days before the wedding. There was one of Hugh with his arm around Tamsyn and a few of Tamsyn alone. Daniel scrolled to look at the one of them together. In that particular image, Hugh wasn't smiling; he looked tired and perhaps somewhat bored. Tamsyn, however, looked very much her usual self. There was a secretive smile playing about her lips, a knowing look in her eyes. Daniel had thought her flirtatious at the time. Studying it now, he saw she was leaning away from Hugh rather than toward him. Of course, it was a random snap, one of a thousand moments he'd spent with the two of them in the last few months, but it brought home an uncomfortable truth: he had never really known either of them.

In the last ten years, Daniel's life had taken many unexpected turns. He had gotten an education he'd never dreamed of, embarked on what to many was a dream career, and had been best friends with one of the greatest young actors in England. It hadn't seemed extraordinary at the time, merely a series of small, incremental steps that had led him to this point in his life. What was extraordinary, he realized, was the fact that he had been friends with someone who may have been capable of brutal rape and murder. And perhaps not even once, which was difficult enough to accept, but twice.

For the first time, he wondered what had happened to Lizzie Marsden. For years after her death, he had stifled every memory of that night. The encounter itself had been brief but disturbing. He and Hugh had gone out for sushi and then returned to Hugh's house to watch a film on television, a new BBC production of Trollope's *Kept in the Dark*. Hugh had turned down the part of George Western and wanted to see if he had any regrets, though Daniel had never known him to second-guess himself about anything. They had sat down to watch it, criticizing the bland moments and the occasional miscasting, when Lizzie Marsden had knocked at the door.

Daniel didn't know which of them had been more surprised by her sudden appearance. It was clear that Hugh hadn't been expecting her. She was a little drunk, which gave her a more vulnerable quality than her usual aggressive manner, somehow softer around the edges. Her hair spray had worn off, and her blonde hair, sheared to just below her chin, was tousled perfectly, as if after a night of lovemaking. Her lipstick, which must have been put on in a taxi, was not perfectly applied, and if she hadn't been quite so beautiful or dressed in an Alexander McQueen gown, she might have seemed like a normal girl. Daniel had been aware of an attraction to her in that moment, which he'd tried to shake off. She was a barracuda who had slept with him once without batting an eye, merely to be able to say she had done it, and she would chew him up and spit him out if he let it happen again. He and Hugh had stood at the door, trying to decide what to do with her, as she thrust herself between them and walked into the room.

Hugh closed the door behind her but made no effort to follow as she walked into the sitting room and tossed her coat across the arm of the sofa, smiling. She hiked up her skirt to a dangerous level and sat, swinging her perfectly sculpted legs up onto the sofa and crossing them at the ankle. Daniel remembered looking at Hugh, who watched her without a word in that chilly aristocratic way of his, and his next thought was that perhaps he should leave. Perhaps Hugh wanted to be alone with her, although he hoped not. As far as he knew, they treaded carefully in that department. He had always thought it would be a little incestuous to sleep with the same women.

Lizzie laughed suddenly. It was a beautiful laugh, and Daniel thought it was the best part of her.

"Pleased with yourself, are you?" Hugh asked.

"I can't believe you're both here. Talk about a dream come true." She heaved a great sigh. "Where's the vodka, boys?"

"How about a cup of coffee instead?" Daniel asked. The last thing on earth he wanted was to watch this girl get even drunker than she already was.

"Killjoy."

"What's gotten you in such a good mood?" Hugh asked. He neither moved toward the drinks table nor any further into the room.

Lizzie stroked her leg coquettishly. "I was at Annabelle's tonight, and Chelsea Drummond walked in with Viscount Blakeley. She's gained twenty pounds since I saw her last. You should have seen her; it was all in her arse. He couldn't keep his eyes off me. Or anyone else in the room, for that matter. They'll be broken off within the month, mark my words."

Hugh smiled. "Nothing like a wee bit of *schadenfreude* to make the day better."

She crooked her finger at him, inviting him to sit down beside her. "You know what else makes the day better?"

"Oh, I have some idea." Hugh still didn't move, and for a second, there was a battle of wills as they stared laser-like at each other across the room. Then she kicked off her heels and stood up in bare feet, her hands on her hips. A moment later, she walked over and kissed him. Daniel turned and fumbled in his pocket for his mobile, checking it for messages in the urgent hope that he could excuse himself to make a call. He would have left already, but they stood between him and the door.

"Not so fast, Richardson," she said. She walked over and tried to kiss him, too, but he took her hand and pushed her back. "How would you like to have the best fuck of your lives, gentlemen?"

"That's enough," Hugh said.

She shrugged and headed for the drinks table, pulling a bottle from a silver tray. "Who else wants a drink?"

Hugh took the bottle from her and placed it back on the tray. "Not tonight, Lizzie. You need to go home and sleep this one off."

"There's only one thing I need." She lifted her hand and began to undo the hidden zipper in the side seam of her dress. "Anyone going to give me a hand?"

"What do you think you're doing?" Hugh asked in a patient tone.

"I think I'm going to have my way with my two favorite boys."

"I hate to spoil a good party, but I have to go," Daniel said, shaking his head.

"Come on!" she cried. "It will be the best time you've ever had."

Hugh reached out and put his arms around her, startling Daniel. Then he zipped the dress and went over to get her shoes. "That's not how it works. When I want a good rogering, I decide for myself who the lucky girl will be."

"Have you got this?" Daniel asked him, opening the door, anxious to bolt out into the cool night air.

"I'll ring for a cab," Hugh answered. Then he turned to Lizzie. "You can stop this ridiculous display, my dear. Nobody's interested in taking advantage of a drunk girl. Or being taken advantage of, for that matter."

Lizzie shot him a vicious look, and for a moment Daniel paused on the step, waiting to see what would happen next.

Hugh took out his mobile to make the call, never taking his eyes off Lizzie. He requested a taxi, giving his address to the party on the other end. Then he cupped his hand over the phone and looked at Daniel. "I'll be right out."

"You're making a mistake," Lizzie said. She slid her feet into her shoes and grabbed her handbag.

Hugh raised a brow. "I'll take my chances."

Daniel nodded at Hugh, relieved to know the situation was in hand. As he made his way down the front steps, he noticed the couple next door returning from a black tie event. The woman, in her late forties or early fifties, wore a silver Grecian-style gown that clung to her shapely body, with a diamond necklace nestled snugly between her breasts. The man with her caught his eye, and he turned away, taking a sharp gulp of air. A couple of minutes later, Hugh stepped outside, and Daniel said good night and walked all the way home.

The following day, two constables had knocked at his door, informing him that Lizzie had drowned in the Thames. He answered questions both at his flat and later at the police station, as had Hugh, and apart from the odd remark between them now and then, the circumstances had never been mentioned again. Not for the first time, he wondered if he should have stayed and put Lizzie in a cab himself, or perhaps even taken her home. He had been disgusted by the entire display, wanting only to extricate himself from the situation. Sometimes he blamed himself. If he had seen her home, there was a good chance she would not have been found dead hours later. Eventually, he reconciled it in his own mind: Lizzie Marsden had been on a collision course with death, and if she hadn't been so drunk and fallen into the river, she would have overdosed on drugs or been killed by a jealous lover. She never would have changed, and all of the regret he had that he was even remotely involved with someone on the last night of their life didn't alter the fact that sometime, somewhere, her time would have been up. It was an ugly but nevertheless true statement, if a small salve to his conscience. He had sometimes wondered how long it had taken for Hugh to bundle the girl into a cab. He'd even suspected that once he was gone, they had gone at it like rabbits. And why not, he thought. People could do as they liked. But never once had it occurred to him that Hugh had killed her.

He'd heard it said once that every murder was related to either money or sex. Now, as he sat next to Carey in the cab and pocketed his mobile, he tried to understand Lizzie's death. If it had been murder, what was the motive? The only thing he could imagine was that she might have threatened to tell someone that she'd slept with both of them that night. Personally, he would have hated that on a number of levels. It was a scandal that could have damaged both his career and Hugh's, and would even have tainted the Ashley-Hunt family by association. If Hugh had something to do with her death, he decided, that must have been the reason why.

But what of Tamsyn's murder? he wondered. Sex could be a logical motive there too. She had been raped, but if Hugh was involved, had she blackmailed him as well? Money as motive he could understand. She was a poor girl making it on her own in London. But why would she have wanted to marry Hugh? He looked at Carey, who, judging from the look on her face, was lost in her own equally morbid thoughts.

He hoped they would find a journal or something else among Tamsyn's things to shed light on the situation. They needed to know the truth, both of them, if they were ever going to be able to put this all behind them.

The cab slid to a stop on the corner a few doors down from Hugh's house, and Daniel helped Carey out before paying the driver. It was late afternoon and sunny, but he felt no desire to wait until after dark, when they would either have to trip around in blackened rooms or turn on lights and arouse someone's suspicion.

"How will we get inside?" she asked.

"I'll see if there's a key under the urn or something," he answered.

"Wouldn't that be a bit obvious?"

"It's worth a try."

Carey stepped back and tried to shield him from view as he stooped down to look under the heavy urn, using his shoulder to support the weight of it and running his fingers along the bottom. He eased it back down and sighed.

"No luck."

He narrowed his eyes and then reached up to the lintel, running his hand along the top until he came into contact with something hard and metal. He smiled as he took the key in his hand and held it out for her to see.

"I can't believe that worked," she said.

"Come on," he said, putting the key in the lock. "Let's see what we can find."

Although Daniel had entered the house on innumerable occasions, it was unsettling coming in without Hugh's knowledge. He was betraying his best friend. He wondered for a second if it was even possible that he had jumped to the wrong conclusion. The clippings of Noel and Hugh were circumstantial evidence at best. Perhaps Tamsyn had seen him in the magazine and liked his face. Daniel rubbed his forehead, which had suddenly begun to ache. Without a doubt, the stress was getting to him.

"We should ring Inspector Murray," Carey said, echoing his thoughts. She stood in the center of the room, looking at him.

"We will, but we're already here. We'll look for a diary and then go. Five minutes and no more."

He looked around the familiar room. He had last been here on the night before the wedding, having a private toast with Tamsyn and keeping her company while Hugh took care of some last-minute business before they were to leave the country the next day. At the time, he hadn't asked what sort of business it had been. He had simply been glad for some time alone with her. It was painful to admit it now, but he had harbored some small hope that she'd have a change of heart before she pledged herself to Hugh in front of everyone they knew.

"Right," he added when Carey was silent. "You know what sort of journal she preferred." There was little evidence of Tamsyn in the room, other than one small, heart-shaped picture frame holding a photo of Tamsyn and Hugh together that an associate producer had taken in Dorset. "We'll probably have to search upstairs."

Daniel knew then that he would never have been able to be a detective. He had no idea how to sort through people's lives and homes, even for an urgent reason. He led Carey up the staircase to the bedroom where her sister had lived for the last few months of her life, in order to disturb what little of her there was left.

"Have you ever been here before?" he asked.

"No. Tamsyn and I didn't see each other much in the last few months. I was trying to finish a difficult term. We met for coffees a few times. I should have been more involved. If I had been there for her—"

"Maybe you should wait downstairs," he said, cutting her off before she could go any further.

"No," Carey answered. "It can't be any easier for you."

He hesitated as he reached the top of the stairs. "Study or bedroom?"

"Study."

Across from Hugh's bedroom was a smaller room he used for his hobbies. Of course, it had none of the posh appointments of his father's, but it was a fascinating room nonetheless. There was a large wood-and-iron settee that doubled as a bed in an emergency, though it had doubtless never been used, and two chairs in the corner.

A hefty mahogany desk was positioned against the wall across from the settee, which served as a repository for some of Hugh's personal interests. The desk was covered in odd, antique accessories that seemed snatched from Darwin's laboratory: filmy test tubes and vials; bell jars covering old nests and petrified eggs; ancient, dusty books; mounted fish and a harrowing red squirrel with bared fangs that had been rendered lifelike by an adept taxidermist. There were hundred-year-old spectacles folded reverently over a 1930s edition of a John Stuart Mill book. Moths and butterflies, pinned to a velvet backdrop and protected by a thin layer of glass, hung on the wall. Daniel had been in this room once before, but he had found the artifacts creepy and the occasion had never arisen to come in again. By the look on Carey's face, she felt the same way.

"There's nothing here," she said. "We'll have to look in the bedroom."

"There's almost nothing of Tamsyn in the entire house," he said, almost to himself. "I wonder if he's cleared her out already."

Even in the closet, few of her clothes were hung beside Hugh's. However, her familiar duffle lay on the floor under her dresses. Daniel picked it up, opening it at once.

"Here we go," he said, extracting an orange notebook, possibly even the one he had seen her writing in on their drive. He scanned the pages. Seeing Tamsyn's handwriting was painful so soon after reading her diaries. Unfortunately, she had written nothing that could shed light on who had killed her.

Carey took the pack from him and rummaged through it. "Two books, some bracelets, her favorite chocolate bars. How could anyone have so few possessions? She must have abandoned her things when she moved in with Hugh. There's no other explanation."

Daniel flipped through the journal again, but it contained nothing more than a few wisps of poetry. It wasn't the damning evidence for which he had hoped. He handed it to Carey. She turned a few of the pages before putting it back in the pack and returned it to the spot in the closet where she'd found it.

"This isn't getting us anywhere," she said.

"There must be something," Daniel said. "There's got to be some clue to explain why all of this happened."

"I can think of one."

"Which is?"

"You only saw what you wanted to see," Carey answered. "To you, she was sexy and fun. I knew the side of her that had truly been broken. I've been thinking that she developed Borderline Personality Disorder after the rape. Of course, I didn't diagnose her myself. I mentioned her once to my old psychiatry professor."

"What is Borderline Personality Disorder?"

"It's a syndrome that develops after a severe trauma. The victim shows signs of intense emotional ups and downs, impulse control problems, and eroded self-image. Even violent tendencies."

"Tamsyn wasn't like that."

"You're wrong. Six months after Emma was born, Mum forced her to come back to try to work it out. She took half a bottle of sleeping pills, trying to end her life."

Daniel was stunned into silence.

"That's why they never made her come back again. They had to accept her on her terms from then on."

"Why didn't you tell me?"

Carey brushed her hair away from her face. "I knew how much it would upset you."

He sat down on the edge of the bed and looked at her. "Do you think Hugh knew?"

"I don't know. Tamsyn managed to keep the truth from you." She sighed. "What now? Are you ready to quit?"

"No. I still think she would have had a diary. Someone who kept one faithfully as a child wouldn't have abandoned the practice later."

"Hugh could have destroyed it, if there was one."

An idea was starting to form, and he looked at her. "You don't suppose she would have kept it on a computer, do you?"

"Where would it be?" Carey asked.

"The laptop is usually in the credenza downstairs in the media room. Hugh likes to surf the net while watching the telly."

"She wouldn't do that. It would be too risky for her to write incriminating things on a shared computer."

"She was a risk taker," Daniel replied. "If you're right, it might have even given her a thrill."

He took the stairs two at a time, with Carey right behind him. They went down the corridor, through the kitchen, and to the back of the house, which, for the previous owners, had once been a large, conservatory-like room for dinner parties that had probably been featured in *House & Garden*. Hugh had redone the room in dark paneling and thick leather chairs, and before Tamsyn had come along, the two of them had watched countless action films sprawled across them. A credenza stood to the left of the fireplace, and Daniel slipped open the door and took out a laptop. He lifted the top and turned on the power.

"I hate this," Carey said, as they waited for the computer to boot up.

"I don't like it any better than you."

A few seconds later, they were in.

"She's made a log for her favorite websites," Carey said, clicking on various icons. "Where would she keep something private, though? Online? If that's the case, we'll never find it."

"Something's telling me to look in plain sight." Daniel clicked on *My Documents* and they read through the list together: *Clothes websites, Emily Dickinson, Favorite Restaurants, Gloves and Hats, Wedding Ideas*. He hovered the mouse over *Emily Dickinson*. "Let's try this."

A document opened, the first few pages of which were poems by the late American poet. Carey frowned and then pointed to the number of pages in the document.

There were a hundred and eighty seven.

"I don't think Dickinson was that prolific," she said, "And even if she was…"

"Bingo," Daniel murmured, scrolling down. The first entry he stopped at arrested both of their attention.

Success! I was bolder than I thought today, actually having a conversation with Daniel Richardson on the ferry. I liked him more than I expected, but I have to stay focused on the goal. I've waited ten long years to make them pay for it. This is my chance, and I can't do anything to jeopardize it, no matter what.

Hugh was sitting inside with a drink. I could see him through the windows, and I wonder if he was looking at me. If he saw me, will he remember? If he remembers me, I won't be able to get close to him, but if not…

I stopped the conversation with Daniel about twenty minutes before we arrived in Dover. I had to distance myself from the two of them before landing. I threw the hat in the trash, changed into jeans and a T-shirt, and pulled my hair back in a knot. I even took off half my makeup to try to look younger. Who says a theatre background is useless? They got a cab together, and I followed some distance behind in another. It cost a bloody fortune, but I was able to stay close enough to see where Richardson was dropped off. Now I know where he lives. All I have to do is figure out what to do next.

"Dear God," Daniel whispered. "It's true."

Carey closed the screen and logged on to the Internet.

"What are you doing?" he asked.

"Emailing it to myself. I'm not going to sit here and read the whole thing like we have all the time in the world. We have to get out of here."

Just as she attached the document and hit send, the screen went black. They both jumped.

"The battery's gone flat," she said. He could see she was trying to get hold of herself.

"Check your mobile to see if you got it," he suggested.

She pulled her mobile from her pocket and sighed with relief. "I did."

"Then let's get out of here."

They left the house, locking the door and putting the key back exactly as they'd found it. Once in the street, he hailed a cab.

"Get in," he said.

Carey stepped inside and slid across the seat for him to get in beside her. Instead, Daniel closed the door.

"What are you doing?"

"I'll come by later. I have something to take care of first."

"You're going to see Hugh!" she cried.

Instead of answering, Daniel tapped on the roof twice and stepped back as the cab pulled away. From the back window, Carey was shooting him daggers. But the truth was, he was going to have to confront Hugh, and after what he had just learned, he didn't want her anywhere near the bastard.

THIRTY-THREE

BENEATH THE FOOTHILLS OF the Sierra de la Ventana mountains, six hours southwest of Buenos Aires, the Campo de Polo stretched across the secluded grasslands for miles. Its remote location was of particular interest to Hugh, who had wanted to visit the polo camp for several years. It was founded in 1910 and trained both beginner and intermediate riders to play. He did not aspire to be a professional—one could hardly remain undetected even in Argentina if one were to participate in a nationally or globally televised sport—but it had the feel of a good spa about it. It would do him good after all he had gone through.

He had always loved riding and knew he would train as an intermediate, at least. The accommodations, small private cabanas, were humbler than he preferred, but it would suit his purposes. There were regulation polo fields on perfect Bermuda grass, and even an indoor arena for practice on rainy days. Purebred racing ponies were raised on the ranch, and there was a fine selection from which to choose. He had spent hours comparing the mounts available. He favored a sinewy brown thoroughbred named Sultan, and hoped the horse would still be available by the time he arrived. Polo wasn't the only diversion that the Campo de Polo offered. After chukkas, cocktails and empanadas were served on the verandah each evening. There was an enormous pool where he would take a swim before retiring for the night. The physical demands of polo would keep his mind off everything that had happened, and when he tired of it after a season or two, he would take the train to Buenos Aires and find a flat.

Buenos Aires would be most stimulating. There was a surging expat population there, escaping hectic city life and careers in favor of the inexpensive lifestyle and slower pace. He'd considered other locations, like Bangkok or Portugal, but dismissed them after doing his research. Bangkok would be an amusing diversion at first, but he couldn't see himself living in Asia for the rest of his life. The culture was too different, and he knew he would long for England after a year or two. Portugal, while more familiar, was simply too close to Britain, and he would have a far greater chance of being discovered there. Argentina was not only on the other side of the world but in a different hemisphere. It had the romantic allure of Spain, with the added virtue of complete and total anonymity.

His bag was already packed. The passport tucked in the pocket of his coat bore the name Richard Marquardt. He'd had it made after Lizzie Marsden's death in case it ever became necessary to leave the country. That day had now arrived. Arrangements had been made. Tonight, he would take the ferry from Liverpool to Dublin and fly Aer Lingus to Puerto Rico before flying south to Argentina. He would travel light, bringing only one bag. Clothes could be bought, flats rented. He hated the thought of leaving his house, but there was no other choice. For the last several months, since Tamsyn had been back in his life, he had been moving money into an overseas account in anticipation of just such a move. Then DCI Murray had honed in on him. He could have gotten away with Tamsyn's murder, but killing Murray was a bridge too far.

He sat in his parents' brick-walled garden with a cup of coffee, looking at the arbor of climbing roses his mother had worked so long to achieve. Although she employed a gardener, she labored here every day. It was a full, mature garden twenty years in the making, and she was enormously proud of it. Dinner parties were held under the stars, with twinkling lights twined on the pergola that dripped with ivy and honeysuckle. It was quiet now, for the middle of the day. He sat back, looking at the pavers that led into the more formal areas of the garden, with small, discreet cherubs gracing the path. The parterre, with its symmetrical box hedges and gravel paths, was small but entrancing. Many days he had walked those paths, often after a fight with his father, to escape the anger in the house. It calmed him. He resolved to find gardens in Argentina. They would remind him of his mother and all that was right in the world.

It was hard to imagine that it would be his last day here, and for all he knew, the last time he would ever see his parents. The thought brought conflicting emotions. His father's gruff demeanor was more than a veneer. Noel had never gotten over his modest upbringing by a single mother or the poverty and the deprivation of life without a father or proper home. He was driven to leave a legacy, a dynasty even, and he had been harder on his son than anyone else. No matter what Hugh did, his father never seemed to approve. No role was great enough, no film would gross as much as his father's had. Hugh was competitive and would have liked to best him, but so far it hadn't happened, and now it was too late.

He pulled his mobile from his pocket and studied it. He wanted to talk to Daniel one more time. When he disappeared, he couldn't look back. He tried not to imagine it. Much easier, he thought, to focus on polo and days spent working up a sweat on the back of a sleek thoroughbred. Still, he wanted to talk to him. He dialed the number, mumbling a curse as it rang to voicemail. He didn't leave a message. He pocketed the mobile and lifted the cup to his lips just as his mother stepped out of the house.

"What a nice afternoon," she said, walking over to him. She pulled her hat forward to shade her eyes from the sun. "May I join you for a moment?"

"Of course."

She set her gardening shears on the table in front of him and sat down, pulling off her gloves. "I was going to cut some roses for the table. The boxwoods need trimming, but Wilkins would never forgive me if I touched them. You remember what happened last time."

"It looked a bit wobbly there for a bit, didn't it?" he answered. "You wouldn't want to incur his wrath."

"Again," she said, smiling. "Once was enough."

"Well, it's all recovered now. Your membership in the Royal Horticultural Society is in good standing."

She leaned forward and lowered her voice. "Do you know, the Simpsons have box blight? Everything's been infected. Their garden may take years to recover."

He felt a catch in his throat that the greatest rumor she could impart was the state of the Simpsons' garden. How would she feel when his crimes were revealed to the entire country? She would never get over it.

She didn't seem to notice that he hadn't answered and sat back, changing the subject. "Listen, darling. I wanted to talk to you about something. Your father and I were thinking of taking two or three weeks in Avignon. The Smythes have offered us the use of their farmhouse." She patted him on the arm. "You're welcome to come with us, of course. You could use some sun."

"I'd rather stay in London, but I think you should go," he replied, relieved. With his parents safely off to France, he wouldn't be missed for at least three weeks. It was an unexpected good turn of events, at a time when things had been going very poorly indeed. "It would be good for you to get away. This has been a strain on you too."

"I don't like to leave you at a time like this."

"You know as well as anyone that there's really nothing to be done. It's a process. And everyone grieves in their own way."

She paused, looking up at the house for a moment as though someone might be listening. She was like that when she was trying to tell him something important, making certain his father wasn't within earshot. "I haven't wanted to say anything, and forgive me if I am over-stepping, dear, but I felt that perhaps you didn't love her."

Hugh looked up into her eyes and saw something he didn't want to see. He tried to come up with a coherent response, settling on a bland, meaningless sentiment. "Love is different for each person."

"I even wondered if she was holding something over you," she ventured.

"Like what?" he asked before he could stop himself. When his mother didn't reply, he answered for her. "She wasn't pregnant, if that's what you were thinking. Besides, people aren't bothered by things like that these days, you know."

"I wasn't thinking of a pregnancy."

He flinched. Could she possibly have any idea of what had happened between him and Tamsyn? Or, for that matter, Lizzie Marsden? But that was impossible. There had been no clues left behind. He'd made certain of that.

"There's nothing," he said. "I just haven't wanted to talk about it."

"Of course, of course," she replied.

She wouldn't bring it up again, and while that in itself was a relief, he was going to swan off to Argentina and she would be left behind to deal with the fallout for years. He hadn't realized the extent to which his actions would have an impact on everyone. He didn't particularly care if his father was infuriated by the whole business, but his mother was another matter. It would kill her.

Hugh took a gulp of air. How had everything turned out like this, anyway? He thought back to that night in Wales, which he remembered in great detail. Marc had been reluctant, but he had wanted to prove something, though he wasn't sure what. He had wanted to seize control of something, and Tamsyn had been the nearest target. If it hadn't been her, would it have been someone else? He had never forced anyone again, but the desire for power continued to consume him. He had funneled that desire into appropriate channels, like building his career and working on his house, but at his core, he was restless, unfulfilled, and angry. Lizzie Marsden had been sucked into the vortex the night she died. If she had shown up at his door on any other night, there might have been an entirely different result. Hugh lived with the fear that something like that might happen again, but the situation hadn't presented itself until Tamsyn burst into his life and forced his hand.

"Well, I'll leave you to it," his mother said, interrupting his thoughts.

He reached out and took her hand, glad at least that she couldn't see his desperate thoughts. He wanted to fold her in his arms, but of course she would know something was wrong. She probably already knew it. He released her hand, and, in that moment, he gave her up forever.

"I'm going to ring Daniel," he said.

He gave her the briefest smile, which was no indication of how emotional he was beginning to feel, and then went inside the house. His father was probably at the club, and his mother wandered into the back of the garden. He went up the staircase, his shoes making no sound on the carpeted steps. Once in his bedroom, he shut the door. He couldn't leave England without hearing Daniel's voice one more time. If it weren't impossible, if he could have spoken freely without judgment or shame, the one thing he would have wanted to tell him was that he didn't kill Tamsyn. Not really. She'd been leading him on a death march, and no one could survive that. Not him, and certainly not Tamsyn Burke.

Suddenly, he heard a commotion in the street below. He avoided looking out of the windows at all costs, knowing if he did it would be on the BBC within the half hour. He refused to give the press more fodder for their sensationalist stories; however, the mild roar outside convinced him that something out of the ordinary was happening. He lifted back the curtain just enough to see Daniel fighting his way through the crowd.

Hugh let the curtain fall back into place. He should have been pleased. Daniel was exactly the person he wanted to talk to, but this was a bad sign. Either he had figured out what had happened or he thought he had. Even Inspector Murray had gotten it wrong. He sighed, slipping the mobile back into his pocket. He had wanted to talk to him on the phone; a final, remote goodbye, leaving their relationship intact and preserving, at least in his mind, the friendship they had shared for so long. Seeing him in person made everything so much harder. And if Daniel knew anything even close to the truth, all hell was about to break loose.

THIRTY-FOUR

DANIEL STEPPED OUT OF the taxi down the road from the Ashley-Hunts' house, not because he didn't want Hugh to know he was coming but because the paparazzi were camped about, trying to get a glimpse of the film star or one of his famous parents during their time of grief. It seemed the longer Hugh avoided them, the more frenzied they'd become. Daniel had barely taken three steps before someone shouted his name and the focus turned toward him. Undeterred, he muscled his way through the crowd, impeded by microphones thrust in his face and reporters stepping in front of him trying to get an exclusive interview or even a short remark. He shook his head, saying only, "Excuse me," and made his way over cables and cords, enduring flashes by the dozens. He'd had no idea that the press were so thoroughly encamped around the house. It was yet another downside to acting. One's life simply wasn't one's own.

Once Daniel had fended off questions and shouts, he opened the gate, walked up to the front door, and rang the bell. It was an unseasonably warm day and he wondered if the curiosity seekers were as faithful on rainy ones. A long minute passed before the door finally opened.

A man, obviously a plainclothes guard, answered the door. He had a gun strapped to his belt and appraised Daniel thoroughly. "Yes?"

"I'm Daniel Richardson, a friend of Hugh's."

"No one is scheduled to visit today."

"He'll see me."

As he replied, Hugh came walking down the stairs. "It's all right, Finch."

"Go back upstairs, sir. He'll be allowed up after I've checked him."

"Send him to my father's study when you're done."

Finch closed the front door and then looked at Daniel. "Raise your arms, please."

Daniel hesitated before complying with his request. The security guard patted under his arms, then ran his hands down to Daniel's waist, feeling around it before brushing the back of his hand down his chest in a smooth, long movement. He checked his pockets and ran his hand down his legs and ankles, probing for a hidden gun or knife. Of course, there was none. He had never carried a weapon in his life.

Finch nodded and stepped aside, and Daniel went up the stairs. He had always loved coming to this house for family suppers and parties, for nights spent watching television or playing video games when they were younger, and to pick Hugh up when they were older and went on the town. It had always been something he had enjoyed. Now, every step was torture. Hugh had killed Tamsyn, and probably even Lizzie Marsden.

Daniel didn't know what he was going to say to him, but it didn't matter. It was time to clear the air and he wouldn't leave until he did.

Hugh was nowhere in sight as he approached the study. He went forward, palms sweating, to the open door at the end of the corridor. He stepped into the familiar room, where he had drunk wine and chatted with Hugh's father not two months before. The desk dominated the center of the room, and everything was in its place. Behind the desk, the French doors were open to the balcony. The Persian rug, a deep claret red with a swirling mass of whirls, made him feel dizzy and disoriented.

This was the first time he had been alone in this room. He moved away from the doorway, wanting to keep some space between himself and Hugh when his friend arrived. Glancing up to be certain he was alone, he walked over to the desk and stood behind it. The old walnut shined as if it had been freshly polished. There were a few volumes stacked on one corner, and a chestnut leather diary lay open to reveal pristine white pages of that precise week. None of the days had entries. On both sides of the desk there were three drawers, and Daniel reached for the one on the top right and slid it open without a sound. Nothing of particular importance was inside. There were papers, on top of which sat a silver magnifying glass. Hearing footsteps in the hall, he slid it shut again and walked over to stand in front of the desk.

Hugh walked up to the doorway and leaned against the frame, arms crossed. "You're looking grim."

"We need to talk," Daniel said, feeling his nerves pulsing in his body. He wasn't the sort to confront anyone, least of all about murder. Yet he had loved Tamsyn, and she had been brave enough to face Hugh head-on when she died. He could do no less.

"Want to sit?" Hugh asked.

"No," he answered, shaking his head. "I want to talk. I want you to tell me everything."

Hugh gave a small smile and walked into the room, settling himself in one of the leather chairs. A breeze blew in through the French doors, ruffling the light, sheer curtain.

"'Everything' would include a very broad scope of topics, old chap. What exactly do you want me to tell you?"

"Let's start with the truth."

Hugh tapped one of his shoes lightly upon the floor. "The truth is a difficult thing, Daniel. And let's be honest. Sometimes you're better off not knowing it."

"I don't even know who you are anymore."

"Of course you do. I'm the one you grew up with. I'm the one who gave you the shot at having a better life. I'm the one who's closer than a brother."

"I may have done Alex a disservice."

"Well, you might be a bit hasty there. And frankly, I'd be careful if I were you, because whatever you say in this room cannot be taken back."

Daniel suddenly realized he was shaking. "You killed Tamsyn!" he said. "I just want to fucking know why."

"It's not as if I wanted to, you know," Hugh replied. "I didn't go looking for her. And in case you've forgotten, it was the other way round. She became a threat I had to deal with."

Daniel was taken aback. He hadn't expected Hugh to admit it so quickly. He'd thought he would have to cudgel him over the head with facts and drag the truth out of him.

"How did you find out?" Hugh asked.

"I went to Wales with Carey," Daniel said. "She took me to the light-house and told me that Tamsyn had been raped by two English boys. Later, I found newspaper clippings of you and your father in Tamsyn's room. They'd been there for years. She recognized you the night of the rape and decided that one day, she would do something about it."

Hugh raised a brow. "Did you find out about the child, too?"

For a moment, Daniel was silenced. "I didn't know you knew."

"When I figured out who Tamsyn was, I put a detective on the case. He brought me photos of the girl. She's obviously Hayley's bloody brat. You don't even need a DNA test to see that. The dark hair, the hazel eyes."

"But—"

"I wasn't the father, but it didn't matter to Tamsyn who got her pregnant. She was after me. She judged me at fault for what happened to her."

"Why did you rape her?"

The question hung in the air, and Daniel could see that Hugh was struggling with his answer.

"We were kids, Daniel. Just kids. It was just a single night when everything went horribly wrong. It never happened again."

Hugh was telling the truth, he could tell. For a moment, Daniel could see it through his eyes: Hugh had made one mistake and would pay for it for the rest of his life. He couldn't imagine living with something like that. But in spite of the fact that Hugh had suffered, Tamsyn had suffered more.

"She tried to kill herself, you know."

Hugh stood. "No, I didn't know."

"When did you realize who she was?"

"I recognized her on the ferry," Hugh replied, "but I wasn't sure where I'd seen her before. It was when you brought her to Dorset that first day that I knew. If you recall, she stood on the doorstep as bold as you please."

"Fucking hell."

"That's one way to put it."

"You shouldn't have even spoken to her, let alone encouraged Sir John to hire her for the film. The whole thing makes me sick."

"It was her own fault, Daniel," he said. "The stupid bitch should have known she would never get away with it. It was an incredibly reckless thing to do."

Daniel reached out and grabbed him by the collar. "Shut up. Don't talk about her like that."

"Touched a nerve, did I?" Hugh asked, holding his hands up. "Well, she wasn't worth it. She was a liar through and through. She would have killed me when I wasn't looking and then taken everything I had. She betrayed you. She betrayed me. She was just like Lizzie Marsden, trying to bring us down."

"Stop," Daniel warned.

"And for the record, it didn't happen the way you're ~~imaging~~ imagining it, either."

"I said, stop!"

Hugh pulled away from his grasp. "You're not the only one who is hurt here."

"What on earth do you mean?"

"I lost something too, that day. I knew when it happened that I would lose you both. The worst part was knowing that you could take her away from me. She wanted you more."

Daniel's mouth dropped open. "You didn't even want her."

"Well, technically, I did, but you don't want to know what for."

Daniel punched him squarely in the jaw and stepped back, shocked at his own anger. He shook his hand, his knuckles stinging from the punch.

"Shit!" Hugh cried, rubbing his jaw. "That hurt. You have a better right hook than I thought."

"You killed Lizzie too."

"Of course I did. You know what a bitch she could be. She was going to blab to the tabloids to take us both down. She was fixated on the fact that my father had grown up poor and liked to rub it in. Someone was bound to kill her, sooner or later."

"Life's just one big chess match to you, isn't it? You're moving people around like pawns."

"I was trying to keep you from getting hurt."

"You weren't thinking of me. You were thinking of yourself."

"Aren't we sanctimonious? You would have let Lizzie fucking ruin us and gone happily back to Brighton to sell fish and chips. And this time, you would have let Tamsyn kill me and then taken her into your bed and turned a blind eye."

"She wouldn't have," Daniel protested, but he knew he was wrong. Tamsyn had been hell-bent on revenge and would probably have killed Hugh just as soon as the opportunity presented itself. He stood just feet away from him, fist still poised in the air in front of him, watching Hugh flex his jaw.

"See," Hugh said. "You can't even convince yourself."

Daniel shook his head, trying to decide what to do. He couldn't let Hugh get away with killing the girl he loved. Or could he? Could he walk out the door and leave Hugh to the police investigation? Was it his place to avenge her death? It was hard to believe any of it, in fact: how Tamsyn had planned to exact revenge on Hugh over months, even years; how Hugh knew all along and had the nerve to let her playact her dangerous little drama; or even how he, Daniel, had been caught up in the life of a man who raped and murdered as easily as jingling coins in his pocket. "*All we like sheep have gone astray*," he recalled from the *Book of Common Prayer*. How could he not have realized that something was seriously wrong with the one person with whom he had spent more time than any other in the last ten years? Hugh was his best friend. Now, even knowing the truth, it was hard to believe.

"Ironic, isn't it?" Hugh asked. He stepped behind his father's desk and opened the upper left-hand drawer.

Daniel suddenly realized both Hugh and his father were left-handed. He had opened the wrong drawer. Before he could react, Hugh pulled out a pistol and pointed it directly at Daniel's chest. "You're the last person I ever wanted to hurt."

"Give me the gun."

"You know, I had higher hopes for you. I thought our friendship was strong enough to last through anything."

Daniel reached out; to do what, he did not know; but Hugh darted out of his reach.

"Wait," he said. "It doesn't have to end like this."

"How does it end, then?" Hugh asked. "I let you turn me in to the police? Spend the rest of my life rotting in prison?"

"Don't be stupid. Just give me the gun."

Hugh cocked the pistol and looked him in the eye. Daniel could see the fear and the regret, but before he could react, Hugh lowered the gun and fired. The bullet shot into the thick muscle of Daniel's thigh. He cried out, tumbling forward onto the rug. Hugh placed his heel against Daniel's shoulder, pinning him to the ground.

"What a fucking mess," Hugh said. "Why couldn't you have left it alone? I'll have to tell Finch you tried to kill me."

Daniel didn't reply. His leg was on fire from the bullet. He turned and looked up over his shoulder at Hugh. His life, his career; nothing mattered but to stop Hugh from killing again. And he would definitely kill again; probably beginning with the guard downstairs. Bullet or not, he had to do something.

Hugh raised the gun, but Daniel came up underneath him, pushing Hugh's leg up with him. As he rose, his leg searing with pain and blood seeping down his trouser, he lifted Hugh nearly off his feet and up against the open doors, onto the balcony. Hugh seized hold of the curtain, but the rod broke off the wall. He teetered against the ledge for an instant, the gun clattering onto the ground below. He fought to grasp the railing as he slid over the side. There was an ugly moment as his long limbs, admired by thousands of women around the world, went over the rail, and Daniel's oldest friend fell to the unforgiving concrete below.

Daniel heard the screams of the journalists in the street as he sank down on the balcony, trying not to lose consciousness.

THIRTY-FIVE

THE MOMENT DANIEL LEFT her in Westminster Abbey, the room felt strangely empty. Tamsyn turned away from the door, the white satin of her wedding dress rustling with the small movement. It was all she could do not to run after him. She turned over in her mind all it had taken to get to this point: ten years of plotting, and even then she had been forced to rely on luck. Still, she had succeeded. She was minutes away from fulfilling the vow she'd made to herself that dark night at the lighthouse in Llandudno, the promise that she would get revenge on the English boys who had raped her.

Marc Hayley was Emma's father. She had known it as soon as she'd seen the dark-haired infant. But it hadn't really mattered. The rape had been Hugh's idea. He was the one who'd chatted her up and had driven her away from the beach and away from any chance for a normal life that she would ever have. He had raped her and then held her down while Marc raped her too. Hayley had been reluctant, even trying to stop what they all knew could not be stopped. He would pay as well, though not with his life. Hugh was another matter altogether.

It was still frightening to remember the rape. The powerlessness. The fear. The sweat that broke out all over her body. The persistent shaking that could not be stilled. The whites of Hugh's eyes had seemed yellow in the dim light; yellow and round like a full moon, his breath hot against her cheek.

She remembered the gulls gliding through the steamy summer air above them, and the smell of the sea and damp grass. It soaked through the T-shirt that she'd put on over her swimsuit. She hadn't put on her shorts, tossing them into her bag lest she slow down the mood and the boys went off to flirt with another girl. Even now, she could close her eyes and feel the hard grit of sand and rocks on her buttocks as Hugh jerked off her bikini and seized her hair to hold her down. He was half mad that night, a monster driven by the desire to dominate, and it happened so quickly she was still bewildered that the boy she had thought so charming could change into something she didn't even recognize.

At fifteen, she'd still had baby fat. She still dreamed of meeting a lovely boy and sitting on a beach, reading Emily Dickinson and T.S. Eliot together under a golden moon. She had hoped to go to university to study English, and perhaps one day to write herself. Instead, she was wrestled to the ground, stripped naked as only an adolescent girl can be, her wrists pinned down, and violated again and again. She would always feel dirty, as though streaks of semen would perpetually drip down her pale, shivering thighs. No matter how many times she closed her eyes to sleep she would never wake without a gasp, remembering. The pain would never leave her. She had never had any choice but to find him and kill him.

Daniel Richardson had nearly ruined everything. When she'd attracted his attention on the ferry, he was only meant to be a means of getting to Hugh. Yet he was so unexpected, so different from anyone she had ever met. He was genuine and interesting. He was funny, and wicked, and self-deprecating in the best way. She felt something for him that she had never felt for anyone else, though she couldn't act on it. He loved Hugh, and astonishingly, he loved her.

He loved her. She knew it. But there was nothing she could do about it now. Love, as much as the world would have one believe otherwise, wasn't more important than revenge. In her weaker moments, Tamsyn thought of Daniel and what a relationship with him would be like, but she wasn't certain normal bonds were even possible for someone like her, someone forged by the tragedy of her past.

She could have killed Hugh the first night she'd spent at his house in Dorset. He had gone to bed and shut the door without locking it. Perhaps, she had thought at the time, it had even been an invitation of sorts, although she was certain he hadn't recognized her. And now here they were, she and Hugh, in Westminster Abbey, about to marry in front of everyone they knew. He would get his punishment soon enough, and she would reap the revenge she had long desired.

"Great dress," a voice said behind her. It was smooth and rich, the sort everyone loved in his films.

She turned to look at Hugh. "I'm glad you like it."

He looked at her for a long moment, the only sound in the room the ticking of the clock on the wall. He was standing just inside the door, several feet away. "Are you sure you're ready for this?"

"Are you?" she asked. She glanced at the bouquet that sat on a table next to where he was standing.

"We don't have to go through with it, you know," he said.

"Hand me the flowers, will you?" she answered, ignoring his remark.

He frowned but picked up the posy of budding white roses, which had been wrapped in thick laps of green ribbon around the stem. "Are you worried about the expense?" he asked. "It's nothing, I assure you. You just shouldn't do anything you aren't fully prepared to do."

Tamsyn met his eyes. "I've burned my bridges. What about you?"

"Oh, I'm always prepared." He stepped closer.

She felt a frisson of fear. It wasn't the Hugh of the last few months that stood looking her in the eye. It was the primal Hugh who had raped her and left her stranded on the isolated beach in a ripped bikini and a bloody, stained shirt. She itched to grab the bouquet. In the stem, she'd wrapped a long, thin, razor-sharp knife; it was her contingency plan in case something went horribly wrong. But she forced herself not to reach for it yet. She would take it from him when he came closer and stab him in the heart before he knew what had happened.

Hugh gave a small laugh and raised a brow. "Well, it's your choice, Tam. I gave you the chance to walk away."

"I was never going to walk away."

"I have to say, I couldn't believe the nerve it must have taken you to walk through that door in Dorset last fall. I quite admired that. If anyone thinks you aren't a good actress, I would sincerely like to set them straight. Tell me why you did all this. That's all I want to know."

"I've been planning to kill you since the day you raped me."

He laughed, apparently surprised. "Well, you've had plenty of chances. The question is, why have you waited? Are you hoping that two hundred people will watch you do it?"

"I couldn't care less who sees me do it."

Suddenly, he went still. "You waited until now because of Daniel, didn't you?"

"You sound jealous, Hugh."

"Oh, I'm jealous. I'm completely fucking jealous, but not about you."

"You're jealous of him," she said, raising a brow. "Everyone thinks you're so alike: best friends, actors. Only you're nothing like him, are you? You're the broken one. You're the one who couldn't get your own father to love you and you have to prove yourself over and over."

"You don't know what you're talking about."

"I know exactly what I'm talking about. You wish you were Daniel. Even your parents love him more than you. You've spent your life trying to keep his love when you don't deserve it. He would hate you if he knew what you were capable of."

"You know, I currently have something more pressing to deal with—like a fiancée who brought a knife to the wedding." Hugh loosened the long green ribbon and pulled the knife from the stem of the bouquet, holding it close to her face. "I could kill you right here in Westminster Fucking Abbey, with everyone you know on the other side of that door."

"I didn't expect to come out of this alive." Tamsyn stood her ground. "Although, to be honest, I thought if you knew who I was, you might try to kill me in Fiji."

"'Bride goes missing after romantic boat ride.' How unfortunate for the grieving young widower. Instead of starting a life together, it ends tragically." Hugh lowered the knife and brushed it with his finger. "Not that it hadn't crossed my mind."

"If you knew, why did you go along with it?"

"What, I'm going to turn down a woman who would screw me and plot my death in the same breath? You should have gone to Vegas, baby. No one plays the odds like you."

Tamsyn stared at him. "You have to pay for what you did."

She cursed herself for trembling. As a young girl, she'd once gone to Norway on holiday with her family, and she could still remember the huge whirlpools churning beside the ship as they'd gone through Saltstraumen. Her father had told her it was the strongest tidal current in the world. She'd stood next to him on the deck, riveted by the sight of those enormous, violent swirls of water like the ones that Jules Verne had surmised could pull down an entire ship. It was the most beautiful, deadly thing she had ever seen. And here she was again, standing in a maelstrom now, about to be swallowed whole.

It wasn't until after she knew she was pregnant that she'd come across his photo in a magazine. She would never forget that moment. It was as if the wind had been physically knocked out of her. She had known the boy was rich—the way he dressed and spoke assured her of that—but she'd had no idea he was the son of a film star. Yet she didn't tell anyone who it was, certainly not her parents. They'd become the enemy after daily rows over whether or not she should have an abortion. She didn't want to carry the child to term, but they thought it would be a mistake and that she would regret it.

Instead, she regretted her daughter, and her fury with Hugh Ashley-Hunt only grew. For weeks after she'd found the photo, she stared at it, withdrawing into a world of imagined scenarios. She knew she would kill him. Even if he wasn't the one who got her pregnant, he was the one who had destroyed her life, someone who deserved to die.

But after a few years, another idea had taken hold. Killing him was not good enough. She wanted to humiliate him first, and then take his life.

And she had done it. The ferry, getting close to Daniel—everything had all fallen into place. Her initial plan to shoot Hugh no longer seemed the best option; poison would be a more insidious, painful death. And by waiting until a few weeks after the wedding, she would inherit his fortune. Money would not erase the pain that Hugh had inflicted on her, but millions of pounds would make the pain and suffering easier to bear.

Then there was Daniel. She knew he loved her, and after Hugh's death, nothing would stand in their way.

"You know something?" Hugh asked. "If you hadn't walked through the sodding door that day, you could have saved us all the trouble."

He dropped the bouquet onto the floor. As Tamsyn reached to snatch the knife, he grabbed her roughly and pressed his lips against hers. She tried to pull back for air, but before she could, he plunged the knife into her and then, just as quickly, pulled it out and stepped back.

Her chest was instantly on fire. She couldn't speak. She was aware of nothing but pain as she crumpled to the floor. This was it, she thought, the end of everything. She wouldn't get to kill him after all. She tried to move her head, but the effort was too much. Within moments, everything was quiet and cold and still.

———

The Montgomery Curse, according to the Ashley-Hunt family legend, was so called due to a series of family catastrophes that had culminated with a tragedy more than twenty years ago. It had begun on a crisp October day in Hampshire. Noel Ashley-Hunt had left his wife and young son, Hugh, in London for a weekend of stag hunting in the country. His brother-in-law, Garrett Montgomery, had invited him and a few others, including Garrett's father, Richard Montgomery, for the weekend. Noel was not an accomplished hunter, but he relished a day in the country like most men. There is something bracing and rejuvenating about walking through scrub and brush in boots and hunting garb, enjoying the cool autumn weather and the change of seasons, that releases one from the ordinary problems of life.

Not that Ashley-Hunt wasn't content. His life was just as he wanted it at that moment. Caroline had been safely delivered of a son, who was a delightful tot of two that year. His career was firmly established, and they had recently signed the deed on the property in Gloucestershire that had a house he was certain they would enjoy for the rest of their lives. Things were not as sanguine with the Montgomery clan, however. He knew from his wife that Garrett was experiencing financial difficulties. In fact, he had been surprised to have received the hunting invitation in light of what he had heard, but when he discovered that his wife's father was to be among the party, he assumed that Garrett planned to take the opportunity to pump the old man for an advance on his inheritance while scoring points with his set.

If the weather had not been so perfect that fall, Noel might have declined the offer. Garrett wasn't his favorite relative; he was known for his long and boring elucidations on the state of government and occasionally religion, a topic Noel avoided altogether. But the weather was indeed perfect, and he had just finished a tiresome film set in Hungary. He was tired of eating goulash and cabbage and Wiener schnitzel. He was in the mood for good English beef and roasted potatoes, and for two days mucking about in Hampshire with the possibility of bagging a red deer.

He had arrived for the weekend the evening before, along with Garrett's father and one other guest, John Burton. Garrett's wife had made a quite decent meal for supper, after which they had retired to the library to enjoy a good bottle of Glenfiddich and a cigar. The mood was jovial among the four men. Garrett hadn't ruined the evening with talk of money. For his part, Noel was relieved. He didn't want to be caught in an awkward situation when he had come for the purpose of relaxation.

The following morning, two other friends arrived early and the hunting party commenced. The first day was unprofitable, huntwise, though Noel quite enjoyed the trek through the forest, finding a delightful stream where he might want to return to fish. He appreciated a break from the incessant activity of London. It was on the second morning, an hour after they had gone into the forest, that he heard a shot. He was some distance away and thought one of the lucky fellows had spotted a stag. He had decided to continue to explore on his own when he suddenly heard shouting. Richard Montgomery had been shot, and Garrett was in a panic. His father had moved into the line of fire and taken a bullet straight through the heart. Police and emergency crews were summoned, but it was too late. The inquest was held a few days later, exonerating Garrett of wrongdoing. It was an unfortunate incident, part of the Curse.

It was not until years later that Hugh stumbled upon a different version of the story. Noel kept a shelf of leather-bound books in which he wrote impressions of his life. They were not diaries, per se, but notes, perhaps for a future autobiography. One day, Hugh began slipping them out of the study to read. It was quite enlightening, in more ways than one. Noel, though reticent and even gruff in the presence of his son, was quite forthcoming in his memoirs. It was some months after Hugh had first begun to read the journals that he discovered a section about his grandfather's death that weekend in Hampshire.

Garrett's asked me for money, Noel had written. *His father has refused his request for another bailout and decided to take a hard line with him.* Noel, too, had refused Garrett's request. He didn't want to sully their relationship with financial obligations that might never be repaid. And as much as he enjoyed a weekend in the country, if Garrett was forced to sell his property and find something more on his level, Noel would still have other friends who could extend such offers in his stead.

Garrett had been furious, according to Noel's account, and a wicked argument ensued. The only reason Noel had not left Hampshire in the middle of the weekend was because his father-in-law especially asked him to stay. When the old man was shot, Noel knew at once that it hadn't been an accident. Yet he refused to say as much to the police.

Hugh had read this with a great deal of interest. Was his father afraid of Garrett? Did he think turning him in would spark an angry confrontation that would result in his own death? The truth, however, when Hugh finally read it in his father's own words, was chilling: *As much as I cared for Richard, alerting the authorities to the true nature of the shooting would have ruined my career. I didn't want to be known as the actor who had a murderer in the family. I believed, too, that Caroline's portion of the inheritance would be beneficial to Hugh one day, and therefore I made the best decision I could on the spur of the moment.*

The Montgomery Curse was not, as Hugh had once believed, a series of misfortunes that befell their family. The curse was that a Montgomery would do what a Montgomery must if someone stood in his way. Tamsyn, like Lizzie Marsden before her and Chief Inspector Murray after, was an impediment to the future Hugh had planned for himself. He had no choice but to remove any obstacle that threatened his well-being. Tamsyn had been that obstacle, and he had killed her without remorse.

———

Now, it was done. Tamsyn lay in front of him, lifeless. Hugh wrapped the knife in a plastic bin liner and went to dispose of it. There were drops of blood on his coat, but in the frenzy that would ensue, no one would notice. When he came back and crouched over her body again, he would get covered in blood anyway.

For one hollow moment before he screamed for help, he let himself bask in the glow of success. Tamsyn didn't have to die, but she, like any other obstacle he faced, had now been dealt with. Like her, he had gambled it all in a single moment. And the odds, as far as he was concerned, were that everything would go his way from that moment on.

THIRTY-SIX

DANIEL STOOD UNDER AN ancient yew tree at the graveyard some distance from the group of mourners and lit a cigarette. His resolve not to smoke had evaporated in the aftermath of Hugh's death, along with much of his desire to keep on living. He knew he was not welcome. He knew, too, that he should hate him for everything he'd done, but ever since Hugh died, he had been wracked with an emptiness he'd never known before. That first night, after he had been released from the hospital without being charged, he had dulled the pain of being shot by drinking half a bottle of Scotch. It was impossible to reconcile the Hugh who had murdered three people with the friend he had loved so much. Daniel remembered their juvenile antics at school; the long, lazy holidays spent in Gloucestershire messing about in the village; the years when they were making homes in London and settling into their careers. Every good memory he possessed, it seemed, included Hugh, and losing that part of his life was as painful as losing Tamsyn, if not more so. It had occurred to him that she had been his first attempt at independence from Hugh, as though the friendship, unbeknownst to him, had somehow begun to erode. Standing here now, watching Noel and Caroline Ashley-Hunt with friends and relatives—including, damn him, Marc Hayley—Daniel felt completely at sea. Carey hadn't answered his calls. Tamsyn and Hugh were dead. His career, which had once meant so much to him, felt stifling. He was overdue to report to the set of his next film, but he dreaded it with his entire being.

The vicar intoned a final prayer and even from a distance, Daniel knew it was over. Police kept the paparazzi from the scene, but they raised their cameras from a distance hoping for a cover shot. The crowd began to disperse, peeling themselves away from the fresh mound of plowed earth and leaning on one another for support. Caroline looked particularly fragile. For one brief second, Daniel caught Noel's eye, and then the elder Ashley-Hunt turned his back and took his wife's arm. Even after everyone had gone—the family, to what would likely be a long seclusion; friends to various pubs for a fortifying drink; the vicar to check his schedule for the next item on his checklist—Daniel lingered, feeling empty. He couldn't approach Hugh's grave. He would see it one day when he could bear it, but just now the wounds were too fresh.

He thought of Tamsyn's daughter, and of what explanations might be given to her for what had happened. He tapped his mobile. There was no one but Carey with whom he could discuss the tragedy, but she hadn't returned his calls. If he hadn't confronted Hugh on his own, none of this would have happened. He was in limbo, as a Catholic would define it: literally, the edge of Hell.

He lost track of how long he stood there. Certainly long enough to intensify the throbbing in his leg. Tired from the exertion, he looked at his watch. Another difficult task lay ahead. He had to go to Scotland Yard soon to give a final statement regarding the case. He would probably face some difficulty with Inspector Murray, who hadn't wanted them to meddle, and they were certain to want more information about how he and Carey had come to be in Hugh's house. He would shoulder responsibility for everything. It was the least he could do.

The sun was hot, a welcome change from most of the last month, when it had rained almost incessantly. After a moment, he took his leave and walked to his car, the warmth radiating through the dappled leaves onto his back.

———————

Scotland Yard looked more imposing than usual, if only because Daniel loathed having to relive everything. He'd started awake each night since Hugh died, sweating and panicked, and had come to the decision to leave London for a while to rethink his life. His bags were already packed. This would be the final hurdle. He forced himself to open the door and went up to the desk to speak to a sergeant.

"Daniel Richardson," he said to the officer at the desk. "Here to see DCI Murray."

The constable looked at him long and hard for a moment and consulted his computer before replying. "DCI Murray was killed this week in the line of duty. Your appointment today is with Detective Chief Inspector Michael Hardwicke, who has taken over the Burke case."

Daniel was stunned. He had avoided the news, with its endless loops of sensationalist stories rehashing Hugh's death. He was shown into a room with a table and hard metal chairs. He pulled out a chair, wondering how everything had turned out like this and wishing Carey was sitting beside him. They had come to rely on each other, or so he had thought. A few minutes later, a young sergeant came in and closed the door behind him.

"May I?" he said, putting his hand on a chair. "I'm Detective Sergeant Ennis. I worked with Chief Inspector Murray."

Daniel nodded. "Of course."

"I'm not really here in an official capacity," the sergeant said, sitting at the table opposite Daniel. "Inspector Hardwicke has been detained, so I thought I would stop in. How's the leg?"

Daniel shrugged. "It'll heal. Fortunately, he missed a major artery. What happened to Inspector Murray?"

"You don't know?" Ennis paused. "He was strangled in his car. From his notes, he was investigating Hugh. It's clear that Hugh got to him first."

"I'm sorry," Daniel said, stunned. "He was a good man."

"He was probably the best detective I'll ever work with," Ennis answered. "He had a dog..."

"A dog?"

"A pup, really. He asked me to get it for him a couple of weeks ago. I had to go back to his house to get the poor fellow."

Daniel looked at him for a moment and realized that Ennis was struggling almost as much as he was. The sergeant stood and went over to the counter, where there was a pot of coffee. He poured two cups and brought them back to the table.

"For lack of anything better," he said, placing one in front of Daniel.

"Thanks."

Ennis took his seat and tasted the coffee. "He was an unusual man, Murray. He lost himself after his wife died, from what I hear. Buried himself in his work. He didn't really talk things out, about cases, I mean. He was a thinker who ruminated over every little detail. He was a talented detective. I don't know why I'm even telling you this."

"It must have been a shock."

"I wish I'd had longer to learn from him." Ennis drank the last of the coffee and crumpled the cup in his hand. "You might be interested to know that Carey Burke was here."

"She was?" Daniel sat up in his chair. He might be able to see her, he thought. Ennis dashed that hope immediately.

"She's left London, I'm afraid." He consulted his watch. "She took the train back to Wales about an hour ago."

Daniel set down his cup. He felt even worse knowing he had missed her.

"I told her something I think you should know too. We uncovered the source of the death threat that Ashley-Hunt received a few days before the wedding."

"I'd forgotten about that," Daniel said, leaning forward. "If Hugh was the killer, who would have sent him a death threat?"

"A family friend of the Burkes' . . . Nick Oliver. Do you know him?"

"Oliver?" Daniel repeated, stunned. "Yes, I met him. But why would he have threatened Hugh? He wasn't close to Tamsyn."

"It was a manipulation on his part. If he could scare Tamsyn and Carey into thinking there was a true threat to Ashley-Hunt, they might have come back to Wales. He was fixated on Carey, wanting their relationship to be more than it was. He had no idea what was going on between Hugh and Tamsyn. The police picked him up yesterday. He was released on a caution."

Daniel shook his head. "What a bloody mess. It's hard to believe that Hugh was capable of killing someone, but I think it's almost worse that Tamsyn was."

"According to Miss Burke's journals, she had been plotting to kill Hugh for a very long time," Ennis said. "She didn't realize how dangerous Hugh really was. If she'd tried to make him think her child was his, it would have fueled the fire."

"He told me the minute he saw the photos that he knew that Emma was Marc Hayley's child."

"Yes. And it happens to be true," Ennis answered. "A DNA test was done two days ago. The results were positive."

"What will happen to her, then?" Daniel asked. "The Burkes won't lose her, will they?"

"No, she'll stay with her grandparents. It's possible that Hayley could still be charged with rape, but that decision has yet to be made."

Daniel sat there for a minute. "I thought I was helping, somehow. If only I hadn't bollocksed everything..."

"Don't blame yourself," Ennis said. "Pursuing facts in a case doesn't change them. Hugh murdered at least three times in his life, and he would have killed again."

"You know about Lizzie Marsden?"

"We believe that's how Inspector Murray knew Ashley-Hunt had killed Tamsyn. He was pursuing a new theory in Lizzie Marsden's death." Ennis tapped his finger on the table. "Hugh might have gotten away with Tamsyn's murder, but Murray was closing in. And you were getting too close with your, shall we say, informal investigation."

"I didn't go to his house to kill him," Daniel said. "I wanted him to turn himself in."

"I'm not suggesting you should have taken the law into your own hands, but you did stop him from killing again. No matter what Hardwicke says, and he's liable to fall on you like a ton of bricks, you have to feel good about that."

Daniel sighed, unconvinced, as Ennis tossed his cup in the bin, nodded, and left the room.

———

Two weeks later, Daniel was ensconced in a cottage in Cornwall, hundreds of miles from anyone he knew. He had been there only a short time, but already he had a routine.

The house, which he had chosen from a dozen offered him by an estate agent, was modest by any standard. It needed a coat of paint, both inside and out, and the hinges on the doors shrieked like gulls every time they were opened. There were two bedrooms, a narrow sitting room, and a kitchen so small only the most rudimentary of meals could be prepared there. In the mornings, he made coffee and then walked into the village for scones and ham and bread, and then he retreated back to the cottage, where he'd set up a makeshift writing area on the small table where he could pound on his computer for a few hours a day. An idea for a screenplay had come to him; nothing serious or thought-provoking, but surprisingly sardonic and funny, and he was pleased with the start he'd made. He had no expectations that it would be successful, but if nothing else, it kept him from thinking about all of the loss he'd experienced over the past few weeks.

A photo rested against the mantelpiece of the small fireplace, newly taken, of Carey and Emma, along with a note Carey had sent with it: *"We're all fine here, and hope that you are finding peace once again. I'm sorry for leaving without saying goodbye. Carey."* He took it down now and looked at it for the hundredth time, relieved that she was beginning to heal.

He had placed his career on hold. He had backed out of the new film, relying on the sympathy of the producers involved to release him from his contract due to the intense emotional upheaval that had occurred in his life. And he felt nothing but relief. He wanted to speak to no one but the middle-aged woman in the shop where he got his food and the fishermen he nodded to when he went for long rambles on the rocky beach. Behind the cottage there was a field, long and sprawling, that backed against a small wood where he sat each afternoon, contemplating everything and nothing. At night, he lay in bed swathed in white sheets, staring out at the stars until he was too tired to keep his eyes open. It was a start. Away from the noise of London and the expectations of his family and the world, he could begin to rebuild his life one day at a time.

After lunch, he sat at the computer, engrossed in his characters, who might have borne some resemblance to himself and Hugh in better times. He scratched his chin, which he hadn't shaved for days, and pushed up the sleeves as a knock sounded upon the door. Daniel looked up, surprised. In the fortnight he'd been in Cornwall, no one had come to the house. He collected the post from Mrs. Bates at the shop where he purchased his food. His mother, who had threatened to visit, had been assured via numerous emails that he needed to get away from everything and had at last given up her repeated requests to come see him. He stood, stretching his back from the long hour he'd spent in the hard chair, and went over to the door. When he opened it, Carey stood at the threshold.

"My God!" he said, without even opening the door for her to enter. "What are you doing here?"

"I wanted to make sure you're all right," she said.

"I've been worried about you too."

"I wasn't surprised when I heard you left London."

"There are too many memories around every corner. I couldn't take it. But what about you? Have you decided what you're going to do?"

"I can't go back," she answered. "I can only go forward."

His manners suddenly remembered, Daniel opened the door wider for her to come in.

Instead, she shook her head.

"It's nice out here," she said.

"It is," he agreed. "I was just about to take a break."

He pulled a blanket from the back of a chair, and leaving the door open, led the way to the garden and spread it on the ground. They wouldn't talk now, he knew. It would take days, maybe weeks, before they would be able to discuss what they'd been through, but at the moment that didn't matter. She was here. He sat down on one corner of the blanket and she on another, not touching. He worried that she was too fragile for that just now. In fact, he realized with a start, he was too.

Daniel watched as Carey looked out over the wide expanse of field as if she might never move from the spot. He felt a ripple of anticipation being near her. Her dress, a cotton sheath covered in a riot of violet flowers, brought Tamsyn to mind. He supposed he would always think of them together. In a way, being with Carey would keep Tamsyn alive; for both of them, no doubt. It was a pleasant thought. He stretched out on the woolen blanket beside her and felt the warm sun on his face and breathed in the salty sea air. The first day of summer had arrived.

ACKNOWLEDGMENTS

Many thanks to everyone who helped and encouraged me as I wrote *The English Boys*:

My fabulous agent, Victoria Skurnick, believed in me and brought out my best.

The wonderful editors, publicists, and crew at Midnight Ink: Terri Bischoff, Amy Glaser, Sandy Sullivan, Katie Mickschl, and so many others made this process rewarding and fun.

Dear friends Lori Naufel, Cindy Gross, Leslie Purcell, and my Book Club girls cheered my progress along the way.

My grandmother fostered my love of books and reading. She put a copy of *David Copperfield* in my hands when I was young and continued to guide me through a very English literary education, sharing her own poetry with me and encouraging my desire to write. After she passed away, my aunt took over, and we formed our own book club of two. I miss you both and owe you a debt of thanks.

To my wonderful family, particularly my daughters, whose abilities helped elevate my writing and made this book possible. As first readers, Caitlin's finely tuned literary instincts and Heather's sharp editing skills made the book stronger than ever. I'm proud to be the mother of two such talented young women.

And special thanks to my husband, Will Thomas, a great writer, whose love and encouragement mean the world to me; without them I could never have written this novel.

© Justin Greiman

ABOUT THE AUTHOR

Julia Thomas (Oklahoma) is a graduate of Northeastern State University and an educator. *The English Boys* is her debut novel.